LOVING
SCOTT HARRINGTON

Bound By Dark and Dangerous Affections

Pam Reaves

Dedications

For Novella Harrington Reaves
(The greatest love of my life)
September 14, 1912 – March 3, 2002

Special Thanks

Mary Reaves Jackson: For the details, connecting the dots, and passing along such rich and fascinating family history. I never grow tired of hearing your accounts.

Natasha Ramsey: For your invaluable insight and guidance. You are truly a treasure.

Gertrude Hack: For your invaluable and unwavering support.

The National Constitution Center – Philadelphia, Pennsylvania: For authorizing the use of the shackles shown on the front cover.

Toni Ramey Webster – He sent you to read my heart.

The Family Tree of Scott Harrington

Mr. Montague
Owner of the beautiful and rebellious slave Fondella

Fondella is sold to James Seamore, Sr.

James Seamore, Sr. – The father of Fondella's two sons:
(1845: Walter)
(1846: Scott)
Jacob & Molly Harrington, also owned by James Seamore
and are forced to raise Walter and Scott as their sons

Fondella escapes from the Seamores while on a trip to
Boston

(January 1, 1863)
The Emancipation Proclamation is signed by
President Abraham Lincoln

(1863) Walter and Cora are married
(no children)

(1863) Scott and Lillie are married
(one stillborn son)

(circa 1863) Scott meets his mistress Belle

(1866) Scott marries again - Iris Davis
(Children: Herbert, Irene, Beulah, Fannie & Naomi)

(1904) Scott marries for the third time - Mary Marks
Mary Marks brings two daughters to the marriage:
(b: 1893 – Maude)
(b: 1895 – Beolia)
Scott and Mary have four more children
(b: 1908 - Leotia)
(b: 1910 - Walter)
(b: 1912 – Novella)
(b: 1914 – Scott Harrington, Jr. – stillborn)

"Why does the slave ever love? Why allow the tendrils of the heart to twine around objects which may at any moment be wrenched away by the hand of violence? ...I did not reason thus when I was a young girl. Youth will be youth. I loved, and I indulged the hope that the dark clouds around me would turn out a bright lining. I forgot that in the land of my birth the shadows are too dense for light to penetrate.

There was in the neighborhood a young colored carpenter; a free born man. We had been well-acquainted in childhood, and frequently met together afterwards. We became mutually attached, and he proposed to marry me. I loved him with all the ardor of a young girl's first love. But when I reflected that I was a slave, and that the laws gave no sanction to the marriage of such, my heart sank within me. My lover wanted to buy me; but I knew that Dr. Flint was too wilful and arbitrary a man to consent to that arrangement."

- Harriet Jacobs, Edenton, N.C.

Prologue

"Hallelujah, hallelujah, oh my Gawd, sweet Lawd Jesus. Did y'all hear that? Word is out. The word is out. The prayers of the righteous done prevailed. Y'all hear that? People goin' 'round sayin' President Lincoln went ahead and signed that executive order folk been talkin' 'bout for months. They say he did it on the first day of January – that be New Year's Day. Don't know what that quite mean, but they sayin' a lot of slaves already free. I do believe that day done come. Come on, come on – we gotta get up to the house."

He hesitated at the irritating distraction, but refused to move away from the body lying beneath his. In an effort to concentrate, he lifted his head and turned it slightly to face the door. The keen sense of hearing he relied on to alert him of threat was now elusive, making it impossible to discern the nature of the chaos. In the end, lust prevailed over reasoning and he chose to proceed with what they were doing prior to the disruption.

"It's almost Noon and some drunken fool still stumblin' 'round in these woods talkin' outta his head. He better get hisself together and quiet down fo' them bosses put a whip to his back. He 'posed to be workin' and here he is runnin' through these woods like a mad man."

"Oh forget 'bout him. Now tell me what you want me to do cause I ain't goin' no further 'til you say it.

"Yes Massa. I have no reservations in telling you that I desire whatever satisfies your imagination. You know that I love you more than anything and live for these moments. My heart beats only for you."

He was really getting excited over the idea of getting what he wanted once again. *Finally made my way through all these fancy petticoats. I think she be ready just like I am. This here belongs to me. I'm Massa and she knows it.* At first he wasn't sure if her shivering body was a reaction to the wintry weather, or what they were doing, but after caressing and kissing her in all the ways and places she liked, he was confident that she trembled in his arms with pure pleasure.

Whoever was shouting and running through the woods didn't seem the least bit concerned about the slave boss' whip.

There it is again – that irritatin' yellin'. Sounds like more than one person. Why is this bunch of fools runnin' 'round in the woods hollerin'?

"I swear fo' Gawd. What is all that foolishness 'bout? Nobody ever come down in this part of the woods but me and you. Now of all times, they 'runnin' down here yellin' some crazy mess 'bout freedom. Yeah, ain't we all dreamin' 'bout that day."

The yelling continued. "Get everybody, gather up everybody. Come on y'all – hurry up. Massa wantin' all us up at his house."

Before all the commotion started, he was staring down into her face, observing the predicable reaction to what they were doing. He was familiar with the expression on her face, and knew what was about to happen. Melanie was getting ready to start moaning and calling out his name. He liked to see her like this. She was quite beautiful in this state, looking all soft and rather innocent although what they were doing was neither soft nor innocent.

She didn't even resemble the cold and impersonal woman who walked up on him about an hour ago while he was chopping down trees. That woman looked all prim and proper. Her expression was pinched, looking as if she smelled something distasteful. Ah, but once they were alone a totally different woman emerged. The woman now lying in his arms was as exciting to him as he obviously was to her.

What they were doing was dangerous. As a matter of fact, he could be killed for what he was doing with her. Yet he didn't care because now he was in the position of master and his willing slave was willing to do anything he wanted. He wanted her to plead and beg for more of him – and she did. He wanted her to touch him in ways she would never touch any man – and she did. He wanted her to surrender her dignity to him – and she did. He wanted her to call him "Mr. Harrington" or "Massa" – and she called him both. Yes – she was doing all of that until all hell broke loose.

Walter was still trying to catch his breath when he burst through the door. He wasn't shocked to find them in a compromising position.

"Scott, you've gotta get yo self together and come up to the house with me. You'll never believe the news goin' 'round. If the reports are true, my dream has come true."

What on earth was Walter talking about, and why would he interrupt at a time like this? He knew good and well what Scott was doing in the shack with Melanie. Hadn't Walter told him on a number of occasions he didn't want anything to do with Massa Seamore's nieces? They were dangerous, and any slave caught messing around with them was playing with fire.

Walter tried to avoid them as much as possible, but they could be relentless and vicious to the point of blackmail. He didn't want to admit it, but there were times when he intentionally guided the sex-hungry misses in Scott's direction. Scott seemed to get all excited about messing around with them and forcing role reversals wherein they became his slaves, but Walter wanted no parts of it. Of course there were times when he used his sexual prowess to his advantage, but that had nothing to do with pleasure. His sexual dalliances were for the sole purpose of getting something important. Scott wasn't just playing master, but was the master at this dangerous game. None of that mattered now.

"Forget her. All that noise you hearin' outside is 'cause of the rumors just gettin' 'round to these parts. We just heard the President signed that executive order freein' slaves on the first day of the New Year. Member back a few months ago when he threatened the Confederate States of America with that preliminary order sayin' that if they didn't return to the Union he was gonna go ahead and sign an executive order to free the slaves? Well, they held out and didn't return, so President Lincoln made good on his promise. C'mon, we gotta get up to the house to see what Massa gotta say about what all this mean. It ain't like no major battles were bein' fought 'round here anyway. Plus, here and there you run into a freeman. So I don't know what, if anything, is gonna change. Come on, let's go and see what he's gotta say."

Melanie's attempt to get dressed was clumsy at best, and she was embarrassed as well as furious at the intrusion. "Scott, wait a minute. You just can't leave me down here all by myself. I won't have it. Walter, turn your head. It ain't proper for you to look upon a white woman and you know it."

He glared down at her with disgust as she moved awkwardly trying to get up from the palate he constructed at her directive. The crude frame was covered with fancy linens stolen from her mother's linen armoire. Nothing about their make-shift bed looked inviting now. His patience was wearing thin. "Get up Melanie. I gotta go with Walter."

"Don't you dare call me Melanie. You had better apologize. I'm Miss Melanie to you."

He was starting to really get irritated. Here it was again, with her putting on airs the minute somebody else came around. He wasn't having it.

"I said get up and get up now."

"I'm gonna tell Uncle James that..."

"You're gonna tell him what? You down here beggin' and pleadin' with a nigger; callin' me Massa and Mr. Harrington and doin' anything I tell you to do. That be what you gonna tell him?"

He had called her bluff. Turning back to Walter he said, "Let's get outta here. You say they've started freein' slaves everywhere? Well let's just go see exactly what that mean."

Chapter 1
Maude

It was November 14, 1914, and a low-hanging branch snapped sharply across Maude's face as she ran through the thickly wooded area stretching along the small community known as the "Gulf" located on the Deep River in Chatham County, North Carolina. The stinging wound to her cheek felt like a cut from Mr. Harrington's straight razor.

She kept running. The finger placed up to her cheek to inspect the severity of the cut had blood on it. Although the cut and blood were causes for concern, she shook her head back and forth as if to self-rebuke. Turning around to go back home so Momma could take a look at the razor thin cut that felt like her entire cheek had been sliced open was not an option.

Oh Gawd, poor Momma's not in any shape to help anybody 'bout now. She's needin' all the help she can get herself. If anything, I'd better stop frettin' over this cut and pick up some speed. Gotta get over to Mama Mame's place quick and in a hurry before somethin' awful happens. I couldn't live with myself if I let somethin' bad happen to Momma and the baby.

The emergency back home had escalated to the point of critical. She was now on a mission, and sprinting through the woods at top speed was responsible for her heavy breathing that had just as much to do with anxiety as it did with the race against time she was running. Ducking and dodging through the wooded path was an obstacle course, causing the terrible ache in her long legs to intensify and compete with her pulsating chest and throbbing head. The wind whipped through her thin wool coat and chilled her bare legs to the bone. The steady stream of tears she kept wiping with the back of her hand was a reaction to the bitter wind whipping at her face, as well as mounting fear over the possibility of tragedy.

"Ouch, this damn thorn!" Her coat sleeve was ripped but she kept running. Terror wouldn't allow her thoughts to linger on the damaged coat. Fear wasn't an emotion she was used to feeling or comfortable with. To the contrary, she reveled in the reputation that preceded her throughout the Gulf. Folk around the county were always complimenting her on being wise and strong far beyond her years. Momma came from strong stock, and she was proud whenever they compared her to Momma in that way.

Now was not the time for tears, and nothing short of bravery was going to keep her focused and running. All alone in the woods, it was left up to her to encourage herself. "Maude ain't no time to be pityin' yo self. You gotta get over to Mama Mame's place and get there in a hurry. If things go wrong, Mr. Harrington's gonna have your hide and everybody in the house is gonna suffer that man's wrath. Suck it up gal and keep runnin'."

The marathon race through the woods was exhausting, leaving her dazed and distressed with brain fog. Was that the low growl of some ferocious predator she heard? Her head was turning in every direction as she tried to determine where and what the noise was coming from. There was nothing in front of her. She looked over her shoulder to the left – nothing, and then over to the right – still nothing. *Sweet Jesus, supposed its one of them Carolina panthers they say be lurkin' in these woods.* It sounded like another growl and whatever was in the woods was gaining on her.

Spinning around to see if the threat was behind her, she stepped into a hollowed hole covered by grass and began to fall. "Oh hell no, I just cut my face, tore my coat, and now about to fall flat on my face. I'm not goin' down…" She stretched out her hands to break the fall, refusing to land face down in the dirt, fallen leaves, and whatever else was lying around in the woods.

While she was lying there trying to pull herself together, the story Momma and some of the old folk told about how a panther chased Momma's brother, Zachery, through the woods popped into her mind. Legend had it that when he finally cleared the woods, he hopped over the fence, tucked his body into a ball, and rolled straight into the house. Grandpa George, who heard him screaming for help, was waiting with his rifle, and as Zachery was rolling through the yard towards the door, fired a round of shots, hitting the panther while it was in mid-air. Everybody still got a kick out of the way Uncle Zachery impersonated Grandpa, when he said, "Damn cat, nobody mess with George Marks' boy – nobody and nothin' mess with my chillun." Uncle Zachery said dust and dirt were flying everywhere as the big cat's body hit the earth with a loud thud, skidded across the ground, and landed just outside of the fence surrounding the house.

The crackling sound of tree branches and dried leaves beneath her body brought Maude back to the current crisis back at the house. She felt her arms and legs. Thankfully nothing was broken. Standing up on shaky legs, she took off running again, all the while praying and asking God to spare her life. "Not now Lawd, Momma's in trouble back there. Please not now. Just let me get her some help and I promise I'll do whatever it is you want outta my life. Just don't let that noise be no panther 'bout to devour me."

Her prayers were answered. Finally she reached the wooded area that looked familiar. She made one more turn and Mama Mame's small wood-framed house came into view. The swing on the porch was creaking as it moved slightly from the breeze.

Inside, Mama Mame was dozing off in her rocking chair. Awakened by the loud banging at the front door, she almost fell out of the chair. Always alert for some odd reason, she popped up out of the seat like a spring had been released beneath her.

She knew what the frantic knocking meant. Either somebody was hurt and needed medical attention, or some girl was in labor and needed her to usher the baby into the world.

"Who is it? Hold your horses and give me a minute. I'm movin' fast as I can." The banging continued. "Mama Mame, please, please hurry. My momma is gettin' ready to deliver that baby, and Mr. Harrington's over there lookin' like he's gonna kill everybody if that baby's not brought into this world right."

"Oh Lawd, that be Maude, so my gal Mary must be in labor. I sho' nuff' hope everything be alright with her bein' up in the age and all. Sides, that man of hers prob'ly givin' her a fit 'bout somethin'. That there man...Lawd Jesus I declare sometimes..."

She remembered being just as surprised as everyone else when she found out that Mary had gotten tangled up with and decided to marry the ex-slave Scott Harrington.

Chapter 2
Mary Marks

Mary Marks' family had been living in the Gulf for as long as Mama Mame could recall. The Marks' only daughter grew into what folk around the county called a "handsome" young woman. She was tall, with a body type considered thick, but shapely. Her facial features were soft, and framed with wavy/crinkly hair, the color of copper.

The gentle voice belied her true character as town folk marveled at the way she worked on George Marks' tiny farm. They said she was as physically strong as her brothers. She was the only one in the family who could read although she never went to school. Family and neighbors relied on her to read their important papers and write letters. Mary was a pillar of strength.

The Marks family lived quietly and none of them ever seemed to get involved in any trouble to speak of. Being devout Christians, everybody was shocked when word started spreading throughout the county that Mary was married to Scott. No one even knew they had been courting. Her new husband was the last man anyone expected her to be with.

When the name Scott Harrington was mentioned people took notice. He stood approximately six feet five inches tall. His frame was thin, but cushioned with well-developed muscle from working on the plantation since the age of six. His complexion was the color of light caramel with skin as smooth as satin. By the time he was 30 years old, silvery white hair generously crowned his head. His almond shaped eyes were light gray and framed with eyelashes so thick and long, women envied them.

Thought of as one of the most arrogant men in the county, he was also considered unapproachable, appearing to look down his long thin nose at others. Whenever anyone approached, he waited for the other person to acknowledge and speak to him first. If they failed to address him as "Mr. Harrington," he immediately took offense, and the piercing eyes glared at the other person as if they were an irritating insect he wanted to squash beneath his boot.

Besides his brother, the only men to whom he seemed willing to humble himself were his employers, the Seamore family. The Seamores were much more than employers, and that particular piece of gossip was the basis for the sizzling rumor mill that revolved around his life.

A history of lust, lies, deceit, and ownership was the relationship that best described the Harrington brothers and the Seamores. The Seamores owned Scott and Walter Harrington until word reached the Gulf that President Lincoln had signed the Emancipation Proclamation. Freedom didn't end the relationship, and for generations to come, the twists and turns grew even more complex.

People around the Gulf found it odd that Scott, who wasn't even born a free man, was arrogant, difficult, and standoffish. On more than one occasion, someone started the conversation with, "He's got some nerve expectin' the world to refer to him as Mr. Harrington. He even makes his wife Mary address him as Mr. Harrington. Now I ain't one to gossip, but I heard he always been like this. Rascal made two wives 'fo her call him Mr. Harrington. Why that arrogant weasel strut 'round like he actually be a legitimate member of them Seamores." Then someone like Mama Mame who knew the details of his family history would whisper, "You know, he actually be a part of the Seamore family, though he don't be a legitimate part."

Now seeing Maude standing before her, obviously upset and explaining the chaos and emergency unfolding over at the Harrington place, she could no longer dwell on history.

"Mama Mame, all hell just broke loose. I tried to get Momma to let somebody come over here and get you much sooner. But no, she up there tryin' to wait on Mr. Harrington and he knows she's in pain. I pleaded with her and she kept tellin' me the pains wasn't comin' close enough. Fo' we knew it, water started runnin' from everywhere outta her. Her pain so bad she's cryin', moanin', and hollerin' some kinda bad. She could hardly breathe when we was tryin' to get her back to bed. Oh Mama Mame, it don't look good at all."

"Well hurry up gal and get my stuff. It's in the back room. No, no, no. Baby, it's in the other room. Get a move on you, we gotta get outta here and over there to yo momma. I'm on my way out to the barn to hitch up my ol' mule. Meet me 'round the front of the house."

As Maude came running through the front door out on to the porch, Mamma Mame was yelling. "Hop up on this wagon here gal, I ain't got no time to stop. I gotta get to Mary. Lawd if that Scott Harrington gets me riled up, I'm gonna tear him in two as soon as I finish deliverin' that there baby." Maude leapt on to the wagon while it was still in motion.

Cracking the whip, Mama Mame kept yelling. "Get up ol' mule and get outta here. Get me to my Mary's place to deliver that baby." As the wagon made a sudden turn, Maude's body landed up against Mama Mame, who never lost control over the mule and wagon. "Whoooooaa there mule, straighten up – straighten up."

After she caught her breath Maude had to ask, "You think we gonna make it in time?"

Now wasn't the time to show fear. "Chile, we gonna make it or die tryin'. I ain't tryin to kill us, so we gonna make it. Get up ol' mule."

As soon as the wagon pulled up to the Harrington's place, Maude jumped down and ran into the back bedroom where Mary was lying in bed soaking wet from sweating and breathing heavy with labor pains.

Walter, Beolia, Leotia, and Novella were standing around the bed with anxious expressions on their faces. Leotia was wiping Mary's brow and trying to comfort her as much as a six year old could comfort a mother who was in labor and about to deliver a baby. As she frantically looked around the room to take in what was going on, sixteen year old Maude was grateful that despite their very young ages, they had been conscious of Mary's pride and covered the bottom portion of her body with a blanket. Still, she could see Mary's legs bent up into a position intended to make delivery of the baby easier. Yet this delivery was anything but easy. As her contractions increased with frequency and intensity, Mary's legs trembled beneath the blanket. Any attempts at remaining calm for the sake of the children were futile as she lay writhing in pain.

"Otie, Vella let me get next to Momma please. She's mighty uncomfortable, but she's gonna be alright shortly." She then turned back to the bed. "Momma, Mama Mame's on her way in with her equipment. She's gonna deliver this baby and you'll feel better real soon. Okay?" Mary could only shake her head up and down.

He was standing erect, silent, and looking out of the window with hands shoved into the large pockets of his denim coveralls. His jaw bone was prominent, and you could tell his teeth were clinching as he puffed on his pipe. He continued staring out of the window without ever flinching as the cries rang out in the background. He seemed oblivious to Mary's travailing labor.

Growing more irritated at the sight of his indifference, Maude started muttering to no one in particular. "Don't make no damn sense. Momma's in pain and he actin' like nothin's goin' on in here."

He still wasn't responding, but just kept looking out of the window, rocking back and forth, and puffing on the pipe. Just when she thought she couldn't take it any longer, and was about to give him a real good piece of her mind, Mama Mame burst through the door huffing, puffing, and talking fast like she did in these types of situations.

"Scott Harrington, where's my Mary, and why on earth are you just standin' there lookin' outta this window instead of bein' back there in that room with her?" He turned sharply and shot her one of those piercing looks that should have made her back off. She wasn't intimidated and as she moved towards the back bedroom, whisked by him pushing an elbow in his direction as if to shove him aside. "Oh never mind, just move outta the way man."

Instead of giving into the urge to strangle her, he went over to a stack of large crates located near the bedroom and sat down. As far as he was concerned, it wasn't proper for men folk to be there at the birthing and he wasn't about to go into the room and see things a man wasn't supposed to see.

Maude made the younger children leave the room and went to work helping Mama Mame who was already barking out orders. "Get me some water; make sure you sterilize that knife;

where the devil is that gauze cotton I told y'all to keep 'round here? I need somethin' for her to bite down on when these Gawd-awful pains hit."

The rapid succession of orders was making Maude even more nervous, but she was following them like a pro. She never forgot the promise she made early in life to never let Momma down, and was even willing to die for her if need be.

"Momma, we gonna get you and that baby through this. Don't you worry none. Mama Mame and me gonna see to it."

Her true feelings were not in alignment with her words of comfort. Quite frankly, the worried look on Mama Mame's face had her worried. With nerves already frayed, she almost jumped out of her skin when Beolia asked the same question she was terrified to ask. "Mama Mame, is everything alright?"

Something was wrong. Mama Mame didn't answer the question but kept working and coaching Mary to push one minute and to rest the next. Pushing, panting, and trying to follow instructions, Mary was moaning and squirming around in pain that didn't seem solely connected to giving birth. "Oh my Lawd. Please help me. I can't, I can't, I..."

Something was definitely wrong, but she tried to hide her mounting fear. "Momma just keep squeezin'. Squeeze as hard and as often as you need to Honey. Me and you, we're made from strong stock, we can get through this."

Mama Mame was now talking out loud to the unborn baby. "Come on now, no time to back-up little one, this here is yo day, and you've gotta come forth." She looked up at Mary and said, "Baby, you gotta give Mama Mame one of them pushes like there's no tomorrow. Come on and yell as loud as you need to, but by Gawd push with all yo might."

Mary reached back over her head and grabbed the hands of Maude and Beolia, squeezing until both of them were sure all of the fingers on the hand Mary was holding were broken. Neither one of them would let go, and held on for dear life as Mary screamed like she was calling out to someone over in Raleigh. She gave the big push Mama Mame demanded, and finally the baby was out.

Except for Mary's heavy breathing, the room was deafly quite. Mama Mame was looking down at the baby she held in her hands dripping with blood. "My dear Jesus, help me out here." She then laid the baby on Mary's stomach. The midwife was acting peculiar and quite frankly the praying had Mary so concerned, she tried to sit up to see what was going on. Why was it taking so long for Mama Mame to make the announcement she wanted to hear? Maternal instinct sounded the alarm. *What on earth is Mama Mame doin' to my baby?* Pushed to the emotional edge, her disposition changed and she started making demands. "My baby, what did I have? I wanna hold my baby now. Where is my baby – give my baby to me right now?"

Instead of the anticipated announcement, Mama Mame stuck her little finger into the baby's mouth trying to clear it of any obstructions that could be preventing the baby from breathing, but nothing happened. She then covered the baby's nostrils and mouth with her mouth, and started breathing hard like she had been demanding Mary to do earlier. Still nothing happened. Finally and solemnly she started to pray, "Dear Jesus, I knows you know what's best, and so I commend this here precious baby boy back into yo presence."

"Oh my Gawd – my baby didn't make it. My baby is dead. You tell me right now, is my baby dead?" Mama Mame just shook her head.

It started out as a whimper. "No, no, no," that grew in volume and turned into agonizing screams. "My baby, oh Gawd no, my baby, I want my baby. Please, oh please, I want my baby. Oh my Gawd, why, why, why? Where's Mr. Harrington? I want Mr. Harrington." He made no attempt to move anywhere near her.

Maude was on her knees beside the bed, still holding on to one of Mary's hands and crying. Beolia had let go of the other hand, and was still breathing hard. She was staring off into space unable to move or speak.

Leotia, Walter, and Novella were terrified, not knowing what to do, and unable to understand what the praying or screaming was all about. But even in their innocence, they knew something awful had just happened. Since Mary wasn't in a position to hold and assure them there was nothing to be afraid of, they turned to Scott for comfort.

His eyes didn't look as though they were focused on anything around him. He was still sitting on the stack of crates with his head back against the wall. It looked like he was just staring at the wall. Moving closer, they saw tears streaming down his cheeks. His body was shaking and trembling. The sniffling noises sounded like a combination of crying and difficulty with breathing.

Something dreadful had just happened. Poppa's body was moving around in a strange manner and the sounds coming from him were frightening. Pandemonium had set in. Now terrified, the volume of their screams was competing with Mary's sobbing. "Oh Gawd, oh Gawd. Where's Mr. Harrington? I want Mr. Harrington. Oh please Gawd – no." Mama Mame's eyes were bloodshot from crying, and she moved about as if she were in a trance.

Finally pulling herself together for the sake of the family, Mama Mame wrapped the lifeless baby in the blanket that had been prepared for his arrival. She then walked into the hallway where Scott was sitting. She stretched out her arms and handed the baby to him. "Scott Harrington, let me introduce you to yo son, Gawd rest his precious soul."

He took the baby, looked down into his lifeless face, went back to the stack of crates, and sat there saying nothing to no one. Back in the bedroom, Mary lay crying with Maude sitting on the floor next to her still crying. By now, Leotia, Walter, and Novella were reduced to whimpering and holding on to the midwife's skirt for some measure of assurance. Scott was rocking back and forth, and crying with the dead baby in his arms.

He finally got up and walked over to hand the baby back to Mama Mame. He couldn't think of anything to say other than, "Here."

"No, not now. Let me go to my wagon and get the box. I'll be right back."

She returned to prepare the baby for its burial. "Arrangements need to be made. I can never get used to this. Lawd knows I can't. Gotta be a way to keep babies from dying whilst they tryin' to come into this world. Gotta be a way."

He walked back to the closed bedroom door. "Maude, she cleaned up yet?"

"Yes sir. Beolia, help me get this stuff cleaned up."

Beolia complied, but still couldn't find her voice. Even if she did, she didn't know what to say. Maude opened the door.

At first he looked lost and confused; looking as if he didn't know what to do next. Then a familiar expression came over his face. He was dismissing them from the room. Pulling Beolia along with her, Maude left.

They stared at each other before he walked over to the bed. He got in fully clothed and held her in his arms as she broke down crying. He continued to hold and comfort her. "I know. I know it hurts. Gone and cry Honey. Cry all you want. I'm here."

Just as the sun was peeking over the horizon the next morning, he got up to ready himself for work down at the mill. He woke Maude up first. "Make sure you feed the chickens and collect some eggs too. Don't forget to chop enough wood for a cuppla' days. Stack most of it up next to the back porch and get a fire lit to knock the chill off the house. Yo momma and them chillun need breakfast too." Before leaving the house she heard him saying good-bye to Mary, who was still in bed weak from delivery, and depressed over the loss of her baby.

Gradually Mary got up out of her bed of mourning and started moving around, but was slow. Although she desperately tried to hide her grief from the family, the sadness in her swollen red eyes told of the depths of her loss. Maude hovered over her trying to help out and lighten the load in some way. The younger children clung even tighter, too young to understand what was going on around them. Walter kept asking, "Momma is the baby gonna come back another time?" Novella's constant question was, "Where's the baby, where's the baby?"

The never ending questioning although innocent was keeping the loss fresh. She would sneak off to a corner to cry and talk to God. *Oh my Gawd, I'm achin' so bad. My heart is broken and I can't stop this pain. I wanted this baby so bad fo' Mr. Harrington.*

How am I gonna go on? Iffin he ain't happy, he's gonna go back to doin' them bad things that break my heart.

Turning to Scott for comfort was out of the question, and they knew better than to invade his space. The day the baby was delivered was one of those few occasions when his mountain of defenses was down and he allowed them to get close. After that day he reverted back to the hardworking, serious, arrogant, and unpredictable man whom everyone was familiar with.

By the next week he was expecting Mary to wait on him hand and foot, and she did so without complaining. Maude was disgusted by his insensitivity once again when she overheard him say, "Mary, time to get up and see what needs to be done 'round here. I'll be waitin' fo' my lunch when they ring the bell down at the mill."

"Yes Mr. Harrington. I know I got a lot to do and everything will get done on time. Don't you worry none, I'll have yo lunch down there by Noon."

Maude started throwing things around the room out of frustration. "He's an insufferable ol' fool. A damned devil be more like it. What Momma see in him I'll never understand. Let me make myself busy fo' I get outta here and go to school. Iffin' I don't do somethin' to take my mind off of him, I'm gonna start cussin' him out no matter what Momma say."

Sometimes Maude really thought he was the devil himself, but then at other times, he acted as if he actually cared about Mary. After the day the stillborn baby was delivered, every night before they went to sleep, he held Mary not saying much, but occasionally kissing and stroking her until she fell off to sleep.

The first night she stumbled upon this scene, she was shocked to discover him in a moment of intimacy. Thinking Mary was asleep, she decided to sneak into the room for a goodnight kiss. From a distance the glow illuminating from the light of the oil lamp could be seen. Then she heard his voice.

"I'm sorry. Don't worry tho' 'cause you gonna have another chance to give me a son. Now don't that feel better?" He even sounded different. He was speaking in a tone of voice that Maude was unaccustomed to hearing.

Curiosity got the best of her, and she had to see what they were doing. Peeking through the crack at the door hinge, she saw him stroking Mary's face. As Mary looked up into his eyes, he moved his lips to cover hers and kept them there in a lingering kiss. She had never seen Mary react to anybody like this. She seemed mesmerized by his voice and what he was doing to her.

Maybe this is why Momma's so in love with him, but this don't even resemble the rattle snake we all have to deal with most of the time.

Even though she had discovered another side of him by accident, she still couldn't get over his refusal to talk when she knew Mary wanted to talk about the baby. He did allow her to name him Scott Harrington, Jr. This baby's birth would be the first in the family to be recorded. Others would know that Scott Harrington, Jr. was a real person, who made an entrance into the world although he never took a breath. *How ironic it is that the first baby to be born into this family whose birth was recorded didn't even get to live.*

Back in 1913, she recalled how excited the grown folk around the county were when word got out that some things had changed, and going forward people's births and deaths would be put into some official town records. *One of these days when Momma's strong again and feel like talkin' I'm gonna remind her that little Scott Harrington mattered to a lotta folk and his life is officially recognized by the State of North Carolina. There's proof down there where they keep them official records. Her baby boy is more than a note in the family bible. She don't have to feel bad 'cause that arrogant man of hers don't wanna talk about his own son. He can lay up and feel all over her, talkin' 'bout how she can give him another son, but he can't let her talk 'bout the one she's grievin' over. What a selfish bastard.*

As the months passed, it seemed as if Baby Scott Harrington became a tragic memory from which Scott was distancing himself. Other than that night when she came upon them during their moment of intimacy, Maude rarely saw any real display of affection from him towards Mary.

That husband of Momma's is a real piece of work as far as I'm concerned. Lawd, I swear fo' Gawd, I don't see what Mama see in him. Yeah he be the handsome devil some of them older women talk 'bout. But his attitude is so stinkin' I can't see how anybody can get beyond that despicable attitude to even appreciate his looks. Can't say a word against him to Momma though. She loves her some Scott Harrington, and ain't gonna put up with me or nobody else disrespectin' him. But that there man got somethin' goin' on in the dark and I smell a rat. Yeah, he's up to no good and rotten to the core.

He frequently disappeared after supper and didn't return until late at night. At times like this, he abruptly pushed his chair back from the head of the table and mumbled something like, "Goin for a walk – be back."

Mary would nod her head in acknowledgement, but Maude often caught a certain look in her eyes. It wasn't the same sadness as when she lost the baby, but was a different kind of pain, more like hurt emanating from disappointment and rejection. She couldn't quite explain what was going on inside of Mary's head or heart at times like these. Once when she got up the nerve to ask, Mary's explanation didn't explain very much. "Baby I can't tell you 'bout this kinda pain, but I sure hope to Gawd you never have to know what it is."

Still confused and curious, she asked Mama Mame about it, thinking the connection would be made for her since for some reason Mary couldn't or wouldn't give any further detail. Once the question was out, Mama Mame tightly clamped her lips together and rolled her eyes before speaking. Making an indignant noise, she responded with, "Humph, that Scott Harrington must be back to tanglin' with that ol' polecat who ain't worth the dirt she walk over. He just can't do right by a dignified lady like my Mary. Prob'ly 'cause he know he ain't good 'nuff for her. Mary luvs him though and so I gotta make peace with that."

Maude was still confused, but too afraid to get in the middle of grown folks' business as Mary had warned her against. In time she would find out about that ol' polecat.

It was a muggy August evening after they had finished eating supper when he pushed back his chair from the table and sure enough mumbled the dreaded announcement, "Goin for a walk – be back." He got up, walked over to the fireplace, picked up one of the oil lamps placed near the hearth, and lit it.

Aw hell no – this is ridiculous. I don't care what Momma say, I'm sayin' somethin' to him 'bout walkin' outta here actin' like he just can't wait to get to whatever or whoever he be runnin' after.

She rose from the table, knocking the chair over while trying to catch up with him. Alarmed, Beolia stood up along with her, trying to get to her before she got to him.

"Maude, sit down and sit down now!" The harsh command shocked her and Beolia. Mary meant every word of her command and wouldn't tolerate a challenge. Maude leaned over to pick up her chair and sat back down sulking.

As she sat there, looking down, and staring at food on the plate, a soft, but firm hand patted her on the shoulder. "Don't you worry none 'bout your momma, she's in Gawd's hands. It may hurt baby, but it ain't gonna break me."

Beolia sank back into her chair like a limp doll grateful Mary stepped in before Maude had a chance to openly confront Scott.

Focused solely on getting out of the house and to his destination, he was completely unaware of the commotion his departure had caused. By the time Mary restored order at the supper table, he was already out of the house and had disappeared into the night full of the sound of crickets, a clear sky sprinkled with stars, and his oil burning lamp to light the way.

Chapter 3
Scott Harrington and Belle

He was on his way to see the woman who had cast her spell upon him shortly after becoming a free man. She was downright bewitching. She looked white, but didn't act like the white women he knew. She certainly wasn't like any of them when it came to sex. Once they were finished, they immediately went back to being prim and proper, but not her. She was fiery all the time and didn't care who knew it. Her lustful spirit and appetite were as ravenous as his, and she wasn't afraid to let him know it.

Once he had her, he couldn't get her out of his system. She wasn't good for him, but he wanted her. She was trouble, but the kind he was willing to have. Her reputation was bad, but he didn't care. Her name was Belle, and when whatever spell she cast upon him called, he answered. He didn't care who got hurt or was left abandoned in order to get to her.

A flicker of light was coming from the oil lamp sitting next to her on the porch, and the cheap wind chimes were moving slightly in the muggy summer breeze. "Good to see ya Belle. Let's go in."

The absence of emotion wasn't an issue, and did nothing to diminish her joy at the sight of him standing before her. She had known him since her teenage years, and was well-acquainted with the impersonal demeanor she could count on turning into something totally different the minute he became aroused. He kept coming back regardless of who he was courting or married to, and that was the only thing that mattered to her.

None of them don't mean a thing to him. He can't get enough of me and that ain't never gonna change. They don't look like me, and they sho' can't please his manhood like me. No matter what they do, he keeps comin' back to me.

Although it felt as if a knife had pierced her heart on those occasions when the word had gotten out that he was married again, there was always a sigh of relief whenever he unexpectedly showed up. His overwhelming aura negated the emotional pain he habitually inflicted upon her. All she ever thought about was their next time together. So whenever he came around, she didn't waste time asking about his day, whereabouts, or life outside of the forbidden world they created.

In response to his command, she jumped up like some smitten young girl and ran behind him to the corner of the house partitioned off as her bedroom. The sound of the buttons from her blouse hitting and spilling all over the floor was neither a distraction, nor warranted assessment of the damage to her clothes. She loved the combination of danger and erotica he skillfully brought to the boudoir. He pushed her and she fell back on to the bed with him on top as he took her to their version of heaven.

While he slept, she stared down at his long and muscular body glistening with tiny beads of sweat. She couldn't help but appreciate the perfectly chiseled facial features. *Sweet Jesus, how could this beautiful man not be all mines after all these years? I done everything I can think of to get Mr. Harrington away from them other gals who keep stealin' him from me. One day though*

I'm gonna finally win this here man so pleasin' to the eye. 'Cept for that gal Lillie, I got more time in with him than any of them and it's gonna pay off – just wait and see.

She refused to consider the lunacy of her reasoning when it came to marriage and why he kept choosing someone else. He had, on more than one occasion, the opportunity to marry her after the death of a wife, but chose not to. Delusion would not allow her to grasp the reality that the women he married shared similarities, and none of them were anything like her. Narcissism convinced her that she was the better woman, and her self-absorbing conclusion was based on the complexion of her skin, long silky hair nearly reaching the bottom of her back, a voluptuous body she was certain no man could ever turn down, and the wild and crazy personality people spoke of. She took the wild and crazy reference as a compliment, when town folk meant it as a warning to strangers to keep their distance.

Her daydreaming was interrupted as he stirred. He then opened his eyes looking as if he wasn't coming out of sleep, but had merely been lying there resting with them closed. The simple announcement sounded as if the two of them had just finished having a cup of coffee. There was no inference to a sexual liaison.

"Gotta go, I'll see ya soon."

She wasn't ready let him go and tried to entice him to stay a while longer. He grabbed a fist full of hair and pulled it back while staring into her eyes as if he could see into her soul. She thought he was admiring her great beauty and was once again wondering how he could resist her. She would have died had she known his true thoughts at that moment.

The once flawless looks that captivated him the moment he laid eyes on her were beginning to harden. The corners of her mouth, now creased, turned ever so slightly downward making her look as if she was perpetually pouting or wining about something. The expressions that he saw in her eyes were a combination of cold and calculating, reminding him of those he used to see in the eyes of the overseer and other bosses over at the Seamore's plantation. He was fully aware of her self-assessment and the willingness to destroy anyone who got in the way of whatever she wanted. His attraction to her had no bearings on his mistrust. He would never entrust his best interest to her.

She's crazy and wild, and I can't understand fo' the life of me why I can't get her outta my system. Oh well, she's good fo' one thing...

Now it was she who interrupted his thoughts asking in her most coquettish voice, "Mr. Harrington, what you be thinkin?"

"Nothin' sweet Belle. Gotta go." He got up, dressed, and walked out on to the porch to light his oil lamp.

During the walk back home, the familiar tortured, empty, and guilty feelings came back to gnaw at him. He lamented over his infidelity to the women whom he pursued and conquered, only to betray their loyalties with the wild, reckless, and selfish Belle. The minute he got up from her bed, agony wiped away any lustful satisfaction he shared with her. He was struggling with conflicting feelings about the women in his life.

Walking through the night he made yet another empty promise to himself. He would never go back. "Oh Gawd, I've gotta get rid of this awful demon keepin' so much misery in my life? She's causin' me to do things I don't wanna, but Gawd help me I'm gonna get away this time."

He groaned as the tragedies in his life in which she had played a significant role came to mind.

He wasn't only thinking about her and his wives, he was also thinking about his children. The general consensus was that he had forgotten about the recent death of Scott Harrington, Jr. They were all wrong. The lifeless face of the baby still haunted him. As a matter of fact, he had experienced a similar scene with another dead baby before. It was the year after he became a free man. Frequently, his tortured soul took him back to that period in his life.

Chapter 4
Scott Harrington and Lillie

For years the rumor mill had been buzzing with stories and theories about why his wives died young or during childbirth. The hot topics revolved around Belle, who caused his first wife, Lillie, to go into labor prematurely and die while giving birth. According to Lillie's people, she was in route to their neighbor's house to get some eggs when Belle spotted and decided to follow her. When she caught up with her, she viciously attacked Lillie.

"Hey you, I heard you married to my man Scott Harrington. Hey, hey, you hear me talkin' to you? I know you hear me talkin' to you and you better not ignore me, come here."

Lillie was frightened. Here she was pregnant and standing face-to-face with the wild and crazy woman everybody kept telling her about. Rumor had it that this negra, who looked white, had claimed Mr. Harrington as her man, and would fight any woman who came near him.

She was out of her element and didn't know how to respond to Belle's aggression. "Yes ma'am, Mr. Harrington, he's my husband. We got married as soon as Massa Seamore set us free."

"Hah, you little mouse don't you know you can't keep him away from me? Look at ya, you be plain as a piece of wood. A little dark fo' my taste. Fo' Mr. Harrington too – prob'ly why he keep comin' back to me. Did you know that? He still comin' back to my bed."

Lillie was really frightened now. She had never heard a woman speaking with vulgarity about what she was doing with a man intimately. "I'm sorry, I don't understand Miss. I thought..."

Belle got up close and started poking at her protruding stomach. "You thought what? You think that baby in there's gonna keep him away from me, huh?"

Lillie had to get away from this crazy woman. Not knowing what else to do, she started to back away, but Belle kept coming, reaching over to grab her arm.

"Let me go, let go of me. I'm gonna tell Mr. Harrington on you. Let me go..." Belle gave her a forceful shove. "Oh Lawd, what're you doin', what're you doin'? She went tumbling down the embankment hitting rocks and bushes along the way.

When the fall ended, she looked up to see Belle standing there laughing before turning away. She was left alone and hurt.

"I gotta get some help. Oh my Gawd, this pain in my back and stomach be feelin' some kinda awful. Help, help, help." No one answered her cry. She then managed to roll over to get up on her hands and knees, and started crawling back up the embankment. "Just a few more inches and I'll be back at the top of this..."

Before reaching the top, she tumbled back to the bottom. The searing pain was back again, but this time she felt a warm, sticky liquid between her legs. "Oh no, please Gawd, oh no." Looking down, she saw the stains, but had to lift her dress up to confirm the worst. Yes, the liquid between her thighs was blood. She struggled once again to make it back up to the top of the embankment.

By the time she reached home, she was in labor. Her kinfolk called upon the midwife, who wasn't able to save the baby or Lillie. It was a slow and agonizing death. According to those who were there, the baby was breached. Each time the poor little thing kicked, his body was pushed back up against Lillie's heart, crushing it. She was grabbing at her chest, and gasping for breath in between agonizing screams. By the time it was over, rumor had it that only the bottom portion of the baby's body had been delivered vaginally. The midwife kept working until she was able to remove the baby's entire body from Lillie's corpse. When she removed the deceased infant, the umbilical cord was wrapped tightly around his neck.

In death, Lillie's eyes were frozen wide open with fear, her mouth was slightly open from trying to breath, and a hand was still over the chest area where her heart would have been located. Her family was devastated. She had lived to become a free woman, married the charismatic boy whose father was Massa Seamore, only to lose her life shortly thereafter.

Belle tried to prevent him from leaving her, and showed up at the mill to give him her version of what happened. "Mr. Harrington, I knows you upset and all, but that wasn't my fault. She came up to me and started a fight, tellin' me I better stay away from her man. I tried to get away from her but she kept followin' me. She grabbed me, but when I turned around, she slipped and fell. I tried to save her, but she kept fightin' me so bad, I had to leave her."

"I know you and I know my wife. You lie, and I don't ever wanna see you again. Ya hear me? Don't mention Lillie or my baby in vain. Stay away Belle – just stay away. Look, I only come to you fo' one thing, that's all. Sometimes you ain't even good at that. I go to my wife for everything else. Now you gone and messed that up. What I get from you, I can get from any woman I want 'round here."

His cruelty was shattering. He even said she wasn't good at sex. Rejected and dejected, she went back home hoping and praying that within a week or two he would miss being in her arms and come back to her.

While he stayed away, she was miserable and tried to ignore her sorrows by making other men fall for and pursue her. None of them had his commanding presence; none of them possessed that mysterious thing he possessed which could make anybody bow to him; none of them could make love to her like him and; none of them made her heart ache like he did. She could not ignore the truth. She didn't want most men. She wanted him. Although her reputation preceded her, men still begged for her hand in marriage. She delighted in turning them down, and was ready to move on to the next suitor who would adore her.

Chapter 5
Scott Harrington Finds a New Wife

After two years, she finally heard something. He was getting married, and his second wife's name was Iris. She was a tall handsome woman, whose personality was similar to Lillie's. Her father was a deacon at Mt. Calvary Baptist Church, and the entire family was active in the church. When Belle heard the gossip in town, she thought she was going to die from humiliation and heartbreak.

She was walking through town, dressed in all her finery, when a group of women who were gossiping in front of the General Store saw her coming their way. When she was close enough, they made sure to raise their voices loud enough for her to hear the devastating news.

"Did y'all hear 'bout that handsome man Scott Harrington? He just got married again to a good Christian woman. Heard he had some pol' cat he used to mess 'round with and she killed his wife and baby. He let that murderin' trash go and found hisself a good woman."

They dissolved into a fit of giggles when she tripped over and tore the hem of her skirt. The news had shaken her, and it was good to see the high and mighty Belle become unglued, nearly falling flat on her smug face.

Why would he do this to me? I could've made him happy after he finished grievin' over that gal Lillie.

She was so sure that once he had gotten over the loss, and stopped blaming someone for Lillie's untimely death, he would realize that he loved her, and they could finally get married. What on earth was he thinking?

When she saw Iris, she thought to herself, *Mr. Harrington be crazy if he thinkin' that plain woman gonna satisfy him. Both of them gals he married ain't nothin' but bible-totin' church mice. He done lost his mind when he can have the most excitin' woman in the county; prob'ly in all the State of North Carolina.*

The humiliation was too much to bear and now everybody knew he preferred another plain woman over her. She became sullen and withdrawn. In the past, she could justify why Lillie won his hand in marriage. They grew up together on the Seamore plantation and she was willing to bet it was an arranged marriage. That was all before he knew her. *Ain't no way he would've married her iffin he had known me first. Time was just on that little church mouse's side.*

I can't understand fo' the life of me why he would be so stupid and go and marry another one of them dull Plain Janes instead me. That be totally stupid when he can have anything he want outta me. I'm gonna show Mr. Scott Harrington somethin'. Just wait and see. This be his loss – not mine. I can get any other man to marry me iffin I be wantin' him to.

She was finally learning to deal with the hurt and humiliation when the unexpected happened. It was late at night, and while lying in bed restless and unable to sleep, she felt an eerie presence in the room. The air was so thick it was difficult to breathe. She could hear whatever it was in the room with her moving around, but was too afraid to open her eyes to see what was happening.

At first she thought it was one of those bad spirits she had been asking the Geechee woman from South Carolina to cast upon one of her many adversaries. *Oh my Gawd – that dang Geechee got things mixed up and done sent some bad spirit here to kill me. This thing be in here with me and circlin' my bed. I can't even get outta here and run. It be breathin' heavy like they say a dragon do. Ain't no way I'mma get outta here alive. Gawd, I can't even move.*

She was paralyzed, trapped, unable, and afraid to run from the house out into the night. Too terrified to open her eyes, she started begging for her life. "Please don't do this. Did that Geechee send you over here? I'll give you whatever you want if you just leave."

She could feel hot breath on her face. *It's over. I'm gettin' ready to die.* Giving up, she wanted this night of terror to be over. Convinced the end was near she opened her eyes slightly and darn near fainted as she looked into gray eyes glistening like broken pieces of glass. Oh *my Gawd, it's a wolf in here and he's bout ready to eat me alive.*

The scream for help was cut short when she heard that soft, but familiar voice. "How ya doin' Belle – it's been a long time."

She closed her eyes and opened her arms. "Mr. Harrington sir, I be the happiest woman in the world tonight. You have finally come back to me."

She made a promise to never let him go again. As a matter of fact, she was going to see the Geechee again and pay her to work roots that would forever bind him to her. Yes sir – she was willing to do anything to keep him from walking out of her life again.

During their lengthy marriage, Scott and Iris had five children. He never stopped sleeping with Belle, and the town folk had plenty to gossip about. During a conversation down at the General Store, three of the town's gossips, Sylvester, Jasper, and Willie, were overheard discussing their favorite subjects, which were Scott, his marriages, and affairs.

"Well, well looka here. If it ain't Massa Scott Harrington hisself walkin' this way."

"Ya know Willie, that fool would like nothin' better than fo' all of us to call him massa. Well it'll be one cold day in hell 'fo I call 'em massa anything. Them slavery days be over and he better start actin' like it."

Jasper couldn't wait to add his two cents to the gossip session. "I knows fo' myself he still messin' with that woman Belle. Seein' her even when his wife be with child. He don't care none. He carry on scandalous with that floozy. She ain't got no respect for nobody. Killed his first wife and baby, yassuh, she sho' did."

Iris was hurting and feeling quite miserable. Everytime she thought she had recovered from one rumor, somebody else was bringing yet another to her. The church gossip, Marguerite, who lived way across town stopped in to see her one afternoon.

"Afternoon Sister Iris. Was on my way back home from visitin' my kinfolk and thought I'd just drop by since this be on my way home."

Iris blanched. This wasn't true, but she didn't want to call out Marguerite on her lie. "Afternoon Sister Marguerite. Thanks fo' stoppin' by. Always good to see ya. Can I offer you a glass of water, along with a piece of my pound cake?"

"Don't mind if I do. Umph, umph, umph. Sister Iris, don't believe I've ever tasted anybody's pound cake that melt in the mouth like this here butter pound cake. How's yo family?"

"Everybody's just fine."

"How's Mr. Harrington doin'?"

"Oh he be just fine. He's workin' awful hard down at the mill, but he be just fine." Iris wasn't giving her the opening she wanted, but Marguerite wouldn't be denied the opportunity to get it out.

"Did he tell you I saw him just the other day? Lawd this cake is some kinda good."

Sister Marguerite knows my house ain't on the way to hers and she really ain't interested in how my family be. She came here to gossip and help me Jesus I knows whatever she's gotta say ain't good. Sensing where the conversation was headed, Iris made her answer short. "No."

Marguerite would not be denied an opportunity to deliver the humiliating news. "Prob'ly nothin' but I seen him over at that woman name Belle's place. I reckon he was fixin' somethin' in her house. You think that be the case Sister Iris?"

The dangling sentence found the two women staring at each other for what seemed like an eternity for Iris. She couldn't let Marguerite see her fall apart.

"You're right, he was prob'ly just fixin somethin'. Here let me take that plate for you. Oh my goodness, it must've been good 'cause you've eaten every crumb."

"Thanks fo' stoppin' by Sister Marguerite. Let me help you up here. I gotta finish my housework and I know you gotta be on yo way."

"Oh did you hear about…"

"I'll be seein' you 'round Sister Marguerite."

She couldn't believe Iris was treating her so harshly and throwing her out. "Well I never. She just about slammed the doe in my face. So much fo' bein' a good Christian woman. Ain't my fault her husband runnin' 'round with that Jezebel."

Tears spilled down her cheeks while she stood leaning back against the door she had just pushed Marguerite out of and then slammed in her face. "Dear Gawd, not another bad report. Please – not another bad report. This is gettin' to be too much to bear. Lawd, I have no idea on how to handle this kinda stuff. It's killin' me not knowin' what to do or how to straighten this out. You've gotta tell me how I'm gonna get to the bottom of this. Momma and Poppa taught me not to question my husband and he don't like people, especially women folk, questionin' him."

She and Momma Lucy were in the kitchen cooking when she started the conversation. "Momma, don't the Bible say women are to obey their husbands and that the husband is the head of the house?"

"Yes and don't you ever go against the Bible. You don't wanna wind up in hell for disobeyin' Gawd's word. Gal, that man of yo's be the head of household and you obey him, ya hear me? I don't want Gawd to pour out His wrath on you just 'cause you disobeyed His word."

"Yes Momma, but what if what the man be doin' hurts his wife some kinda bad?"

"The word is the word and you had better listen to me and obey Gawd. No ifs, ands, or buts."

Somehow Momma's answer don't sound right. She knows the Bible though, and I guess I've just gotta let Gawd work out whatever's goin' on between Mr. Harrington and this woman name Belle. I'm gonna mind my own bizness and do everything in my power to make the best home for him and my children.

She knew what he had been through as a child and teenager, and concluded that another good Christian woman was exactly what he needed to get rid of the demons that refused to stop following him. Whenever he disappeared and then re-appeared reeking of strong perfume, she explained away the ache in her chest by justifying his behavior.

"Dear Lawd, he can't help it. Mr. Harrington ain't like me. I was born a free woman, and he was born a slave. He's like a wild colt that be needin' to run free whenever he feel like it. He likes good Christian women. I know he do 'cause once he became a free man, he married that gal name Lillie, who everybody say was sweet and kind. Wasn't Mr. Harrington, but that wicked woman named Belle that caused young Lillie to die."

"Lawd, I'm tryin to be an understandin' wife, but this ache just seems too much to bear. Momma says I'm supposed to do like the Bible say and obey him, but somethin' in me wanna speak up for myself."

"I remember when I first met Mr. Harrington. Oh he was so charmin'. I had to pinch myself when Poppa told me he wanted to come courtin' me. It felt so good to have a man like that wantin' me. I remember it like it was yesterday."

The first time she saw him was at Mt. Calvary's Sunday afternoon picnic. He wasn't a member of the church, but happened to come upon the picnic area. She took it upon herself to be the first to greet him.

"Welcome, I mean hello. I'm sorry, I'm sorry. Havin' trouble gettin' my words out sir." He didn't do or say anything to put her at ease, but continued to stare – waiting for her to get whatever she wanted to say out. Extending her hand out to him, she proceeded. "Good afternoon sir... I mean Mister, Mister..."

"It be Mr. Scott Harrington, and how you doin' on this fine Sunday afternoon Miz...?"

"I'm Iris Davis sir."

She escorted him around to meet the other church members. "Y'all this here be Mr. Scott Harrington and he come to join us fo' the afternoon."

His only comment was, "Afternoon." It became apparent he wasn't a sociable man, and not the type to initiate conversations. She remained close by, under the watchful eye of her father, to fill in the gaps for his lack of conversation. The very least she could do was to make him feel like he had at least one friend.

As the afternoon grew late she was exhausted. *I've gotta admit – I'm interested in this man, but his spirit so strong, frankly I'm quite exhausted. Whew Lawd – can't believe I'm sayin' this, but can't wait fo' this picnic to be over.*

Just before the picnic ended, she got the shock of her life when his single-worded conversation turned into a full exchange with Samuel. "Mr. Davis sir, I would like yo permission to court Miss Iris here. If you agree I'd like to come to this picnic y'all give here next Sunday to keep company with her."

Samuel looked if he was trying to size him up on the spot. Then he turned to look at Iris, who looked frightened, but wanted the company of this young man. He turned back to look at him again. "Well Scott..."

He flinched. *Now I just told this ol' man my name is Mr. Scott Harrington and he gonna disrespect me and call me Scott. Didn't I just call him Mr. Davis? Can't worry 'bout that none now. Got mo' important things on my mind.*

He wanted her, so he couldn't challenge Samuel. In order to get his way, he decided to overlook the lack of respect he charged Samuel with. He ingratiated himself by displaying the ultimate respect when he answered Samuel's questions with "Yes sir" or "No sir." The suave worked.

The courtship was nothing like she imagined, but then again, she had no experience with boys and really didn't know what to expect. His spirit was strong, and he possessed a quiet, but mesmerizing charm. Like the time he walked her back home after the Sunday afternoon picnic. Just before she went into the house, he pulled her into his arms and held her in a way she could only describe as electrifying. The only thing more stimulating than his embrace was the way in which he stared into her eyes. "What's the matter – you tired?"

Heck no I ain't tired. Those piercin' gray eyes of yours got my knees bucklin'. Good thing you holdin' me up in them strong arms you got there Mr. Harrington, 'cause I would likely be on the flo' at yo feet 'bout now if you wasn't.

"I, I, I guess so. Didn't realize I was this exhausted." She was lost in him and didn't stand a chance.

This man was able to draw a woman into a realm that was difficult, if not impossible to define or explain. He was not the stereotypical suitor, but his methods worked. Within six months after he started courting her, he asked Samuel for her hand in marriage, and within six months after the wedding date, his disappearing acts started.

The first time was after supper with the family on a Sunday. The comment came out of nowhere. "Goin for a walk – be back."

The silence was uncomfortable and Samuel was suspicious. "Y'all not even finished yo food. What're you talkin' 'bout Scott? Y'all ain't been here that long and we got plenty to talk 'bout and might even do some singin' too." The inquisition did nothing to discourage him.

"Said, goin' for a walk – be back."

Iris was terrified Samuel was going to further challenge him, and tried to provide a cover. "Just let me finish up Mr. Harrington and we can go."

"No, you stay and I'll be back."

Samuel was backed into a corner. Although he had his suspicions, he couldn't very well go against everything he had taught his daughter. Her husband had just given her an order and she was to obey. However, she wasn't as naïve they thought. Her female intuition had already kicked in. She knew what was going on, where he was anxious to go, and who he was anxious to get to. The rumors had been spreading throughout the Gulf. Belle was back.

There was too much going on for her to dwell on his infidelity. The persistent nauseaousness, mood swings, and change in appetite were symptoms she wasn't accustomed to. None of the pre-menstrual remedies were working, and her period wasn't showing up. Unable to get rid of the mysterious symptoms was making her depressed. The thought of what he was doing with Belle, and trying to figure out a way to bring his attention back home added more stress and left her exhausted.

Momma Lucy couldn't give her answers this time, but pointed her in the direction of the midwife. Once the midwife diagnosed what was causing the lethargy, nauseousness, and odd cravings, she came to the conclusion the discomfort was well worth it. She was pregnant and thrilled at the thought of a baby putting their marriage back on the right track, and forcing him to settle down.

"Mr. Harrington, you ever think 'bout havin' a family?" She held her breath, concerned that her question was too direct and would make him angry.

"Naw – I really don't think 'bout it one way or another. Why you askin?"

"'Cause we gonna have us a baby. That means we're gettin' ready to have a family."

"I guess I'm ready."

As happy as she was, her joy in no way matched his when the midwife announced they had a son. He named him Herbert Scott Harrington.

Dear Gawd, You must be lookin' out for this family. I know how much Mr. Harrington wanted a son. Maybe bein' a poppa was all he needed to take his mind off of that woman.

He was paying attention to home again, and seemed happy with his growing family. The changes weren't grand gestures, but rather subtle differences in the way he was treating the mother of his child.

Because he wouldn't discuss certain things like how the death of his first son affected him, she didn't know all of the details responsible for the welcomed changed.

He was trying to make amends thinking he had been given another chance. He was convinced Herbert was a reward to replace the stillborn baby Lillie delivered and died with. Although he didn't consider himself a religious man, he believed the God Iris and her family constantly spoke of had forgiven him and blessed him by replacing Lillie and the baby with Iris and Herbert.

That was all Belle's fault. Had she not been messin' with me and keepin' me comin' over to her house, things would've been different. That woman sho' know how to work a man and keep him comin' back whether he be wantin' to or not. Got me a good Christian woman and a boy now so I can live a clean life. Don't be needin' her no more. He was wrong.

Iris was pregnant again. "Mr. Harrington, you'll never guess what happen to me today."

"Don't reckon I be able to, so tell me. What's goin' on with ya now?"

She ran over to him, grabbed his hand, and placed it on her stomach. He tried to pull back, uncomfortable, for some reason, with the gesture. She wouldn't let go and kept it firmly planted against the tiny bulge. "We be gettin' ready to have us another baby. That's what happened to me today. The midwife say I'm with child again."

As her body swelled with pregnancy, the disappearing acts resumed. She was learning to recognize the pattern. He had a life with another woman he was unwilling to let go of. By the time their fourth child was born, her tolerance was spent.

Lawd, I just don't know what to do 'bout this misery he keep bringin' into this house. You gotta move this thorn from my side. You gotta sho' me what to do'. I don't think I can keep quiet much longer.

I'm tired of prayin' 'bout this. Ain't nothin' changin' 'cause I ain't doin' nothin'. Well it be time to do somethin' 'bout it and I'm gonna confront the devil. I ain't gonna continue to live in this torment. If them ladies back in the bible days can do somethin' 'bout their situations, I'm doin' somethin' 'bout mine.

She found out where the adversary lived, and decided to confront her. When she showed up, Belle was looking out of the window. To her disappointment Iris looked much different than she remembered. She stood on the other side of the road looking strong, and amazingly beautiful. Her eyes were set as if she was determined to have her say, and she moved with an unexpected confidence.

Determined to be the aggressor and scare the daylights of out Iris, she ran out of the house and into the middle of the road to confront her. *Maybe if I tell her how her man's still comin' over here every chance he get, she'll back down. Now she can see fo' herself what I look like. She be a plain woman and can't compete with the likes of me.*

"Whatcha doin' comin' 'round here? Look he comin' over here every..."

"Shut up. I don't wanna hear it. Look, I don't know what kind of trash you workin' with woman, but I want you stay away from Mr. Harrington. I been hearin' 'bout you for some time now, and quite frankly I'm surprised. The ugly works within you have taken their toll on those looks you take so much pride in. I recommend you look within and ask yo self why Mr. Harrington won't marry yo kind. Know this. I ain't never lettin' him go, so you'll be waitin' in hell for your chance to marry him. Hear me?"

Rendered speechless, Belle stared at her back as she turned back into the woods to go home.

"She come 'round here attackin' me. Who do she think she is? Ain't nothin' wrong with my looks. Her man still wants me and I ain't goin' nowhere. I'm tellin' Mr. Harrington on her and he'll fix her real good. Sides, I know somebody who can put a spell on him and get him fo' me. I swear, the next time she come 'round here..." The door slammed so hard the wind chimes fell off the porch.

Meanwhile, Iris marched back through the woods feeling invincible and completely satisfied. She had stood up to her husband's mistress. "Forgive me Lawd for cussin', but I'll be damned if I was gonna be beaten down like that witch beat down and killed Lillie and her baby. She know who she's dealin' with now and iffin I find out she's not gonna back down, I'm gonna go back over there."

Her private celebration of victory was cut short a few days later. She was reading to the children when he walked up behind them and interrupted. "I need to see you in the other room. Stop what you doin' right now and get in the other room." He was angry, but desperately trying to hold on to his temper.

"What is it Mr. Harrington you wantin' to see me 'bout?"

"You are never to go talkin' to folk outside of this house 'bout me. Is that understood?"

"Understood Mr. Harrington."

His next move caught her off guard. Just as she was passing by on her way to the kitchen, he leaned over, placed a hand on the small of her back, and swiftly pulled her into his chest. Then he was kissing her in a way that left her breathless and feeling wobbly in the legs as she was swooning and leaning up against him.

This is the most unpredictable man on earth. Who would've thought a Christian gal like me showin' a little spirit would get such a rise outta him? Lawd Jesus he's some frustratin' mystery, but You know I love him.

He unintentionally revealed his attraction to the fire in a woman, especially one whom he considered a lady – not the kind like Belle, who was always stirring up trouble and strutting around using her looks to get a man to do whatever she wanted him to do. It was a good thing he gave her this precious memory because, it would be among the few she clung to during the hardest and most painful battle of her life.

Fifteen years into the marriage she was plagued by health problems, and the symptoms weren't prenatal. Immune to her failing health, he was demanding as ever, and it was impossible to please and keep up with him. The persistent feelings of exhaustion and nauseousness were consuming her thoughts more than thoughts of pleasing him.

Nothing she did brought her back to the condition she needed to be in to care and fight for her family. She no longer had the patience to deal with the children. "Can y'all please just give Momma some time by herself? I'm not feelin' too good these days and all this noise is just makin' me feel worse."

In response to her pleas for privacy, they went into action, becoming helpful and overly protective, especially Herbert. "Look, y'all hear Momma, she ain't feelin' well. So leave her alone for a while. Beulah and Irene, take them chilluns out fo' a walk or somethin'. I'll help Momma back to bed and finish cleanin' up this house."

Scott expressed concern about her health as well, noticing the significant weight loss and other disturbing changes in her appearance. Her sunken eyes reminded him of the hollowed sockets in the head of a skeleton. He couldn't take the pitiful sight before him any longer.

"Iris, you walkin' 'round here with no strength in yo legs. I see you reachin' out for stuff just to hold you up on yo feet. That ain't right. That ain't how somebody 'posed to be walkin' 'round in their own house. You need to go and see the midwife. Maybe she can give you somethin' to perk you up again. I'm tired of seein' you like this. A woman 'posed to keep herself fixed up fo' her man. Go see the midwife soon as you can."

He left her standing there feeling sick, helpless, and ugly. She wanted him to take her in his arms and comfort her. Instead he turned away and left the house.

The next day, Irene and Beulah went with her to see Mama Mame. There would be no answers to ease her fears. The only medicine Mama Mame could offer was words of comfort and a warm embrace.

"Sweet Iris, I can't figure nothin' out this time. I think you better go over and see Doc Moore. You're not pregnant, that's fo' sho', but you need to see a doctor that got more stuff to work with than me. Let's just hope this thing that's got you be one of them stubborn flu bugs. Here, let Mama Mame give you a big ol' hug and a kiss that'll hold you til you get to Doc Moore's. I be keepin' you in my prayers though. Now make that 'pointment with Doc Moore, keep prayin', and everything's gonna be alright – you hear me gal?"

"Thanks Mama Mame."

As they were walking back home, she was making plans to go over to Doc Moore's as soon as possible. She was clinging desperately to her faith, but even it was attached to something foreboding, warning her that life would never be the same after she saw him. *It just can't be somethin' bad. It can't be. I gotta a lot of livin' to do fo' my family. Doc Moore has gotta have an answer or better yet – a cure.*

She exerted the little bit of energy that was left by keeping busy with chores around the house until he came home that evening. When he arrived, he came straight to the kitchen, and without making small talk, walked over to her. Placing an index finger under her chin, he lifted her face searching for a consoling expression to ease his fears. "What did she say?"

She searched his face looking for reassurance, support, or any evidence that he loved and wouldn't abandon her in her hour of need. His eyes were void of the confirmation she was looking for.

"She don't know what's wrong with me Mr. Harrington. Says I'm not with child, but I need to go see Doc Moore as soon as possible. Oh Gawd, she couldn't even tell me what's wrong. I'm terrified. Mr. Harrington, I fear you're 'bout to lose a second wife."

He wrapped his arms around her, and drew her so close to him her face was pressed into his chest. They stood silently for a moment before she gently pushed back and squared her shoulders. "That's enough of this pity party. Let's get ready to eat supper."

The thread of hope he had been hanging by all day finished unraveling. There would be no positive outcome. She interrupted his thoughts and yelled out in the direction of the other room, "Come children, it's time to sit down to supper with Poppa and Momma. Come, come, fo' it get cold."

He tried to enjoy supper, but the fear was driving him crazy. He hated fear. He hated starting over, and hated becoming close to (or wanting to become close) loved ones only for them to leave him for one reason or another. All of the fears and demons that followed him out of slavery and into what was supposed to be his freedom robbed him of an appetite. He couldn't force food down, even if he tried to.

The mental monsters were beating him up and he was losing his composure. *Damn it Scott, get it together. She ain't dead yet. Maybe that ol' white doctor can save her. What in the world am I gonna do with these chilluns once she's gone? This can't be happenin' again. Gawd must got somethin' against me to keep lettin' stuff happen. Didn't He think slavery was 'nuff? Didn't I suffer 'nuff humiliation at the hands of even my own daddy?*

His emotions were suffocating. He had to collect himself before anyone in the house realized what he was going through. They had no idea how much he struggled with, and hated fear. Besides Walter, he had never spoken a word to anyone about the countless fears the System of Slavery instilled in the slaves. A man didn't talk about his fears – he just lived with or fought like hell to conquer them. The master, overseers, and field bosses were relentless in their attempts to strip the slaves of human dignity. He was determined to never let them know he ever entertained the emotion of fear. He was especially bitter about James Seamore who, in his opinion, was the biggest hypocrite of them all.

He knew me and Walter was hizzin, and bein' the hyprocrite he was 'til the day he died, kept tryin' to act like he was doin' us a favor by throwin' us crumbs, but takin' away everything important to us. Soon as somebody white come by, he actin' like we just like any other slave. Even stood there when the overseer was threatnin' to sell me or Walter and separate us fo'ever after he drove Fondella away.

Now sitting at the dinner table with his family and learning an early death was about to take his second wife, the fear of his fears being exposed was too much to handle. Panic was getting the best of him.

"Goin' for a walk – be back."

"Mr. Harrington, I really don't wanna be left alone. Please stay." While waiting for his response, she was silently praying. *Lawd Jesus, I just need to get to Doc Moore so's he can fix me up and I can fight fo' my family.*

The chair scraped the wooden floor as he got up. "I ain't feelin' good either. Gotta get some air. Goin' for a walk – be back."

The next morning she was lethargic and didn't have the strength to make the trip to Doc Moore's place. So she sent Irene and Beulah to ask if she could come later in the day when she was feeling strong enough to take the walk. They ran all the way.

Doc Moore was a portly man who stood about five feet five inches in height. Most of the coloreds believed he was about as compassionate as any white man could openly be without getting into trouble. Although he wasn't one of them, they took comfort in knowing he would at least treat them like human beings – even with some dignity. He caught a lot of heat for having anything to do with them. Nonetheless, he went as far as to work with the midwives throughout the county and even provided them with medicines and equipment to care for their patients.

It was difficult for Doc Moore to understand what Irene and Beulah were trying to explain to him because they were talking at the same time. He was able to determine that the emergency had something to do with Iris' health. Irene finally ended with a plea.

"Doc Moore, can we please bring Momma here this afternoon, sir? She's feelin' somethin' awful and time's a wastin'. 'Sides, she don't look good at all – almost like a ghost."

He knew things must be serious because the coloreds went directly to the midwives before coming to him, and Mamma Mame was the most sought-after. *That ol' Mama Mame is some talented gal. If the good Lord had made her a white man, she would've been a very good doctor. But fate decided differently, so the old girl has to be satisfied with being a midwife and doctor to the coloreds throughout Chatham County. Oh Lord, if Mama Mame can't help Miss Iris, she must be in serious trouble.*

There were no patients to be seen that afternoon so he decided to close the office. "Come, come Harrington girls, Doc Moore will go over to your momma's house to see what's going on."

Iris heard a horse braying and knew it must be Doc Moore. "Thank you Jesus. The way I'm feelin' it was gonna be mighty hard tryin' to get over there to Doc Moore's place to see 'bout myself. I just gotta get better for Mr. Harrington and my children."

It was difficult not to show concern over her ghastly appearance. During the examination she broke out in a sweat. "Beulah, Irene, will one of you get me a cool wet towel so I can make your momma comfortable. Go on now, hurry up."

Irene handed him the cloths. "There, there. Now doesn't that feel much better? Now I'm going to leave you with some tonic which is a mixture of herbs rich in vitamins. This should give you some of your strength back while we're figuring out how to proceed."

Doc Moore tried to comfort her with optimism, but he had seen the same look of death on the faces of other patients. No amount of medicine was going to heal her. "Sweet Iris, I'll stop in to check on you in about a week or so."

"You girls, if you need me before then, just come and get me."

"Have a glass of water Miss Iris. I promise to come back in a few days."

The ride back home seemed unusually long as he was thinking about his visit and coming to terms with the inevitable. The second Mrs. Harrington was also going to die young.

Chapter 6
Iris' Long Goodbye

Iris' death was so unlike Lillie's. Lillie went into labor and died while giving birth, and although agonizing, everything was over within hours. Iris' decline was slow and agonizing. After Doc Moore's initial visit, there were a few times over the next five years when it seemed as though she was rebounding and on the road to recovery. But just when they started believing she was going to survive, there was another relapse. Eventually the bouts of recovery were coming far and few in between. When it seemed she couldn't lose any more weight, she did. Eventually she became bedridden and Herbert, Irene, and Beulah had to assume responsibility for cooking, cleaning, washing, and trying to keep up with Scott's demands.

The sicker she became, the more frequent his disappearing acts occurred. She was heartbroken knowing that during the long good-bye he was self-medicating in the arms of Belle. Whenever he sat next to her sick bed, he was awkward, not knowing what to say, although occasionally he would hold her hand. He tried to avoid eye contact, but whenever she did catch the far-away look in his eyes, it looked haunted. She had always put his needs, as well as the needs of the children before her own, but now his apparent self-pity and fear were irritating to her.

She knew death was imminent and had to use whatever time that was left to face it with courage. She gave directions rather than took them from him. When he was struggling with his fears, she spoke of them.

"Mr. Harrington, I knows you feelin' scared 'bout all this, but all this fear is makin' me quite frustrated. The good Lawd's 'bout ready to come and get me, but before He do, I want you to promise me you will not see my children suffer for the sake of your own flesh."

"I gave this heart of mine totally to you and did just 'bout anything a good Christian woman could do to please her man. I know you frequent that woman Belle, Gawd knows why when I tried to be the perfect wife to you, but you do see her on a regular basis. Now I'm askin' you to do this one thing for me and that is you will never marry her 'cause she's evil and I hate to think I'm leavin' my children at the mercy of some mad woman. If you disregard my wish, I'm prayin' right now the good Lawd won't let you rest and there'll be no peace in this home. I've said what I gotta say, and now I'm tired and ready to go home to be with the Lawd."

He was shocked at the candor with which she confronted him. She even called Belle by several unpleasant names. Unlike Lillie, she wasn't afraid of his hot-blooded mistress. She was only afraid of losing him, and that was his only leverage. Now that she was losing her life, she no longer feared him.

Although he couldn't imagine himself in any position wherein he took orders from a woman, he granted her deathbed wish. "I promise never to marry her. She ain't my type no way."

He was silent about the compromise with his ever-present demons. While he could promise never to marry Belle, he craftily avoided any promise to never see her again.

Iris Harrington passed away just after her forty-fifth birthday. He had the Undertaker to lay her out in repose wearing her favorite navy blue dress. It had white lace around the collar and the cuffs of the long sleeves. Her hair was parted down the middle, pulled back into a chignon, and covered with a net. The Undertaker tried his best to make her look the way she did when she was healthy, but anybody could tell the sickness ravaged her body before taking her life.

The church gossipers, including Marguerite, made sure they came to view her body.

"Lawd so glad she outta her misery. Sho' 'nuff suffered long and hard. Did ya hear he was still seein' that woman all the while. She knew 'bout it too. Heard she even stood up to her. Lawd Gawd, don't know what I would've done in her place."

They were so busy gossiping and inspecting Iris' corpse, they didn't realize he was standing nearby and overheard the conversation. He wasn't going to allow them to continue their gossip session right there in front of the coffin. He stormed over to them to set them straight and throw them out.

"Don't go callin' on the Lawd in here. Y'all just came over here to signify, but I'm puttin' both of y'all outta my house right now. You ol' hags prob'ly the biggest demons down at that church full of hypocrites. Get the hell outta my house now!"

"Mr. Harrington, we didn't mean no harm, we're so sorry for your loss. We just came to pay our respects."

"You lie. Ain't nothin' respectful 'bout either one of you. Both of you are ugly, gossipin' fools and don't have a man to try and figure out what to do with him. But I know one thing, y'all gettin' outta my house right now."

The narrow wooden coffin remained in the house for viewing for two days, with the church members and other friends visiting to pay their last respects. The short funeral was held at Mt. Calvary, and she was buried in the small burying ground for slaves and coloreds in the back of the church.

After the burial, he went home and headed straight for the bedroom to smoke his pipe and think. *Here I be again, alone – another woman been taken away from me. What kinda curse is this? Don't a man ever get redeemed? I knows people done far worse than me and they don't seem to be spendin' the rest of their lives sufferin' and bein' paid back for Gawd knows what. I gotta get outta here.*

Getting up from the chair, he started with his standard parting words. "Be back in a…" Then he remembered there was no wife to whom he had to explain his impromptu disappearance.

Where Poppa be goin' at a time like this? I'm hurtin' so bad, I wish just once, he could be here to comfort us. I wonder if he's goin' over to that woman's place. I heard Momma talkin' 'bout her and how she was causin' so much misery for her.

As Beulah watched him close the door, she sighed with resignation, heart-broken that their grief wasn't important enough to keep him home. In him, they could neither seek nor find solace. She joined Herbert, Irene, Naomi, and Fannie around the fireplace.

"I know y'all hurtin' bad as me at this moment. Maybe I can share some words of comfort to help ease this hurt we all feelin'."

"Go ahead Beulah, read us some scripture. How 'bout the one that talk 'bout how this here pain we're feelin' is but a short time that one day will feel like it was but for a night, and that joy is promised in the mornin'."

"That sounds good Irene. Here it is. It says, weepin may endure for a night, but joy cometh..."

No this isn't what we be needin' to hear right now, we need somethin' else. I'm gonna read Momma's favorite scripture.

> "But now thus saith the LORD that created thee, O Jacob, and he that formed thee, O Israel, Fear not: for I have redeemed thee, I have called *thee* by thy name; thou *art* mine.
>
> When thou passest through the waters, I will be with thee; and through the rivers, they shall not overflow thee: when thou walkest through the fire, thou shalt not be burned; neither shall the flame kindle upon thee.
>
> For I *am* the LORD thy God, the Holy One of Israel, thy Saviour: I gave Egypt *for* thy ransom, Ethiopia and Seba for thee."
>
> Isaiah 43:1-3

They were crying by the time she fininshed reading, but in their hearts could still hear Iris saying, "Babies, don't ever forget that Gawd has claimed each and every one of us as His own. Since we all belong to Him, them trials and tribulations that are a part of life, they're not the same as the ones people that don't believe and trust in Him suffer."

"Trust Momma when she tell y'all Gawd will always put His lovin' arms around you and protect you. The enemy will certainly come into your life to destroy you, but Gawd, He's the one with the real power, and He'll never let you drown in the seas of heartache and sorrow. He don't forget His own. I have my trials and tribulations, but I hold fast to these scriptures and want y'all to do the same. You never know what's gonna happen in life and sometimes, all you will have is the scriptures to get you through."

Herbert spoke up. "Y'all we gotta 'member these here words. I know the good Lawd gave this passage of scripture here to Momma so she could leave these same words of comfort to us after she left this earth. As we live this life, we gotta figure out how to apply these words to those things Momma say we colored folk gonna have to endure throughout life. I tell y'all the answers is right here in these here words."

They huddled together trying to comfort each other and wondering where Scott was.

Chapter 7
Fondella's Boys

He left the house with every intention of seeing Belle, but while in route changed his mind. As hard as it was to fathom, the kind of comfort he needed was far greater than his need for her.

When Walter opened the door, it was if Scott was looking at himself. The only difference was the face in front of him was not afraid to smile or show emotion. Walter pulled him into his embrace.

"I knew you would come and I've been waitin' for you. This be 'nother one of them hard times for you brotha, but you know I'm here to give whatever support I can."

He was most comfortable with Walter. They were not allowed to know Fondella, and the only memories they had of her were the stories they heard or were told to them by the older slaves living on the Seamore Plantation.

Fondella was a spirited and rebellious slave. She was said to be Mulatto. Standing at least six feet tall, she walked around perfectly erect as if she was royalty and everyone else on the plantation were her subjects. Her features looked nothing like the other slaves. On her head was a glorious crown of curly hair, which the other female slaves described its texture being as soft as cotton. Her blue/gray eyes were so piercing that people, both coloreds and whites, were afraid to look directly at her.

She was frustrating for the Seamores because while James Seamore was captivated by her beauty, he couldn't tolerate her rebellious behavior for fear of the other slaves becoming emboldened and following suit.

Mrs. Seamore hated her with a passion and seized every opportunity to voice her contempt. "James, where did you get her, and why bring her to our plantation. We already have twenty slaves and can't afford to care of another one. She looks like trouble, and I don't want her anywhere near me. I recommend she be sold with haste."

"Frankly Missy, I don't think anybody knows too much about her. Old man Montague's health is failing. He told me that he wants to make sure his wife's brothers can handle their plantation once he's gone. I think he's just trying to make sure everything is in order while he's still around. You can't blame a man for setting his house in order before something happens to him."

It didn't take them long to realize that Mr. Montague sold her for almost nothing because she was problematic, untamable, and just too much trouble.

Her beauty kept Mr. Montague from dealing with her in the manner in which the law and social mores required. Although he employed a brutal overseer who was anxious to break her, he wouldn't let him anywhere near her no matter how rebellious she proved to be. He couldn't stand the thought of the whip or any other form of lash violating the prized beauty he was infatuated with.

At almost anytime throughout the day, he could be found staring at her as if in a trance. He conveniently showed up wherever she was. The rumor mill was abuzz. Out in the fields, the overseer and other workers ridiculed him.

"Ol' man Montague thinks he's puttin' one over on everybody. He damn near kills himself trying to keep me from breaking her. He don't even realize we all see him sneaking down to her quarters every night. Sometimes he can't even wait 'til the nighttime. He rushes everybody out of the fields before the sun goes down so he can hurry up and spend time with her."

"Yeah, Miss Montague knows what he's up to, but too afraid to say somethin'. I heard about the time he bought her jewels for Christmas, and low and behold, here comes Fondella struttin' in to serve dinner wearing the matching earrings. She's so arrogant she stopped directly in front of the Misses and stared at her, daring her to say something. Montague looked like he was gonna wet his pants tryin' to get Fondella outta that room."

A round of laughter followed the field hand's account of what happened at the Montague's Christmas dinner. As hard as he tried to hide his feelings, everybody knew he was obsessed with Fondella and had made a fool of himself over her on more than one occasion.

He had been sleeping with her from the time he purchased her off of the selling block at the age of 16 until she turned 20. Whenever he came near her, he couldn't speak without stuttering, and was so clumsy he fell over everything trying to stay close. His insecurities had him standing guard for hours trying to keep the overseer or any other man from touching her.

As time passed she became more and more difficult to deal with. He was trapped in a constant state of frustration, wishing she could understand what he felt for her, and be grateful she wasn't treated like his other slaves.

He was reduced to begging. "Why can't you appreciate what I do for you? I give you more than I give any slave on this property. I even gave you jewels that I was supposed to give to my wife. So you have got to start obeying the orders of these white people and stop making so much trouble. I'm telling you if you don't start acting proper, I'm gonna have to put the whip to you myself. I can't keep making excuses for you. These men are chomping at the bit to teach you a lesson, and I've got a good mind to turn you over to them."

Her response was a blank stare. *Massa's intelligence must be way smaller than his appearance iffin he thinkin' his pieces of jewelry mo' valuable than my free spirit. He may own my body, but my mind and spirit belong to no white man, fo' they remain in my safekeepin'.*

That jewelry be beautiful but I knows he didn't pay much fo' it anyways. He knows that other white massa that get jewels from them ships comin' in from the other side of the world. Heard'em talkin' myself. I'll do whatever I wanna do. Treatin' me better than other slaves ain't sayin' much now is it?"

She was far more intelligent than anyone gave her credit. Although her tongue could be poisonous, she never voiced her true feelings about her leverage over him. She knew exactly when and how to exercise her power.

She also knew that notwithstanding the feelings expressed to her deep in the night down in her slave quarters, she was considered property rather than human, and would not accept his hypocrisy. The most effective way to pay him back was to be rebellious and make everybody's life hell on earth. As she aged, she became more bitter and vicious about her status in life. As he aged, he became more exhausted in trying to control her. In the end, and notwithstanding the ache in his loins and heart, he felt it best to sell her to some unsuspecting slave owner who thought with his head. That slave owner was James Seamore, or so he thought.

James Seamore didn't make it a practice of sleeping with his slaves because it was bad business. He was determined that emotions would never influence his decisions on how to deal with chattel he paid good money for.

His recent deal with Mr. Montague didn't require him to pay much for the female slave. Being a frugal man, paying any amount of money for human chattel was an investment from which he wanted to yield a profit – not trouble. Sleeping with his latest acquisition was the furthest thing from his mind.

He pulled up in front of the Montague house and waited for his property to be brought out to him. To say she was different was a gross understatement. His throat started to tighten for no reason. At that moment he knew that he was in trouble.

Lord have mercy on my soul. If she has this effect on me by just walking towards this wagon, then surely ol' man Montague had to get rid of her. Who on God's good earth can handle an extraordinary creature such as this? Something's wrong. Ain't no way a slave supposed to look like this or have this affect on a white man.

The power of persuasion this slave woman possessed was undeniable and she displayed it effortlessly. Right then and there the selfish part of him took over and he decided to have her for himself. For the second time Fondella was assigned to private quarters for the satisfaction of her master.

The first night in her new quarters it was she who made James Seamore surrender. Under the pretext of making sure she was in bed by curfew, he paid her a visit. As the door opened, he saw her standing over a small table lighting an oil lamp. She looked up to see who the visitor was. Her hair was all over her head and the illumination from the oil lamp picked up the glistening effect of her blue/gray eyes. She was much taller than him.

His discomfort became even more noticeable as he stared at the silhouette of her body through the long muslin nightgown. His attempt to sound authoritative fell flat, and his voice quivered as he spoke.

"You ready for bed gal?"

"Yes massa, I'm 'bout ready." His throat felt like it was getting tighter.

"Well hurry up because you have get up to the house before the sun comes up and fix breakfast for my family. What're you waiting for? Hurry up and finish whatever it is you're doing and get into bed. I don't know what you got away with over at the Montague place, but I won't tolerate disobedience. So don't try it."

Now how am I supposed to hurry up and get in this bed when he's standin' there starin' at me and not makin' a move to leave me alone. She knew better than to voice her thoughts.

"Yes massa." He still didn't move.

Just what I thought. He's standin' there like a damned fool, wantin' me and too proud to say somethin'. Pretendin' like he orderin' me to do somethin'. Well, time to show'em just how weak his flesh be, and who really be in charge here. She reached up and started to unbutton her gown.

"Nigger, what the devil do you think you're doing?" Yet he did nothing to stop her, as she knew he wouldn't. When she finished unbuttoning the gown, she stepped out of it and was standing before him completely naked. He started walking towards her even though he kept telling himself he should put the bull whip to her for making such a brazen move on a white man.

Never taking her eyes off of him, she opened her arms and he walked right into them.

"Sweet Jesus, what in God's name am I..." As soon as she closed her arms around him and locked her lips over his, he was lost. He pulled back one last time trying to resist her. "Damn you nigger. Oh God help me – am I the slave or the master?"

This ain't complicated, but I'll help Massa out. She kept it simple when she provided him with the answer. "Both."

He surrendered.

Over the next two years, she gave birth to two baby boys, and James Seamore fathered both of them. He wouldn't allow her to keep the babies. In order to have complete access to her, after the birth of each son, he sent the baby to be raised by the slave girl Molly and her husband, Jacob, who lived in other quarters.

Molly's complexion was the color of coffee beans; her hair was coarse; and she stood about five feet tall. So everyone knew the two boys whose features were nothing like those of Molly or Jacob, were Fondella's boys, and their father was James Seamore. No one openly spoke of the obvious, but the whispers continued regardless.

"Either Massa think we dumb, or he just don't care none, 'cause ain't no way two niggers the color of Molly and Jacob

Harrington gonna produce light skinned boys with curly hair and gray eyes."

"Now Mavis, I reckon he just don't care. He be too concerned with havin' her. He's so spell-bound, he could care less what the missus or any of us slaves think."

"Guess you right 'bout that Georgia. What we gonna do 'bout it anyhow?"

They were going on vacation up north to visit with friends in Boston. Mrs. Seamore was anxious to get away for awhile and even more anxious to get James away from Fondella.

"Make sure we take enough girls to take care of me while I'm up in Boston." He nonchalantly suggested Fondella.

"I don't want that negra going up to Boston with me. She's too unruly and I'm not going to have her embarrassing me. Take two girls that know how to treat a white lady. Everytime I look at that she-devil, I want to pull out a whip and rip her to shreds."

She-devil or not, he wasn't going to leave her behind in North Carolina. He had seen how the field hands, as well as his friends, looked at her. The minute he was out of town, one or more of them would be beating down the door to her slave quarters.

"Now Missy, I know she can be a handful, but she's as strong as an ox and can get more done for you than any two girls. So if you take her, it's like taking four girls instead of three. C'mon, you know I'm right. Please just do this for me. I promise to buy you anything you want if you just agree with me on this."

"Oh, alright, but she had better learn to stay in her place – I mean it."

She was going to Boston with them, and he would find a way and a place to spend in her arms. She drove him mad, and madness in her arms was worth the risk as far as he was concerned.

True to her rebellious spirit, Fondella took the trip as an opportunity to run away, and no one ever heard from her again. One of the other slave girls said she could have sworn she saw Fondella running off one night with some young, white aristocratic looking gentleman.

Standing before Massa Seamore, the slave girl was truly shaken. He was threatening to have her whipped and worse if she lied to him.

"Goddamnit nigger, you had better tell me the truth. Now where is she? I know you've seen her, so you had better tell me the truth."

"Massa, I, I, I..."

"You had better find you tongue in a hurry and tell me everything you know. If you don't, I swear, I'll take a whip to you myself gal, and when we get back home, you will be sold by the next day. Do you understand me? I'll make sure you never see your family again if you live past the whippin' I give you. Now where is she?"

"Massa, I'm tellin' you the truth, whilst y'all was out with yo friends on that first night we got here, this white man who look like he was rich eyed Fondella. Later on, I saw him talkin' to her just outside the door to that private room you got for her."

"James, how despicable of you. Here you are up in Boston still panting after that beast. Well, I never..."

A sly smile appeared on slave girl's lips. *Yeah, I'll bet you never. Missy, you thought you knew him real good. You so certain 'bout where you stand in Massa's life, you thought he was gonna make all three of us slave girls sleep together on the skinny little cot. Po' woman. You powerless to do anything 'bout his fixation on Fondella. Must feel horrible knowin' Massa's heart belong to that beast and beat very little fo' you.*

He was too furious to address the obvious revelation. "Continue gal and you had better get it right. What rich looking white man are you talking about?"

"Massa, as I was tellin' you fo' the missus got upset, there was this rich lookin' white man that eyed her on the first day we got here. He was takin' her outside in the back and sittin' there talkin' to her. Some nights he brought food with him and shared it with her. I even heard him readin' some stuff he say he wrote for her 'bout the big wide world and how he wantin' her in it 'long side of him. That last night when y'all was havin' the big party, I saw them runnin' off. That's the whole truth massa, I swear fo' Gawd that's the whole truth."

He returned to North Carolina a broken man. Some young white man actually did what he fantasized about, but never had the heart to do – running away with the beautiful Fondella to a place where he could be free to be with her, regardless of what anyone thought, or what the law was.

When he couldn't bear another day of suffering in silence, he turned his attention to the next best thing – their sons. While they weren't treated like his white sons, everybody knew they weren't treated like the other slave children. They had Fondella's spirit and accepted his preferential treatment. His gestures were received, but never worthy of appreciation. As far as they were concerned, it was he who owed the debt and didn't deserve their gratitude.

Early in life they learned that Molly couldn't connect with them maternally no matter how hard she tried. Jacob wasn't a man who was comfortable with demonstrating his feelings for anybody. He was always on guard and could never let Massa know what he was feeling or thinking. Sensing the dysfunction in their quarters, from the very beginning, they clung to each other, and didn't trust anyone else.

By the time they reached their early teens, they had discovered their power over the opposite sex, as well as men who were intimidated by their soaring height and good looks.

Walter, despite his good looks, didn't use his leverage in the same way that Scott did. "Brotha', you can have them fast gals, but me, I wanna have a life with a sweet girl. I know it's hard to bring this anger under control we got 'bout Massa and how he kept us from Fondella, but anger will eat away at you, and I'm tryin' to live. I ain't tryin' to shrivel up with bitterness."

"Ever since I heard President Lincoln signed that preliminary order, I've had my hopes up 'bout livin' as a free man. I'm prayin' one day soon we're gonna be free and when that happens, I'm ready to start livin' with a sweet colored gal as my wife. All I want is freedom and peace."

Walter's dream sounds good, but I ain't countin' on no President Lincoln signin' no papers that's gonna turn us niggers free. Heard them white folk talkin' sayin' he be more intent on preservin' the Union than freein' us niggers.

In the meantime, I'm gonna have as many of them gals that come my way. Most of 'em say they want somebody to be massa over them anyways and I, for one, ain't got no problem with that. 'Sides, I got sweet Lillie. Whenever I get tired of them gals who just wanna be with a man and really don't have no feelins for him, I go to Lillie. She always accepts me with opened arms. She be a good gal and knows how to obey a man.

Walter got his wish and President Lincoln did exactly what Scott wasn't counting on him to do. At the ages of 18 and 17, respectively, Walter and Scott Harrington became free men.

On the day Scott learned he had become a free man, he was down in the woods again in the shack with Massa Seamore's niece, Melanie Hollinsworth. She was all his and begging for more. Just when he had gotten through all the fancy petticoats they were interrupted by total chaos.

There was screaming, and he could tell people were running in every direction. Even the sounds of branches and dried leaves crunching beneath their feet were unsettling.

"What the devil's goin' on? What kinda fool is runnin' through these woods screamin' 'bout freedom?"

He tried to go back to what they were doing, but the hysteria around them wouldn't allow it. Not only were the people who were running through the woods frantic, Melanie was becoming hysterical as well.

"I can't be found down here with you. Jesus Christ, I'm gonna get into serious trouble if they find me down in here with the likes of you. Oh dear Lord, how am I gonna get out of here without somebody seeing me?"

Her hypocrisy and hysterics were getting on his nerves. "Look Melanie, just you calm down right now. Sounds like they too riled up to pay much attention to us."

Just then, Walter burst through the door with an explanation for all of the chaos. President Lincoln had signed the Emancipation Proclamation.

"Did you just say we're free men?"

"I'm not sure, but that's what everybody's runnin' 'round yellin' 'bout. Massa wantin' to see all of us up at the house to explain what's goin' on. Come on, let's go see for ourselves what's got everybody upset."

"Melanie, get up and get outta here."

"Don't you dare talk to me in that tone of voice. You are to refer to me as Miss Melanie, or I will tell Uncle James…"

"Tell Uncle James what? You down here callin' a nigger 'Massa' and doin' anything I ask you to do? Is that what you gonna tell him. I said get up and get outta here."

The brutality with which he was now dismissing her was more than insulting. However, she wasn't about to tell anybody that minutes earlier she had been in his arms telling him how much she loved him, begging him to make love to her, and calling him Massa.

As soon as the slaves were gathered in the front yard of the main house, James Seamore made the official announcement. "It seems that Mr. Lincoln has signed a document they call the Emancipation Proclamation. Y'all know that although North Carolina hasn't seen too many battles, we've been in this Civil War. President Lincoln warned North Carolina, as well as the other slave states, that if they didn't return to the Union, he was going to proceed and sign an executive order to free all slaves."

"Well, it seems like the Confederate fighting spirit made the states hold out and Mr. Lincoln exercised his power and went ahead and signed the Emancipation Proclamation. It's my understanding that it happened on New Year's Day. It's taken a little longer for word to reach these parts, but states have already started releasing their slaves."

"I've only got about twenty slaves anyway. We're gonna have to figure out what to do with y'all. So y'all need to start thinking about what you're gonna do with your families. I can keep a few of you on to work around here or down at my family's tobacco mill if you wanna stay."

A sea of blank faces stared back at him. *Damn – these niggers are confused. They don't know what the devil all this mean. How am I gonna explain this to them. Where are they supposed to go? Where are they supposed to live? I don't even know what to tell 'em myself. Let me try again.*

"Y'all free people now, I can't make you stay here and you're free to do whatever you wanna do. You can take your whole family and just walk on away from here if that's what you want. Mr. Lincoln signed the papers that said so."

Nobody walked away. It was if he announced how much longer they had to stay out in the fields working. They went back to doing exactly what they were doing before the announcement. They weren't prepared to leave because everybody, including the Seamore's, had to figure out what all of this meant.

"Scott and Walter, would y'all boys please come in for a minute. I need to talk to you about something."

Out of curiousity, some of the slaves stopped what they were doing. An elderly slave leaned over to another man and whispered, "I told you so. All these years I been tellin' y'all them there his boys."

Once they were inside, he didn't admit to paternity, but made offers he was sure they couldn't refuse. They accepted his offer of land owned by the Seamore's, as well as lifetime employment at the family's mill.

Walter built his home in a secluded and beautiful spot located deep in a wooded area. He lived there peacefully with Cora, who also grew up on the Seamore Plantation.

Scott moved into a house on a piece of property closer the Seamore's. As soon as he became a free man, he asked Lillie to marry him. He overheard on many occasions, James Seamore and his friends talking about owning women through marriage. As their husband's property, they had to obey him. This was the perfect relationship as far as he was concerned, and he was in a hurry to make it happen. Although she knew about his reputation with women (slave and free) Lillie couldn't resist him, and accepted his offer.

The crackling sound of the fire as Walter threw another log into the fireplace brought Scott out of his daydream about the past. Sometimes, all that seemed like it happened so many years ago, it was somebody else's life, while at other times he wanted to go back in time. At least while they belonged to James Seamore it wasn't much they had to figure out. All they had to do was to follow his orders and those of the overseer. *Sometimes I wonder if that was better than freedom.*

They continued their visit by talking about how now things were so different from the old slavery days. Walter was at peace with his life since becoming a free man. Scott was complicated. He was charismatic, but no one could quite put their finger on the reason why. While he could have his pick of any number of women, he only married a certain type – his polar opposite. Yet despite their gentle and kind dispositions, as well as an eagerness to please him in every way, he continued to remain entangled with Belle. Despite her allure and fiery temper, he refused to allow the femme fatale to get too close to him.

Walter couldn't condone his actions, but understood their origin. The residual scars from the effects of slavery had created a complex man who constantly acted out and directed his frustrations at those who had nothing to do with, or no control over the System of Slavery. He could not detach from certain affections that constantly haunted and called out to him. He was bound to answer the calls.

Reflecting back on the position he caught Scott and Melanie in when he came to tell him they were free men, Walter also recalled that her and her sister, Sandra, simultaneously and secretly started their affairs with Scott when he was only fourteen years old.

Although they were considered among the most beautiful and eligible young ladies in the county, they preferred to sneak off and enjoy Scott who spoke of his resentment over their hypocrisy.

"Walter, they be some deceitful women. Moanin' and groanin' like I'm the best thing ever happen to'em while we in the woods where nobody can see us. Tellin' me I don't even have to call'em "Miss." 'Just call me Melanie or Sandy is what they say to me. Both of 'em know what I'm doin' with the other one. Yet Melanie keep swearin' she loves me. Then as soon as they get back in front of their people, and their white friends, they start actin' like they some kinda angels and treatin' me like any other slave. But I'll tell you somethin', when I got'em down in them woods, I make'em serve me like I'm the massa. I show 'em no mercy."

His anger was further fueled by James Seamore's tolerance of his nieces' behavior. "Let me tell you somethin' else, that ol' man knows what them gals doin' with us in private. He knows, but he be the biggest hypocrite of 'em all. Just like he went cryin' and whinin' after Fondella, but wasn't man 'nuff to keep her here with us, he know his nieces whinin' and cryin' after us. He's too damned hypocritical to step in though."

As a teenager who had no sexual encounters prior to his relationships with Melanie and Sandra, at first he enjoyed the attention, as well as the sexual experience. But he grew tired of their insatiable sexual appetites one minute and verbal castration of him the minute they were in the presence of white people. To get through the humiliation, he looked forward to and retaliated in the area where he knew they were totally at his mercy (having sex down in the woods in the old shack where he ruled).

So as a free man, he remained enslaved to dark and dangerous affections, the origin of which was the twisted love/hate/ slave/master relationship with the Seamores, not to mention dysfunctional sexual relationships with older women who begged for his love in secret, but verbally and emotionally castrated him in public.

Walter coped differently. He knew they wanted their sexual liaisons with the slaves heated and uninhibited. So he was intentionally inhibited and boring. They really didn't care and left him alone. They preferred to be with the hot blooded and power-hungry Scott. He was eager to fulfill every sexual fantasy they could conjure up. They came to Walter only when Scott was being watched closely by the overseer or James Seamore.

Walter couldn't bring himself to rebuke him because he was guilty of strategically driving them into Scott's arms. *Brotha, you seem to like these dangerous games these gals like to play. I ain't tryin' to feel the whip 'cross my back, or worse. No sir. You can have all you want outta them misses. They way too much trouble fo' me.*

If Scott didn't trust anyone else, including himself, he knew Walter's loyalty was a given and a promise never to be reneged. He couldn't bear to think of a day when Walter wouldn't be there for him. Whenever he was at his wits end, he went to the one person who could console him. *Gotta see Walter. He knows just what to say. He understand what be inside of me. He know what them years on the Seamore property did to us.*

Now Iris was gone and he had no one to vent with but Walter. He had too much on his mind and Belle couldn't even satisfy what he was longing for right now. *Walter always there with me and fo' me. Can't bear to think of life without him. Hope that day never comes.*

They were standing at the door saying their goodbye's when Walter pulled him close to him. With his arms wrapped around Scott, he held him until his body relaxed. He then planted a kiss on his forehead.

"Ya take care of yo self now. Can't nothin' destroy you if you don't let it. We made it outta that particular place in time. You gotta leave that stuff behind and stop draggin' it through life with you. Let it go. Brotha, I would've lost my mind if I held on to everything we went through. Kill it and leave it where it belongs – in the past."

Preparing to face the world again, Scott started to stiffen up. "I'll be seein' ya soon". With that, he left to go home. The perfect peace he found only in Walter was over.

Chapter 8
Life without Iris

When he returned home, the children were already in bed, and the flames in the fireplace had been reduced to embers. Pulling off his heavy boots, he fell into bed with a sigh. While lying there staring at the ceiling, he was wondering what life was going to be like now with children and no wife. Sleep finally won the battle against anxiety and exhaustion, although it was a restless slumber.

The knock at the door startled him. He sat up rubbing his eyes with his fists. It was Herbert. "Poppa, time to get up and go down to the mill. I'll get Beulah to bring yo lunch by 'bout 12 o'clock Noon." He looked down and realized he never took his clothes off the night before.

"Okay, I'm gettin' up right now. Make sure everybody do their chores, ya hear me?"

"Yes sir."

Herbert, Beulah, and Irene helped Fannie and Naomi to wash up and get dressed. Irene gave instructions for breakfast. "Y'all come sit down and eat. I fixed grits just the way Momma used to fix them with a touch of cream and plenty of sweet butter."

Before leaving the house, Beulah placed his lunch inside of the small metal pail. The lunch pail was then placed in the middle of the table.

"Herbert, as soon as the recess bell rings, I'll run Poppa's lunch pail down to the mill so he can eat. There – everything is all set. Can't risk bein late gettin' Poppa's lunch down to the mill."

While Irene and Beulah had been attentive students with respect to household responsibilities, the special touch that belonged exclusively to Iris was glaringly missing. Scott made attempts at interacting with them, but felt awkward trying to display emotions that were uncomfortable for him. He tried telling stories, but they weren't interesting. He couldn't read, so that was out. Frustrated, he gave up.

He demanded that Irene and Beulah handle the emotional stuff when Fannie and Naomi wouldn't stop crying.

"Beulah – Irene will one of y'all see what's the matter with them chillun? I don't know what they cryin' fo', but somebody better get them to stop that noise fo' I pull out my whip – I mean my strap."

Before either one of them could respond, Herbert stepped in. "Here, let me take care of this. "Y'all just follow my directions. Momma taught me what to do in these situations."

"Boy, I said fo' Irene or Beulah to take care of that. That stuff ain't fo' no man to be takin' care of. Let'em do what I say."

"Oh no Poppa, I'll do it – Momma showed me how."

"Listen here – I'm yo poppa and you do like I tell you to do. I don't wanna hear another word outta ya. You're gettin' on my last nerve and I'm 'bout to do somethin' that ain't gonna feel real good to you."

The relationship between Herbert and Scott was disintegrating into one of constant conflict. He kept asserting himself into matters and in ways that, as far as Scott was concerned, were disrespectful. *That boy needs a strap taken to him. I'm gettin' real sick and tired of him talkin' back at everything I say. One of these days he's gonna be real sorry for gettin' smart with me. I'm gonna give him a beatin' he ain't soon to forget 'cause that's exactly what he's itchin' fo.*

The relationship took a serious turn for the worse when Herbert confronted him about his disappearing acts.

It was a Saturday afternoon when Herbert hitched the wagon to the mare out in the barn. He rode into town and purchased sacks of flour, cornmeal, and dried beans at the General Store. *Gotta stop by the Jenkins' place 'cause Mr. and Mrs. Jenkins said if we ever need meat, they got plenty we can have. I'm gonna ask for some pork so I can fry fatback, fix some greens with them good ol' ham hocks, and have plenty of that hot and spicy sausage for breakfast. This way I can spend all of the money Poppa gave me on the flour, cornmeal, and beans. That'll save us some money and Momma always said not to spend money when spendin' wasn't called for.*

During the ride back home, he was entertaining himself with singing. "If I can help somebody as I pass along; if I can cheer somebody with a word or a song; if I can help somebody from doin' wrong, then…"

He abrudptly stopped when the door to a small house opened and Scott appeared with Belle, whose arms were wrapped around his waist. She then moved around to the front of him and they started kissing.

"What the devil?"

Although he had heard the rumors circulating about his father for years, he had never seen him behaving like this – not even with Iris.

"There my momma was witherin' away durin' her last days on earth, and he couldn't think of nobody but hisself. Didn't even want to face the truth that she was dyin' with a broken heart and he was never nowhere to be found."

He sharply pulled on the reins, confusing the mare. The horse took off running. It was a miracle that the horse and wagon came to an abrupt stop just short of the porch rather than crashing into it.

Everything happened so fast they were shocked at and unprepared for the intrusion. Scott saw the fury in Herbert's eyes and attempted to jump in front of Belle, not knowing exactly what Herbert intended or was capable of doing. "What the devil do you think you doin' huh? Belle stay behind me, stay behind me. Answer me boy."

Herbert's arms were flailing wildly about, striking out at and landing punishing blows to both of them, all the while screaming, "How could you do this to Momma, how could you do this to my poor momma? She never done nothin' but love you... how could you?"

Eventually Scott was able to subdue him, but only to the extent his blows no longer caught the frightened and somewhat bruised Belle, who had scurried back into the house and was witnessing the fight through the window.

"Get yo self together, ya hear me? Why you here, and what're doin' messin' 'round in grown folks bizness?"

Although both of his arms were restrained, Herbert continued kicking.

"Why Poppa, why, why..."

"This ain't the time nor place to talk 'bout this. I'm yo poppa boy, and I don't be owin' you no explanation."

Herbert noticed Belle peeping through the window. Trying once again to break away from Scott, he lashed out at her. "You good-for-nothin trollop, you're a whore, and you look like the filthy trash people been talkin 'bout all these years. You look like some made-up Jezebel travelin' with that carnival what come through Chatham County. You will never have him – don't you know that – you will never have him."

To her disappointment Scott never said a word to challenge his boy's name calling. Tears started to form in her eyes as she was struggling to regain her composure. "That boy don't know what he be talkin' 'bout. His daddy keep comin' back to Belle, so I ain't gonna let them hurtful words he tryin' to throw at me, ruin my day."

Meanwhile, out on the porch, Herbert was yelling. "I hate what you did to Momma, and I hate y..." Before he could finish the word "you" she heard the resounding slap across his face.

"Don't you ever talk to me like that again, else I'll hang you up like they did in them old slavery days, and I'll take to your back with my razor strap, ya hear me boy? There won't be a strip of flesh left on your back when I get finished with you."

"Poppa, you won't ever hear me talk to you like this again, you can count on that."

Herbert then jerked away with such force Scott stumbled back dangerously close to the window through which Belle was still peeping.

Then jumping onto the wagon, he pulled out of the yard and on to the road. The horse trotted erratically down the dusty road, kicking up so much dirt, they couldn't even see him – they just heard him coughing as he became lost in the cloud of dirt.

Scott went back into the house to calm down. "I'm gonna kill that boy when I get home. I swear I'm gonna kill'em. Belle jumped and everything rattled when his fist landed hard on the table. "Nobody's gonna disrespect me like that or raise his hand up to me. He's gonna be sorry he even tried. Just wait 'til I get home."

Irene and Beulah heard the horse and wagon approaching the house and could tell something was wrong. The wagon wheels were squeaking some kind of awful. Herbert was driving fast and/or recklessly. The crashing sound sent everybody running out of the house to see what was going on.

His appearance was shocking. There was dried blood around his mouth, sweat pouring down his face, and his shirt was soaking wet.

Irene spoke up first, "For the love of Gawd, what happened to you?" He didn't answer, but then again he didn't have to because by looking at him, they could tell that he had been met with violence, but by whom?

"What happened, Herbert?"

"Stop askin' me questions and just do what I tell y'all to do. I ain't got time to be runnin' my mouth with y'all. Beulah, stop yo whinin' and help me. If you ain't gonna help, then just gone on back in the house."

Instead of running into the house, she picked up her long skirt to avoid tripping and ran after him. She grabbed him by the arm. "Now Herbert Scott Harrington, you gonna have to tell us what just happened. You're scarin' the daylights outta Irene and me. Please tell us what happened?"

"I'll tell y'all soon as y'all help me to get these sacks of food in the house and store them away, but right now we've gotta get this stuff off of this wagon and into the house."

He was giving out orders and throwing the sacks off the wagon with so much force, they had to struggle to keep standing upright in order to catch them. By now they were out of breath trying to follow his orders, and crying so he forced himself to gain enough composure to calm them down. While he was furious with Scott, he didn't want them upset, frightened or even worse, thinking he was anything like their father.

"Oh Gawd, I'm so sorry. Look y'all, I seen Poppa with that woman Belle. I just lost it – she was hangin' all over him like he belonged to her. I never even seen Momma hangin' on him like that. 'Sides, Momma ain't hardly cold in her grave and here he go messin' round with that woman. I tried to take her head off and Poppa's head off too."

Their eyes grew wider as he recounted the violent exchange blow by blow. Irene put him on notice as to his fate as she described what was going to happen upon Scott's return. "Oh my Gawd, Poppa's gonna kill you when he comes back home."

"If I don't kill him the minute I lay eyes on him again."

When he arrived, they were shocked that he didn't even mention what happened, but went straight to his rocking chair. He sat staring into the fireplace, and there wasn't even a fire burning.

"Poppa, you alright?" Irene thought maybe he had been so deep in thought he didn't hear her and repeated the question. "Poppa, you hear me? I asked you if you're alright."

She sounded too demanding and he took offense to her line of questioning. "Damn it gal, do I look alright? You had better mind yo tongue. Get outta my face and go start gettin' them chilluns ready for bed. I don't feel like talkin' and don't want no bother." He didn't mention Herbert.

It was not Scott's, but Herbert's disposition that had everyone in the house on pins and needles. No one could figure him out. Over the next few weeks, he continued to do his chores. He rose early in the morning, chopped wood, made the fire, and got Irene and Beulah up to help prepare Naomi and Fannie for school. They kept asking the same question they had asked of Scott, "Herbert, you alright? His answer was short. "I be just fine." He didn't appear to be just fine.

When Iris was healthy, he would sit with her and discuss the Bible for what seemed like hours. When she passed away, he was the one who kept them focused on her favorite scriptures in an effort to draw comfort. After the fight, no one saw him pick up Iris' bible and he never mentioned a bible verse again.

"Herbert, why don't you read some scripture to us."

"Don't feel like readin' no scripture Irene. That stuff don't work for everybody, and I ain't interested. Y'all can read if y'all wanna, but I got things to do 'round here."

They couldn't deny that Scott expected a lot out of him and that he did have plenty to do, but his answer meant something other than what he was actually saying.

It looked like he was starting to come around when he announced he was going to be helping Mr. Jenkins out for a couple of hours a day.

"Beulah, maybe he's startin' to come 'round if he's feelin' strong enough to start workin' for somebody else when he got all this stuff Poppa make him do right here at home."

"I don't know if I agree. Maybe he just don't wanna be 'round Poppa too much. He was some kinda mad when he caught him with that woman. Must've been madder than the devil hisself 'cause how else he gonna have the nerve to actually fight with Poppa. Maybe workin' over at the Jenkins' place will keep his mind off of things? I sho' hope so. I miss the old Herbert."

Scott noticed the change as well, but was determined not to mention the fight. He was still simmering about Herbert standing up to and attacking him in front of a woman. He was also dealing with a revelation. During their fight, he realized the full measure of his son's strength and that he was dealing with a formidable opponent. He was uncomfortable with this acknowledgement and apprehensive when any attempts at discipline could turn into humiliation in front of the other children.

The next day after the fight, he made an attempt to approach Herbert because he was hell bent on putting him in his place. Just as Herbert was about to leave the house, he stepped in front of him to block his path. "Where you think you goin' boy without askin' me?"

The non-response made him even angrier. "Well, where do you think you goin'? Don't just stand there lookin' at me all simple. Answer me. Where you think you goin'?"

Herbert tried to go around him, but he was determined to back him into a corner.

"Boy, I intentionally didn't deal with you when I got home yesterday 'cause I was gonna have to kill you. Like I told you, don't you ever…"

"Don't I ever what? What you gonna do to me huh? Kill me? Go on and do it 'cause I don't care 'bout nothin' no more. Go ahead Poppa, I ain't afraid."

"Boy who the devil you think you talkin' to?" He became physical and started jabbing him in the chest until Herbert was standing with his back up against the wall. Despite the tears filling up in his eyes, he wouldn't back down.

"Go on and do what you gotta do. You ain't changin' my mind 'bout how I feel. Meant every word I said, so you better go ahead and finish me off 'cause a lotta stuff inside me already dead."

Herbert's disdain hurt him to his heart. There was no telling what was going to happen next since it was obvious he was willing to endure punishment rather than give in to threat. Still his pride wouldn't allow him to humble himself. He was Mr. Scott Harrington, and if there was going to be any reconciliation, it was Herbert who would have to take the first step.

I ain't gotta solve this right now. He like his momma. That boy can't stay mad fo' long. Just watch, he'll come 'round in a day or two. He's gotta learn he can't go messin' 'round in my bizness.

Scott would be waiting on an apology for the rest of his life.

A few days after the fight, Herbert went back to the Jenkins' place. "Mornin' Mr. Jenkins. I heard folk 'round here sayin' you be needin' somebody to help you out 'round yo place. I'm lookin' fo' work. I'm young and strong and ain't askin' fo' much money."

"Son, I don't know 'bout that. You sho' it's a good idea? I know how yo poppa is 'bout stuff like this. Ask him first and then come back to me."

"Please Mr. Jenkins. You've gotta let me do this. Whatever you can pay me sir be good 'nuff?" He wanted the job in the worst way because after the fight, there was no way he could continue living with Scott. He had to leave the Gulf forever.

His resentment had been building for a very long time. Everything just came to a head the day he caught Scott at over at Belle's place. Up until then he felt compelled to hide his growing resentment about the way Iris was treated. Besides, she would never allow him to disrespect his father. He never knew about her confrontation with Belle, and believed she was too afraid of losing Scott to fight back or let anyone else fight back for her.

For as long as he could remember rumors had been circulating throughout the Gulf about the tawdry and scandalous affair. It tore him up to see Iris suffering in silence from the pain and humiliation inflicted by Scott and Belle.

Lawd I just don't understand the justice in all this misery. How come he get to live and Momma she gotta die such an agonizin' death? Just don't seem fair. How come he raise so much devil and get away with it? Momma, she's a good woman and don't deserve to suffer like this. I know she tell us that You never make a mistake, but this just don't seem right.

Putting his heart and soul into Iris and the girls was the only way he could control the growing resentment. As long as she was alive his focus was on taking care for her, and compensating for the love Scott denied her. Once she was gone, all he had to focus on was Scott. He battled internally wanting to love him as he desired, but tormented by the reality of his resentment. *Lawd Jesus, I wish I could just love him or hate him. I hate bein' betwixed and between the two. I wanna feel one way or the other.* While he acknowledged some twisted pride in his father's legend, he couldn't stand the reality of the legend's impact on his family. After the fight, he was clear on what he had to do. The only way to end the cycle of pain and suffering was to leave.

He was honest with Mr. Jenkins regarding the real reason he wanted the job. "Mr. Jenkins, know what?"

"What is it boy? What's on yo mind?"

"I really hate leavin' Beulah and 'em, but iffin I'm gonna get 'way from him, I gotta break all ties and they're tied to him. I love'em, but I ain't willin' to keep stayin' 'round here puttin' up with him. I just can't take it no more. Momma gone now and I can't find good 'nuff reason to stay here, knowin' I'm most miserable 'round him. You think I'm selfish fo' that sir?"

Mr. Jenkins had always viewed Scott as a self-righteous bigot who thought he was above all the other coloreds living in the Gulf. "Boy, I gotta be honest with you. Yo Poppa, he be one arrogant son-of-a-bitch. He think 'cause that white man be his real daddy, he better than all the rest of us. I swear fo' Gawd, I don't know how he fool hisself into believin' somethin' so crazy. That man held on to him as his slave 'til the day Mr. Lincoln made him set him free. Then, 'spite all his arrogance he wanted to stay there on that Seamore property after he was free. He'll deny it, but he was too scared to leave. He got some strange affection fo' that family that even he can't figure out hisself."

Herbert felt awkward listening to the criticism, and made a half-hearted attempt to provide an explanation. "Mr. Jenkins, I heard a lotta them slaves was scared to leave at first. So Poppa wasn't much different than anybody else."

His logic made the older man pause. "Yeah, you got a point there boy. He's still an arrogant SOB."

"Now Mr. Jenkins, you know I ain't 'posed to be laughin' with you talkin' 'bout Poppa like that. Anyhow, explain to me why was he still so attached to them Seamores after becomin' a free man? Scared to leave is one thing. Bein' attached to a daddy that denied him is another. That sounds mighty strange to me."

"Boy, the story that been goin' 'round is that on his deathbed James Seamore finally acknowledged them boys as hizzin tho' they already knew that 'cause they been hearin' the same rumors everybody else been hearin' throughout the years. Anyway the ol' man, on his deathbed, gave orders to his white boys to make sho' them colored boys of hizzin be comfortable fo' life after he was gone. I reckon that had a lot to do with his guilt. Gotta give it to James Junior and that Clayton – they did just what they daddy told'em to do. They keepin' them Harrington brothers employed as long as they willin' to work. As a matter of fact, they pay 'em the same money they pay to some of them white men. Nobody wasn't 'posed to know that either, but the word got out anyway. The contact 'tween them white and colored brothas been some kinda twisted and strange. Yassuh – twisted and strange do say so myself."

Fascinated by what he was hearing, Herbert wanted to know more. "But why is my Uncle Walt so different than Poppa?"

"It was said that yo Uncle Walt just always had a different spirit than yo poppa. Word was that Walter was fine with havin' little to nothin' to do with them Seamores after they set 'em free. He just wanted to live in peace as a free man with no reminders that he was once considered his own daddy's slave. Although he was the quiet one, folk still knew behind that quiet spirit was a man full of resentment toward his daddy who he felt was a hypocrite."

"Both of them boys grew up hearin' that James Seamore claimed to have loved their real mammie. Her name was Fondella and she was one of the most beautiful women a person ever laid his eyes on. She was so unruly nobody could do anything with her. They couldn't tame her. Matter of fact, it was said she ruled Seamore and his wife hated her for it. As time went by, he stopped carin' what anybody thought 'bout him and how he was crazy 'bout Fondella."

"He was so crazy he only wanted her fo' hisself and forced her to give her babies away to another slave so he wouldn't have to share her with the babies she had by him. The minute she dropped the load, the baby was taken outta the house and down to the shack for them slaves Molly and Jacob to raise 'em. Jacob was some kinda bitter 'bout that. Of course, that kinda ugly truth be 'nuff to make anybody bitter and them boys got a lotta stuff pinned up inside of 'em. Both them boys cut from the same cloth. They just act different about the same mess they dealin' with. Both of 'em hold him responsible for drivin' her outta North Carolina."

"Now yo poppa, on the other hand, was more out with not bein' pleased with James Seamore. Although the ol' man occasionally made some sorry attempts to show favoritism towards them boys, yo poppa felt like Seamore was only throwin' 'em crumbs. He wasn't treatin' 'em like he was treatin' his white boys and Scott was mad 'bout that. Don't know fo' the life of me how he 'xpected to be treated like a white boy, but damned fool did. He was bitter 'bout the fawning over him that some of them white people like Seamore's nieces did when nobody else was around, but the minute they got in the company of other white people, they treated him like any other slave."

"Oh my Gawd, Mr. Jenkins, you tellin' me Poppa's been a handful all his life? Sounds like he was makin' life hard fo' a lotta people way back when."

"Yeah boy – Yo Poppa learned early on that he held some strange power over them white gals and some of them white boys was scared to death of him. So his revenge was to become even more arrogant and self-righteous than all of 'em. He knew his poppa was tryin' to have some kinda 'lationship with him and Walter after he couldn't have their mammie, but he was 'shamed of him 'cause he was too much of a coward to fight for the 'lationship he wanted."

"Now I ain't makin' no 'cuses fo' that Mr. Seamore, but I don't think yo poppa ever even considered what might happen iffin Seamore treated them 'xactly like he was treatin' white folk. A white man could get in a lotta trouble treatin' coloreds like they treated other white folk. Everybody knew 'bout lynchin' coloreds and white people who spoke up 'bout what was goin' on, but yo poppa wasn't tryin' to understand anything other than what he wanted. He wanted his white daddy to stand up for him and Walter, but Seamore knew 'bout some real bad things that had happened to white folk who got too close to the coloreds."

"What did Mr. Seamore know Mr. Jenkins?"

"Yo poppa was the one who actually told somebody else about how he overheard James Seamore and another white man talkin' 'bout a man name Louis Taylor's twin babies who were found drowned in a small stream located deep down in some woods. Accordin' to the folk who knew 'bout Louis Taylor, seems he came here from some place up north called Connecticut to claim a tobacco farm his dead uncle left to him shortly after that day Lincoln set them slaves free. When he arrived in the Gulf, everybody was busy buzzin' 'bout his wife. Folk 'round here had never seen a white man who was married to a colored woman, but Louis Taylor was."

"From the time they moved to the Gulf until the vicious murder of their two babies, life in these parts, for them, was hell on earth. One day the wife, Flora, had gone out to the detached kitchen to check on flour she had risin' for some biscuits she was gettin' ready to make. While outside, she thought she heard noises up in the main house, but decided she wasn't really hearin' things. Them babies wasn't cryin' and she wanted to believe nothin' out of the ordinary was goin' on in the house. Still, her spirit was restless."

"Somethin' kept tellin' her to go back to the house in a hurry. As she was gettin' near the inner backyard, she was sho' somebody was in there with her babies. Well she took off runnin' and screamin', not even knowin' 'xactly why she was screamin'. Just as she threw open the back door, she saw two white boys runnin' outta the front door, each with a baby in his arms."

Herbert was now leaning in close to Mr. Jenkins as if to hear him better and Mr. Jenkins was only too happy to continue the suspenseful story.

"That Flora, she ran after them white boys with the straw broom she had picked up without missin' a stride. She was screamin' and swingin' that broom, and at one point even connected her broomstick with the shoulder of one of them boys, but they was too fast for her. They disappeared from her sight. She then took off runnin' in the other direction, screamin' for Louis. When she finally found him deep in the tobacco fields, she so upset she could barely talk coherent 'nough to tell him what had just happened."

"He then jumped onto one of his tobacco wagons, and drove back to the house to pick up his rifle. Folk say he went lookin' for them white boys, determined to punish 'em. He searched for his babies fo' days. To make matters worse, his friends was unwillin' to talk too much about who they thought took his babies. They was 'fraid what would happen to them and their families if they opened they mouth. Finally, the owner of another farm close by came quietly to Louis to tell him his workers discovered the bodies of the two babies floatin' face down in a small stream located down in the woods on his property."

This was some brutal story Mr. Jenkins was telling. If this was true, no wonder James Seamore and other white people were afraid to get close to colored folk. But of course, Scott didn't want or care to understand anybody else's fear.

"Mr. Jenkins, go on and tell me more. Whatever happened to Louis and Flora Taylor?"

"Well son, they took one of their tobacco wagons down to the stream and got them babies outta that water. They wrapped each baby in some white cotton cloth and dug two small graves next to the stream. After that, them people got outta North Carolina faster than you can bat an eyelash. Didn't try and pack too much stuff up. Left that there house 'xactly like it was the day them babies got stolen outta there. Everybody 'round here got the message loud and clear – some stuff just wasn't 'ceptable, and there was hell to pay if you got outta line."

"Do you know that even knowin' what happen to white folk who get tangled up with coloreds, yo Poppa still didn't care? He didn't care about the fear of white folk. James Seamore owed him and Walter much more than he could ever give them in a lifetime. Far as he was concerned, he didn't have to be grateful fo' anything James Seamore gave 'em. I tell you boy, them Harrington boys and them Seamores have one strange connection. 'Yo poppa act like the devil hisself. I guess 'cause the devil been torturin' him all his life."

Mr. Jenkins offered to pay Herbert a meager salary. He made contact with a relative who followed the white family for whom she worked to New York. She agreed to get Herbert a job with the family if he could find a way to get to New York on his own.

"Boy the money I pay you don't begin to be 'nuff to get you up there to New Yawk, but if you can find a hide-away spot on one of them box cars attached to a freight train, you be good to go."

Herbert was nervous because he had never been out of the Gulf, much less going all the way up north to live and work with people he didn't know. When he considered the alternative, he couldn't bear the thought of trying to get through life with a father he had a love/hate relationship that seemed to be getting more strained every day. He still wanted to love him, and the inability to connect with this man whom he viewed as larger than life left him with an aching feeling in his chest that he wasn't going to carry around for the rest of his life.

The stubbornness he inherited from Scott wouldn't allow him to give reconciliation one more chance. He wasn't willing to risk loving him any longer. So, notwithstanding the ache over leaving his sisters, he proceeded with his plans to leave the Gulf forever.

As the planned date of his departure was getting closer, Herbert reverted back to the brother whom Irene and Beulah knew and depended on.

Least I can do is love 'em good 'fo I leave 'em forever. I've gotta do what I've gotta do. Ain't no turnin' back. The little ones will have Irene and Beulah to look after 'em.

He started encouraging conversation again and reminiscing about the good times. "Y'all 'member when Momma and 'em used to have those picnics after church every Sunday during the summertime? That fried chicken was some kinda good. I used to hide some like I had finished eatin' and go and ask for more. I was hidin' 'nuff for a few days." Irene and Beulah couldn't stop laughing at his stories. They assumed things were finally getting back to normal.

They even welcomed the return of his bossy ways – telling them how to do house work and other chores. Irene started fantasizing. *Now if we can just get him and Poppa back on one accord, maybe we can be a real family again.* Her fantasies were a million miles apart from his intentions. He was intentionally giving them the relationship they shared in the past because he was preparing to sever it forever.

It was months later when one day Irene and Beulah arrived home from school to find no Herbert. This was strange since he never hung around after school to talk to friends. There was no time to even make friends. So he usually beat them home, and had at least started supper by the time they arrived.

The conversation started out as small talk. "Beulah, I wonder what's takin' Herbert so long to get home. I know he like goin' over to Mr. Jenkins and all, but he had better get home and get his chores done before Poppa comes home."

"Yeah, I know what you mean. Things seem to be gettin' a little better 'round here so I'm prayin' to Gawd Herbert don't go and do somethin' stupid and mess things up again between him and Poppa. Lawd, Irene, I thought Poppa was gonna kill that boy when he got home that day they had the fight. Couldn't believe Herbert had the nerve to attack Poppa and that woman. He was crazy with anger. Gotta say, Poppa shocked me. He came home and didn't say a word."

"It's gettin' late so we'd better start supper so Poppa won't kill all of us if things ain't on the table like he want. Herbert had better get his behind home 'fo Poppa start talkin' 'bout pullin' out his strap and puttin' it to Herbert's backside."

As the hour moved closer to the time when Scott was due to arrive, they were wringing their hands in total nervousness, now certain there was no way to avoid the big fight that was sure to occur when he arrived and found out that Herbert didn't come home.

Irene could have sworned her heart stopped beating when the door opened. He stood there almost as tall as the doorway, taking in his surroundings. Although the table was set for supper and the children were seated, the first thing he noticed was Herbert's empty chair. "Where's Herbert at?" They stared at him speechless and not wanting to get Herbert into trouble.

Poppa is sure to kill Herbert this evenin'.

"I asked y'all where's Herbert?"

Irene cleared her throat, "Uh Poppa, we don't know, he never came home from the school house."

He walked into his bedroom and then emerged with a large black thing that looked like the whips the old folk said the masters used on their slaves. Irene and Beulah did everything to suppress the whimpering sounds they were making, trying to avoid all out crying.

Irene found her voice first. "Poppa please don't do this. He must've gotten tied up over at Mr. Jenkins' place or somethin'. I don't think he's tryin' to be hardheaded. I'm sure he'll be home soon. Poppa, you can't..."

"Gal did I ask you what you be thinkin'?"

"No sir, but..."

"No – I didn't ask you what you be thinkin' and I don't wanna hear it. I'm gonna tear his hide into shreds. He's been walkin 'round here for months with that attitude that I ain't gonna stand fo'. Now he thinkin' he can come in here when he be wantin' to. Well, I'm gonna string him up high and wide, and then take this here whip and cut 'em to shreds."

They cried out in unison, "No Poppa."

Beulah was beyond distraught and forgot to restrain herself. Running over to him, she reached out to grab his hand. He lifted it as if to strike her, but wound up pushing with so much force, she stumbled back into Irene's arms and they both tumbled to the floor.

"Gal, you lost yo mind or somethin'? I told you I don't care what y'all thinkin'. I'm the head of this here house and nobody bet' not disobey my orders. Don't you dare put yo hands on me, ya hear me? If I had the time, I'd put some of this whip to ya. You better pray I change my mind 'bout whippin' ya when I get back here with that boy."

They watched in horror as he stormed out of the door.

He was exhausted when he returned late that night, and didn't bring a beaten Herbert home.

The next morning he went over to the Jenkins' place. Mr. Jenkins was out in the yard when he arrived.

"You seen him?"

Mr. Jenkins kept sweeping. "Seen who?"

"Jenkins, you know who I'm talkin' 'bout and I ain't got time fo' yo cat and mouse game, so I'm gonna ask again. Where's my boy at?"

"I ain't seen yo boy. He was 'round here a couple of days ago, but I ain't seen him since."

There was nothing else he could do but turn and walk away. Mr. Jenkins wasn't going to be of any help. Maybe Walter knew something.

"I can't find my boy. He didn't come home yesterday. I looked over at that fool Jenkins' place. I think he know somethin' but he ain't 'bout to tell me. Had a good mind to give him an ass whuppin', but was tryin' not to lose too much time in findin' Herbert. He ain't been 'round here, right?"

Walter looked down at the whip in his hand. "No, ain't seen him, but I'll tell you this. Lookin' at what you got in yo hand there I don't blame Jenkins if he's hidin' that boy, and I wouldn't tell you if he was here. Brotha' you can't be whippin' these chilluns like they 'yo slaves. Don't you 'member how you felt everytime that overseer threatened us? Don't you 'member seein' the raw meat of them men that disobeyed them down in the fields. Brotha, I knows you ain't forgot how we even seen them whip some of them women folk that was with child. Now them slavery days been over fo' some time and here you tryin' to punish yo chillun the same way they used to whip them slaves. What on Gawd's earth are you doin'?"

Scott didn't answer. Again, there was no alternative but to turned around and walk away. Herbert had escaped, and he never saw him again.

Chapter 9
Finally – Scott's and Belle's Time

Herbert was gone and the atmosphere in the house felt like they were living in a tomb. Irene and Beulah walked around for weeks crying.

"What y'all walkin' 'round here cryin' fo? I'm gettin real sick and tired of hearin' all that whalin' like y'all givin' birth or somethin'. There's plenty work 'round here for y'all to do, so stop that slobberin' right now, fo' I give y'all somethin' to cry 'bout."

His threats only served to produce more tears. He couldn't control them with domination and became exhausted. So he tried his hand at comfort.

"Look y'all he'll be back. He get hungry 'nuff, he'll come back here with his tail waggin' between his legs. He ain't never been nowhere and how far can he get 'way from here? Y'all just be patient. He'll be back."

Although his comfort was not as warm as Herbert's or Iris', it was something at least. They were eager to respond to his ministrations no matter how awkward. He forced himself to sit and listen as they sat around the fireplace sharing their plans for the future. Beulah described in detailed the big house she wanted to live in.

"One of these days, I'm gonna live in one of them big houses just like the Seamores. I be thinkin' if I make myself real pretty and dress real fancy like I see some of them ladies do in town, a boy's gonna come down from up north and marry me."

"Beulah, what boy from up north comin' down here to marry you? How y'all gonna get a big house like them Seamores, tell me? Don't no colored folk get houses like that."

"You're wrong Irene, I hear people talkin' 'bout how some colored folk livin' almost good as whites. I heard people talkin' 'bout this thing they call "Reconstruction" and they say some coloreds are doin' rather well fo' themselves. I also heard 'bout some white teachers come down here helpin' educate folk so they can live better. Well, me and my husband gonna be included in that number. You just watch and see."

"You dreamin' Beulah, that Reconstruction period ended back in '77 or 'round about then."

He was left to wonder how they developed such imaginations to come up with stories about people and places that were totally foreign to him. He couldn't imagine thinking about the things they described in their stories. He could only think about what was happening in the present and certainly didn't want to think about anything prior to becoming a free man, although it was impossible to forget. He often wondered what Herbert was doing and imagining.

Can't understand for the life of me why I keep losin' my sons. After that first boy was stillborn, I believed down in my heart Herbert was some kinda miracle. He was gonna be my chance to have a 'lationship – the kind me and my slave daddy Jacob didn't have and the kind me and my real daddy, ol' man Seamore couldn't have. No matter how I tried, nothin' ever worked out so I could be close to my boy.

I used to watch how Seamore made so much to do over his white boys. Since me and Walter couldn't have it with him, I was gonna make sure any boy I fathered had it. Belle messed up my chance at havin' my first boy. I used to think she won't get to mess up my next chance at havin' a boy. I'll see to that. My boy's gonna get what the ol' man and Jacob refused to give me and Walter. All I needed was another chance. Damn it if Belle didn't go and mess that up too. She just had to follow me outta that house and climb all over me.

So notwithstanding his promise to love the next boy, he stumbled around aimlessly trying to learn how to father without his slave/master mentality. When he realized Herbert wasn't coming back, he grieved as if he had lost his first born again. His grief zapped him of any desire to be with Belle.

I don't even wanna see Belle. Got no desire to lay down with her. I'm cravin' somethin' she can't give me right now. I done lost my boy. Got nothin' but gals 'round me now. Who gonna know I'm a strong man that make strong boys? Lawd, I gotta find me a decent woman who can give me more boys. Belle sho' ain't decent. She's good fo' one thing and one thing only.

It had been weeks since Iris passed away, and she still hadn't seen him. Impatient, she went down to the mill to see if she could draw him back into her web before someone new came along. More importantly, she didn't want to take a chance on letting him marry someone else again.

As additional insurance, she had been faithfully visiting the Geechee woman from South Carolina, and paid her to work roots on him. She didn't care if the root doctor's practices were good or evil. Whatever it took to keep him coming back, she was willing to try. The Geechee promised her that the roots and spells she created were effective and he would never marry anyone else again but her. Not trusting anyone, especially one who was dealing in witchcraft, she had to keep her eyes open for any possible threat of another woman.

"Mighty fine evenin' Mr. Scott Harrington sir don't you think?"

He couldn't hide his irritation with her for showing up unannounced and without his permission. "Hi. What do you want?"

"Too fine a evenin' to go straight home to no woman. I was thinkin' maybe you could keep me company for awhile. Don't you be missin' the way I make you feel?"

"No."

She was hurt by the rejection, but had to be persistent. She then slipped her arm into his and once again tried to convince him to change his mind.

"I'm sho' I can change yo mind if you just relax and come home with me. You know deep down inside you wanna."

He was tired from a long day's work and exhausted over the state of affairs at home. She was tap dancing on his last nerve and he had to stop her. Shoving her away, he gave her a blistering tongue lashing.

"I won't be seein' you no more. Matter of fact, I don't wanna see you no more. When I'm ready, I'm startin' over with a good woman. Somebody different than you. You think you can control me with what's under yo skirt, you a bigger fool than I thought you were. Don't even know why I ever bothered with the likes of you."

Once again he walked away with the intention of never seeing her again. "We'll see bout that Mr. Harrington. We'll see who be the bigger fool."

The separation lasted for about six months. His daughters started to come alive again. Although he couldn't comfortably engage in their conversations and penchants for playing games, he did find comfort in just sitting, watching, and listening to them. Six months was just enough time for them to believe he was really changing for the better, but he was struggling with his addiction.

He was itching to see her again, and the itch wouldn't go away. So one Saturday morning while they were busy with chores, he announced, "Goin' out – be back in awhile."

When he arrived at her place, she tried to show him that he wasn't welcomed. She wasn't willing to fall into his arms whenever he decided to just walk back into her life.

"How ya doin' Belle?"

"I'm doin' fine Scott."

He recoiled at her use of his first name only, and that was the response she wanted. He decided to let it go.

"I been wantin' to see ya, so thought I'd stop by and we could keep company."

"Good to see ya, take care."

He leaned over and looking her straight in the eyes said, "I'm not playin' with you. Go into the house and get ready."

She got up, obediently went straight into the bedroom, and submitted to whatever he wanted.

Belle was a very happy woman. She finally had him all to herself. His daughters didn't count. *They don't matter 'cause I'm gettin' ready to become the lady of their house.*

She made candies, put several pieces in handmade burlap pouches, and sent them to the girls in an effort to establish a relationship.

"You know Mr. Harrington, it would be real good for yo girls if we all could have supper together on a regular basis. They be needin' a woman's touch in y'all's house and all. I can teach them how to be beautiful ladies so they can hurry up and snatch a husband."

He was determined that her fantasy would never be her reality. He was never going to let her anywhere near them, and she was kidding herself to think otherwise. While he listened to her suggestions, he always came up with some excuse as to why the suppers or picnics couldn't happen. Furthermore, she didn't know that her gifts never reached them. As soon as he was out of her line of vision, he tossed them into the woods.

I knows she's mixed up with that Geechee and I ain't 'bout to go placin' my chilluns in the midst of that witchcraft mumbo-jumbo everybody say the ol' woman practice. I don't accept that roots mess, and I'm much too strong a man for any of that trash to work on me. Now my gals, I ain't playin' with their lives. Belle, she be one of them old demons that keep followin' me, but she'll never get to my gals.

If she be wantin' to think she's finally gonna be my wife, that be her bizness. I ain't never promised her nothin' close to marriage. She be all the woman I got right now, so I can try and make the best of things with her.

He tried to please her with long walks just to get out of the house and a break from her suffocating attempts to get closer. On an occasional Saturday night, he joined her at the Juke Joint she operated with her cousin Amos. The rowdy and disorderly atmosphere wasn't his cup of tea. He wasn't a drinker, and actually hated being around drunks. But the moonshine Belle and Amos sold brought in enough money for her to survive financially, and so he couldn't complain.

The music was played with instruments the musicians made by hand, and he would find himself patting his foot to the beat. Still, he could live with or without it. *This Juke Joint is Belle's world. Harlots like her like this kinda place. Me – now I can do with or without it. Keeps me from havin' to take her any place where decent people go.* While the dates at the Juke Joint meant nothing to him, she was on top of the world.

She was beside herself when he celebrated Christmas with her. Mrs. Seamore gave him and Walter handmade snuff boxes, although they didn't chew tobacco. They were certain James Seamore begged her to give them the pitiful gift just to make himself feel like he had done something for them. So when he handed his box to Belle, she acted as if the gift was a proposal of marriage. "Oh my Gawd Mr. Harrington, this is the most precious thing you've ever done fo' me. This is so beautiful. I love you so much for thinkin' 'bout me in such a special way on this Christmas Day. Things are really gettin' sweet between us and I think we gonna be together forever. Merry Christmas Mr. Harrington."

He didn't bother to respond to her declaration of love or wish her a Merry Christmas, but she didn't care. He was different this time, and she interpreted the difference as getting closer to him and one day becoming the next Mrs. Scott Harrington.

She had good reason to believe he was finally hers because she was the only woman in his life. Initially she was nervous and afraid that one day she would wake up and he would be married again. However, as far as she could tell, other than working and going home to his daughters, he spent most of his time with her, and so constantly worrying about other women finally became a thing of the past.

From the looks of things, age was mellowing him. He was spending more time with her and it was clear he was going to do the right thing by making her his wife. His daughters were growing up and he felt comfortable with leaving the younger girls with the older ones so he could spend nights at her place. In all the years she had been with him, she had never enjoyed having him spend days and nights with her.

Me and Mr. Harrington finally got a real life. He's been seein' how I'm a good homemaker, and it makes perfect sense to make me his wife. I got him and he belongs only to me. I make him feel like no other woman ever been able to. I look good fo' him and nobody in this county can touch me when it come to my looks. He don't ever look at another woman. Only got eyes fo' me.

To make things even better, I'm still payin' that ol' Geechee to put more roots on him. Them roots are my insurance. May always told me I needed Geechee Insurance. I got me some and he ain't never gonna get away from me now. I see that witch on a regular basis. Her place be one scary and filthy pig's sty, but I ain't carin' what it look like in there. She just better keep my man in my bed or else...

She was right. The Geechee's house was a scary place to visit, with its dirt floors, strange aromas, and jars filled with odd looking things. Sometimes Belle wondered if the old woman was using human body parts, instead of the chicken feet, livers, and other animal organs she claimed were potent. If whatever the Geechee was using kept Scott with her, the scary visits were well worth it. When she realized how long they had been together without interference from other women, she was confident of the Geechee's powers, and frankly didn't care if those strange parts did wind up being human remains.

Despite all of the roots, spells, and witchcraft, he once again did the unthinkable. Out of nowhere he made the announcement that pushed her over the edge.

"Belle, I won't be seein' you no more. Found myself a decent woman and I'm marryin' her. You been good to me, but it be time fo' me to move on and make a new start fo' myself."

"Why you no good bastard – you comin' in here tellin' me 'bout you found a good woman and startin' over. What the hell you think I been to you all these years? I changed myself to act like one of them ugly women you think you gotta be with. No sooner than you get with 'em, you come crawlin' back to my bed. You damned fool...."

Before the slap connected to his cheek, he grabbed her arm and twisted it around to her back. "Ouch, you hurtin' me. Let me go."

"You crazy witch. You got what you wanted. Pantin' after me like some female dog in heat. You know what a female dog is don't ya Belle? Don't you? Comin' after me when you knows I'm married to a good woman. Now when I let go of ya, you bet not try nothin' like that again or else I'm gonna break yo arm. Ya hear me?"

"I know, I know, please don't leave me. I love you. Mr. Harrington, I'll do anything to make you happy, but please don't leave me. Look, I'll even get down on my knees and beg if that'll convince you how much I love you."

She wasn't even given the courtesy of a response as he stared down at her. He just wanted to leave, and shook his leg as if to get rid of a bothersome pet. Further humiliated, rage replaced the pleas that fell upon deaf ears as she kept holding on to his pant leg.

The obscenities started again. "You better not leave me. I'll make you and her regret this day. I gave you everything and you owe me the rest of yo life. I swear I'll destroy whatever woman you think you're gonna marry."

The internal war between insanity and despair raged on in the midst of her ranting and raving. How could he so easily walk away, especially since she had done everything to prove she could be just like the women he married? She compromised and tried to emulate them, although, in her opinion, they were inferior, just to be with him, but even that wasn't good enough.

She had faithfully visited and paid the Geechee to work roots on him and couldn't understand why the supernatural was ineffective. In the midst of her tantrum, she made a mental note to visit the Geechee and have it out with her for failing to deliver an eternal life with Scott.

As he was leaving for what he (once again) decided was the last time, she was still lying in the the floor kicking, screaming, crying, begging, and threatening – all to no avail. His mind was made up and nothing could or would deter him from what he wanted.

Months before the announcement he found the good woman he had been searching for and with whom he wanted to spend the rest of his life. Her name was Mary Marks. No matter what type of woman Belle tried to become, she wasn't the type he wanted to marry. He had very definite views about "good girls" and "bad girls", and was never going to marry a bad girl.

Belle could care less about the distinction between good and bad girls. The Geechee was supposed to deliver Scott to her, but apparently the roots weren't working. She didn't take kindly to being swindled out of money, and it was time to have it out with the old root doctor.

When she arrived at the Geechee's place, she was still enraged over having once again lost the love of her life. The old woman was going to pay dearly for taking money she had worked too hard for and not get the results she wanted.

The door to the shack was barely on the hinges. Security wasn't an issue because the Geechee wasn't afraid of anything or anyone – it was the other way around. There were plenty of people who wanted nothing to do with her roots. Belle, however, was too fixated on Scott to dwell on fear, and was also comfortable using any powers available regardless of who possessed them. Since the Geechee's powers seemed to have lost their effect, she was willing to do battle. Splinters flew everywhere when she kicked the door open.

"Geechee where are you? My man done left me again after all these years, and you was supposed to keep that from happenin'. Damned witch, where are you? You can't hide from me and I come here to get some results or I'm gonna tear this whole place up with you in it. Ya hear me? You had better get your frail tail out here right now and explain what happened."

The root doctor emerged from a back room holding a large jar with some big white crinkly matter soaking in a solution. Her complexion was dark bronze; her hair was course, sprinkled with gray strands throughout; and the expression in her hazel colored eyes was mysterious. She spoke the English-based creole language of the Gullah people.

"What hunnuh come breakin' down my do' fo' and yellin' like hunnuh crazy fool?"

"Mr. Harrington done left me again and you gonna get him back for me right now." She lunged forward and they came together scratching, biting, and pummeling each other. The Geechee would not be handled so violently and no one, especially Belle, was going to forcibly take her to the room where she kept medicines, potions, and jars with the strange organs and chicken feet.

"Gal git off me. Hunnuh know who hunnuh foolin' wid? I can make hunnuh hell hundred times worse than it already iz. Yo better take yo hands off'uh me right now b'fo' I release every demon in hell upon hunnuh."

Belle did know better because she had dealt with this woman many, many times before. Yet insanity prevailed and her sweeping motion caused the shelf overcrowded with the Geechee's diabolical wares to collapse, sending bottles tumbling to the dirt floor. The putrefied liquids flowed in every direction causing mud to form. The place smelled ten times worse than the stench people normally complained about.

Had she been thinking clearly, she would have started running from the hateful look in the Geechee's eyes, which clearly confirmed that a fatal mistake had just been made. The thought of losing Scott negated the consequences of her actions so she continued to attack.

"I'm gonna kickin' your sorry behind 'cause it don't look like you got any more power than an ol' hen."

Their violent dance continued until she calmed down enough to remember that if there was any hope of getting him back, the prospect was in the hands of the Geechee.

"Look, I know I lost my head and messed yo place up. But you gotta do somethin' to bring him back. I can't take this. You gotta help me, you just gotta do somethin'. Can't you come up with a root, spell, curse or somethin' that will make it impossible for him to leave me? I've seen what you can do to people."

The response was a cold stare as she pointed at Belle's crotchet purse. Once paid, she led her back to a room and gave instructions as to what was needed.

Belle, in her delusional state, was ecstatic and confident she was going to win the love of her life back. As she sashayed out of the house, she was unaware of the piercing stare fixed on her back.

Yessuh Gal. Yo'll rue the day ya put ya hands on me missy.

Chapter 10
Another Mrs. Harrington

After the death of two wives and the loss of two sons, he had finally found another "good girl" to marry. It was about a year before he left Belle when one day Walter asked him to help fix a wagon belonging to his friend Zachery's father, Mr. George Marks.

When they arrived at the Marks' farm, George, Zachery, and his brothers were at the wagon, trying to remove the broken axle. Walter and Scott immediately joined in. Just as they were finishing up, Mary came out of the house and went over to the large barrel of water they kept in the icehouse. She filled a bucket with water and re-appeared to offer them a cold drink after working all afternoon in the hot sun.

"Excuse me, I know it's awful hot out here and thought maybe you gentlemen could use a cool drink of water."

"No Mary, we fine baby. You go on back in the house. As a matter of fact, it's too hot out here fo' you. We'll help ourselves to some water later."

"Poppa I really don't mind. Y'all been out here most of the morning and I think these gentlemen could use a moment's rest, plus a cool drink. Here, let me start with you."

She started moving around the circle offering the bucket of water to each man who held a cup. When she approached one of the two strangers, their eyes locked until she became uncomfortable and turned her attention back to the bucket of water. The man standing in front of her could hold a stare. Her parents had taught her that it was impolite to stare. *Oh my, who in the world is this handsome stranger? He be one fine lookin' man. Real pleasin' to the eyes. Poppa and 'em would be shocked if they knew what I'm thinkin'. He has sparked my interest and it goes far beyond handin' out cups of water.*

Although she wanted to get a better look at him, she kept moving around in the circle of men until each one had filled his tin cup. After everyone had been served, she walked back up on to the porch. Only when she had opened the door to go inside did she turn around to look at him once more. *Oh my Gawd, he's starin' at me and prob'ly knows I find him quite attractive. This is embarrassin' to say the least. He's gonna think I'm some shameless hussy.* Mary Marks had just had her first encounter with Scott Harrington.

He was impressed with her hospitality and quiet demeanor. When she lowered her eyes and turned away to avoid the impropriety of staring, he found the demure gesture attractive. *This here is a gentle woman – a real lady. She reminds me of Lillie and Iris. She be 'xactly what I need in my life. I truly miss the comfort of a gentle woman. Belle, she's so taxin' on a man. Make a man feel like he's gotta have her, but then she never can get enough. Would suck the life outta me if I let her.*

The dichotomy of Scott was his attraction to the purity and innocence of a woman, as well as the promiscuity and reckless abandonment of Belle. Although he was accustomed to Belle's more worldly behavior, and recognized her efforts to be a different type of woman (like his deceased wives) the result was not the same.

This handsome woman whom he just met, however, was refreshing – the type of woman who had the cleansing effect he still wanted in his life and home. He was going to get to know and have George Marks' daughter.

This type of gal, she requires a man to marry her. She ain't the type that's gonna settle for lettin' a man have her the way Belle let me have her. 'Sides, I don't want her like that. I need her to turn my place into a home again. Here's another chance to have the kinda woman I deserve. Ain't nothin' nobody can do to stop me, especially Belle.

"Walter, who was that tall woman that gave us a drink of water? She kinda handsome don't you think? You think her poppa will let her take company from a man like me?"

"She's Zachery's sister, Mary. He told me she was married and livin' over in Durham fo' awhile. Her man died and she came back to live with the family. Zachery says she's a strong woman that work hard. Say she's real smart too. She's the only one in the house that can read. I'll ask him for more information and get back to ya."

Walter came back several days later with more information. "It's true what I heard 'bout her. Seems she's a widow and got two daughters. Their names be Maude and Beolia. Zachery say she teach Sunday school down at the church where they belong."

"Now brotha I gotta warn you. You need to be real careful 'bout how you approach and handle her. Iffin' you wanna get to know her, you can't be treatin' her like you do Belle. She ain't that kinda gal."

"I know she be different – could tell it the first time I laid eyes on her. She sounds like my Lillie and Iris, and that's the kinda woman I want and need in my life. I'm gonna be different this time. Trust me."

The more he learned about her, the more he was convinced that some higher power had placed her in his life and was rewarding him with a chance to redeem himself of past transgressions. He had to have her, and therefore became the charismatic man he knew was impossible for women to resist.

He sent word through Zachery requesting a meeting with George Marks. "Mr. Marks, I wanna ask you iffin I can start seein' yo daughter. I like what I see and I think I'm the kinda man she be needin' in her life. I understand she's a widow, and I've lost two wives. We prob'ly be real good company for each other if you would allow it."

"Looka here boy, my gal be a good Christian woman and can't be unequally yoked. I been hearin' 'bout some fast woman you messin' 'round with and I don't want my gal gettin' hurt. She been through 'nuff and got two little chillun she lookin' out fo'. If you comin' 'round tryin' to use her in any way not honorable, you need to keep lookin' 'cause I ain't havin' nobody hurt my gal."

"Sir, I understand you wantin' to protect your precious daughter. I admit I've made quite a few mistakes in my life. Mistakes I ain't particularly proud of. But I be wantin' me a good Christian woman like yo daughter in my life. That be what I really want. Anybody ain't 'posed to be in my life, I done got rid of 'em and I'm a changed man. I got a good home already fo' a good woman to come in. I'm just askin' you to do what yo Bible tell you to do. Extend mercy and forgive me my past. My intentions are honorable, and I'll make yo daughter glad she married me."

George agreed to the trial courting period. "Mary gal, that man Scott Harrington, he came to me askin' iffin he can keep company with you. I gotta tell you, I have my reservations and told him so. He wouldn't let it go though. Admitted he's made a lot of mistakes he ain't proud of and that he's a changed man. Can't keep kickin' a man when he admits to his wrong-doin' and swear fo' Gawd he done changed. I told him I would talk to you and iffin you wanna, I will allow it. Now you be careful and iffin he ain't treatin' you right, you drop him outta your life right away. George Marks ain't havin' nobody messin' with his chilluns."

The first date was supper with the family. After being widowed for some time, she relished the thought that a man like Scott was interested in courting her. He was so different from her Daniel.

She met Daniel Hawkins from over in Raleigh when she was 16 years. He came to the Gulf to spend the summer with relatives. Their quiet and uneventful courtship led to him asking George for her hand in marriage. She didn't return to Gulf until after he passed away. He remained etched in her heart as a good man who was simple in his expectations. Unlike Scott, Daniel didn't demand the high maintenance that his successor would require in his marriage. Working hard and spending quiet time with Mary and their children was enough.

She was intrigued, and yes anxious to get to know him. *I can hardly contain myself. He wants to court me. He's so different from my Daniel, but his different is excitin'. I've never had anybody in my life like him, but maybe I need somebody like him to make me feel alive again.*

George's stern eye and willingness to step in at anytime kept him in line. He managed to court her properly. Everything about her was refreshing, while life with Belle was just too much for any man to handle on an on-going basis.

Miss Mary is like a breath of fresh air. Her spirit be light and she don't demand much. Nothin' like that hellcat Belle. All she be wantin' to do is party, drink, and lay with a man. I ain't never been comfortable goin' down and hangin' out at that Juke Joint what she love so much. Only place I could take her though. Couldn't take her 'round 'spectable folk 'cause they know too much 'bout her. 'Sides told Iris on her deathbed I wouldn't do nothin' crazy like marryin' Belle.

The relationship with her had put a strain on his relationship with Irene, Beulah, Fannie, and Naomi. They were jealous of his time with her, and resented the thought that she prevailed over Iris in the competition to win his love and fidelity. She was the reason Herbert walked out of their lives for good. They swore to never accept her.

"Poor Momma, she never stood a chance against a woman lookin' like Belle. Some folk say they've never seen a woman 'round the Gulf as pretty as her. I think that's why Poppa refused to give her up. He just couldn't say no to that pretty face. Irene, I wish I had long straight hair like that."

Irene hated the years they witnessed him preferring to go with her rather than stay at home with them. "People used to tell Momma how pretty she was too, but Poppa must've thought Belle's looks were prettier. It seems like no matter how pretty a brown girl is, some men still prefer the high yellow ones. I can't stand most of 'em myself. They think lookin' like that give them power over men that the rest of us don't have."

They were stunned to find out the woman he announced who was coming for supper on Sunday wasn't Belle.

"I'm bringin' somebody over here for y'all to meet. Her name is Miss Mary Marks, and she's gonna be my new wife. She's the Widow Hawkins with two youngin'. Her and her gals comin' over here on Sunday and I want y'all to fix some stewed chicken, rice with gravy, and turnip greens. Oh yeah – make sure to fix that cornbread like y'all's momma taught y'all to make. I want us to finish supper up with somethin' real sweet like that apple/peach cobbler Iris used to make special for us. Bring out the good china that woman she used to work fo' gave her – the ones she loved so much."

The china was worn and chipped when it was given to Iris, but it was authentic. She was proud to own something rich white people owned. They couldn't ever recall hearing him mentioning china, and were amazed that he even knew about the china, or would want to impress someone to the point of using it. His attention to detail was the seed of discord that would give him more family drama than he bargained for.

Poppa done once again chose another woman over us. He's forgotten 'bout Momma and throwin' us away. She must be somethin' else if he givin' up that woman Belle for her. How in the world is Miss Belle gonna take all this? Belle, who had become quite complacent in her relationship with him, never saw it coming.

When Mary arrived on Sunday afternoon, they were surprised to see that she had many of the features they remembered about Iris, and she looked nothing like the woman people described when describing Belle. They tried not to like her, but it was hard to criticize her physically when she reminded them so much of Iris.

"My momma was the best cook in the entire Gulf 'cause everybody said so."

Mary overlooked the intended slight, and Irene was disappointed to discover that her attitude was ineffective.

"I'm certain she was. Yo poppa has told me a lot of good things about yo momma and I think I would have liked her a lot. I know I like her cookin' if what you ladies have fixed is anything like what she used to cook."

It was apparent she was the strong silent type and would be much more difficult for them to deal with than Belle. It was easy to hate and tear Belle down – history, rumors, and fact made it easy to do that.

Mary was one story, but her daughters were another. Maude could be a hellion. Frustrated that Scott was still bringing new women into their lives, Irene resigned herself to the reality that they may never have his undivided attention. *Of course he just had to bring some little demon into this house expectin' us to put up with her. Poppa just gotta have a bad girl some place in his life – this time she be six years old and lookin' like she every bit of twelve.*

For the most part, their courtship was supper together on Sundays, but whenever the meals were at Mary's place, Beulah and Irene refused to attend. Naomi and Fannie only went because they were forced to. They were hoping their silent boycott would discourage him from making any permanent commitments. Their plan failed, and the next major announcement was that he had set a definite wedding date.

He laid down the law before Mary, Maude and Beolia moved in. "All y'all chilluns in here had better obey Mary. She's runnin' this house now. She'll tell everybody what to do – exceptin' me."

Beulah and Irene bristled at having to answer to another woman. They had no choice because if they were going to live under his roof, they were going to obey Mary, whether they wanted to or not.

On March 9, 1904, Scott Harrington and Mary Marks became husband and wife. The first awkward moment occurred on their wedding night when he announced that going forward she was to refer to him as Mr. Harrington and never Scott. "We married now and you gotta call me Mr. Harrington."

"I don't think I understand Scott."

"I said we married now and the Bible says the man is the head of the house. I'm head of the house. You will call me Mr. Harrington outta respect and teach the chilluns to respect the head of the household. They can't hear you callin' me Scott. That ain't right and we gotta do things right iffin we all gonna live here."

The subject never came up before because he didn't know how Poppa George would react to his condition of marriage, and didn't want to risk losing what could be his last chance to have a woman like Lillie and Iris. He was willing to wait. Once his wife, she would be obligated to honor his directive.

If calling him Mr. Harrington gave him the respect he wanted, she was more than willing to oblige him. She never called him by his first name again and justified his request rather than challenge it. She knew of several couples where the wife referred to her husband as "Mister."

The new living arrangements, as well as the additional people, were not favored by everyone. Irene and Beulah hated the hellion Maude. She was always hovering around with a look on her face that dared anybody to cross her. They secretly made fun of her.

"Beulah, that gal be one big black ox. She looks meaner than an ox too – especially when she get mad and her nostrils start flarin'. She always lookin' at somebody like they wrong for even speakin' to her momma. They come to live in our house. She better act like she grateful for Poppa puttin' a roof over their heads?"

Maude wasn't moved by their obvious disdain. "You know what Beolia, them two can come this way and try and disrespect Momma if they wanna. They gonna be some kinda sorry when I finish whuppin' up on them. They don't know who they messin' with. They better stay away from Momma and you. I'll hurt 'em and hurt 'em bad."

"Maude, remember what Momma told us. We are all to get along. We're one family and we've got to love them because they're our sisters."

"I don't care what Momma say, they ain't my sisters. They can't stand me and I sho' can't stand them. You'd better not tell Momma what I just said either."

It was during one of Scott's and Mary's visits with Walter and Cora when the atmosphere in the Harrington household shifted in a major way. As soon as they left the house, Irene confronted Maude about cleaning out the hen house. After inspecting the work, she returned to the house and informed Maude that the job was unacceptable.

"You didn't clean that house out like Poppa want it cleaned out. You need to get back out there right now and do it like I told you to. Don't even look like you touched the place."

"I cleaned that dang hen house out. Looks better than it prob'ly looked in a long time. I ain't goin' back out there when I know I did my best."

"I'm tellin' you, you had better get yo big behind out there right now and clean up that hen house like I told you to. Nobody want y'all here anyway, but since Poppa forced y'all on us, you gotta learn how to earn yo keep."

"Done all I'm gonna do."

Irene wasn't going to accept back talk. Fed up with the attitude Maude was giving, she started punching her in the chest, trying to push her back in the direction of the hen house. "Get back out there and clean it up the right way."

The warning was short – too short to contemplate Maude's next move.

"Heifer you just put your hands on the wrong gal." She drew her arm back as far as she could before releasing a fisted blow to Irene's cheek. The punch was so powerful she landed in the dirt on her backside.

Beulah was furious and grabbed Maude by a thick kinky plait, spinning her around, "Why you big disgustin' ox you, how dare you hit my sister?"

Beolia took off running in the direction of the kitchen to look for something to use as a weapon to get them away from Maude. She need not have worried because Maude was boiling mad at this point, and in spite of the searing pain pounding in her head from having her hair pulled, stomped her foot down and it landed on top of Beulah's foot.

"Owwwww. Owwwww." Just as she screamed out in pain, Maude landed the same punishing blow to her jaw. "This one's for you. You think you and your sister can whup me, huh? Come on. Get up."

Now terrified, they managed to get up off of the ground, and run back into the house. Their bedroom door was barricaded just in case she came after them. She wasn't interested.

"Maude, are you okay? Oh my God, I can't believe the two of them attacked you like that. I thought they had hurt you really bad."

"I'm not surprised. It's been comin' since the day we got here, and I've been ready since the day we got here. I ain't puttin' up with them thinkin' they can push us 'round or treat us any kinda way."

When Scott and Mary returned home, Irene and Beulah, who were both wearing swollen and bruised cheeks, told their version of the fight.

"Go and straighten that gal out 'cause I ain't havin' no fightin' goin' on in here."

"Yes sir, Mr. Harrington, I'll speak to her right now."

"What on Gawd's earth you doin' gal? Have you lost yo mind fightin' Mr. Harrington's girls? They're grown folk and you had better give me a good reason why you think you had to go punchin' on them young ladies or else I'm gonna put some fire to that behind of yours myself."

"Momma, I swear, I didn't start nothin' with them. Irene told me to go and clean out the hen house and I did. I made sure I cleaned it good 'cause I wanted to stay out there and away from them. Then when I came back into the house, they started lyin' on me sayin' I didn't do it right. Both of 'em started callin' me names like big black ox. When I wouldn't go back, Irene started pushin' me. I didn't touch her first. She's the one who started pushin' me. Then Beulah jumped in and tried to fight me too."

Mary knew her daughter enjoyed speaking her mind too much than to hide behind lies. So temper notwithstanding, she knew Maude had boundaries.

"Oh my Lawd. This foolishness is wearin' me out. Look Maude, if them young ladies bother you, I want you to come to me and I'll speak to Mr. Harrington 'bout the matter. But I don't ever wanna come back home to find out you fightin' yo sisters, understood."

"Ain't none of my sisters, Beolia be my only sister."

Beolia chimed in, "That's right."

Mary gave them a look of consternation. "I make myself clear Maude...and Beolia?"

"Yes Momma." Beolia just shook her head up and down acknowledging that like Maude, she understood the warning.

"Good. Now Maude, get in that house and apologize to Irene and Beulah – and mean it."

Chapter 11
Scott Harrington's New Family

Irene and Beulah were busy making plans to leave home at their earliest opportunity. Irene was the first to leave. She met, married a man she barely knew, and moved to Asheboro. Beulah was franctically searching for a man to rescue her from a life of loneliness and isolation. Now that Scott was focused on his new family, she, Fannie, and Naomi were convinced they would never regain his attention. Loving him without the distraction of a new family was hard enough. Now they would never have the chance to be close to him. Someone else was always commanding his attention.

On January 8, 1908, Mary, Maude, Beolia, and Scott celebrated the arrival of Leotia Harrington. While Scott seemed pleased that his family was once again growing, he reminded Mary of his true desire.

"Ya know Mary, I still want a boy so bad. I can't wait 'til you give me a son."

"I know Mr. Harrington. I'll be one happy woman when that day arrives. I know how much havin' a son means to you and any wife who loves her husband the way I love you would be the happiest woman in the world when she has given you something so important."

After years of yearning for a son, on March 15, 1910, his dream came true. Mary gifted him with a son. He named his healthy baby boy after the two most influential men in his life; his brother, one of the greatest loves of his life, and his father, the greatest love/hate relationship of his life. He named him Walter Seamore Harrington.

Mary understood how important it was for him to incorporate his birthright into their family. Fondella was an elusive character in stories that were told to Scott and Walter by others who knew or knew of her. Because of James Seamore's obsession, they were left with nothing but a yearning for the woman they never knew. James Seamore was flesh and blood although he denied it until his deathbed confessions.

The Gulf's grapevine now had new gossip to spread. He had the nerve to name his son after his father/master, but their gossip was irrelevant. He didn't care and would never bow down to discuss James Seamore with town folk.

Walter Seamore Harrington was another chance to bond with a son, but inwardly he struggled with uncertainty. *Will it be different this time? I sho' hope and pray things won't ever deteriorate to the point where my boy will one day just up and walk away from me, never to be heard from or seen again? I ain't gonna never let that happen again, 'cause Belle be outta my life fo' good now.*

The folks throughout the Gulf couldn't imagine anything eclipsing the birth of his son. Even Belle, from a distance, understood the magnitude of his male pride and what it meant to finally have a son again. Although she was still visiting the Geechee, she was lying low, feeling useless and terrified that he was settling into his latest marriage, and enlarging his family.

He's now got one of the things he most wanted in life – a son, and he won't stand for me tryin' to get some of his time right now. I've gotta play this real smart and just bide my time. I'mma keep goin' to Geechee and let her keep workin' her roots. One day, he'll be mine – all mine.

Since Belle and everybody else in the Gulf thought fathering a son was his zenith, they were totally unprepared for his reaction to the next addition to the family.

On September 14, 1912, Mary gave birth to a daughter whom they named Novella. Once again, the Harrington's newest arrival was the talk of the town. This time he was acting as if the birth of his daughter was the second coming of Christ. He was bragging to anybody and everybody about her.

"Mary, that new baby gal of mine, she's prob'ly the most beautiful little gal you ever laid yo eyes on."

She couldn't ever recall having seen him react to anyone like this. Maybe, just maybe, he was finally satisfied with fatherhood. She was aging and her body was changing. She wasn't sure she could deliver on the promise to give him more sons.

Sitting with his new baby on his lap and showering her with compliments became a favorite pastime. "I don't know what you gonna be one of these days, but Vella, I do know my baby gal is gonna be a great lady who will reign over the lives of many. You be different, I can't 'splain it, but you be different. Yo Poppa been a fool many times in his life, but he knows a great lady when he comes to be in her presence."

The gossip about the baby girl who had accomplished what no other woman had been able to was circulating throughout the Juke Joint. Belle was agitated everytime the conversation came up, and appalled that he was running around town talking about a baby being the prettiest girl he had ever seen.

What kinda fool gonna go runnin' 'round town talkin' 'bout a baby like she's a pretty woman? What makes her so special? If she be lookin' anything like that plain momma of hers, she can't be lookin' like too much. Humph – I don't believe it.

Her visits to the evil root doctor were increasing with frequency. "Geechee, I'm gettin' impatient. What be takin' you so long? I want my man back. You takin' too long, and that plain woman over there still givin' him babies. You need to hurry up."

She was unmoved by Belle's urgency. "Hunnuh gotta stop rushin' me. Geechee know warruh to do and when to do it. Dis take time and yo need to give me mo' money. Iffin hunnuh want dis to work, hunnuh gotta wait. The right potion take time. 'Ent ready yet. I workin' wit' all kinds of t'ings. Next time I bring dat there man back, 'e 'ent ever leavin' no more."

Belle had no alternative but to wait. The thought of him conquering his fixation and finally able to resist her was too much to take. She wanted drastic measures taken.

"Ol' woman, just hurry up and make whatever it is you workin' on so powerful that woman will have no choice but to let 'em go." She then stepped closer and said with all seriousness, "Even if you have to kill her. Yeah – as a matter of fact, I want her dead."

"Go bring me a piece of her clothin'."

She didn't go into detail about what she was going to do with the clothing and Belle didn't need any. Her only focus was the destruction of Scott's third marriage. She was now obsessed with getting her hands on whatever the Geechee needed to curse Mary. Since he was no longer coming around, she couldn't ask him to get what she needed, and he would never do it even if he was. She wasn't allowed to have a relationship with Irene and Beulah, and couldn't approach them for help. There was only one solution to her problem, and that was to steal what she needed.

Mary was taking down laundry when she discovered the damaged undergarments. *Well this is strange indeed. Who would want to tear my clothes?*

She went back into the house to make inquiries. "Maude, Beolia have y'all been playin 'round out in the yard and messin' with my clothes? Some of my undergarments have been torn."

"No ma'am. Momma that's crazy. You sure Poppa's gals didn't do it?"

She didn't want to believe they were capable of such maliciousness, but had to ask if she wanted to get to the bottom of things. He was furious and blew up.

"Fannie, Naomi, get in here this minute. Y'all know who tore up yo momma's clothin' that was hangin' out there on the line?"

Their delayed response had nothing to do with guilt, but rather the discomfort of hearing another woman referred to as their momma.

"Y'all hear me talkin' to ya? I asked who tore up yo momma's clothes. If anyone of y'all did this, I'mma have yo hide. Speak up. Now."

"Oh no Poppa, we don't know who would do such a terrible thing. I swear on my momma Iris' grave, we don't know who did this, but it wasn't us."

Although he had no actual knowledge of whom or what had damaged the clothing, a chill crept up his spine as soon as the name Belle popped into his head. He tried to dismiss the thought since he had been able to stay away from her since 1904, approximately nine years. She wouldn't be so bold as to come on to his property and destroy his wife's clothing. His heart was palpitating as he considered her relationship with the Geechee.

That crazy Belle and her Geechee can't harm me and my family. I'm Mr. Scott Harrington and they knows not to mess with me.

As a precautionary measure, he warned them to be on the look out for intruders. "Okay, we don't know who did it, but iffin' I find out, they gonna wish they never stepped foot up in my yard. Just be careful. When y'all put clothes out there on that line, make sure to keep a watchful eye out."

A triggering event had occurred. The thought of her was intoxicating and tormenting. He was finally on the right track and didn't want to jeopardize his family again for his addiction to her. But addiction is a powerful thing. It started calling out to him, and he had to answer. Once again he was on the slippery slope into hell with the destructive Belle.

About a week before Mary's clothing was damaged, Belle, Amos, and several other men were drinking at the Juke Joint. The conversation started with the Gulf's favorite topic. One of the drunken men in the group, who was speaking with slurred speech and slobbering all over himself, brought up Scott's fascination with his youngest daughter. Although the Gulf was full of women who adored him, there were plenty of men who were intimidated by and jealous of him.

"That arrogant fool, Harrington, always goin' 'round makin' all that dang noise over his missus' new baby? He's actin' like nobody else's baby mean nothin'. One of my friends said he heard him tell somebody else only he could make a baby this beautiful. That proud rooster thinkin' nobody can make pretty babies but him."

Belle replied, "She can't be all that pretty 'cause her momma be a plain woman."

The comment from another man is what put things into motion. "No it be just like Scott, or shall I say Mr. Harrington, say it is. My cousin Lena Mae say she went over there to sit for a spell with Miz Mary and saw the baby. Say when she looked down in the little angel's face, swore she seen a halo. Say the baby Novella is much prettier than Scott been splainin' – much mo' pretty. Say there somethin' special 'bout that little gal."

She had never heard anyone describe any woman in the Gulf in such terms – not even her. Her cheeks were as red as the pickled beets they sold at the Juke Joint. Sweat starting running down her face, arm pits, and back. The profuse sweating on her face was mixed with a steady stream of tears.

To add insult to injury, one of the drunken men pointed to her face, and could hardly get out what he was trying to say because he was laughing so hard. "Damn Belle, what be happenin' to you gal? You look like one of them raccoons with all that black stuff 'round yo eyes."

The place was in an uproar with laughter. She couldn't take being the butt of the ugly joke and hearing about another woman's extraordinary beauty. It was time to destroy Mary Harrington.

By the time they were closing down the Juke Joint, she had convinced a group to join her in sneaking over to Scott's place to have a look around. They lit oil lamps and made their way through the woods. She wasn't sure what she was going to do once they arrived, but she had to go. There was a queasy feeling in her stomach at the anticipation of running into him. *If he catches me and these fellas on his property he's prob'ly gonna take his shotgun and blow every one of 'em away and strangle me with his bare hands.*

Once they arrived, she was pleasantly surprised. Getting the pieces of fabric was going to be a lot easier than she thought. There was laundry gently swinging in the breeze on the clothes lines extending from the house to the big trees at the opposite end of the yard. She snuck up and tore several pieces from the undergarments since the material was sheer. They ran back through the woods laughing. Her faith was restored and she was looking forward to happily-ever-after with Scott.

Now Geechee gonna bring Mr. Harrington back to me for good. She's got what she be needin' to destroy that woman that took him from me. Events would not unfold as expected, and she would not get the exact results she was looking for.

Against his better judgment, he decided to confront her. *Oh my Gawd – I've been able stay away from her all this time. Now she's hauntin' me again. Every intoxicatin' second I ever spent with that woman keeps playin' over and over in my head. I'm doomed. I ain't never gonna get out from under her spell at this rate. Damn.*
While he struggled with temptation, feelings of guilt kept popping up out of nowhere reminding him of the peaceful life he was contemplating ruining. Before the incident with the damaged clothes happened, he had been doing a decent job of making peace with the life he created with Mary. She had given him Walter, who was now walking around the house imitating him with antics like puffing on his pipe and sticking his hands

down into the pockets of his overalls. She had also given him Novella, who stole his heart and attention.

I can't take this no more. I gotta get her outta my system for good. I'll tell her to leave me and my family alone. I don't need her kinda excitement. Ain't no place in my life fo' the likes of her. I've been able to resist her this long. Can't turn back now. I don't know what she's tryin' to pull now, but it ain't gonna work. I'm gonna let her know that.

As he stood looking at the den of immorality that had been beckoning him, he was bracing himself to put this crazy, intoxicating, frustrating, sensuous, and bewitching woman in her place for good. Squaring his shoulders, he walked up onto the porch and through the door, but nothing happened as planned. He walked straight back to bed in the corner, took off his clothes, pulled back the covers, and got in.

Aroused out of sleep, she turned over as if the last nine years never happened, and welcomed him with opened arms. "Why Mr. Harrington sir, I'm so happy to see you. I've been waitin' for you."

That ol' geechee got it right this time. He be back and back for good.

Mary could never quite put her finger on when the change for the worse started. For years he seemed content, especially after the births of their children. Things on the homefront should have been getting better, but that wasn't the case. With trepidation, she watched as he became sullen, distant, and distracted with each passing day. She turned to prayer.

"Dear Lawd Jesus, you know what be troublin' my husband. Please give him peace. I truly love that man, and it hurts me to see him so unhappy. Show me how to please him in every way. I don't wanna lose him."

There were times when she just had to ask what was bothering him. "Mr. Harrington is there anything in particular you wanna talk about?"

"Nothin' Mary."

She knew better. Her marriage was starting to follow the same path folk spoke of his previous marriages. She hated gossip, but could no longer dismiss the grapevine. Initially she was confident he was being faithful – that is the until disappearing acts started.

Grandpa George was furious, and called for a meeting. "Listen here boy. My Mary was in damn good shape when you got her from this here house, and I ain't 'cepting that she gonna start bein' mistreated now. I told you 'fo I gave you my permission to take company with her that you had better treat her right. 'Parently you was givin' me a bunch of hogwash when you said you was a changed man. Now I'mma say this again. If you can't do right by her, send her back to her momma and me. If I gotta get my rifle out to deal with you that be fine with me too."

"Nothin's goin on Pa George."

George was now well up in age, senility had set in, and he was no longer a threat. Family members watched his strange behavior and conversation in confusion and horror. He constantly spoke of life as a slave, acting as if he were living in that desolate period one minute then immediately reverting back to the present. He no longer remembered places that and people who should have been familiar to him.

Scott could tolerate listening to his sermons knowing he couldn't remember what anybody said five minutes earlier. George became even less of a threat when eventually Mary had to admit him to a nursing home with other coloreds who were talking out of their heads, urinating on, and unable to feed themselves.

The turn of events was taking its toll. It was impossible to satisfy Scott's never-ending demands. He turned to Belle again in his futile attempts to forget the mounting family life obstacles that besieged him.

Staying connected to the children was even becoming difficult. His rare tender moments were when Novella climbed up onto his lap to play the patty cake game he had taught her. "Oh my special little gal, you gonna be that great lady one of these days. Poppa feel it in his bones."

He was a tormented man with a tormented wife. Even with the growing knowledge of what he was up to, she fought to stay strong for the children, and care for her mother who was devastated by the changes in Grandpa George. Things still didn't happen in a logical order. Before the year 1913 ended, her mother passed away, George was hovering near death, and she was pregnant again.

Maude was learning about adult matters that were frankly making her very angry. Beolia was upset about the rumors circulating throughout the Gulf as well.

"Maude, what is Poppa doing with that woman they call Belle? Some boys at school were laughing about her saying that she's hotter than a skillet and Poppa likes it like that. What are they talking about?"

She didn't understand much more than Beolia, but knew that whatever he was doing with the other woman wasn't proper and it was tearing Mary apart. Whenever someone started a conversation about seeing him around town, she saw the look of embarrassment Mary deseparately tried to hide.

She was sick to her stomach watching Mary fighting to hold on to her marriage, splitting her time between home and the nursing home where Grandpa George lived, and being a mother to young children. All the while Scott was disappearing whenever he got good and ready to, and daring anyone to say anything to him.

"Beolia, don't pay no mind to that trash you hearin'. Mr. Harrington..."

"You mean Poppa?"

"Like I said, Mr. Harrington got hisself mixed up with some loose woman who everybody say is crazy. She been chasin' after him fo' long as most folk 'round here can remember. They say she killed his first wife and her baby. Him and his dumb self can't control what's in his pants and now he done brung his mess into Momma's life. I can tell you this. The whole thing stinks in my nostrils and most of the time I can't stand him. If that crazy witch come anywhere near Momma, I'm gonna give her the whuppin' she been askin' for, but everybody seem too afraid to give to her."

"Oh my God Maude, you're talking about fighting a grown woman."

"Yeah, I guess you're right – I'm talkin' 'bout givin' her a grown woman's ass whuppin."

"Girl, you had better watch your mouth. You can't be talking about Poppa like that."

"He ain't none of my poppa. My poppa be Daniel and he be dead. All this stuff Mr. Harrington got goin' on is gettin' worse and you watch – it's all gonna come to a head one day and one day soon. Damn fool can't even control hisself and Momma carryin' his baby."

"And Beolia, gal, why you always talkin' so damn proper? I like hearin' you and all, but when I'm mad, I ain't tryin' to hear no proper talk. All I wanna do is cuss him out. Maybe give him the ass whuppin' I'm itchin' to give his tramp."

"Maude, you had better stop speaking such filthy language."

"See what I mean? Filthy language – oh please Beolia, I'm talkin' trash gal, but I'm gonna do somethin' 'bout it too. Just you watch and see 'bout that too."

As Mary advanced in her pregnancy, it became more difficult to get around. Maude was worried that she stayed sick a lot of the time.

"Baby gal, yo momma be alright and don't you worry none. These bouts of sickness just goin' on 'cause I'm really too old to be havin' babies. I gotta keep tryin' til I give yo poppa another son. That be his heart's desire, and I declare, I'm gonna give him one. Iffin the good Lawd could just give us one more boy I'll be satisfied iffin He fix it so I can't have no more babies. This body of mine feelin' mighty tired these days."

Poor Momma, she sick as dog most of the time and still thinkin' 'bout keepin' him happy.

In the wee hours of the morning of November 14, 1914, Mary awakened to her first labor pains. Maude was nervously pacing the floor and seething because Mary wouldn't even think about letting her go to get Mama Mame until he had his breakfast.

Is everybody in this house crazy? Mr. Harrington needs to be stayin' here with Momma, or gettin' his hide over to Mama Mame's place. But we all sittin' up here worryin' 'bout him and not Momma.

"Momma, please let me go and get Mama Mame before somethin' awful happens."

"Maude, just do what I say. Make sure Mr. Harrington's breakfast is ready on time. Don't worry 'bout me. These pains ain't close enough or strong enough for you to go runnin' over to Mama Mame."

Suddenly things took a drastic turn for the worse, and she had to be helped back into bed. "Oh Gawd, the baby's comin'. Maude, Maude, you gotta get over to Mama Mame's. Somethin's happenin'. Feels like..."

Water started running down her legs.

"Beolia, get somethin' to wipe this water up while I get Momma back into bed."

Beolia had returned with the rags and was mopping up the water around Mary's feet when they noticed the liquid was turning another color. At first it looked stained, but as it continued to run down Mary's legs, became thicker and red. She was bleeding.

"Maude baby, I can't wait no longer. I think I'm in trouble. Hurry up now and get Mama Mame." The pains were now excruciating and everyone in the house was terrified – even Scott.

"Beolia, help me get dressed and look after them youngins while I run and get Mama Mame." They were running around the room with both of them dressing Maude. As if she could make Maude move even faster, Beolia finally gave her a hard push out of the door and into the yard. She was running in a desperate attempt to save Mary and the new baby. By day's end, however, they were in mourning. Mary would never have a chance to give him another son and home was never the same.

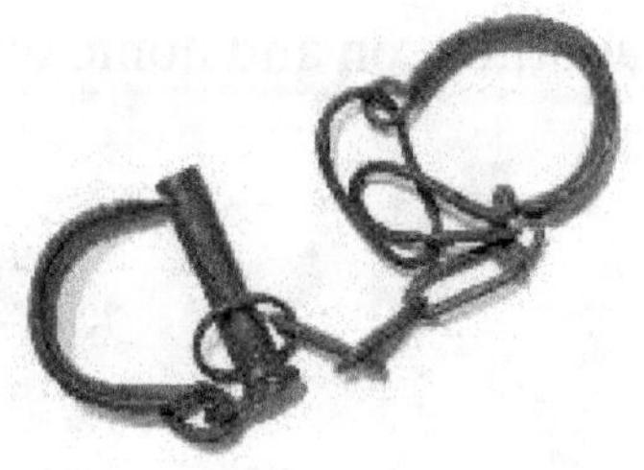

Chapter 12
Maude Finds a Beau

It was the summer of 1915, when Maude started working at the tobacco farm where she met Henry Oakley. Henry was a giant young man. He was as tall as Scott, but looked as though he weighed twice as much. He was the color of dark chocolate and had a set of pearly white teeth that flashed constantly because he laughed constantly.

He noticed early on that Maude had a temper, and was too serious for someone her age. So he made a point of endlessly teasing her, trying to get her to lighten up.

"Miss Maude gal, don't you ever smile? What be so serious that you can't find nothin' to smile 'bout? Can't nothin' be that serious. C'mon – give ol' Henry a smile. C'mon, c'mon, let me see it, let me see it. There it is. Stop fightin' me gal – you know you wanna laugh. There it is – see there; I knew you wanted to laugh."

"You just mind yo bizness Henry and I'll mind mine. Got plenty to be serious 'bout and ain't got no time fo' yo foolishness. Ain't none of yo bizness anyhow."

"Oh yeah, well I be serious 'bout one thing and that is to get to know you better. Why don't you go down to the Juke Joint one Friday night with me? I promise you we'll have us a real good time. Dat moonshine they serve down there be the best in all the Gulf."

"Ain't nothin' I want at no Juke Joint and iffin that be where you hang out, I don't want nothin' to do with you no how."

He kept trying and she couldn't resist his persistent teasing. He was playful, loved clowning around, and everybody at the farm found him hilarious. His persistence paid off and eventually she found herself reduced to fits of giggles.

"Henry, I know you wanna be more than friends and you be wantin' to hug and kiss and all that stuff. But I just got too much goin' on at home to get involved like that. My momma, she had a baby 'bout a year ago and she ain't been the same since. Mr. Harrington, he ain't a patient man and he want everything his way. He just ain't there fo' Momma like a husband ought to be. So I gotta look out fo' her, know what I mean? I ain't got time for huggin' and kissin'. Maybe you should start courtin' one of them other girls on the job."

"Look Maude, I think that be mighty strong and good of you to be lookin' out fo' your mammy like that. Ain't nothin' mo' pleasin' to a man when he see a strong gal like you takin' on this big ol' cruel world. Look, if there be somethin' I can do to help out, just let me know. Okay?"

She took him up on his offer. "Look, go ahead run yo other errands. I'll sit with Miss Mary. She seem to like my jokes more than you do anyways." Mary did like Henry at first. With everything that was happening, one of the bright spots was seeing Maude starting to enjoy life with a young man.

Henry asked Mary for Maude's hand in marriage. She was offended by their lack of respect for Scott, and scolded them.

"Henry, I think you may be a fine man for my Maude, but Mr. Harrington is the head of this household. He's been raisin' Maude since she was six years old. I can't give y'all my blessin' lest you go to him first and get his approval."

"...but Momma."

"Maude don't try back talkin' me gal, I mean what I say. I don't like it already you told Henry to ask me instead of Poppa. You are not to disrespect him, and I don't care if you think you be old enough to get married. I have nothin' more to say until the man over this house approve of this marriage."

Maude hated having to ask him for anything, but knew Mary's mind was made up.

When Beolia heard the news, she was torn between being happy for Maude and struggling with the thought of living in a home without her close by. She didn't have the stamina or boldness to stand up to Scott on any matters, and worked hard at loving him. While Maude refused to call him anything but Mr. Harrington, she called him Poppa. He knew she was a much gentler personality, and that she wanted to be close to him. He didn't have to be on guard with her because in her he found yet another adoring female.

Now that he had the power to keep Maude in the house, she was praying for his typical response. She wanted him to be difficult and forbid Maude to marry. She was being selfish, but this time she didn't care. *Do forgive me Maude, but I just can't imagine trying to live here without you to protect me and Momma. Maybe you can find a husband down the road when I'm older and strong enough to take care of myself.*

To everyone's surprise, he didn't have any objections and gave his blessing. He did so, in part, because he was getting rid of the one person who didn't fear him, and wasn't afraid to challenge him. Quite frankly he was tired of the constant battles, and she didn't seem to be getting tired of challenging him. He was so glad to get her out of the house he was willing to reward her for leaving. His gift to the newly married couple was a burlap sack filled with some of the gold coins James Seamore had given to him and Walter years back when he met with them immediately and privately after announcing they were free men.

I will never understand that man. Just when you think you got him figured out, he go and do somethin' nice for you. Lovin' Mr. Harrington is 'bout one of the hardest things in this life to do.

Chapter 13
The Chickens Come Home to Roost
(Part I)

Belle was gloating and convinced the Geechee's powers were starting to unravel his marriage to Mary. She couldn't help rejoicing about the turn of events. *Geechee told me that after three wives, he still be in love with me. Don't really want them church mice when he can have a real woman. Yeah, Geechee said she had a vision wherein them spirits she talk to told her I'm the reason his sons keep dyin' or walkin' outta his life. They ain't my sons, so he keep losin' 'em. Nothin' gonna go right fo' him 'til he's with me. Too late now, she done lost the last son and she be too old to give him another one. Serves her right stealin' what belongs to me.*

Unfortunately, Mary still had all the leverage. She had given him a daughter whom he adored. Belle was jealous of Novella, whose beauty and personality were blossoming with each passing day. The more she heard about his adoration for Novella, the angrier she became at her untouchable opponent. She couldn't even admit to herself the insane jealously she felt over a toddler. However, nothing was going to stop her from destroying the woman she blamed for giving Novella to Scott. She was furious with Mary and decided it was time to get rid of her once and for all.

Destroying Mary became her fanatical focus. She was going to remove her from Scott's life. Novella and anyone else who loved Mary was going to pay for coming between her and Scott.

She wasn't satisfied with the root doctor's results thus far, and wanted Mary destroyed immediately.

"Geechee, when you gonna get rid of my last enemy? I been waitin' all my life and I'm even gettin' up in age. You need to finish off that woman layin' up over there with Mr. Harrington. I need her outta my way right now. Kill her – I mean it – kill her."

"Eb'ryth'ing iz gettin' ready to happ'n that posed to happ'n. Old Geechee's spells are gettin' ready to do dem' own work. When I finish folk won't know warruh hit tuhr'um. Gal, yo won't ever have to come back dis way. Eb'ryth'ing will be settled."

"I wish I could better understand that mumbo jumbo you be talkin'. After all these years I should be better at figurin' out what the devil you're talkin' 'bout. Hard to understand that Gullah talk, but long as I get what I want, I'll just have to trust you'll come through for me. Dang crazy lady."

Once again she was oblivious to the severity and dire consequences of her offensive language. The Geechee kept mumbling, but now more to herself. "Geechee gettin' ready to put somethin' on yo dat yo won't ever be forgettin'. The chickens are comin' home to roos' yo eegnut witch."

Belle gave up talking and shoved more money at her. She was so careless with handing payment over to the Geechee some of the money fell to the floor. She neither apologized nor attempted to pick the crumbled dollar bills up. As she was leaving, she shouted over her shoulder, "Just hurry up and do somethin'." Unaware that the Geechee still could hear her, she spat out, "Damn ol' hag", but didn't hear the response.

"Fsutt'n yo eegnut witch."

The next morning she awakened with a dizzying headache. When she swung her legs over the side of the bed and attempted to stand up, she crashed to the floor. *What on earth is goin' on? I must really be tired. Gotta get myself together here.*

After a few minutes of struggling, she was finally able to get up from the floor and move around. *Now that's more like it. I must've had too much liquor. Must've been some kinda party where I can't even remember gettin' drunk.*

Nothing else unusual happened for the remainder of the day to remind her of the shaky start earlier that morning. There were no more incidences until the following Sunday morning when she awakened with an excruciating headache – much worse than the last time. Her vision was blurred and there was an awful ringing in her ears. She managed to stand up, but then everything went black and she crashed to the floor.

When she came to, she screamed for help. "Please, somebody help me, somethin's wrong with me. Oh Gawd don't let me die in here alone. Please, somebody…"

Miserable and frightened she crawled back into bed and was forced to stay there until Amos stopped by to see why she hadn't shown up at the Juke Joint. While lying there thinking about the strange attacks, she had a reveleation. *Oh my Gawd, that evil bitch must've turned on me. I bet she's workin' some roots on me. Whatever be wrong with that crazy witch? I asked her to destroy Mary Harrington. Why would she turn on me? Sweet Jesus, let Amos get over here in a hurry to see 'bout me. I'm sure he know somethin's wrong by now.*

Amos finally arrived. "Jesus Christ – what happened to you? You look like death. You need another drink or somethin'?"

Her hair was soaking wet from sweating and it was plastered to her head. Her eyes were bloodshot with swollen lids. She didn't have the strength to fight with him for insulting her looks.

She was shivering and complaining about freezing one minute and swearing she was burning up the next. "Get me some help. Somethin's wrong you stupid fool. Do somethin' – just don't stand there talkin' 'bout me like I ain't in the room. Get outta here and get somebody to help me!"

"Okay, okay. Jesus Christ Belle, I'm gonna get Mama Mame. She won't wanna come, but we gotta get some help."

She was out of her head and delirious. Her combative relationship with Mama Mame over the years was the furthest thing from her mind. She stopped yelling and started pleading, "Please hurry up and get her. I'm scared to death. Oh Amos, please do get help before I die."

After he left, she was lying in bed feeling alone, frightened, and forced to face the ugly truth – the Geechee was out to get her.

My Gawd, askin' that old witch to work roots on my man to keep away them other gals always tryin' to take him from me wasn't no worse than some of the low down dirty things she's been doin' most of her life. Matter of fact, what I asked her to do don't no way in hell compare to the reign of terror she been spreadin' all throughout South Carolina, North Carolina, and Georgia. She would never do anything like this to May. She was more than willin' to do any and everything May asked her to do. I'm May's daughter, so why would she do this to me?

She should have known that dealing with the devil reincarnated as the Geechee would be her ruination. But dealing with the evil root doctor was the only way she knew how to get the results she wanted. May had taught her the value of "Geechee Insurance."

Gawd I wish May was here right now. I bet she could get the old witch to reverse this curse. May I thought you would never die. Considerin' everything you and that ol' woman did together, I thought she worked some kinda spell that would make you live forever. Don't seem like she's ever gonna die.

As she lay helplessly waiting for whatever was about to happen, she started thinking about the day things changed forever. Before that awful day, they lived well – better than most white people because her and May were once considered white, and they were the family of a very wealthy and powerful white man.

Chapter 14
May Granger

Oakland Hall Plantation was one of the largest in Lincoln County, and the owner, Doctor Stephen Granger, was one of the most affluent men in the State of North Carolina. May Granger was the love of his life. He was a man who loved to flaunt his wealth, as well as his wife and daughter Belle. He had everything a man could ask for. Everybody loved or pretended to love May and couldn't get enough of looking at her. Her extraordinary beauty, however, was responsible for a bloody and brutal feud that no one in Lincoln County ever forgot.

Doctor Granger had been visiting relatives in Virginia and was supposed to stay for about a month when life for just about everyone in Lincoln County changed.

He was missing May terribly and decided to return home a week earlier than planned. He couldn't wait to get back to Oakland Hall and surprise her with an exquisite sapphire and diamond necklace. The enormous blue sapphire would rest in her cleavage with surrounding diamonds sparkling as if a million stars had landed on her voluptuous chest. She was worth every material possession he bestowed upon her. Jewels notwithstanding, she was his most prized possession and he was the envy of every wealthy man in Lincoln County.

It was around 11 o'clock at night when he arrived at Oakland Hall. "Damon, just go on around to the stables to put away the horse and carriage. I can walk back to the house from there. I need to stretch my legs and the walk will do me some good."

"Yessah Massa. Want me to help you with yo bags?"

"No, I'll fetch them in the morning. I just want to take a quiet walk up to the house. It's such a beautiful night. Besides I want to surprise Mrs. Granger. I reckon she misses me as much as I've been missing her."

Damon didn't respond, but just kept staring straight ahead as Doctor Granger spoke. Had he been facing the slave, he would have gotten his first warning that things at home were not as peaceful and inviting as he thought they were. Damon didn't want to get caught in the middle of the events he knew would be unfolding throughout the night. So he kept his mouth shut and continued staring straight ahead.

Once the horse and carriage pulled into the stable, Stephen jumped down, making sure not to drop the boxed jewelry. He wanted to unwind before he reached May. He was excited just thinking about her and how she drove him crazy.

I don't think there's a woman in all of North Carolina that's as sensuous as my May. Every man in these parts would die to have her, but she's married to me. Can't believe I pulled that one off, but I did and don't regret anything I've done. It's nobody's business anyway, and she's everything I've ever wanted and more.

He opened the door and stood in the foyer taking in the panoramic view of his mansion. It was breathtaking, but the woman waiting for him upstairs was even more breathtaking. He smiled, anticipating what would be taking place for the next hour or so.

About halfway up the stairs he heard voices. *Maybe she's not sleep after all. Sometimes she suffers with insomnia, and will keep the slave girls up with her until she falls off to sleep. I wonder what they're talking about this time of night.*

The next voice he heard froze him dead in his tracks because it was that of a man. *What in God's name is going on here?*

"May, you know how much I love you. Anything you desire I can give to you, but I don't want to keep coming over here whenever he's out of town. I can't relax always thinking he may show up unexpectedly. We can't continue taking chances like this. I want to be with you whenever I feel like it."

"Linwood, will you stop worrying about that. He's away – up in Virginia visiting with his family and isn't expected to return until sometime next week. Let's just enjoy the time we have together."

"But I want you with me all the time. I can give more than he ever could. My family has done exceptionally well in the iron ore business and we're considered among the wealthiest in Lincoln County. I have more slaves than he does. If you leave him, I promise you won't miss a thing. Just leave and I'll prove everything I'm promising you tonight."

Linwood was Stephen's arch rival. He had tremendous wealth, a huge mansion, and more slaves than anyone could count working his plantation. He was a handsome man and his wife, Audrey, was a good looking woman. She didn't compare with May and that's what set Stephen apart from his aristocratic friends and neighbors. May was his leverage. No matter how rich other white men were, they envied him because of her. She was envied by most women and the heart's desire of every wealthy man.

One of the double doors banged into the wall as he stormed into the bedroom. They scrambled to pull up the covers to hide their nudity. His wife was having an affair with Linwood Smith.

"You son-of-a-bitch. How dare you come into my house and bed my wife. Well you're going to meet your maker tonight."

He abrudptly turned to the opposite corner, moving towards the armoire. May started screaming because she knew what he was going after.

"Oh my God, no Stephen no. Oh my God. Get up Linwood, he's going for his rifle."

Linwood jumped out of the bed and lunged at Stephen. He was much larger and stronger, and was able to wrestle him to the floor face down.

"Calm down, calm down. I'm leaving right now. Just calm down and I'm out of here."

"Not before I kill you, and her. Let me go you son-of-a-bitch." He started struggling to turn his body over so he could have a better chance of getting out of Linwood's grip.

Linwood humiliated him even more when he pushed his face down into the floor. "I'm not going to let you kill me tonight or any other night. Are you mad man? You want everybody to know another man is sleeping with the wife you so gallantly parade around in front of all of us? Think about how my wife is going to react. I've got children to protect."

"You dog, get off of me. Get off of me. I'm going to kill you and I mean it."

Linwood was determined there wouldn't be any dead bodies lying around when the sun came up and started giving orders. "May, hurry up and get me something to tie him up with."

"Linwood, are you crazy? I can't do that. He's my husband. I can't do..."

"So what do you propose I do with him? Let him go so he can get up, get his rifle, and kill me? May, please hurry up. Just do as I tell you to. I'm not going to hurt him. I'm just going to tie him up so I can get out of here."

She was confused, but had no choice but to follow his orders. When he finished, Stephen was still struggling trying to get loose, but to no avail. The look on his face was terrifying and she didn't want to be left alone with him. "Linwood, don't leave me alone. What am I going to do when I have to untie him?"

"For God sake, I don't know, but I've got to get out of here. I can't have my wife finding out about this. Oh God, what is everybody going to think if they find out about this?"

She was finding it hard to even process the cowardice words of the man who had just professed to love her more than her husband. A few minutes ago he was making all kinds of promises. Now here he was just thinking about saving his own neck and marriage. He put his clothes on and left without saying another word to May or Stephen.

She removed the handkerchief away from Stephen's mouth, and the venomous assault was launched. "You filthy negra." She was stunned, and couldn't remember the last time that word was directed at her.

"Sweet Jesus – Stephen, what are you saying? You can't mean..."

"You heard me – you filthy negra. How could you? After all I've done for you. I never told a soul about your damn secret. Not one soul in Lincoln County knows you're not one hundred percent white. You're a negra-- nothing but a damned negra. I loved and married you in spite of that. I made you wealthy and the envy of everybody in Lincoln County and this is how you repay me? Well your hell has just begun. I want you out of this house now. Get your bastard and take her down to the slave quarters with you."

"Oh my God, what are you saying? Belle is our daughter. Don't you dare speak about her in that tone of voice."

"You had better start moving right now. You're a negra and as far as I'm concerned that makes Belle one too. I want you down in them slave quarters right now. From this night forward, you are a slave and I am going to treat you like one. You can get off of your high horse right now because by daybreak everybody around here is going to know who you really are. They're going to see you brought down to your lowest estate. You just watch me."

"Stephen, I can't believe you would do this to me and your daughter."

As soon as he finished untying the remaining rope, he grabbed her by the arm and started pulling her towards Belle's room.

"You're hurting me. Please stop this madness. I'm so sorry. I promise to never lay eyes on him again. Just forgive me. It's you that I really love. Please Stephen. Please..."

"I said to shut your filthy mouth. I'm going to do more than hurt your arm. Get down this hall right now and get her up and out of my house."

Things got worse once they arrived in Belle's bedroom. "Get in this damn room and get her up. I want the two of you out of here."

The arguing woke Belle up. "Hello Daddy, I'm so glad you're home."

"Get up. Don't you ever call me Daddy. You and your nigger mother are my slaves and you're getting out of my house right now."

"Momma, what is Daddy talking about? What's going on?" She was crying, but no one would do anything to calm her down, or explain to her why Stephen looked so mean. May was too upset to help her get out of the bed, so he yanked her up by an arm.

"Owww, that hurts Daddy. Please let go of me. You're hurting me."

He was oblivious to their pleas as he pulled them down the stairs and threw them out of the house and into the night. "When I'm finished, you are going to be begging me to put you out of your misery with a bullet between your lying eyes."

The slaves came out of their quarters. Earlier that night when Damon told them Dr. Granger had returned a week early, they knew something awful was going to happen. They were confused, however, because they kept hearing the words "negra" or "nigger" and thought she had somehow turned her indiscretion into a lie on one of them. They were shocked when the front door opened and Doctor Granger tossed her and Belle out.

"C'mon Miss Granger, I'll take you down to my quarters. Then in the monin', we can get you and young Miss Belle here situated. Maybe Massa will have simmered down by then."

"Jessie you'd better watch your mouth girl and shut up this minute. She's no damned Miss to anybody and all of you had better start referring to her as May. She's no more human than you niggers."

Jessie backed off and the other slaves stood expressionless in response to his statement reducing them to less-than-human.

Things were no better the next day. Before daybreak he brought one of the overseers to the slave quarters. "Get up May. Mr. Perser here is going to take you to other quarters.You can't stay here with Jessie and her family. It's already crowded in here."

She was now treated like a slave and made to serve him as one. He took pleasure in berating her in front of the other slaves. She was forced to call him "Massa." He demanded that she and Belle speak like slaves, and never again as if they were white. To make matters worse, he forced her to submit to his perversions as he raped her on a regular basis. When she thought him incapable of humiliating her more, he found a lower level to stoop.

To his detriment, however, he had under-estimated her tenacity and was ignorant to her taste for blood. The savage beast had been aroused, and she wasn't going to take the punishment without relatiation. She was ready to seek revenge and shared her thoughts with Jessie.

"Jessie, he knew I wasn't white when he met me. This isn't – I mean this ain't fair. He was the one telling – I mean tellin' me not to ever tell anybody I was Mulatto. He knew it, but said he loved me and wanted me to be his wife anyhow."

"The niggers – I mean y'all just don't know what it's really like to live with him. He bought me jewels and was only too happy to parade me around in front of his rich friends. As soon as we got back home, he was always worked up and couldn't wait to get me into bed. Then in the bedroom he would demand that we copulate in the most disgusting fashion. I mean he wanted to do all sorts of dirty things. Then you know what?"

"What is it May?"

"The minute it was over, he immediately fell out of bed onto his knees and started beggin' the Lord – I mean the Lawd to forgive him for his dirty thoughts and deeds. I had to lie there hearin' him praying for forgiveness for doing what he wanted to do with me. Then in a couple of days the whole sick and twisted thing would occur all over again with him beggin' me to do certain things to him and then beggin' the Lawd afterwards to forgive him for those same acts."

"Now he's determined to make me pay for being with Linwood. I thought he cared about me too. But Jessie, he was only thinking about himself. He left me there to deal with Massa all by myself. Oh God – I mean Gawd, I'm most miserable, what am I ever gonna do?"

"Miss Granger, I feel so bad fo' you and little Belle. I can't imagine livin' like you been livin' all these years and now him makin' you a slave just like the rest of us. Lease we used to it. You richer than most white folk 'round here. This here tribulation he done brought upon you is mo' than a woman can take."

"Jessie you've got to stop calling me 'Miss Granger'. He'll have you beaten within an inch of your life if he hears you calling me that. So from now on, I'm May and if he wants to treat me like a slave so be it. But I'll tell you this, if I ever find a way to get him back, I'm gonna make him regret the day he turned on me."

"That damned Linwood is gonna pay too. There he was one minute pretending he doesn't like sneaking into my bedroom while Doctor – I mean Massa was gone, beggin' me to leave and come with him when he had no intentions whatsoever to make me his wife. He went runnin' off into the night worried about what his wife and everybody was going to, I mean gonna think if they found out about us. If I ever find a way, I will make all of them sorry they hurt May Granger."

"Well May, if you be serious 'bout that I got the perfect answer. I know 'bout a woman they call "Geechee" and she be one of the most feared root workers in these here parts. You know what roots are?"

"No, I can't say that I do, but tell me 'bout 'em."

"Well, this woman they call Geechee, she was sent up here by her Massa's from the low country of South Carolina. She come from this place they call the Gullah Country. She so terrible they were scared to death of her. So as soon as they could, they got her outta South Carolina and sold her to somebody up here. They say root workers like her got knowledge of the spirit world, and can reach into it and make the spirits do things human beings not capable of doin'. I hear them root workers practice their witchcraft and that stuff throughout Georgia and South Carolina. Now them witches makin' their way up here. I reckon pretty soon ain't no place gonna be safe from 'em."

"Jessie, I'm dead serious. If it takes the rest of my life, I'm gonna get him and every other man that ever used me back. They fall for beauty and wanna use it only for their selfish pleasure. Then the minute a woman don't do like they want her to do, they wanna treat her like she ain't even human. Well I'm gonna show all of 'em just what a beautiful woman can do to 'em. I can't wait to pay him back. Can you take me to meet her?"

"Yeah – my brother Isaiah, he know how to sneak over to that plantation where she be at. He'll make arrangements fo' you to meet her. You gotta be serious now. I'm tellin' you – once you start messin' with her, ain't no turnin' back. She ain't nobody to be playin' wit."

"I'm dead serious. Massa turned on me in the worst way. He has humiliated me, turned me into his slave, and come down to my quarters to rape me whenever he gets good and ready. Then Linwood, he used me and ran out on me when we got caught. I'm gonna show them what happens when you mess with May Granger."

"Then I'll make the arrangements."

"Thanks Jessie."

She was shaking so bad, her teeth chattered while standing in the woods in the middle of the night, waiting and terrified at the unknown. Before her conversation with Jessie, she had never heard of geechees, galluhs, or roots. The whole thing sounded spooky and dangerous, but it seemed like the perfect way to get revenge on Doctor Granger, Linwood, and anybody else who crossed her.

She didn't hear any leaves rustling or footsteps approaching, but was startled when suddenly the Geechee was standing in front of her. Her dark complexion was in stark contrast to her hazel eyes. May had never seen anybody's stare as piercing as the odd looking woman now standing in front of her. Her sharp features gave her a bird-like appearance. She didn't bother to smile or shake May's hand.

"Warruh hunnuh wunt wid me gal?"

"I'm sorry, I don't understand, what did you say?"

"I 'ent got no time fo' you to wais. Warrah hunnuah wun wid me?"

"Oh, what do I want with you. I'm sorry. My name is May Granger and I need you to help me to destroy my enemies? I've got a lot of 'em. My husband, Doctor Stephen Granger, he's the main one. He threw me outta my house and is now forcing me to be and live like a slave. He threw our daughter out with me."

"Yo lawfully man be a w'ite man and hunnuh look w'ite to me too. So huccome you sayin' dis' Doctor Granger makin' yo his slabe? Dat strange talk. W'ymekso?"

"I know this sounds strange and all, but you see, I'm not all white. Doctor Granger found out I'm Mulatto when I first came to these parts. He wanted me, but didn't want anybody else to know he was in love with a Mulatto. So he swore me to secrecy and I've been living as a white woman ever since. We even have one daughter."

"So 'smattuh?"

"Oh my God, I'm sorry, I don't understand. What did you say?"

"So if he already had this inflummashion, why he makin' yo his slabe attuh all dis' time?"

"I was sleepin' with his arch rival, Linwood Smith, who owns the Rosewood Plantation. Doctor Granger came back from Virginia a week early and caught me in bed with Linwood. To add insult to injury, when he tried to get his rifle, Linwood wrestled him to the floor and tied him up. He hates me so much now he's willing to enslave and humiliate me. I want you to help me pay him back for every despicable thing he's done and is doin' to me. Please help me."

"Lemme tink 'bout it. Gal yo should'uh knowed bettuh. Dem w'ite mens don' like nobody to duh t'ings like dat to 'em buhhime dey back. Puhaps he more mad a him'own self fo' lettin' you git to'em like dat. Now he don't wun't no boddum outta you.

Fsutt'n he gonna make you fuhr'ebbuh pay fo' makin' him a fool right dey in his own house."

"Just tell me what to do and I'll do it."

"Well, we gonna give dem trubble the likes dey 'ent seen 'fo'. I got potions dat hab dem ack like wild animals. I got spells dat hab dem crawlin' 'round like ravin' dogs. Geechee can do enny tink you want. Don't madduh to me, we can do eb'ryt'ing and enny t'ing you wantin' to bring him and his w'ite friends down to the mud. I kill dem iffin dat be what you want."

Initially she was feeling pretty good knowing that Stephen was going to pay for humiliating and disowning her. When she got back to her quarters, however, she started having second thoughts about getting involved with the woman. She wasn't comfortable with spirits, demons, spells, and witchcraft. Maybe there was another way. *I ain't never heard a woman speak so violently in my life. She's willin' to do some of meanest and nastiest things I've ever heard. I didn't even know a woman could behave and think so viciously. Jessie said I better not be playin' with this woman. Yeah, I think it may be best to leave her alone. She's terrifying to say the least.*

Before going to sleep, she decided not to go that route. She would find another way to pay Stephen back.

Nothing changed. He treated her far worse than the other slaves. Nothing she did satisfied him. He ignored Belle. When she didn't think he was capable of inflicting any more pain, he found yet another way to discredit her. He claimed he didn't know she was Mulatto and that she had tricked him into marrying her.

His accusation was the furthest thing from the truth. From the very beginning she was completely honest, fearing he had mistaken her for being white. When considering the consequences, there was no way she was willing to take a chance on hiding the truth. In the end, he convinced her that it didn't matter. He was determined to have her and devised the scheme to fool everybody.

Now he wanted to make her pay for her crime of passion and blamed the whole charade on her. The marriage was annulled on the basis of deceit. It was only for selfish reasons he wouldn't allow those who wanted to lynch her to have their way. His preference was to commit her to a lifetime of daily torture.

He brought a woman name Betsey to Oakland Hall and introduced her as his new wife. The slaves were called to the front yard of the mansion to be introduced to the new Mrs. Granger. The first words out of his mouth were intended to humiliate May.

"Where's my nigger May. I can hardly see you back there. If I recall, you have a hearing problem. Come on up to the front here with your bastard. I don't want you to miss a word of what I'm about to announce."

There was complete silence. The slaves were embarrassed for her as they witnessed the depraved level to which he was willing to stoop in order to humiliate her in front of them.

"Now that May can hear this loud and clear, I want all of you to meet my precious wife. This is Mrs. Betsey Granger, and she is from a prominent family that lives down in Georgia. Mrs. Granger is a good Christian woman, who comes from pure lineage and is to be treated as such. May, you will serve exclusively at Mrs. Granger's pleasure as her personal nigger."

Betsey looked down at the woman her husband had assigned to serve her. If she had met her under any other circumstances she would have never guessed the woman standing in front of her was a slave. She immediately picked up on Stephen's attraction to her although he was trying his best to humiliate her. *This wench must have been sleeping with Stephen before he married me. Oh well, she's at my beck and call now. I plan to run her so much she won't have any energy left to please him and she'll look too haggard for him to even want to lay eyes on her.*

"Girl, get my things from the back of the carriage. Then I want you to take them upstairs and arrange them in the armoire properly. You will then separate my most personal garments and put them away. When you have finished, you are to fix lunch and bring it to the wrap-around porch. Now hurry up and do as I say. Time is of the essence."

May hesitated because she was trying to process the long list of directions. Her eyes started to tear up, but she was determined they wouldn't spill down her cheeks. Betsey wasn't sympathetic. The slap was so hard May thought her neck had been broken.

"Nigger, did you just hear what I said? You had better hurry up and carry out my instructions. If you don't move now, I'll put the whip to you myself."

The smirk on Stephen's face as he watched his new wife berate her was the last straw. The last laugh was not to be his because his introduction of Betsey sent May back to the Geechee. It was time for revenge.

Six months later, Betsey was found hanging from a tree in the woods. Both of her wrists were slit. There was a note addressed to Stephen explaining that she made a horrible mistake in marrying him and coming to North Carolina. For reasons she could not explain, shortly after moving to Oakland Hall, she constantly felt tormented. The suicide note went on to say that he wasn't the man she thought he was. She was miserable and decided to choose death over living a lie with him.

When May heard about Betsey's suicide she snuck out that night to meet the Geechee. As soon as the root doctor emerged from among the bushes and briars, she rushed up to hug her. The Geechee wasn't accustomed to affection or being embraced.

"Gal, what da' madder wid you?"

"Oh Geechee, whatever did you do to drive Betsey Granger to take her own life? I tell you, Stephen is beside himself. He's mortified that a woman would choose death over life with him. You should've heard him. All of us did. We were in the kitchen when we heard one of the field workers come runnin' into the house. He was yellin' 'bout them findin' Missy Granger down in the woods hangin' from a tree. Apparently she had already slit both wrists, but death was takin' too long. So she got up in that big ol' tree somehow and hung herself."

"That poor field hand couldn't read her suicide note and brought it back to the mansion. Stephen was distraught and couldn't wait to find out what happened. He read the note out loud in front of everybody. Damned fool was so humiliated, he let the whole world know his new wife couldn't bear to live another day with him. So tell me – what did you do? "

"Gal, dem pieces of cloths you bring to me warruh she owned I put 'em on a little ol' dolly I made. Den I took and covered the dolly in some hot spices dat make a lady figgity. Dat mean she won't be satisfied with nutthin'. She libbin in distruss eb'byday of her life. The mo' she suffa, the mo' she blamed dat' man that make you his slabe. Once I got her unduh my spell, she can't git loose. The mo' I tighten dat rope I put 'round dat dolly's neck, the mo' she can't take libbin wid him. She can't take no mo' and so she heng herself. She choose de't and dats what make him mo' miserable. Yaas 'suh, Mister Granger tormented. Warruh wantuh do next Missy?"

May was hooked. She had found a way to make Doctor Granger and everybody else pay without anyone being able to trace the crimes back to her.

"Geechee, can we start a war between him and Linwood Smith where in the end, they both lose? Linwood was makin' a fool of me and left me alone that night. He wouldn't protect me. I hate him just as much as I hate Doctor Granger. I want both of them to lose everything they own. I don't want it all to happen at once, but I want their torment to be long and slow."

"Damn gal, dat be fine wid me."

"Geechee, I ain't never met nobody like you. You tell me what you need and I'll get it in exchange for you bringin' terror to them they ain't never imagined."

The Geechee's next move was made on Linwood. His home actually became hell on earth.

"Massa, Massa, there be a fire in the back of the house."

"Maggie, what are you talking about? Isn't that smell from the fireplace back in the kitchen area?"

"No Massa, the kitchen is on fire. I don't know what happened, but there be flames everywhere. We tried to put 'em out, but its gettin' worse. Please Massa, you gotta get them field hands in here right away or this whole place is gonna go up in flames."

Linwood was running to the back of the house with her beside him. As they neared the kitchen, he could feel the heat. "Maggie, get the house staff out of here and tell them to start drawing water. I'll get us some more help."

He ran out to the front yard overlooking the slave quarters. "Get out here right now. Rosewood is on fire. Everybody get out here right now and start drawing water. Hurry up, hurry up."

"Booker, run over to Phillip Mason's plantation. Tell him to get his slaves over here to help us to put this fire out."

"I'm on my way right now Massa."

Everybody was running around and throwing water on the fire, but it kept raging. Maggie couldn't believe that her beloved Rosewood had been turned into an inferno. "Lawd have mussy, this here fire won't go out no matter how much water we put on it. I ain't never seen a fire this bad. My Rosewood been turned into hell."

Booker returned with Phillip Mason and what looked like everybody who lived on his plantation. Phillip was shocked at the inferno that was once the mansion of Rosewood Plantation.

"For Christ sake Linwood, what on earth happened here?"

"I don't know and don't have time to talk about it. Just put everybody to work until we've brought this thing completely under control. I've got plenty of able bodies and you probably brought just as many."

There were so many people on site water was being thrown on the fire at all times. Despite their efforts, the inferno continued. One of the slave bosses looked up and saw the roof caving in. "Everybody get out of the way, move it, move it. Look up there. A part of the roof is caving in. Oh my God, it's raining fire."

By the time the fire was extinguished only a small wing of the mansion was left standing. People were exhausted and bodies were lying everywhere. It didn't matter to Linwood and Phillip that they were lying amongst the slaves. They were too exhausted to care about who was master and who was slave.

"Massa, you be alright sir?"

"Goddamnit Booker, does it look like I'm alright. Most of my house is gone. It's a wonder we got out of there without somebody getting killed. I don't think I've ever seen anything like this. My wife and children are pretty shaken up about all of this."

After Linwood left to look for his family, Maggie, Booker, and some of the other slaves were standing around talking.

"Maggie, how in Gawd's name did that fire happen? I gotta say I agree with Massa. I ain't never seen a fire like that. Fo' awhile I thought we was in hell. Seem like nothin' we did put the fire out. How could that happen? Slaves and white men was everywhere throwin' water on it, but it refused to die."

"Gawd as my witness, I don't know how somethin' like that happened. None of us that was in the kitchen saw anything that looked like a fire was startin'. We wasn't even cookin' at the time. It seem like all of a sudden a flame started. I went to get Massa and by the time him and me got back to the kitchen, fire was everywhere. As a matter of fact, we never even got back to the kitchen. When we was gettin' close you could feel the heat from the fire. I'm tellin' y'all that fire wasn't started by none of us. It just came outta nowhere. It was as if Satan himself just decided to show up and turn Rosewood into hell."

After Linwood's family was settled down for the night, he went to one of the rooms unaffected by the fire to think things through. He needed to come up with a plan on how to rebuild Rosewood.

I just don't understand. Maggie and her staff have never been careless. I know I have some rebellious niggers around here, but Maggie isn't one of them. She's as loyal as they come and would never allow a fire to get out of control in her kitchen. Sometimes I think she loves Rosewood more than I. How on earth did this happen? Nothing they cook with should have caused a fire that destructive. Damn, Maggie said they weren't even cooking.

It was a month later when she brought back gossip about who started the fire.

"Massa, can I speak to you fo' a minute sir?"

"Yeah – what is it Maggie."

"Sir, I believe I know who started that fire. I heard some of the field hands sayin' they saw Doctor Granger sneakin' 'round out back. They say he had a couple of other men with him. He was tellin' them men 'bout how yo house is built and where everything is located."

"Massa, I think they started that fire. Me and my gals don't use nothin' to cook with that would start a fire that big. Fo' days, I kept thinkin' I was smellin' strange odors, but couldn't put my finger on 'xactly what them strange smells was. I'm figurin' they be what started that fire. What you think Massa? Could I be right?"

"I'll look into this. I just can't accept that Doctor Granger would do something so destructive. Someone in my family could have been killed. I know he can be a mean snake, but he can't be that vicious."

On the night Linwood, Phillip Mason, and their slaves were fighting the fire that all but destroyed the mansion at Rosewood, Stephen was walking his horse back to the house because he didn't want anyone to hear the pounding hoofs of the stallion as he returned to Oakland Hall. He was shaking so bad, he could barely walk and was sweating profusely. *Now that lying son-of-a-bitch knows what it feels like to have one of his most prized possessions destroyed. I hope that house burned down to the ground with him in it.*

Linwood didn't want to believe the gossip Maggie brought to him, but he couldn't stop thinking about what she said. After that night when Stephen caught him and May in bed, he didn't know what was real and what wasn't. Once the news about her got out he was flabbergasted. She wasn't white! Everybody in their circle of affluent friends was gossiping about her. The women were happy to see her topple from her pedestal, and the men couldn't stop gossiping about what it must have been like to be married to a woman like her.

Linwood could answer one of the many questions. When a man was with May, he would do and say anything she wanted. He had no idea he had been at the mercy of a Mulatto. There were no visible signs that would have raised suspicion about her true pedigree. All he knew was that her beauty was spellbinding and his appetite for her was unquenchable.

He was walking among the ruins of his home when he found it. "What on earth is that? It looks like one of my pocket watches. Its solid gold, so it makes sense it would have survived that blaze. Thank God everything wasn't destroyed. I built Rosewood once and I can do it again."

"Let's see here – there is hardly any damage. Wait a minute. This isn't my watch."

"Damn that bastard – it was him. I know this watch and it's his. Look, his initials are even on the back. By God, Maggie was right. He was sneaking around back here and started that fire. He was trying to kill my family. Well if that's the way he wants to fight, then I'm going to give him a fight he won't soon forget."

Linwood summoned Booker to the mansion. He wanted him to run an emergency errand. What he was getting ready to do was vicious and evil, but what Stephen did to him was unconscionable and called for strong measures. He owned the lethal weapon that would get him his revenge.

"Booker, bring her up here to me right away. I've got something I want to talk to her about. Go quickly. I need to see her as soon as possible."

Booker returned with her following close behind. She waited in the foyer until she received permission to enter the room. "Come on in here. Massa's waitin' fo' you?"

Oh yes – she's exactly who I need to take Doctor Stephen Granger down. I always thought he was one arrogant bastard. He thought May was something else. Well I'll bet he's never dealt with a woman like this.

Now with her standing before him, he was already feeling better. He looked her over from head to toe as if assessing her for the first time. However, he knew her very well.

"Geechee, you still messing around with those roots and spells you're always jabbering about?"

"Massa warruh jabberin'?"

He only wantuh talk to me when ebbuh he wanna do harm to somebody. I wunduh who he got it in fo' dis time.

"Look, I don't have time for your smart mouth. Are you still working roots on people?"

"Yassuh, I do wuhebbuh needin' to be done dat people can't do fo' demself. Warruh you need?"

"I want you to bring Stephen Granger down to the dog that he is. Do whatever you want to do with him. I don't care if he winds up being a wild animal. That's the state most befitting for him anyhow. Can you do it?"

"Yass 'suh – I see warruh I can do."

Doctor Stephen Granger was acting strange. His behavior was so erratic, no one except for the slaves bothered to go anywhere near him. His patient list became non-existent. Not only was he becoming emotionally unhinged, his physical appearance was shocking to those people who had admired him in the past. He deserted personal hygiene and stopped shaving. Friends tried to intervene, but he was beyond help. His downward spiral bottomed out the day Jessie came into the library to serve lunch.

"Massa I've got yo lunch sir."

He wasn't sitting in the big wingback chair where he usually took lunch. *Hmmm, where is he? I know he's a strange man these days and don't have much of an appetite. He be needin' some food on his stomach 'bout now 'cause he ain't ate nothin' in a few days.*

She heard the growl before she saw anything, but called out to him again. "Massa, I got yo lunch. It be time to eat sir." The growl sounded like one of the snarling dogs he used to hunt down runaway slaves. The sound was coming from behind her. She turned around quickly. "Mas..."

He came running out from a darken alcove on hands and knees. His matted hair was all over his head, and he wasn't acting human. The look in his eyes was that of a wild animal, and he was foaming at the mouth. He charged at her, and chased her around the room with gnashing teeth while growling.

"For Gawd's sake Massa, whatever be wrong with you? Stop, stop. Oh Gawd, somebody help me. Come and get this man. He runnin' 'round on all four actin' like some kinda dog or somethin'. Booker, somebody, hurry up and get this man away from me."

They eventually caught and restrained him. He was still kicking, screaming, and growling as they carried him upstairs and locked him in the master bedroom.

Everybody in Lincoln County was talking about Doctor Granger's descent. At one time he was the most envied man in the county. In the end he was considered no more than a raving animal. The question remained – how could a powerful man like that wind up running around growling and barking on his hands and knees like a rabid dog?

May was unable to stop thinking about the day he went mad and had to be locked in his room until family arrived at Oakland Hall. They knew exactly what to do with him.

She was anxious to get out of the house. At nightfall she snuck away once again for a meeting in the woods. She couldn't keep still waiting for the Geechee to appear. Just like every other time when they met, the root doctor made no noise as she approached. It was if she appeared out of nowhere.

"Oh there you are. I couldn't wait to see you. Geechee, you've done it again. That was so sweet how you turned him into the dog that he is. You should've seen me. While they was takin' him up the stairs I was laughin' my head off. He looked my way, but didn't recognize me or anybody else for that matter."

Now that Stephen had been taken care of, she was satisfied that his future had been secured in a home with people just like him. His family sent him away and his slaves never saw him again. Sometimes when the new owners were entertaining, they overheard them gossiping about the institution for insane people where he would be spending the rest of his life.

She was anxious to give the Geechee new marching orders. "Now it's time to get the other one."

"May, warruh you wunt me to do to 'em, huh? Warruh you talkin' 'bout?"

"Oh I don't know exactly. I want Linwood to pay for deserting me when I needed protection. I'm sure you got somethin' real good. Think about what kinda massa he's been to you. That should tell you exactly how you wanna make him pay. Go ahead and do it. Whatever it is, make sure it's down and dirty. I don't want him to ever recover."

"Down and du' tty ent' half of warruh I gonna to dat man. Nebbuh liked him eny how. Massa callin' my roots 'jabberin'. Pledjuh be all mine to get rid of 'em. Pledjuh be all mine."

It was Linwood's turn to be dealt with. The Geechee went to work on the master whom she despised since the day he brought her to Rosewood. When they found him, he was sitting under a tree with his chest split wide open. His hands were cupped and in them was a bloody mass with a huge knife sticking out. It was later determined to be his heart.

Once May had tasted blood, she wasn't satisfied with exacting revenge on the two men who humiliated and abused her. She wanted the blood of anyone who crossed her, and collaborated with the Geechee to ensure retaliation was brutal and effective. The Geechee was happy to oblige and carry out her sadistic orders. The bodies of her enemies frequently showed up. If she wanted a man, she went to the Geechee to work roots on him. Once he was lured into her trap, she used her sexual wiles to control and ultimately destroy him. The women from whom she stole him meant nothing to her. In the Geechee, she had found the perfect partner in crime.

Years later she explained to the Belle the importance of having a woman like the Geechee around. "Listen Belle, you old enough to know this stuff now. I don't know how much you 'member 'bout how we got to be slaves. You was just a little gal back then. Yo daddy, Doctor Stephen Granger, knew I was Mulatto when he met me. Yet when he found me with that Linwood, he throwed us outta the house. I was never so humiliated in my life. He raped and tormented me some kinda awful 'til a slave gal named Jessie introduced me to the Geechee.

Now Geechee, she be a woman after my own heart. She ain't nobody to be playin' with. She got me everything I ever wanted. Her revenge on Doctor Granger and Linwood been the talk of Lincoln County ever since. I still get excited everytime I think 'bout how she took revenge on both of 'em. Then, after that she got rid of any enemy I asked her to, and got me any man I ever wanted. Iffin they did me wrong, she made 'em pay dearly."

"You look just like me, but just a touch mo' brown. You still look white though. Belle, you prettier than any gal 'round here. I'm tellin' you, a man can't help hisself when he comes 'round a pretty gal. That go fo' whites and niggers. That's yo weapon gal and it be mighty powerful. But there be plenty of times when you gotta have somethin' far mo' powerful than yo pretty looks. You gotta have the Geechee. She will get you anything and anybody you want in life. Never – ever forget that."

Belle never forgot May's advice. By the time she reached her teenage years, she was in deep dealing with the Geechee and her roots. Unfortunately, she never developed the relationship May enjoyed with the woman.

Chapter 15
The Chickens Come Home to Roost
(Part II)

Now here it was years later, and it had come down to this with Belle lying in what was mostly likely her deathbed. She knew who was responsible, and could only hope Amos would come back soon with help.

He rushed over to Mama Mame's place to plead on her behalf. Both of them took certain things for granted about the good Christian folk in the Gulf. One of those things was that they wouldn't refuse to help someone in need. When he arrived and described Belle's condition, she went into the house and returned with a bottle of tonic. She shoved it at him.

"Here, give this to her."

He took the bottle of tonic, but couldn't believe she was refusing to come back to Belle's place with him.

"Look, I knows most folk 'round here don't think much of me and cuzin Belle, but Mama Mame, she's in awful shape and somebody's gotta help her. We got nobody else to turn to. I'm beggin' 'cause I don't know what else to do. I knows a good Christian woman like you wouldn't just sit by and see somebody die."

He was right. Her conscious wouldn't allow her to ignore his pleas. Exasperated at the imposition from an unwelcomed source, she went out to the back and hitched the mule to the wagon. "Boy, get on the back of this wagon and shut your blabberin' up. I'm goin' but I ain't makin' no promises."

When they came into Belle's room, she was met with the same pitiful sight that Amos left when he came begging for help.

"What be wrong with you gal?"

"Don't know – somethin' got me weak. I feel like I'm dyin'. I'm down and out and can't help myself. Can you give me somethin' to make me well again?"

Mama Mame thrust a spoonful of the tonic into her opened mouth and then applied wet towels to her forehead. "Hold yo head still and stop thrashin' 'bout like you crazy or somethin.'"

Her compassionate nature wouldn't permit her to dwell on her destain for Belle, so she decided to stay. "Amos, make yo self useful and get me a bowl of cool water with some more towels. Hurry up boy and stop lookin' like you scared of everything. Get a move on ya now."

The bath with cool cloths broke the fever and her body temperature lowered. When she finally fell off to sleep, Mama Mame left.

The next morning she felt well enough to get up and move around and about, but didn't feel like herself. Something was different, and the fear of death now loomed over her.

When Scott stopped in later that evening, she was listless and quiet. This was unusual, but he thought it was best to keep his thoughts to himself. *She's lookin' real bad. Gettin' kinda triflin' and not makin' sure she's fixed up when I come over here. She ain't even doin' anything to make me feel good. Ain't no use in complainin' though since I ain't stayin 'round here long to look at her like this.*

After reaching the conclusion he didn't even want intimacy, he got up preparing to leave.

"Mr. Harrington, you think you can stay awhile longer? I'm not feelin' real good and scared to stay here all by myself. Amos is supposed to come over later. If you can just sit here 'til he come, I'd appreciate it."

He wanted to get away from her in the worst way, so he did what he did best – shut her down. "Be seein' you 'round."

The episodes with the strange attacks were happening more frequently and nobody could figure out what was wrong with her. Except for Amos, Mama Mame and Doc Moore were the only ones who visited with her. More out of curiosity than doctorly duty, Doc Moore started making house calls under the pretext of relieving Mama Mame. He was known to be yet another town gossip, and was happy to share the details about Belle's tragic and horrific decline. He had a wide audience, including whites and coloreds throughout the Gulf and Sanford.

"I know there are plenty of people in the Gulf who feel Belle is getting exactly what she deserves. However, I feel so sorry for her. She's become downright deranged. The other day I stopped in to check on her and the poor woman was out of her mind. She swore Scott's first wife, Lillie, and Lillie's stillborn baby were trying to kill her. I tried to calm her down and explain that Lillie and the baby had been dead for years, but she was so out of touch, she refused to believe it. She started yelling at me, saying Lillie and the baby hid out in the woods during the day watching and waiting for her."

"She said to me, 'Doc, I know what I be talkin' 'bout. That witch Lillie and her baby, they wait fo' me until late in the night, then come in here tryin to kill me.'

"Nothing I said convinced her that she was wrong. She went so far as to say, 'Doc them two demons, they go through my house tearin' everything in sight apart tryin' to find me. I ain't gonna let 'em kill me. That be why I got to them first.' The woman has gone completely insane."

From the scratches on her arms, legs, and face, he could tell her wounds were self-inflicted. He told anyone who would listen about another time he went to check on her status, only to find her totally out of her head and hallucinating.

Whenever he tried to comfort her, she started fighting him and screaming, "Get that baby away from me. Get that baby away from me."

They had to subdue her by tying her hands and feet to the bed posts. He couldn't help but to compare the insane woman who had to be tied down to the bed with the beautiful woman who strutted around the Gulf for years, self-absorbed in her beauty, and not letting anyone else forget or ignore her. Doc Moore's gossip was spreading throughout the Gulf like wild fire. Belle had gone completely mad.

On occasion she went into town imagining she was dressed up as she did in the past. In her delusional and physically withered state, she made her face up in the most garish fashion with eye kohl smeared drastically around her eyes, red lip stain applied on the outer perimeter of her lips, and hair so matted and disheveled, it looked like a gigantic bird's nest.

Whenever she overheard the town folk whispering and laughing at her, she became infuriated and lashed out. "What y'all lookin' at, huh? Y'all tryin' to kill me too? Well you ain't gonna do it. Keep lookin' at me and I'm gonna get ol' Geechee to work some roots on y'all too. Watcha lookin' at? Get away from me, get away from me".

After one incident in particular, Jasper of the trio of male gossips who loved any excitement involving Scott and Belle, found Amos and warned him about her. "Boy, you'd better get up there to town. Your cuzin is up there screamin' and fightin' everybody. She lookin' and actin' like some mad woman. Somebody's gonna get hurt iffin you don't go and get her."

During her infrequent moments of lucidity, Amos had to explain why she looked the way she did, and why her place looked as if a tornado had gone through it. Hearing him describe who and what she had become added to her torment. To make matters worse, Scott completely stopped coming around. After swearing to never give him up, reality finally set in. He wouldn't be coming back, and she possessed nothing to entice him back into her life. Gone was the one thing of which she was most confident and for most of her life used to compete with other women– her looks.

"I'm gonna go see that damned Geechee. She messed everything up, but she ain't gonna get away with takin' my money for years and not deliverin' my man to me. She ain't gonna get away with this. She done messed with me fo' the last time."

When she arrived, the old woman was sitting in a rocking chair on the porch. She could tell from the long and angry strides that Belle had come for trouble. She wasn't afraid because their hatred was mutual.

"Here come dat crazy witch to fight 'bout dat man Scott Harrington, who 'e 'ent ever gonna get. He got hisself lawfully lady, but dis t'ing 'e be thinkin' 'e want to tangle wid me 'cause I 'ent brought dat there man to her like 'e be wantin'. Then I 'ent forgot dat time 'e came here breakin' and throwin' my stuff all 'round. Tol' her one day 'e gonna rue the day 'e mezzed wid me. Well, dem chickens done come home to roos'."

When Belle was close enough, she heard the inaudible mumblings of the Geechee. She was burning up with fever, insane with rage, and fearless. Once on the porch, her tirade started.

"Get in that house ol' woman. Time has come for you to pay for not deliverin' my man to me. I'm gonna wipe that there dirt flo in there up with yo skinny behind. I paid you good money, and if you think you ain't gonna pay for stealin' from me, you much more stupid than evil."

The Geechee wasn't moved by the threats being hurled at her, and retorted, "Go 'straight'n fuh hell. Yo don't want to stuhr up mo trubble with me dan yo already be in. Yo in daingus territory gal and don' know what I can do to yo."

Blinded to the glaring look that should have killed her on the spot, Belle snatched her up from the rocking chair by a boney arm and started shoving her into the house. "I said get in the damned house."

Just as she shoved her through the doorway, the Geechee spun around with lightning speed. Belle immediately let go of her arm. The evil before her was undeniable as she saw flames of fire lighting up what used to be hazel colored eyeballs. The look on the old face looked like some demonic beast the

Christian folk around town described in the book of Revelations. The chill in the room felt like the inside of a grave, and a haunting voice that repeated the words "Death is upon you" could be heard.

A wicked smile spread over the Geechee's face. Then her hysterical laughter filled the room as Belle realized just who she was dealing with, and the full extent of the powers that were being unleashed upon her.

"'Smattuh gal, cat got yo tongue? Humph. Now yo know what Geechee be capable of do'n to yo? Yo need be leabe here gal."

Belle stumbled around disoriented, trying to get away from the root doctor, who was now chanting, cackling, and dancing some odd dance as she circled around her.

"You brought this evil upon me that be killin' me. For years, I paid you good money to destroy Mr. Harrington's wives and you cunnin' beast turn on me to destroy me. For Gawd sake – I'm May's daughter. What kind of devil are you?"

"Da kind you paid good money fo, and you ain't May."

As soon as she found an opening, Belle took off running.

By the time she arrived home, her energy was spent. She crawled into bed shaking with chills and from fear. The Geechee was killing her and no one could save her.

Her many enemies around the Gulf were taking delight in her demise. She was quite a spectacle, and was now looked upon as a pathetic and deranged woman whom they rarely saw. For years she reveled in being the talk of the town. She was now hiding out in defeat, shame, and pain.

After she passed away, Doc Moore told people throughout the county about the final day when Amos begged him to come over to her place because the end was near. When he arrived, he smelled the stench of death even before she took her last breath. She was lying in bed and her skeletal frame was convulsing. Her eyes were fixed on something beyond her immediate surroundings. A lone tear was making its way down a gaunt cheek, and her mouth was slightly open as she gasped for breath making gurgling sounds that folk called the "Death Rattles." She was attempting to say something, but he couldn't quite make out what. He leaned over and placed his ear close to lips that were cracked and parched.

With the faintest of whispers, she said, "Scott." He then took her withered hand and held it, attempting to provide comfort during her final hour. Once again, she whispered, "Scott." Then she was gone.

Meanwhile, over at the Geechee's place, she was moving around in the back room humming the tune to a popular Gullah song. Her work was done. She walked over to a shelf and picked up the pretty doll with long black pieces of yarn representing long flowing hair. She ran her fingers over the dried chicken's blood that was smeared all over the doll. One by one, she pulled out stickpins from different areas of the body. She then gave a little chuckle before throwing the pretty, but soiled and punctured doll into a bucket where she kept human waste.

"Yaas'suh, dem chickens don come home to roos' fo sho."

Mary knew the news that was spreading throughout the Gulf's grapevine about Belle's long and agonizing death was true because of his disposition. Whenever she asked what was on his mind, his answer was short. "Nothin'. I'm alright."

She reached the conclusion that she really didn't want the details of his grief over the death of his mistress. She couldn't help but feel a sense of relief knowing the long-term threat to her marriage was finally over.

Maybe, just maybe his attention will come home to where it belongs. Dear Lawd, let that be so. I didn't wish death upon that woman, but maybe You decided to deliver us all outta that mess the devil had my husband mixed up in.

He was tired and confused about the sense of loss that he felt. "Ya know Walter, I'm glad I got that curse off of me. I can't explain for the life of me how she got that kinda hold on me fo' all them years. Everytime I thought I was finished with her, somethin' pulled me back in. I knows them gals I married wanted more than I gave 'em, but Belle had some kinda hold on me. Sometimes thought it must've been love or somethin'. Why else couldn't I turn that wild gal loose?"

"Brotha, some things just can't be explained. No answer fo' 'em. She's gone now. Maybe you be free to give yo wife what she want."

He couldn't deny those inexplicable feelings that kept him going back to her for years although he kept marrying other women. He waived countless opportunities to totally remove her from his life, but remained attached to her in ways he could never understand.

Her death lifted the weight of hypocrisy he hated, but constantly indulged. "I don't know. Maybe I can finally give Mary what she really want outta me. Ain't gotta feel like that hypocrite daddy we had to deal with all them years. Tryin' to prove he loved us, but wouldn't do a damn thing to back up what he swore in secret."

He was now anticipating redemption. Finally without the distraction of Belle, he was trying to build a foundation, and provide the security and serenity of family life. He wanted a life that didn't resemble anything like world he lived in when he was considered the human chattel of the man who fathered him.

Despite his flaws, Mary and the children could see his efforts to be the man they desired and expected him to be. He was awkward, but his efforts were noticeable. The only place where he wasn't awkward with Mary was in the bedroom. In there, she was confident that he loved her, and it wasn't just the physical part either. His entire disposition, conversation, and touch changed. Sometimes she wished they could stay there forever. Loving him was still complicated.

After Belle's death, he never cheated on her again. Because of the events to occur over the next few years, no one would ever know whether his fidelity was a result of triumph over past demons, or if the events consumed so much of their lives, he couldn't have wandered off into another affair even if he wanted to.

Chapter 16
Something Is Terribly Wrong

Mary was learning to relax knowing her marriage was free from the threat of Belle, but she was faced with another threatening issue. Her health was never completely restored after delivering Baby Scott.

Lawd, it don't ever seem like I got enough energy to do anything 'round here. I know Mr. Harrington's attention be on us and all, but iffin' I don't get myself together, no tellin' what he's gonna do 'bout that. He be wantin' a strong wife who can take care of him and his family. Maybe if I just push myself harder, my get-up-and-go will come back. Lawd just give me the strength.

She wanted to believe "The Change" women folk spoke of in hushed conversation was the problem. Her menstrual cycle was erratic and the symptoms were next to impossible to figure out. Sometimes she was bedridden from the horrible cramping. She passed large clots of blood for days, which made her pale and weak. Then for months she would go without having any cycle.

She asked Mama Mame about the persistent female problems. "Baby that sound like the Change, and I know that period in a woman's life feel like somebody else done come in and taken over yo body and your feelins'. Thought I was gonna have to kill somebody a whole lotta times. That's how bad my nerves got shook up. Just you hang in there Mary. This too shall pass. You'll start feelin' like yo self soon."

Mama Mame's diagnosis was the comfort she decided to cling to and ride it out until the Change was over.

Novella was about seven years old when things changed drastically, and not for the better. The pain was becoming unbearable and the increased blood loss no longer seemed connected to a menstrual cycle. She was hemorrhaging.

Maude knew something was wrong. "Momma, you don't need to suffer like this day in and day out. Let me get Mama Mame over here. If she still sayin' it's the Change that's makin' you feel so bad, we can just be patient and hold on 'til things get better, but we need to know that's all it is."

"Baby, I did go to her 'bout this and she told me to ride it out."

Riding it out wasn't acceptable. "Maybe you need to see her more often or somethin'. Promise me you'll go and see 'bout yo self."

She wasn't satisfied with Mary's explanation and decided to go to him. "Mr. Harrington, we need to get Mama Mame or Doc Moore over here as soon as we can. Somethin' just ain't right with Momma and we can't be waist'n time on gettin' help. She needs attention right now. This ain't got nothin' to do with no Change if you ask me."

"Well I ain't askin' you, but she told me herself that she be okay. Stop worryin' me gal 'bout that kinda stuff. Frankly, I'm tired of hearin' bout it. I just want everything to go back to normal. That ain't gonna happen if you keep makin' stuff up, tryin' to make things worse."

This was exactly the kind of response that confirmed his insensitivity. *Lawd I'm tryin', but this bullheaded slave 'bout to make me tear into him real good. I ain't never seen somebody so distant from other people's hurt and misery in all my life. Momma must've bumped her head when she got tangled up with this devil.*

Her irritation with him was rapidly increasing and they were headed for a major blow up, but she didn't care. He was still acting like the insufferable, stubborn mule she kept trying to get along with for Mary's sake. _Here Momma is seriously sick and this most irritatin' man playin' stupid and goin' along with her explanation instead of takin' charge and forcin' her to go see Mama Mame or Doc Moore more often. He needin' somebody to deliver a good swift kick to his behind and Lawd I'm volunteerin' my size ten and a half._

The tenuous relationship was eroding, and Mary was no longer strong enough to referee their battles. He was infuriated with her back talk, and she was just as infuriated with him for his indifference to Mary's declining health.

She was helping Mary from the bed to the chamber pot when she saw blood so dark it was the color of eggplant. _That damned fool been in this house all day allowin' Momma to bleed to death without sendin' one of them children to get Mama Mame or Doc Moore._

As angry as she was with him, there was something more pressing that she needed to take care of before dealing with him yet again for his neglect.

"Henry, go out on the porch and wait for me. I need to change Momma's bed clothing. Beolia, Walter, don't say anything, but do exactly like I tell y'all to do. Go and get Mama Mame. Tell her it's critical that she come over here as soon as possible. Momma's bleedin' real bad. Hurry up. Otie and Vella, help me get Momma and the bed cleaned up."

After they changed Mary's bed clothing and the linens, Maude stomped out to the front porch.

"What on earth are you thinkin' Mr. Harrington? Is it not obvious to you Momma's in bad shape and need medical attention right now?"

"Now Maude you had better watch yo tongue. Mary say this here stuff is just that Change and ain't nothin to worry 'bout."

"Why you stubborn mule, this is more than some damned Change and Momma needs attention right now. I sent Beolia and Walter to get Mama Mame. Don't you dare look at me like that. Yeah, that's right. I sent them over there without askin' you. Goin' to get help is somethin' you should've thought to do long before now. I swear – I can't understand for the life of me why Momma has put up with this foolishness all these years."

"I know you thinkin' you a grown woman and all, but I'm tellin you Maude, you don't wanna cross me. I'll put you and yo husband outta my house right now iffin you don't back down and stay in yo place."

Although he was issuing an ultimatum for her to either shut up or be put out, she refused to back down. Mary was too sick, and she had reached the conclusion that she was either going to kill him or he was going to have to kill her. She wasn't about to just let Mary wither away without doing something about it.

"With all due respect sir, you had better do somethin' 'bout this situation now or I'll make your life one miserable hell. I promise you, I will not let up on you until I'm satisfied Momma is bein' taken care of. Do you understand me?"

He was not going to let her or anyone else know just how terrified he was about what was happening to Mary. He worked hard at convincing himself that Mary's explanations about merely going through menopause was what they were dealing with. As a matter of fact, he needed to believe her in order to calm his own fears. He was also trying to mask his secret dependence on the strong-willed Maude to keep things in order. Therefore, he could do no more than bluff and attempt to scare her back into her place. He wasn't in a position to follow through on any of his threats.

As he was trying to think of a comeback to convince her that he had the upper hand in the argument, they heard Mama Mame's wagon pull up in the backyard.

"That must be Walter and Beolia with Mama Mame. Gal, I ain't got time to fight with you. Let's go 'round back to let'em in."

"Let's do that 'cause I'm 'bout to do or say somethin' you ain't gonna like."

Mama Mame rushed into the bedroom and once inside, tried to hide her anger at him for letting things get out of hand. As she heard him and Maude approaching the bedroom, she was all prepared to admonish him once again for not responding to Mary's needs in a timely manner. She changed her mind when she saw the expressions on their faces as they entered the room.

Uh oh – terrible storm's a brewin' in here. They both lookin' like they seconds away from killin' the other one. I better not add more fuel to the fire. Look at poor Maude. She's shakin' and that mean that gal was just 'bout ready to land him a real good punch. Lawd Jesus, you gotta do somethin' 'fo these two kill each other. Looks like somebody was gettin' ready to die just 'fo me and them little chilluns got back here – and I ain't talkin' 'bout Mary.

She turned her attention to Mary in order to diffuse the argument. "Baby, Mama Mame's gonna bring Doc Moore over here to get you up and well again. We gonna work on this thing 'til my Mary's back to herself, ya hear me?"

"Yes Mama Mame."

Mama Mame couldn't think of anything else to say and was moving about the room as if she was confused and unfamiliar with her surroundings. She wasn't confused, but trying to hide her own fear and resignation to the unfolding tragedy. *Oh Lawd, here we go again, but this one's gonna hurt more than most of us will ever be able to bear. Yassuh, this here's gonna hurt a lot of people for a very long time. Ain't a thing I can do 'bout it, but put this here in Yo hands. No medicine I got gonna fix this.*

She asked Maude out to her wagon.

"Now Maude, I know that man been a thorn in yo flesh for years, but you gotta try and get along with him for Mary's sake. Try keepin' a lid on that hot temper of yours gal. Don't wait for him – if you be thinkin' you need me or Doc Moore, just come runnin' soon as possible."

"Yes Ma'am, but I swear fo' Gawd, if somethin' happens to Momma 'cause of that arrogant fool, I'm gonna tear into his hide myself. I'm gonna put my foot straight up in his…"

"Hush chile. He's still Mary's husband and the only poppa you and Beolia been knowin' since y'all was youngins'. You've gotta honor him with yo respect. Bible says so. He can get on my nerves too, but I can't stand here listenin' to you disrespectin' that man who be Mary's husband, and yo poppa whether or not ya 'cept him. Just call on Mama Mame."

Maude was now convinced that Mama Mame was limited in what she could do. Totally at a loss for what her next move should be, she decided to go back into the house to sit with Mary a while longer.

Feeling defeated for the first time, she lifted her head towards the ceiling and spoke to God. "My dear Gawd, what're we gonna do? I know I don't come to you like the others, but here I am beggin' fo' good reason. Please don't take Momma. My heart is already breakin' into a million pieces, and my little sisters and brother won't be able to get over this separation. Momma's been a good woman who don't deserve this pain and agony, neither death. She deserves a long life, so please step in fo' things get worse. I'm beggin'You, please have mercy on us."

She had no idea that someone was on the other side of the door. Beolia was terrified. If Maude was praying as hard as she was now hearing, things didn't look good for Momma. She too looked towards the heavens. "Lord, I'm not as strong as Maude, and I don't think my heart can take this. Please answer us by making Momma well."

Maude yanked the door open unaware she had pushed Beolia back into the wall. She walked over to Mary's bed and gently kissed her on the cheek. "Momma, me and Henry gonna leave right now, but I'll check on you tomorrow after I finish workin." Mary's eyes were closed, but she nodded her head in acknowledgement because she was too weak to speak.

They were out on to the back porch when Maude lifted her head once again. She didn't care whether or not Henry thought she was crazy. "Lawd, 'member what I just said. I'm beggin' you, please don't take her away from us." Henry didn't think she was crazy. The woman familiar to him was an unrelenting fighter. The defeated stranger he was now looking at was a frightened little girl who was terrified of losing her momma.

"Here Maude, let me take your hand. We can't do anymore today. Let's go home."

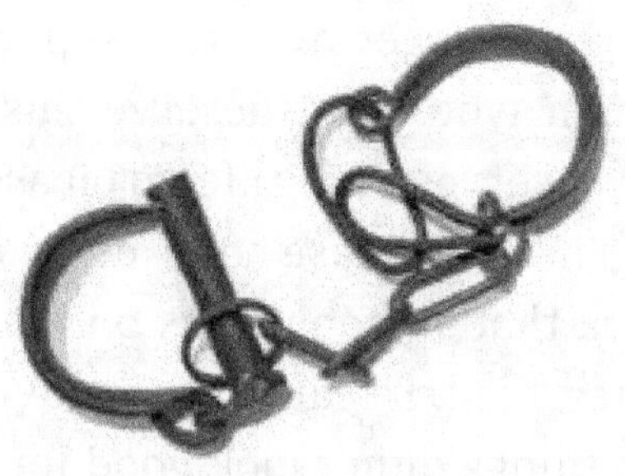

Chapter 17
The Other Scott Harrington

As long as she could remember, Maude had been battling with Scott over the way he treated Mary. Yet she was concealing her own shameful secret that resurfaced every weekend. She couldn't bear the thought of being perceived as anything but strong. So instead of admitting to what happened whenever Henry went on one of his weekend drinking binges, she suited up with the armor of courage and focused on being Mary's protector.

Just can't bring myself to put this added burden on Momma. She's got enough to deal with. Now Mr. Harrington, he prob'ly could care less 'bout what's goin' on between me and Henry. Goin' back to live there ain't even an option. As bad as things are here, I can't imagine goin' back over there to live under that man's roof. He's just too difficult to understand and I'm tired of all the tension in that house. Momma loves him and I truly can't understand that, but it's the truth. She ain't gonna let no body disrespect him either.

Henry's drinking binges started every Friday night and went through Sunday night. The transformation was unbelievable. While sober, he was delightful, considerate, and gentle. Once the drinking started, he stumbled around the house angry at the world. Even worse was his mouth.

"Gawd-damned bitches think they can beat a man down with their whinin' and complainin'. Always tryin' to strip a man of his pride. I ain't havin' it. Did it to me once, but I ain't never gonna let another one strip me of my manhood again."

"What you lookin' at me like that for? I'm talkin' 'bout you too. You don't like it, huh?"

"Henry, you've had too much to drink. I ain't no bitch and you had better stop talkin' to me like that. I don't know what that woman you had before me did to you, but I ain't her, and I ain't expectin' you to be talkin' to me like I'm her either."

One of the reasons she had been able to keep the secret from everyone else was because of her own strength. As big and strong as he was, she usually could hold her own in a fight with him. But she didn't move out of Scott's house to spend her life fighting for her life.

Peace eluded her after each fight was over. She would lie awake crying and listening to his loud snoring. Hiding her hellacious marriage from the world compounded the problem.

I'm so ashamed. I've fought my whole life thinkin' I had to protect Momma from a bad marriage and I wound up in one just as bad, if not worse. If people find out what's goin' on in here, they're gonna laugh me outta town. I'm always runnin' my mouth and jumpin' up in somebody's face ready to do battle, and here I am with a man who starts beatin' me every Friday night. I don't know how I'm gonna keep this secret. People gonna call me a hypocrite 'cause I'm takin' the very thing off of a man I call myself protectin' Momma from. I'm feelin' like a hypocrite myself. All I did when I left was to move away from one mess into another.

Sure enough, it was on a Friday evening when he started drinking. This time, the fight would not end as usual.

"Why I gotta take my time on Friday and care for some sick woman that ain't even my mammy. I'm sick and tired of havin' to stop over there all the damn time. Why can't I just come straight home and enjoy some moonshine and my own wife? No – she busy runnin' straight over to her mammy's house and draggin' me with her. Then I gotta deal with that arrogant-ass slave who thinks he better than everybody else."

She tried to ignore him, but anger was written all over her face. *This ain't fair – I take good care of this house and don't deserve this drunken rantin' and ravin' 'bout Momma. She can't help her situation and he knows it. I'm sorry Lawd, but this drunken fool could drop dead right about now and I wouldn't care one bit.*

The condescending look on her face was too much to handle. When the opportunity presented itself, he snuck up from behind, spun her around to face him, and started choking her all the while ranting. "I knows you angry 'bout me talkin' bout your mammy, but what you gonna do huh? I see that look on your face and I'm gonna knock it off right now. Come here – don't you pull 'way from me."

The life was being choked out of her and if she wanted to live to see another day, she had to fight for that privilege. This was a battle for her life and she had to take advantage of her large frame as well as the ability to throw a solid punch. The first blow landed directly in his eye. After getting over the shock, he responded with a roundhouse slap that sent her flying across the floor. "You crazy bitch, I'm gonna stomp you to death. You damned near put my eye out. You gonna pay right now."

Her eyes fell upon an old broken table leg that he kept in a corner. She sprang for it. When he was close enough, she shoved the splintered table leg into his groin area. "Oooowwww, Oooowwww, Oooowww, sweet Jesus Christ, why you stupid…" She shoved it again into the same sensitive spot. His eyes bulged and mouth popped open in response to the excruciating pain. He looked down and saw blood seeping through his pant leg. "You're crazy. You tryin' to take off my manhood. Gal, I'm gonna kill you. You ain't leavin' this house alive tonight."

Just as he bent over again to inspect the blood-soaked pants, she cracked the table leg over his head. He hit the floor with a loud thud.

"Oh my Gawd, he's right. One of us is gonna die in here tonight. I gotta get outta here before he comes 'round." She ran out of the house and to the very place she swore never to seek solace.

They were taking a nap when she startled them with the sudden intrusion. Her incoherence was equally as frightening as her disheveled appearance. "Momma, Gawd help me, Momma, oh Momma. I think I killed him. I left him lyin' on the floor in his blood. I think I killed him."

"Oh my Gawd, Maude, what happened to you? Who did this? Dear Gawd, what happened?"

"It was Henry. He gets drunk every Friday night after we leave here. He's been beatin' me 'cause he's still mad about what them other gals before me did to him. I spend the whole weekend fightin' for my life. Oh Gawd Momma, he's awful. He says terrible things 'bout you and call me disgustin' names. By the time Monday rolls 'round, he be actin' like the hell we lived through for the entire weekend never happened. Then the next Friday night, the whole thing starts over. I'm so ashamed. Here I am tryin' to be a strong woman and I go home every weekend to take a beatin'."

The secret hell she had been living was painful to hear about. The only comfort Mary could provide was strokes to the back of her head.

"Dear Gawd in heaven, here I was thinkin' you finally got yo self a good man to take care of you and give you a decent life and that man over there beatin' on you. Baby, Momma's sorry she didn't see this. I'm so sorry. Oh my Gawd, I can't do nothin' for my child here in misery."

"Momma, I just couldn't bring myself to tell you 'bout all this mess goin' on between me and Henry. Before tonight I was doin' a pretty good job of defendin' myself. I never saw him come up behind me. We were arguin' and the next thing I knew he had me 'round my neck, sayin' he was gonna kill me."

The deep sigh that escaped her lips wasn't one of relief, but rather the telltale evidence of shear exhaustion. After wiping the last tears away, she turned around to see Scott still sitting in his rocking chair. He had been silent during her tearful confession. The look of fury in his eyes was undeniable. The grinding of his clinched teeth and the rat-a-tat rhythm of his fingers tapping on the arm of the rocking chair were now the only sounds in the room. As if a final decision had been made, he started to rise from the chair. "Goin' out – be back."

Those words had not been spoken since the days when he disappeared to visit with Belle. She was dead now, so there was only one other explanation given what Maude had just told them.

"No Mr. Harrington, please don't go. Let's just stay here and make sure Maude is okay. Mr. Harrington, please don't go over there. I'm beggin' you. That boy be a giant and ain't no tellin' what he might do to you. Please don't go."

To be honest, Maude wanted Henry to pay for what he had done, but Scott's response changed her mind. "I ain't the one you need to be worryin' 'bout. Ain't no tellin' what I might do to him. He be takin' a lot fo' granted, like he's gonna live to see tomorrow after he been messin' with my family. Time to show him what lookin' in the face of death look like."

Mary's pleas fell upon deaf ears. He walked out of the house.

The front door was still open when he arrived at Henry's and Maude's place. He slowly strode through each room looking around as if he were taking a leisurely tour. But this was warfare and he was on the prowl searching for his prey. He didn't announce himself, but stealthly approached ready to pounce.

The whistling sound coming from the top of the moonshine jug as it was ripped away from his lips was as confusing to Henry as the burning pain to his cheek. Disoriented, he peered out into the night trying to determine where the jug landed. He then spun around to face the enemy.

"Who in the hell? Oh it be you ol' man. I'm gettin' mighty tired of yo family and y'all's problems. What you doin' here anyways? You and Maude ain't zackly lovebirds now is you?"

"Looka here boy, I don't ever wanna hear 'bout you hittin' Maude again. Do you understand me?"

"You gotta be kiddin' me. Get this straight ol' man. She be my wife and ain't nothin' you can do 'bout what I do to her. From what I hear, you don't know how to treat your own wife. Matter fact, word is you ain't never knowed how to treat any woman. Don't come 'round here threatenin' me. You ain't welcome in here so leave."

Without warning he found himself suspended in mid-air. Unable to break free from the hand around his throat, he was forced to endure the burning and stinging pain that penetrated his torn flesh as fingernails dug in. The only thing he could do was kick ferociously as the wild animal does when the steel jaws of the hunter's trap sinks into its flesh. Then the deadly threat was issued.

"...And she be my gal. I also heard you callin' my Mary names, so just keep strugglin' and I'll keep you up here danglin' by that sorry neck of yours. In a few minutes you'll strangle to death on yo own spit, iffin I don't snap yo neck first. So what's it gonna be, huh? Boy answer me."

"Let me down. Pl... plea.... please – you stranglin' me to death. Let...le...le...et...let me down Mr. Harrington."

A wood plank at the edge of the porch gave away from the weight of his massive body as he fell to the ground writhing with pain. Scott wasn't finished. He descended the steps, walked over to him, and stood with a large boot on each side of his body.

"Look boy, I'm only comin' back over here for one reason and that's 'cause you done hurt Maude again. When I come back, it be to bury you right here in yo own backyard. You don't ever put yo hands on Mr. Harrington's chile again, or you prepare for yo burial."

Mary and Maude were sitting facing the door frozen with fear, but praying for his safe return. When he returned, he wasn't any worse for wear. There was no evidence of a battle. As a matter of fact, there was a slight smile at the corner of his lips.

"What y'all all worried 'bout. I told y'all I was gonna straighten this mess out. That boy be big, but he's as soft as cotton. Never did think too much of him anyways."

Weak and unable to get out of the chair, Mary held out opened arms to him. "Thank Gawd Mr. Harrington. He brought you back safely home to me and my children. I was havin' all kinds of thoughts 'bout what that big strong boy was gonna do to you. I don't think I've ever been so grateful to see you standin' in that doorway."

"Like I said, I took care of that boy and told him what'll happen iffin he ever says one bad word 'bout my wife or touches my chile again."

Maude couldn't ever remember him referring to her as his child. She didn't know what was going to happen next because she wasn't accustomed to moments like this.

"Now Maude, I don't think you'll be havin' any more trouble from that boy, but just in case, you tell me and I promise it will be over for good. Ya here me?"

Despite her resolve to maintain composure, she broke down crying as he drew her close. Then he kissed the top of her head. "Don't you worry none, Poppa take care of this." Before she could get really comfortable, he pushed her away. "Now gone on home. You be alright."

"Yes Sir."

Once she was out on the porch, she had to chuckle while shaking her head in disbelief. "Lovin' that Mr. Harrington is one confused state for a body to be in. I hope one of these days I'll be able to figure that man out."

Back home, she tried to ignore Henry who was sitting in a darkened corner with head in hands.

"Oh Maude, I don't know what come over me when I get like this. I know I keep apologizin', and keep doin' the same thing over and over again. You must think I be some kinda horrible monster, and I sometimes think that same thing. I gotta get a grip on myself, 'cause iffin' I don't Mr. Harrington is gonna kill me. Told me hisself."

"I don't wanna talk about it Henry. Let's get some sleep."

As she sat plaiting her hair and looking into the mirror she spoke to her reflection. "I still can't believe Mr. Harrington got so riled up and started actin' all gallant and defendin' me. He actually called me his chile. Maybe I'm wrong 'bout him. Obviously the man's got a heart, and at the most unexpected times he be capable of showin' love."

For now, she wanted to dwell on the probability that he did love her, and if he loved her, he had to love Mary. *Why in the heck is this man so darned complicated – especially to the people who love him? Love don't have to be this damn hard.*

Chapter 18

Another Heartbreak

Mary was now declining at an alarming rate, and the hemorrhaging was getting worse. He couldn't hide his frustration with her failing bodily functions. "Mr. Harrington, I know I'm makin' a mess and I 'preciate you helpin' out as much as you can. I truly love you for it." He didn't respond to her apologies.

Walter was furious. "Otie, I don't know why Momma feelin' like she's gotta apologize for what she can't help. Poppa's gotta do his part just like everybody else in here. I'm gettin' fed up with that angry look on his face everytime he's gotta do somethin' for her. His fault she's in this shape anyway."

"I know, but we can't do nothin' about it. I'm prayin' real hard tryin' to keep the devil that wants me to hate him under control."

Sensing the strain in the atmosphere, Novella offered to assume some of the burden. "Let me help y'all. I'm strong and can do a lot 'round here. I know Momma needs my help too."

At school, she was earning a reputation as a track and field star, and never got tired of hearing Miss Washington brag about her abilities. As much as she loved running, the desire to get more practice and participate in track and field had more to do with obligation at home than having fun.

In addition to everything else, endurance and speed was needed in order to accommodate Scott's demands. Mary was too sick to take his lunch to the mill, and Maude wouldn't dare offer to take anything to him. So Novella stepped up and offered.

Another person making sacrifices to accommodate him was too much for Maude.

"Absolutely not – we're already lettin' you do enough and runnin' back and forth between the mill and school is out of the question."

"Yeah, that's just takin' stuff too far." Walter then leaned over to Leotia. "See I told you. He sittin' there hearin' us say why Vella can't run his lunch down to him and he won't step in and tell her not to run herself ragged."

When he finally spoke up, his response made them angrier. "I don't see what's the problem. She be wantin' to bring me lunch, then she should. Somebody gotta do it."

Their exhaustion outweighed the never-ending displeasure with his inconsiderate rulings on family matters. Besides, they didn't have enough fight left among them to win this particular battle.

Walter was frustrated, weary, and worn out as he struggled, without success, to define his feelings. *Who is he? One minute, he's the man I wanna love and the next minute I can't stand the sight of him. I can't believe the way he thinks. Here he is a grown man and expectin' Vella to bring lunch to him. Why can't he just take the damn lunch with him when he leaves the house in the mornin'? Vella just a skinny little gal who loves everybody and want everybody 'round her to be happy. 'Sides, she don't even realize what she askin' for and how she gonna be worn out tryin' to take care of Poppa when he ought to be takin' care of her. Momma always preachin' 'bout how a gentleman should treat a lady. Well there be plenty of times her own man don't act like the gentleman she keep tellin' me I gotta grow up to be.*

Within a year after Novella started missing school recess to make the lunchtime run, anyone with eyes could see the effects of undue pressure on everybody in the house but Scott.

To make matters worse, Henry was back to his violent, drunken binges and Maude's nerves were frayed trying to keep the resurrected secret hidden. She remembered Scott's threat to end his life if he ever touched her again. The tension was so thick, she was sure he was waiting for the opportunity to deliver on his promise to end Henry's life.

As bad as I wanna put an end to fightin' with Henry, I know if I tell him the same mess is goin' on again, he'll make good on his promise. I can just tell he be waitin' for any excuse to tear everything up in sight. Heck I know 'cause I'm feelin' that way most of the time myself. I'm just tryin' to keep it all together for Momma's sake.

Too much was going on for anybody to keep it all together, and Henry couldn't think of any way to handle the chaos other than numbing himself with moonshine. The devil's juice lured him into a false sense of audacity and once again he took it out on Maude.

The door hadn't even completely closed behind her when his eyes immediately went to the bruises and the blackened eye. He sprang from his chair and made a dash for the fire poker.

"No Poppa, you can't go over there. We can't have no more trouble with Momma so sick. Let him sleep that moonshine off and things will get better. I promise I can handle this."

After putting the poker down, he picked her up by the shoulders and placed her away from the door.

"You stay here for the next few days and I mean it."

"Mr. Harrington – I mean Poppa what you thinkin' 'bout doin'? You scarin' me to death. Please – Momma can't take this right now."

"I knows what yo momma can't take, I knows what these chilluns can't take, I knows what you can't take, and I know for damn sure what I ain't gonna take, and that is that animal puttin' his hands on you and doin' 'zackly what I told him never to do again. Now do as I say and stay here 'til I tell you to go back home."

He wasn't to be challenged so she stood with arms wrapped around herself desperately trying to provide her own comfort. When that didn't work, she walked back to the kitchen praying to God he wasn't going to do something they would all live to regret.

No one heard from him for the next three days. Unable to remain patient and do as he directed her to, Maude went down to the mill. James, Jr. was sitting behind a large wooden table looking as if he had been expecting her to show up.

"Afternoon Mr. Seamore, I come lookin' for Mr. Harrington. He left the house a few nights ago, and we haven't seen him since. I was wonderin' if he showed up to work."

"Yes, I have seen him. I asked him to go over to Winston-Salem to take care of something for me for a couple of days." The expression on his face was the look of conspiracy.

Oh my Gawd, these Seamores are involved in whatever Mr. Harrington is doin' and know exactly why we can't find him. Who would've thought Mr. Harrington and these people would be in cahoots with each other? This man lookin' at me here don't wanna tell me what's goin' on, but that sly expression on his face done gave him away.

"With all due respect Mr. Seamore, can you tell me when you expectin' him to return? You know my momma's real sick and we need to know how to reach him."

He got up from his seat, came around the table, and placed a big, burly hand around her shoulder. "Now I don't want y'all worrying about anything. If Mary needs anything, you come back here immediately. We'll take care of everything. I promise you Maude, your poppa will be back within a day or two. Now you go back home and tell Mary not to worry. Everything is going to be okay."

Somehow she knew that she would never see Henry again.

He finally showed up. "Mr. Harrington, can I go home now?" He shook his head. They stared at each other, and before she could ask the next question, he spoke up. "Oh Maude, Henry took a job up north. Says he tired of dealin' with folk in the Gulf." She was too afraid to ask for clarification.

"Yes sir."

While she didn't know the details, she was confident that whatever it was he did with the help of his white brothers, there would be no traces.

This man is one of the most difficult people in the world to figure out. Who knew he had any kind of relationship with them Seamores where he could make somebody disappear forever.

She was feeling beholding to him for saving her from Henry, and once again tried to focus on loving him. That would never be an easy thing to do.

Despite his act of chivalry, things continued to spiral downward. Mary wasn't improving, sickness was ravaging her body, and the end was upon them. They fought to remain in a state of denial, but the heart-breaking truth would not be ignored.

Novella was having the most difficult time trying to give Mary lunch because her condition had deteriorated to the point where she couldn't even handle a liquid diet. "Momma, just try and get some of this broth down. Maybe eatin' somethin' will give you a little bit of strength." Not even the broth was soothing. Just like everything else, it irritated her throat. She started coughing violently and her stomach gave up the bitter contents. The pressure from vomiting caused her to lose control over her bladder and bowel.

"Beolia, Otie, Walter, come quick, Momma's throwin' up and stuff is comin' out from everywhere. Y'all hurry up. Somebody help. Come quick."

When they arrived, she was grabbing everything in sight, trying to catch the spew from Mary's mouth and nostrils. If not for love, the nauseating scent of vomit mixed with bowel would have turned them back. Because of love, none of that mattered. Beolia began barking out orders. "Leotia, hurry up and get water and some fresh towels to clean Momma up. Walter, you gotta leave so we can clean her up. Go on now. We'll call you back if we need you."

"Y'all sure? This stuff don't make no never mind to me. Let me help."

"Walter, get outta here. We said we'll call you. Momma doesn't want or need you seeing some things. Get out now!"

Mary's laborious breathing felt like all of them were taking their last breaths. Weighted with sorrow, Leotia left the room to take the soiled clothing and linen out to the back porch.

Novella slowly walked up to the bed feeling as if she was on her way to the guillotine. Thinking Mary had fallen off to sleep she spoke softly, not expecting a response. "Oh Momma, I love you more than anything, but sometimes I think you'd be better off dead."

Mary opened her eyes. "Baby, you're prob'ly right. Sometimes I think I'd be better off dead too, but you wouldn't."

Beolia was distraught and reduced to tears. She grabbed her by an arm as she was dragging her out of the room. "Vella, why would you say that to Momma, why on earth would you say something like that? You're being so cruel."

"Why are you so mad at me Beolia? Haven't you been thinkin' the same thing? I hear you and Maudie talkin' when y'all don't think nobody is listenin'."

Mary's response was a prophecy of things to come after she was gone.

When Maude arrived, Leotia recounted what took place earlier. She couldn't take anymore, and the emotional collapse happened right before their eyes. Although she was much taller, her head wound up on Leotia shoulders. When it appeared she was all cried out, she broke down again. The sight was too much for them. Walter's fear and frustration turned into anger.

"All this stuff's Poppa's fault. What kinda man let his wife suffer like this? She disappearin' mo' and mo' everyday. What kinda man do that to his wife? Y'all tell me that. Oh my Gawd, what kinda man just sit by and do nothin', but watch his wife die like this. Sometimes I hate him…"

He completely lost it and ran out to the barn. They heard him screaming and things being thrown around, but were too exhausted, broken, and terrified to do anything to calm him down.

Maude's tears turned into determination. "Y'all, I'm gonna get Mama Mame. I ain't waitin' fo' him to make any more decisions. He don't seem to be able to make any good ones anyhow. Ain't nothin' he can do to hurt me any more than I'm hurtin' right now. He can't stop me, and I'm goin' to get some help."

She pulled the wagon from the barn and hitched it up to the mare. During the ride, she reflected on her marathon race through the woods back in November of 1914. Although Mary's situation was again critical, she didn't have a fraction of the energy she had back then, and couldn't run the distance to Mama Mame's place now even if she wanted to. Hard times had taken their toll.

Mama Mame was sitting on the porch with Minnie Gilmore. She knew something was wrong, and it was serious because Maude looked defeated. They stopped talking.

"Good evenin' Mama Mame. Evenin' Miz Minnie."

Before either woman could answer, tears began to flow and once again she let go. Her shoulders were shaking as she sobbed and pleaded for help.

"Somebody's gotta help us. Momma, she's lyin' over there dyin' and Mr. Harrington won't do nothin' to help her. Oh Gawd, somebody's gotta help Momma. Somebody's gotta…, somebody's gotta help us. I don't know what to do. I don't know where to go. Somebody, please…"

She was down on her knees in the dirt with arms outstretched towards them begging, pleading, and crying for help.

They looked at each other, eyes brimming with tears, but were determined to remain calm. They knew all too well about the rumors of the late Belle's visits to the Geechee and how she had paid and conspired with the root doctor to destroy Mary. Being women of faith, they rejected the Geechee's practices, and fought against buying into the rumors. However, the bizarre chain of events had them worried.

Miss Minnie made the decision to counter-attack whatever the Geechee may have done. "I'm gonna get Avery Baines to go over there with us."

"Maude, you gone on home Honey. I promise, we'll be over there by tomorrow evenin' to see 'bout Mary." She was too worn out to question what they had decided. She trusted Mama Mame, and that was all she needed.

Avery Baines was a root doctor, and all the old folk knew about his work, or as he referred to it – his anointing. If anyone was able to undo the Geechee's roots it was Avery. Folk said he was as good at undoing spells as he was at casting them. People hated and feared the Geechee. They looked to Avery to counteract her damage and destruction. At the first sign of trouble, he offered to use his potions to cast protective spells against evil. It was said that even the Geechee recognized his powers and tried to stay as far away from him as possible.

Mama Mame and Miss Minnie were desperate and calling off any demons the Geechee may have released was what Avery

Baines could do, or now in their desperation, they wanted to believe he could.

The next evening Maude, Beolia, Walter, Leotia, and Novella were sitting on the back porch when Mama Mame's wagon pulled up. Mama Mame and Miss Minnie jumped down to stand aside as Avery pulled a long stick out of the back of the wagon. The end of the stick had two branches that formed the shape of a sling shot.

They could tell the strange ritual being performed by the root doctor wasn't anything like what Mama Mame or Doc Moore did to help people. They were confused about why he was needed and what part the odd stick played in the ceremony that was being performed. He placed the stick out in front of him and started walking around. By now Scott had joined them. Oddly, he didn't demand Avery to stop doing whatever he was doing, and leave.

The switch to the light of understanding was flipped and Maude started to comprehend his apparent acceptance. *Oh my Gawd, Mr. Harrington already knows what that root doctor is lookin' fo' and he's scared to death?*

The gasping sounds coming from Mama Mame and Miss Minnie tore her attention away from him. Avery, who was standing at a spot immediately in front of the back porch, was shaking and jerking around as if his body had a will of its own. The part of the stick shaped like a sling shot was pointed at a small mound of dirt that looked like someone had been digging.

Maude tried to calm her fears by minimizing what the root roctor had discovered. *Its prob'ly just some spot one of the chickens dug up.* That explanation really didn't sit well with her, and somehow she knew that wouldn't be the real reason why the mound of dirt was there.

Avery spoke up, but didn't sound as if he was excited about finding whatever they were looking for. "Right there. Y'all, it's right there."

Mama Mame and Miss Minnie ran over to the spot and with their bare hands started digging. Finally, Miss Minnie pulled a sealed jar out from the hole they dug. She brushed away the dirt, and held it up to the sky.

"What in the world do we have here? Sun so bright I can barely make out what it is. Wait a minute. Let me turn a little bit to the east. There, there. I still can't make out what we've got here in this bottle."

"Oh Minnie please. Just hurry up and open the bottle."

She looked frightened although she fought hard to maintain an expressionless face. Scott was now approaching, and Avery was looking as if the bottle contained a poisonous snake.

"Minnie I said open up that jar, and open it up right now."

Miss Minnie unscrewed the bottle and slowly started taking out small pieces of cloth that everyone recognized as torn pieces of Mary's undergarments. A putrid smell was released and permeated throughout the yard. There were stains all over the fabric. Mama Mame and Minnie both looked at Avery for confirmation.

He made the announcement no one wanted or was prepared to hear. "It's already too late. Y'all come to get me too late."

Mama Mame and Minnie collapsed into each other's arms crying and praying.

Scott dropped to his knees moaning in agony. He was remembering the day when Mary discovered someone had damaged her undergarments that had been hanging out on the clothes line to dry. Belle had been there.

"Damn that witch, damn that witch."

Things started adding up for Maude as well. She jumped down off of the front porch and started running. She leapt on him, kicking, biting, and scratching while he was still on his knees in the dirt sobbing.

"You good for nothin' slave, what did you do to Momma? You and that rotten whore Belle did somethin' awful. I hope that bitch's soul burn in the hottest part of hell along with yours. You good for nothin' slave."

Mama Mame yelled out to her. "Stop Maude, stop it right now." She ignored the demand and kept kicking, biting, and scratching.

"Them white folk should've killed your sorry ass rather than set you free. You be the devil himself come to destroy Momma and for what reason? You son-of-a-bitch, I'mma kill you. I swore to you if anything happened to Momma I was gonna kill you."

Everyone else was too caught up in their own raw emotions to notice that Beolia was right behind Maude. But now they were getting an eyeful as they witnessed her all over him as well, with fists and feet flying, and landing everywhere. Maude was still delivering punishing blows to any place on his body where she could. When she stopped kicking, she was scratching him. Some of the scratches on his face were so deep white meat was exposed while others bled profusely. He wasn't even trying to defend himself.

Avery couldn't take the violent and heart-wrenching scene any longer. Rushing over to Maude, he grabbed her around the waist, dragging her away from Scott.

"Gal you gotta get yo self together. You ain't no good to yo momma like this. Come on Maudie, you gotta calm down. That man be in hell right now, trust me, he be in hell right now. You prob'ly can't kick him down any further than he be right now."

She didn't care and wouldn't stop fighting. A barrage of obscenities was hurled at him although her voice had become hoarse.

"You evil mother f..."

Mama Mame ran over to them, throwing a hand over her mouth. "Hush chile, don't talk like that. Don't you dare talk like that. Yo momma don't want that. Don't let the devil take you there. We're Christian folk. Don't let the devil have his way. Rebuke the devil and he shall flee. Rebuke the devil. Yo momma's back there in the arms of Jesus. Don't you dare speak the devil's filthy language."

Avery turned around to see Beolia still attacking Scott as he remained on his knees in the dirt crying and moaning.

"I will kill you, I will kill you."

"Here Momma Mame, you hold Maude, I gotta get the other gal." He picked her up and walked back over to the porch. She was still screaming, "I will kill you, I will kill you."

Walter was trying to hold and console Leotia and Novella at the same time. Leotia, usually the quiet one, was crying, but kept asking, "Walter, what're they talkin' about?"

Novella didn't know in which direction to turn, and just stood there holding on to Walter and crying. "Momma, I want Momma. Stop fightin' y'all. I want Momma."

"Otie, they're talkin' bout that dead woman Poppa was messin' 'round with all them years. Rumor been goin' 'round that Belle was mixed up with the old Geechee woman who been puttin' roots on Poppa's wives before Momma, and possibly on Momma too. People 'round town say the Geechee killed Belle, so I thought maybe them rumors had gotten mixed up and nothin' was gonna happen to Momma cause the Geechee got Belle instead. I swear 'fore Gawd, I could kill 'em 'bout now. When I get the chance, I'll pay that ol' man back for he did to Momma. I swear 'fore Gawd I'm gonna get even with him."

"Walter, what're roots, and what have they got to do with Momma?"

"I really don't know much 'bout stuff like that. Just that some people practice this thing they call witchcraft, puttin' all kinds of horrible spells on other folk, makin' them sick and sometimes even killin' them. Momma told me not to worry 'bout them rumors cause she's in Gawd's hands, and in His hands no devil can do nothin' to her. I just hope all this mess is some crazy coincidence and it's not too late to save Momma. Maybe Mr. Avery got it all wrong and Doc Moore can help Mamma Mame to straighten all this stuff out. Gotta be somethin' somebody can do for us. Mama Mame and 'em be prayin' some kinda hard; that's gotta count for somethin'".

"I hate all this talk about roots and Geechee people. When I get away from this place, I won't ever go near anybody who believes in that trash. This isn't what Momma taught us about living for the Lord, and I don't want any part of this hocus pocus."

Although no one responded to Beolia's outburst, it was the moment of the unspoken declaration to completely separate from anyone or anything connected to the bizarre practices and beliefs people like Belle and the Geechee woman embraced. That was the day they completely and unequivocally denounced the dark world of roots, spells, and witchcraft.

Finally everyone turned to go back into the house. Beolia, Walter, Leotia, and Novella headed straight for the bedroom. When they arrived, Maude was lying in bed, with her head resting on Mary's frail shoulder. Mary was asleep, with one hand resting on Maude's cheek.

They returned to the kitchen to sit, huddle together, and wait although they had no idea what they were waiting for.

Mama Mame couldn't rest until she looked in on Mary herself. She walked into the room and up to the bed. This was how she wanted to remember her – sleeping peacefully. An overwhelming sense of sadness compelled her to take advantage of what could be the last precious moments they shared.

Feeling the gentle kiss to her forehead, Mary opened her eyes and raised a shaking hand up to stroke Mama Mame's cheek.

"How you doin' Mama Mame? It's good to see you. I wish I could get up and keep you company, but I'm so tired these days."

"Hush now Baby. Don't you be worried 'bout gettin' up and keepin' me company 'cause just bein' here with you is all I need. Mama Mame is gonna bring Doc Moore over here tomorrow so he can help us out."

She nodded her head and closed her eyes again. Before they left, Mama Mame and Miss Minnie woke Maude up. "Baby, come see us back in the kitchen will ya."

"Now looka here chile, we know this here's 'bout the hardest thing a young woman can go through, and there're some things that got you boilin' mad, but gal you gotta hold on just a little while longer. The good Lawd ain't never left His chillun forsaken. No matter what Avery say, we gotta look to the Lawd.

Iffin He be wantin' to take Mary, that be His call, but ain't no roots or other demon in hell can take her from us iffin the Lawd ain't ready for her to come home." The intended words of comfort brought on more tears.

Mama Mame and Miss Minnie tersely nodded their heads in Scott's direction as they were walking back to the wagon. Mama Mame was too angry to speak. Miss Minnie was only able to get a few words out. "Evenin' – we be back tomorrow with Doc Moore." He was too exhausted to respond, but then they didn't expect him to.

Back at the wagon Mama Mame and Miss Minnie discussed their next step. "This be real bad, real bad. You gotta send Doc Moore over here to see what he can do to help Mary cross over Jordan more comfortable. Lawd knows I hate to say it, but you and I both know she's in the process of leavin' us."

Mama Mame wiped the tears from her bloodshot eyes with the back of her hand, shaking her head up and down.

"Minnie, I knows that – been knowin' for some time, but was prayin' to the good Lawd I was wrong. I'll get 'em over here tomorrow to do somethin', although I don't know what."

Chapter 19
To Be Absent in the Body
Is to be Present with the Lord

It was about 3 o' clock the next afternoon when Doc Moore pulled up to the Harrington place. He was dreading going in based on Mama Mame's latest report. He, too, had a deep affection for Mary, and was hoping there was something he could do to help ease her misery. Before he reached the top step, Scott appeared at the door.

"Afternoon Doc, she's in the bedroom. I'll take you to her."

Despite Mama Mame's report, he was unprepared to see the condition in which he found her. Leaning over to Scott, he whispered, "What in God's name did you let happen to her man? This is not my Mary. This is not my Mary. Why on earth didn't you come and get me sooner?"

He was embarrassed and feeling awkard not knowing what to say or do in response to the accusatory look and reprimand. Doc Moore was holding him responsible. He had seen this same expression on the faces of family and friends, but immediately became dismissive or defensive in order to avert the truth.

Now this white man blamin' me for what's goin' on with Mary. Why everybody blamin' me? She herself told me it was just the Change. This here white man standin' here lookin' at me like I'm 'posed to make her well. That's what he be here fo'. He needin' to be doin' somethin' instead of starin' at me like a damned fool.

Unable to mask his discomfort as arrogance, he abruptly walked out of the room without responding to Doc Moore's inquiry.

"Mary, honey, its Doc Moore, and I've come to spend the day taking care of you if that's alright with you."

She couldn't open her eyes completely, but tried in vain to focus on him. She had no voice and only a raspy whisper came out as she spoke to him. "Thanks for comin'. I'm feelin' mighty tired in my body, but Doc, my soul is ready to take its rest. I'm concerned 'bout my children, but ready to go home to be with the Lawd. He's been mighty good to me no matter what anybody says, but this here body is so tired. I don't have much life left in me. You know what that good book says?"

"Mary, tell me what it says."

"It says to be absent in the body is to be present with the Lawd. So Doc, I can't lose. All my livin' for Him is gettin' ready to pay off. I'm rejoicin' in the Gawd of my salvation, and 'bout to receive my reward."

"I 'preciate all you've done for me and my family. Just one favor though. Whenever you get the chance, please look in on my babies." Even her whisper was getting faint.

"Don't try to talk any more Sweetheart. Just be still and get your rest."

At the door, he turned around once more. Despite her frailty, she looked peaceful. She had turned slightly onto her side with her hands in the praying position and her cheek resting on them. *My God, this angel has already taken her wings and is resting in peace.*

That was the last time he saw her alive. During the night, she completed her transition.

In the early morning hours just before daybreak, they were awakened by his screams. They started running in the direction where the screams were coming from.

As he was sprinting towards their bedroom, Walter was already yelling, "No Momma, no Momma" although he had no firsthand knowledge of what he was going to find when he reached her. It was instinct that bound son to mother telling him she was already gone. He couldn't accept what his heart was saying and kept yelling, "No Momma, no Momma."

Leotia and Novella were crying more than screaming. They also knew the end must have come.

Scott was screaming out in agony and the frightening sounds coming from him were foreign to them. The duration of his shattering screams resonated like echos.

When they reached them, he was still in bed holding her. She looked as if she was peacefully sleeping in his arms, but they knew better.

"No Gawd no. No. No. No. Oh Gawd no. Mary, Honey, wake up, wake up. You can't leave me like this. You just can't leave me. I'm sorry – I promise I won't ever do another thing to hurt you. Just wake up. I don't wanna be by myself. I've been good. I've been good since she died. Please come back to me Mary, please. Oh Gawd, help me." He was inconsolable.

Leotia made the next decision. "Walter, you gotta get outta here right now. Go and get Maude. Hurry up. She'll know what to do.

Her heart skipped a beat as she heard the banging sound on the door. *She's gone. Dear Gawd in heaven she's gone.*

Walter's sobbing confirmed her worst fears. As soon as she opened the door, they fell into each other arms slowly sliding down to the floor.

"Maude, what're we gonna do? I feel like I just died. I don't wanna go on livin', I swear I don't. How could she be gone – how could she? She was so good and lovin'. She lived for the Lawd. This just ain't right."

Dear Gawd, these children can't take no more. They've been called upon to bear more sorrow than anybody should have to bear in a lifetime. I've gotta do this for Momma. It breaks my heart everytime I look at 'em. They've tried to be brave, but this stuff has been killin' them right along with Momma. They're my babies now. I've gotta take care of 'em just the way Momma would want me to. They're my responsibility and I'm gonna see them through this, even if it kills me.

"Walter, I know this hurts some kinda awful. I feel like my life is over too. But I'm gonna take care of y'all. I promise you don't ever have to worry about me leavin'. You know I would gladly give my life for each and every one of you. Now, let's go on back over to the house and help Mr. Harrington start makin' plans for Momma's burial. I'll figure the rest of this stuff out later."

Chapter 20
Moving On After Mary

It had been three months since Mary was laid to rest, but their grief was as fresh and painful as the day she passed away.

"Y'all where's Beolia?"

"She's out in the barn Maude readin'.'"

"Otie, did you just say she's in the barn readin'? Why in the world would she be in the barn readin' instead of in this house?"

"She hardly ever talks to anybody since Momma died. She spends most of the time out in the barn, and sometimes she out there all by herself 'til the middle of the night. One night I snuck out there and found her asleep."

"Where in the devil is Mr. Harrington while she's out there in the middle of the night?"

"He be in here sittin' in front of the fireplace just starin'. He ain't payin' us much attention either."

Listening to Leotia's and Walter's account of how they were grieving and being treated made her angry, forgetting about her exhaustion. "I swear. That's the most selfish, bullheaded man I've ever known in my life. Most of this sorrow is his fault anyway. All he's thinkin' 'bout is how he's grievin' over losin' Momma. Should've treated her right when he had her."

"Now he's miserable and ignorin' y'all. If that ol' man be hurtin' my little sister, he's gonna have to deal with me and that ain't gonna be pretty. He hasn't even had the decency to talk to Beolia and find out what's troublin' her. He just gonna leave her out in the barn by herself to grieve all alone in the middle of the night. Everybody else 'round him droppin' like flies, and the devil himself still goin' strong. It just don't seem fair. I hope enough women have died so's the one's still 'round know to stay as far away from him as possible. Tryin' to love that man is a death sentence if I've ever seen one."

They jumped when she slammed the door and stomped out of the house to find Beolia.

"Beolia, where are you? I've come by to see 'bout you. Please answer me. Come out and talk to me."

There was no response, so she kept moving around in the barn until she found her in a corner propped up against some old stale hay. She had stopped reading and was just sitting in silence staring off into space.

"Honey, what're you doin' in here?"

She sat down in the hay and placed an arm around her thin shoulders. "Come on, tell ol' Maude about it. I know it hurts to lose her. I can't believe she's gone myself."

"Maude, I wish I was with Momma. This is too much to bear. My heart hurts too, too much. As long as I can remember, I've been praying we could be a happy family and live normal lives like other people. Everytime I heard something about that woman Belle, the Geechee woman, and roots, I was sick to my stomach. Momma lived for God, so I just don't understand why that stuff had to destroy our family like it did."

"Now that Momma's gone, I just want to lie down and die. I know Mr. Harrington don't feel the same way about me like he does towards Leotia, Walter, and Vella. He tries, but I know I'm not his, although I want to be more than anything. What am I gonna do?"

Her question trailed off as she broke down crying. Maude pulled her closer. The confidence with which she spoke belied her own grief, "Listen here Beolia, you know Momma wouldn't want you hurtin' like this and feelin' like you got nobody. You know for yourself your sister Maude ain't gonna let nothin' bad happen to you. I'll tell you what, when Mr. Harrington comes home from the mill, I'm gonna tell him I'm taking y'all home with me. I guaranty you'll know you're loved deeply – won't be no question there. You hear me? Now come on and go back to the house with me. This barn ain't fit for you to be sittin' in here all the time by yourself."

Maude was right. He was so self-absorbed in his personal loss, he was oblivious to what anybody else was going through – namely his children.

The day after Mary's burial, he returned to work. James Junior and Clayton could see he wasn't in any shape to be around anybody, and definitely not in any shape to do any work. Although approaching him was the last thing either one of them wanted to do, they had to talk to him before one of the other employees said or did something to set him off into a fit of rage.

"Junior, how are we gonna tell him to go back home until he can handle what just happened to Mary? You know he's stubborn and can get meaner than a rattle snake. I hate to admit it, but I'm always nervous when I gotta talk to him about something. He looks right through you almost like you ain't even standing there talking to him. Daddy used to say even he had a hard time looking him in the eyes."

"I'm not looking forward to telling him to go home either. Now Clayton, you know he's not going to see we're trying to look out for him. Truth be told, we're trying to look out for us too. He'll get all worked up thinking we're trying to boss him around. Any other colored man would fall in line, but nooooo, not Scott Harrington."

"Daddy sure did leave us with a mess. Don't know why he just didn't find a way for us to cut ties after he died. But then again, I've gotten so used to them boys I'd probably ball my eyes out if something terrible happened to either one of 'em. Now our momma was real good at hating them and keeping her distance, but I'm like Daddy. I can't do it. Don't you find that strange?"

"Strange it is. There are plenty of times when I don't understand how we feel about each other. All I know is that Daddy made a mess a whole lot of years ago and left us to carry on. Instead of letting them go back in 1863, he made all kinds of promises, trying to keep them close by. His guilt is our cross to bear."

"Well, ol' Scott is just going to have to get mad when I tell him to go back home for a few days. He's one strange bird. We gotta say something though. If the wrong person says the wrong thing to him, he's liable to go off and kill whoever tries to talk to him."

"I swear that boy has always been difficult to read and understand. Now that he's lost Mary, he's in a darker place than I've ever seen him. He's raw right now and we've gotta be careful on how we handle him. I sure do wish our old man was still here. He would know how to kiss up to him. I just don't get it. Most of the time, him and Walter seem like they okay with everything that happened. Then there are those times when you know they resent Daddy and us, and at times like that, you couldn't pay me to turn my back on either one of them – especially Scott. "

Trying to deal with him after Mary passed away was far more complicated than dealing with him when he brought the Henry Oakley problem to them. Clayton began reminiscing about that night.

"Remember when he came to us about that big black boy they called Henry? Boy I tell you, Scott looked like the devil himself. Wasn't worried about us being white and him being colored. He came in here and demanded we do something about Henry."

James started laughing when he recalled that scene. "Yeah boy – I'm laughing now, but back then I was so scared, I thought I was gonna crap on myself. He was so damned mad I thought he was gonna kill us if we turned him down. But when I mentioned doing away with Henry so nobody would ever see him again, ol' Scott started salivating at the mouth. He was hungry for that boy's blood. Once we all started talking about what we were gonna do, I was actually feeling like he was my real brother – I mean my white brother. He came up with a plan I never would have thought of. I tell you – that rattle snake is smarter and more cunning than any white man I know when it comes to dealing with his enemies."

In the end, they were too afraid to send him home, and gave him another promotion. Maybe working longer and harder hours would take his mind off of losing Mary. Since James Seamore, Sr. gave them more of everything whenever they had a problem, they figured the same would work for him. They knew this much about Scott. He was attracted to money, power, and control as much as they were.

He accepted the promotion, but didn't feel any sense of gratitude. *Ain't gotta be grateful since they the ones who owe me.*

It'll help, but it won't erase what happened. Nothin' will ever erase that, so they'll just be tryin' as long as all of us are alive to make up for what that hypocrite daddy of mine did. Ol' Seamore ain't never paid his debt in full and them Seamores ain't ever gonna be paid in full as far as I'm concerned.

The day he arrived home after Maude found Beolia in the barn, she asked for permission to take them with her.

"Mr. Harrington, I think it's best if I take the children to live with me. You be at work all the time and they really need to be nurtured 'bout now. I wanna take them to live with me."

"Absolutely not."

"So are you gonna tell me why you sayin' 'no?' I mean it ain't like you're here with them and lookin' out after 'em. As a matter of fact, I found Beolia out in the barn cryin' her eyes out over Momma, and it's my understandin' she's been grievin' like this out in that barn all by herself – sometimes late into the night."

"Look, these children are hurtin' with losin' Momma and all. You're so lost in yo own grief and hidin' out down at the mill, so you don't see what they are goin' through. They need a woman to raise them, and I'm the best person to do that. You need to let them come and live with me."

"I told you no and I mean it. These are my chilluns and I say they stay here with me. Ain't nobody gonna take them outta this house."

"What're you doin' to help them with their grief? Don't answer that question – I'll do that for you. You're spendin' time at the mill, hoardin' more money, and for what? Nobody in this house is happy and much of it is because of some Geechee mess you got yo self tangled up in for years and people like that good-for-nothin' witch Belle wantin' what other women folk have. Of course, Momma had to get caught up in somethin' she didn't even start."

"Gal, who you think you talkin' to? I got a good mind to take my strap and…"

"I dare you. You just try and lay a hand on me. I swear I'll make you eat that strap."

The restraints were off and the fight was on. Beolia, Leotia, Walter, and Novella stood by helplessly watching and listening as the two of them battled yet again. It was really getting ugly when Beolia took a deep breath and stepped forward. "Poppa, I would like to go and live with Maude if you don't mind."

The silence was deafening until he partially conceded. "Alright, you can go, but my chilluns are stayin' here."

His distinction was like a slap in the face, but the comment was confirmation she had made the right choice. *Obviously he's never accepted me as his. I should have known better – chasing after his love all these years has meant nothing to him.*

Maude's heart hurt for Beolia as she looked at the pain and embarrassment on her face in response to his rejection. "You go straight to hell. Do you hear me? Beolia don't need you 'cause she's got me."

"Honey, go and get your stuff."

Beolia left the room to pack her things. Walter, Leotia, and Novella were once again reduced to tears. They were still being torn apart even after Mary and Belle were dead.

The cost of loving this man ain't worth it. This fool is way too stubborn to admit he's inflictin' more pain on these children. I'm glad Beolia spoke up. I can't wait to get her outta here. Someday and somehow I'll find a way to deliver the others out of the claws of this fool.

"Maude, please just try to reason with Poppa some more. I know if you explain it to him, he'll see it the right way. Please don't walk outta here with just Beolia. All of us need to stick together."

"Shut up Walter. I don't need her to reason with me. I said y'all ain't goin' nowhere. She's the unreasonable one – always tryin' to boss everybody 'round and have her way. Let her do what she wanna do with Beolia, but she ain't takin' y'all."

Leotia couldn't stand to hear anymore. "No, you shut up Poppa. You need Maude just as much as everybody else in here. She's been there for Momma, you, and all of us. Why're you bein' so pig-headed? You had better think real hard, 'cause if you run her away, who you gonna have to keep things in line?"

He was stunned to hear from the least expected. "Gal, what did you say? I'm gonna take my strap off and..."

This time is was Maude who interrupted. "You're obviously a way bigger fool than I thought. If you touch her, I swear I'll kill you. Now try it."

He looked around and saw nothing but angry faces, and most of them were the children he wanted to keep with him.

Beolia re-appeared with her things. As they were heading for the door, Maude issued another warning.

"Don't even think you can keep me from them."

She then strutted out of the door with a relieved Beolia marching behind her. He was left speechless. Leotia was right. He still needed Maude far more than she needed him.

The first Christmas after everything happened was the worst. There were no individual baskets filled with candies, nuts, and fruits waiting for them as was Mary's tradition. There were no banana and coconut cakes, or sweet potato pies she stayed up late into the night on Christmas Eve to bake. A haunting silence now replaced the noisy excitement that filled the house as she was preparing to exchange and sample desserts with family and friends who stopped by throughout the day on Christmas Day.

The only decorations they had on that first dismal Christmas were the ones Novella made in school out of construction paper. They tried to spread the few pieces of ornaments throughout the house to make each room feel as if the spirit of Christmas was there, but in the end, the sparseness only made things worse.

His attempt was pathetic at best. The miniature glass dolls with the crudely painted on features looked nothing like the beautiful dolls the other girls in school described. Novella was left to wonder about the lyrics to the carol that was sung in the Christmas pageant about old Saint Nicholas bringing toys to all the good little girls and boys. *Were we that bad? Is that why God took Momma, Maude, and Beolia from us? Does He think we don't deserve to be happy like everybody else?*

Walter's gift was even more pitiful than the dolls. He knew exactly where the pocket knife came from. *He's gotta be kiddin'. This knife looks like one of them they use down at the mill. He could've kept this. I don't need no used knife he stole from the mill. This is one miserable life without Momma, Maude, and Beolia. I gotta start makin' plans to get away from here. I ain't never gonna be happy livin' in this house with him. Can't take much more, and I'm sick and tired of being sick and tired.*

Chapter 21
Exodus

In the month of March in the year in which Walter Seamore Harrington turned thirteen years old, he started working at the General Store. Scott only approved because he was hoping the job and time away from the house would give him something to do besides moping around and looking as sad as the day Mary passed away. Occasionally, he caught Walter staring at him and sensed the resentment. Although he recognized this same expression on the face of Herbert, he fought to dismiss mounting suspicions that another nightmare was going to become his reality. He was faced with the possibility of losing Walter just as he had lost Herbert.

Uncle Walt's grief was watching them being swallowed up by grief with no comfort from Scott. This time he wasn't willing to pour energy into pampering Scott and refused to remain silent. He couldn't convince him to move beyond his own loss and support the children he was fighting so hard to keep, so he was left with no alternative but to step in.

Expressing emotions wasn't difficult for Uncle Walt. He showered them with compensatory hugs and kisses since Scott was uncomfortable with giving them. Occasionally he grabbed all of them up in his long arms at one time. "C'mon and give Uncle Walt a big hug. Y'all know I'm here for you anytime. If you need a hug, Uncle Walt is here to give it to you. You need a kiss Uncle Walt will always be here to give you that too. You just wanna cry, Uncle Walt will wipe them tears away."

"Thanks Uncle Walt. I don't know what we'd do without you. Seems like you doin' all the stuff Poppa should be doin'. He ain't payin' nobody no attention. He's spendin' most of his time down there at the mill."

"Look Otie, I know's yo poppa be a difficult man. I been talkin' to him 'bout how he 'posed to be there for y'all at a time like this. I don't seem to be able to get through to him. Believe me when I tell you I'm fightin' to keep from givin' him a good swift kick in the rear end. Only thing keepin' me from doin' it is I know all too well he's got his own demons to deal with."

"He loves y'all though. He just doin' a piss poor job with showin' his feelins'. Them feelin's of hissin' were trampled all over when we was young boys. It ain't easy when yo poppa gives you away at birth and then run your mammy away. Ain't easy when you see him treatin' his white boys one way and treatin' you another; sometimes sneakin' down to our cabin, swearin' fo' Gawd he love us just the same. Ain't easy when that same poppa watch them overseers put the whip to you when they don't think you been workin' hard enough, and he don't do a damn thing to stop'em from beatin' you damned near to death."

"That all be in the past, and I ain't lettin' them demons ruin the rest of my life. I buried them the day I found out Mr. Lincoln declared we was free. Now yo poppa, he be a complicated man, but I ain't. Don't y'all worry though, Uncle Walt be here whenever you need me."

Unlike Scott, he got along fine with Maude. The extreme difference between the two was mind-boggling to her because they shared the exact same history. *How did Uncle Walt avoid bein' a bitter and distant man like Mr. Harrington? Sometimes I thought maybe his twisted nature come outta slavery, but wasn't*

Uncle Walt a slave too? He ain't nothin' like Mr. Harrington, and thank Gawd for that.

"Uncle Walt, you just don't know how much I appreciate the way you stepped in to help us out. I know it seem like I'm all strong and everything, but sometimes I get weary not knowin' how I'm gonna work things out for everybody. I just love you to death for everything."

"Aw gal, you embarrassin' me, but what else you 'xpect me to do. Y'all family and I take care of family. Love y'all to death too."

Once she was out from under the dark cloud hovering over Scott's place, Beolia's transformation was impossible to ignore. Her metamorphosis was the catalyst responsible for infusing life into the dreams of Maude, Leotia, Walter, and Novella. Single- handedly she inspired them to pursue and execute luminous dreams, of which the origins were nightmares visited upon them over and over again, compliments of Scott.

The shy little girl who stood quietly on the sidelines watching Maude fight for their place in the Harringtion household, who shunned confrontation, and sought to love a father-figure who publicly rejected her became an outgoing woman, who was poised and articulate. Maude was captivated whenever she listened to Beolia reading her poems and essays. She had never heard a colored girl read or speak so eloquently. Everybody else was influenced by her charm and oratory gift as well. They wanted to speak like her and use the words she used when speaking.

Not only was she beautiful and poised, she proved to be a strategist capable of mapping out a future that taught all of them a lesson in moving beyond Scott's world.

"Maude, I've decided to leave North Carolina and go away to school up north in this place called Washington, D.C. The letters D.C. stand for the District of Columbia. I want to share my love for reading with other colored children. I'm going to become a teacher."

"Beolia, that sounds wonderful and I'm so proud of you. I gotta ask though. How we gonna pay for yo schoolin'? Heck, where you gonna live and how you gonna eat? We gotta have the answers to them questions too you know."

Beolia had all the answers. "I've been working on this plan for a long time and I've got it all worked out. You've gotta trust me. I've seen how responsible you are and I'm the same way. My friend Lucie mother's sister, Miss Mary, lives in Washington. She works for a rich white doctor and his family. They have so much work for her to do they've decided she needs some extra help. They asked if she knows of someone who can help. She told them she has the perfect person – that being me."

As Beolia laid out her plans, Maude knew she couldn't and didn't want stop her. She would have an opportunity to go after her dreams. *It's what Momma would've wanted.*

Everybody came down to the train station to see her off. All of them were crying and exchanging hugs – that is with the exception of Scott. He hung around in the background pre-occupied with cleaning his pipe, but just as she was getting ready to board the train, he approached.

"Beolia, I'm proud of you gal, and I knows Mary would be proud of you too. Take care of yo self." With that he shoved a pouch full of coins into her hand. At this point, she was feeling like Maude must have felt on many occasions. *Poppa sure is one hard man to figure out. Loving him is a chore.* Shaking her shoulders and clearing her mind of the past, she got on the train headed for Washington, D.C.

After two years in Washington, she sent a telegram announcing her engagement. Maude was so excited, she ran straight to Uncle Walt's house.

"Uncle Walt, Beolia is gettin' married. She met a college man and he done asked her to be his wife. I'm so happy, I don't know if I'm goin' or comin'."

She then broke the news to Leotia, Walter, and Novella. They were all jumping around the room. None of them could remember the last time they jumped and screamed for joy. The news got even better – she was coming back to the Gulf for the wedding.

Maybe, just maybe we're about to break that ol' curse Mr. Harrington been draggin' around with him since he became a free man. Beolia is the first, but I'm determined she won't be the last one of us to make somethin' good outta ourselves.

When she stepped off of the train, they were fascinated by the natural beauty and confidence she exuded. Behind her was a handsome, well-dressed man who looked as confident as she did. As soon as she saw them, a smile lit up her face and she started running.

They locked into a group hug, and were all talking at the same time. It didn't matter that no one could understand what anyone else was saying. Anxious to be introduced to Beolia's fiancé, Uncle Walt stepped in as the voice of calm.

"Shh, shh, y'all be quiet so we can meet Beolia's young man. Go 'head Honey and tell us who this is."

"It's so good to see all of you. I've missed you so much, and couldn't wait for the train to arrive here in the Gulf."

Maude was beaming with pride. *Oh my goodness, listen to her. She sounds like an angel from heaven speakin'.* Beolia had always been reserved and didn't ask for or require a lot of attention. While they knew she was different from most girls her age, they could not have imagined how accomplished and cultured she would become as a woman.

As Maude reflected back on growing up, she recalled that, for the most part, Beolia and Leotia had been the quiet ones. As soon as they arrived at Scott's house, Beolia realized and decided that the best way to get along with everybody was to avoid confrontation. Her loyalties were responsible for jumping into Maude's battles, but it was her preference to maintain peace.

Maude and Scott were the dominant and confrontational personalities. Mary was the strong silent type who kept them from crossing certain boundaries. Everybody else got pulled into the chaos that came with living with and loving Scott.

But all the while, she had been developing a strategy to change her course and put an end to the turbulence of her childhood. She discovered a path out of his complicated world fraught with sadness, secrets, and even death. Nothing was going to stop her from creating the life of her dreams.

Looking at the woman who returned to the Gulf after being away for two years, no one would have ever guessed she was the same Beolia who walked out of Scott's house one night broken and rejected. The woman standing before them was a conqueror. The trials and tribulations of her youth had not defeated her.

"I want to introduce all of you to Mr. Matthew Jackson. Matthew, I'm pleased to introduce you to my Uncle Walt, my big sister, Maude, brother, Walter, and two little sisters, Leotia and Novella."

He stepped forward to take the hands of Maude, Leotia, and Novella, gently placing a kiss on the back of each hand. "I am so pleased to make your acquaintances ladies."

"Hot damn, why Matthew, you don't have to be so formal bein' that you're 'bout to become family."

He wasn't offended, but welcomed Maude's bear hug. Leotia was captivated by him as well. *Why he sounds all good and proper even when he's laughin'.*

He then turned to Uncle Walt and Walter to shake their hands. After the introductions were completed, they took him to meet Scott.

"Poppa I would like for you to meet the man I'm going to marry. His name is Mr. Matthew Jackson. Matthew, I would like for you to meet my poppa. This is Mr. Scott Harrington."

Scott had never met anybody like Matthew and didn't know how to react to a well-educated colored man who wasn't intimidated by him. Matthew was oblivious to the piercing gray eyes and towering height. As a matter of fact, as soon as he started speaking, it was Scott who stuttered. Even the Seamore's didn't speak as eloquently as this young man.

"Mr. Harrington it is indeed a pleasure to meet you sir. I've heard fascinating things about your life."

"Yeah – well, well... Good to meet ya boy."

"Maybe when you have some time, you can tell me more. I would love to hear all about you. Do you think that's possible, sir?"

No one had ever described his life as fascinating and he couldn't fathom what was fascinating about it. Matthew made him feel important and that made him feel good. He couldn't get enough of hearing Matthew's praises and wasn't ready to end the evening, but it was getting late. His performance was exhausting to Uncle Walt, who was ready to leave. "C'mon Matthew. We'd better start gettin' back to my house. They've got a full day for you tomorrow."

Before they settled in for the night, he was ready to give his opinion. "Beolia, you got yo self a fine man. Poppa Scott wishin' you the best."

In response, she took both of his hands and stepped into his arms. He lost the battle with his standard reflex as he relaxed and proceeded to draw her closer into his embrace. This was an amazing woman he was holding in his arms. After everything she had been through since coming into his life, she still wanted his approval and blessing.

"Thank you Poppa. I'm so pleased to have your blessing. I was wondering if you would mind if I ask Uncle Walt to give me away at my wedding. He's been so good to all of us, and he doesn't have any daughters. So I was thinking I could show my gratitude for all he's done for this family by including him in the wedding. You understand don't you?"

His contrary nature lost another round when he overcame the urge to take offense. He didn't have a leg to stand on with an argument knowing there were plenty of times when she was hungry for and seeking his attention, but he wasn't willing to respond favorably. To be honest, there were plenty of times he had been downright mean to her and Maude, irritated at the thought of having to take care of another man's children, even though that man was dead.

Then, he couldn't dispute her claim as to Walter's impact after they lost Mary. Beolia had laid out the rationale for her decision, and he couldn't challenge her without alienating everyone else in the family.

"I'm okay with your decision. I know it'll make Walter a very happy man."

Beolia and Matthew left a lasting impression. Maude was walking around beaming like a proud parent.

"Otie, that Matthew is some fine young man. Thank Gawd every man ain't like Henry or Mr. Harrington. Uncle Walt – he's one of them good men too. He's a very lovin' man and ain't scared to let you know how much he loves you. Gal, I know it's awkward listenin' to me talk 'bout yo poppa like I do, but I swear fo' Gawd, I ain't never seen nothin' like him. Uncle Walt was a slave too, with the same master. Yet he don't go 'round actin' like we still back in them slavery days. I can tell you this – that Matthew has restored my faith in men."

"Beolia went through a very tough time there after Momma passed away. She deserves a good man and a good life. I'm so happy for her. I know the same thing is gonna happen for the rest of y'all. I can feel it. Now my man won't have to be a college man. He's just gotta be a strong man that's kind and loves me. I know I won't ever accept a man like Henry or Mr. Harrington in my life. I've had enough of that mess."

Walter was impressed as well and determined more than ever to save enough money to one day leave the Gulf. *I knew it –*

I knew there was more to life than what Poppa been showin' us. He knows about power and money, but he don't know what to do with power and money. Now Matthew, he knows how to live as good as them white folk, and that be exactly how I'm gonna live. Gonna do much more with power and money than Poppa ever dreamed of. Me and him both lovin' power and money, but that's 'bout all we got in common.

I don't want women folk scared of me like they scared of him. I'm gonna be a successful man like that Matthew and it's gonna happen sooner than Poppa think. That money I'm keepin' over at Uncle Walt's house is growin' every week. Gonna be enough to move on up outta here soon. Walter Seamore Harrington is gonna be a big shot one of these days. Watch and see.

Chapter 22
From the Gulf to the Hills

Maude was the first to act upon Beolia's influence, and she had an announcement to make. "I've been thinkin' a lot 'bout my life. After seein' what Beolia accomplished, I'm more convinced now than ever there's a better life out there for me. I just gotta get out there and find it. So I've decided to go up north. Much further north than Beolia went."

Scott saw the looks of terror on their faces and had to do something to stop her. "No way – Maude you ain't leavin' here. I forbid it. You stayin' right here with your family."

"You've gotta be kiddin' iffin you think you can forbid me to do anything. I'm a grown woman and I come and go as I please, whether it be in the State of North Carolina or not. Now I've done my very best to take care of these children before and after Momma passed away. I even offered to take them to live with me and you put a stop to that. I've thought about it and I'm doin' it. Ain't nothin' you can do to stop me."

"You bein' real selfish gal. You know these chillun need you and all's you can think about is yo self."

"Y'all hear her don't ya? She's leavin' y'all without so much as a thought so's she can run up north and get into Gawd knows what."

"Don't listen to a thing he says. He's just tryin' to scare y'all and make you think I don't love y'all, but y'all know better than that. He's an ass."

"Maude, you stop talkin' to Poppa like that. He just wants you to stay here with us. He don't mean no harm. Do you Poppa?"

"Vella, don't speak fo' me. If she's that selfish, y'all just need to let her go."

"Like I said, he's just tryin' to scare y'all. As a matter of fact, I'll take y'all with me."

"You will not take my chillun outta this house. The only way you get to do that is over my dead body."

"I swear fo' Gawd, you're the most irritatin' man on earth. I'll tell you what, over your dead body ain't such a bad idea."

She had come too far to let him win this time. After months of struggling with what to do with her life, she finally reached the conclusion that the world was much bigger than the Gulf, and if Beolia was brave enough to leave and find happiness, so could she.

Some of her friends had started moving up north to find work and create new lives. They sent photographs back home to show off their fancy clothes and the jazz clubs where they partied. Maude and the friends who were still in the Gulf would look at the photos over and over again, wishing they were living up north and enjoying the good life too. Rather than being envious, she was going to join them.

The letters mentioned the steel mills in a place called Pittsburgh, Pennsylvania, where they were willing to hire coloreds. Maude and her friend, Norma, were convinced Pittsburgh was the place they wanted to be. Maybe they would find husbands who worked at the mills.

As excited as she was about her plans to move, she was struggling with guilt over the thought of abandoning Walter, Leotia, and Novella. Leaving them was almost too much to bear, until she considered what the future would be like if she stayed in the Gulf. There was no way she was willing to spend the rest of her life dealing with Scott.

She received another letter from Pittsburgh. Mabelle wrote about life in a neighborhood called the "Hills."

Dear Maude,

Y'all gotta come up here and see this place. It's much different than the Gulf. They got mills, mines, and other kinds of businesses hiring coloreds all over the place. We even live close to other kinds of people too. Some of 'em are Russians, Armenians, Greeks, Chinese and Jews. We all get along okay. Not perfect, but much better than colored and whites get along down there. Gotta close this letter now, but tell everybody I said 'Hi.' Can't wait 'til you come up here to live.

Very Truly Yours,

Mabelle.

Walter, Leotia, and Novella, got caught up in hearing about the excitement and were anxious to leave too.

It was Norma who came up with the perfect idea. "Maude, why don't you bring 'em along with us? 'Sides, they ain't little children no more and you ain't gotta babysit them all the time. As a matter of fact, they can pitch in and there'll be more of us to help each other out. Think about it. It makes good sense to me."

"In one of my letters, I read that some Chinese people are hirin' teenagers to help out in their laundry businesses and sometimes cleanin' up their homes. Maybe Walter could work at one of the steel mills for a few hours a day. I hear sometimes foremen at the mills are willin' to pay colored boys a few dollars to help clean up."

The relocation to Pittsburgh was the answer Maude had been looking for. *I really don't have the details 'bout how we're gonna make it, but I'm gonna go for it and take them with me. We leavin' this place and all its misery here with Mr. Harrington.*

So now here she was standing toe to toe with him yet again, fighting for freedom and happiness.

"Gal, you can dream 'bout killin' me all you want, but my chilluns ain't leavin the Gulf, and I'm still sayin' you wouldn't be goin' iffin you cared anything 'bout them. You are one ungrateful wench if I ever saw one. After I got rid of that Henry for you, this is how you repay me?"

"You need to stay here so's we can all be here for one another. I need some help with these chilluns and that's what you're gonna do. You need to know your place Maude. I'm real sick and tired of your bad mouth and bad attitude. Why can't you just be grateful, shut up, and try and get along?"

Her only regret was that she couldn't find anything in the room to hit him over the head with.

This insufferable man is only thinkin' 'bout makin' himself comfortable. He can't even see what I'm tryin' to do here – give him some relief and give my brother and sisters a way out of this mess he created the moment he walked into Momma's life.

Backing down wasn't an option. "Look Mr. Harrington, it's time for me to leave the Gulf, and that's exactly what I'm gonna do. Like I said, I'm a grown woman, been one for some time now, and there ain't a thing you can do to stop me."

"Whatever the hell you and your white brothers did to Henry, I didn't ask you to do. I came runnin' over here to get away from the situation – not for you to do whatever it is that you did, and I'm certain I never want to find out the details."

"Now I'm offerin' you a solution to raisin' these children the right way. I'll be leavin' in about a month from now and you can either let them come with me, or you had better be prepared to handle this situation by yourself. I'll come home as often as I can to see 'bout them, but I have to do this for myself. For once, think about somebody besides yourself. You've had your life, allow them a chance at one."

He saw anger on Walter's face, fear on Leotia's, and confusion on Novella's. He was defeated. If he got in the way of what she wanted, the looks of anger, fear, and confusion would haunt him everytime he looked at them, reminding him that he was responsible. He gave in, and by the end of the next month, they were living in Pittsburgh.

Life in the Hills was unlike anything they had experienced. Maude found a job in a laundry within a week after arriving in Pittsburgh. One of the owners hired Leotia and Novella to assist his other housekeeper. Walter was hired to clean-up at the steel mill.

To Maude's surprise, she was told to enroll them in a school where the students were the multi-cultural children her friend spoke of. The rest of them were going to get an education like Beolia.

Momma, they all gonna wind up doin' good if I have anything to do with it. I promise. If you just keep watchin' over us with the Lawd, I know we're gonna make it.

Everyday away from the Gulf increased her confidence. Their dreams, however, were much bigger than their finances. It would be impossible to survive unless they did something creative like consolidating resources.

Their apartment was in a wood-framed house. There was one medium-sized bedroom with two additional tiny bedrooms. A wooden constructed outhouse stood close by since there was no indoor plumbing system or functional sewer lines.

Maude and Norma slept in single beds in the larger bedroom, while Walter, Leotia, and Novella slept in one of the small bedrooms and Norma's two sisters slept in the other. Although cramped, they were happy with the living arrangements. At least they were all together.

Neighbors from the south, as well as the immigrants, used their farming skills to plant food gardens. Through generosity and pooling of resources, everybody in the neighborhood at least had vegetables to eat when meat was a luxury they couldn't afford.

While Maude worked hard, she was also becoming a social butterfly. She no longer had Mary to worry about, or the weight attached to the responsibility of saving everybody else in the house from Scott. So when the workday was over on Fridays, she dressed up and headed out to the jazz clubs to listen to the bands and dance late into the night.

Her statuesque frame and elegant clothes were magnetic. As soon as she walked into the club, all eyes were drawn to her. She walked about as if she owned the joint. Her loud and hearty laughter was infectious and the party crowd loved the energy she brought to the club. She was having the time of her life.

Maude and Norma felt like celebrities the moment they stepped into the club. Usually the first person to greet them was a photographer. "Okay lady with the big smile. Give me one of those spicy poses. Yeah girl, that's what I'm talkin' about. Now hold up that glass like you've got real champagne in it. I swear, them folks back in your hometown gonna think you livin' high off the hog."

He kept teasing Maude as she posed for more pictures and she loved the attention. Not even the blinding light from the photographer's gigantic flash bulb bothered her. She could imagine what people back home would be saying when they saw the pictures. *That Maude and her friends look like they ain't never been po' a day in their lives. They sho' look like they come a long ways from when they was livin' back here in the Gulf.*

It was Friday afternoon and the workday was coming to an end. She was already anticipating getting dressed up for another night out on the Hill District's jazz scene. It was to be a pivotal turning point in the direction her life would be taking.

Leotia and Novella were fascinated as they watched her getting dressed for the night out on the town. They giggled over the transformation taking place as she finished buttoning the jacket to the gray flannel suit trimmed with black velvet.

The stately and elegant woman who stood before them was breathtaking. After she slipped on her wireless glasses, she donned a small gray and black pillbox hat. The black birdcage veil attached to the hat added a hint of mystique to her glamourous look.

"Oh Maude, you look like one of them ladies that be in the moving pictures."

She smiled at Novella's compliment, but inside was bursting with pride and excited about the night out. She felt like pinching herself to make sure she was the woman whose beauty her little sisters were admiring. Checking in the mirror one last time, she was more than pleased. She did look like one of those starlets who lived in that place people called Hollywood.

"Now y'all be good and don't be makin' too much noise to get any of these neighbors mad. Make sure you get into bed before it gets too late. Okay, since its Friday night, go on and stay up 'til 'bout 10 o'clock. Love y'all. Now I gotta go. I'm ready for some excitement."

The smooth jazz sounds that greeted Maude and Norma immediately put them in a partying mood. "Now Maude, this is what I'm talkin' 'bout. Don't that girl sound just like that jazz singer they call Ethel Waters? Let's hurry up and get in here before we miss the good stuff bound to happen tonight."

The lighting was dim, and thick smoke made it difficult to recognize anybody who wasn't up close. As she moved towards the table where their friends were seated, Maude felt all eyes on her. *Let'em look 'cause there's plenty to look at. It's been another hard week and I'm due for a good time. I sure hope somethin' special is 'bout to happen.*

"Work it gal. Shake what ya Momma done gave you." She welcomed the cat calls.

She had just about reached the table when she noticed him. He was extremely tall and very good looking. He reminded her of someone, but she couldn't figure out whom. *Damn he's fine and a tall drink of water I can't get enough of. Wonder where he's on his way to, or who he's on his way to.*

This was her night. He stopped right in front of her. Picking up her gloved hand, he lightly planted a kiss on the back. "Why good evening lovely Maude, my name is James Wilson and I'm pleased to finally make your acquaintance. I've been seeing you in here every Friday night and was determined not to let another weekend go by without introducing myself to the woman I'm determined to marry."

Lawd have mercy. I'm 'bout to drop to my knees. They're knockin' together some kinda bad anyhow and I can't stand up much longer. Maude, straighten up gal. You can't let him know how charmin' he is.

When she was ready to speak, she gave him a mischievous grin, and flirted back. "Well, Mr. James Wilson, we can't have you goin' another weekend without the two of us gettin' to know each other, now can we? What do you have in mind for us kind sir?"

"Here take my arm and let me start showing you just what I've got in mind. You do know you're gonna be mine don't you?"

She placed her arm in the crook of his and as they walked back to the table responded, "Maybe it's you whose gonna be mine. Ever thought 'bout that?"

She was everything he imagined her to be. He leaned over and whispered into her ear, "Girl, I'm definitely lovin' that Southern drawl you got there. I'm yours – all yours. "

She kept sneaking peeks at him throughout the night. *My Gawd he's a good lookin' man and I'm pinchin' myself to make sure I'm actually sittin' here with him. I ain't gonna let this rascal know how I'm feelin' though. He's already too cocky, but I love it. I like everything about him. Hope it stays that way.*

Yes, she was captivated. She was impressed with his smooth way of taking charge of what was becoming a first date, and her heart was pounding with the anticipation of becoming his woman. Still, there was something nagging at her and she couldn't quite figure it out. *Makes no never mind to me. Whatever it is, it ain't important. I'm just gonna enjoy this special evenin' with this fine man. I'm havin' too good a time to let any negative thoughts ruin my evenin'.*

She picked up the drink he ordered, took a sip, and threw back her head to laugh at one of his jokes. Yes, life these days was definitely different. The phrase 'almost perfect' danced around in her head, but life up until their arrival in Pittsburgh had taught her to remain reserved no matter how good things seemed. There was always somebody or something she had to be concerned about or take care of.

She rode back to the apartment on a cloud. Coming back to earth and her responsibilities, she stepped into the other bedroom to look in on Leotia, Walter, and Novella. The sound of Walter snoring traveled across the room to where she stood. "Look at 'em. He swear fo' Gawd he don't snore, and he's callin' hogs like there's no tomorrow." Looking further into the room, she saw Novella nestled up against Leotia, both of them seemingly at peace. All was well. *Maybe, just maybe...* "Sweet dreams y'all." She closed the door.

She wanted to believe she had done the right thing by taking them out of the Gulf, but struggled with bouts of insecurity and occasionally questioned her decisions. *Momma, I pray I'm takin' care of them like you would want me to. I know you loved him, but he got too much devil in him fo' me. He was makin' everybody so unhappy, and I just had to get away if I wanted the chance to really be happy. I couldn't leave them behind though, so I brought'em with me. Please show me some sign to let me know you're watchin' over us and that I did the right thing.*

Unfortunately, trouble was on the horizon. Leotia and Novella were unhappy working for the wife of the owner of the laundry. When they arrived after school, she was waiting at the front door with a long list of chores although the live-in housekeeper was at the house all day. They weren't in a position to challenge her directions or complain about her treatment. If they wanted to stay together, they had to help Maude and Norma.

On Saturdays they worked the entire day with only a brief break that was designated as lunch time. They were forced to eat in a small pantry sitting on stools without a table. There was nothing appetizing about the sticky white rice with a few tiny pieces of meat in a small bowl. The measly meal was washed down with a cup of unsweetened tea. Fed up with being the objects of the boss' mistreatment, they went to Maude.

"Maude that woman is mean to us. She makes us work 'til we 'bout to drop and then only feed us scraps. Everytime we ask a question, she starts hollerin' and sayin' stuff like we stupid. One thing I know for sure – I'm not stupid. I don't wanna go back there. Tell her Otie. Tell Maude how that scrawny little woman is mean to us."

There was no way she could give into instinct and confront the woman. Things were different this time. They were hundreds of miles away from the Gulf and she couldn't afford to lose her job. She had no other alternative but to give her boss Leotia's and Novella's resignations.

Two less salaries in the household landed them in big trouble. She wound up in the dreaded position of having to enlist the help of the man from whom she wanted total emancipation. The thought had been lingering since the day she arrived in Pittsburgh, but she refused to dwell on it. Accepting money from him would place them at his mercy once he realized they couldn't make it without his help.

Damn, I've gotta find a way to keep them here with me. I've thought of everything, but nothin' I come up with seems to work. I can't let Otie and Vella go back to work for that woman. I'll wind up in jail if I strangle her.

There's only one thing left for me to do and I'm sick about it. I'm gonna have to ask for some help from Mr. Harrington. These are his children too. He's been hoardin' money ever since them Seamores gave him that raise on his job. It's time for him to take some responsibility.

I don't understand why he's hoardin' money anyway. As far as I can tell, he ain't spendin' much. I honestly believe he uses it as power – somethin' else he learned from them Seamores. Well, he's just gonna have to part with some of it and start sendin' it up here to help shelter, feed, and cloth these children.

Initially he honored the agreement to send money per schedule. Then the missed payments started, leaving her uncertain about how the bills were going to get paid. How on earth could she continue to take care of three children without any help? Whenever he missed a month, she asked the supervisors at the laundry for permission to work overtime.

Walter's part-time salary was welcomed, but the loss of two salaries was being felt in a big way.

Scott had missed sending payment four months in a row and she had to tell them. They knew something was wrong because it was Friday night and she wasn't dressed to go out. The foreboding news was evidenced by the somber expression on her face.

"Y'all know I love you like you were my own children, and I would move heaven and earth for you. I've been tryin' to keep us all together like I know Momma would want me to do, but Mr. Harrington won't send me the money needed to help take care of y'all properly. Whenever I send him a telegram, I'm not even gettin' a response. I'm so sorry, but I'm gonna have to send you back to the Gulf so he can do what he's supposed to do. I'll continue to do what I can, and will come back home as often as I can, but I have no other choice."

Leotia and Novella couldn't hold back the tears. "Maude, let us go back to work. This time, we'll just have to take whatever she throws our way, but we can take it. We know what to expect now, so we'll just go back to work."

"No Otie, I can't do that Baby. I refuse to put y'all back with some strange woman who ain't treatin y'all right. I kept my hands off of her the first time y'all told me what she was doin', but I swear for Gawd, the next time I wouldn't be able to restrain myself, and will break every bone in her body. Look, I promise I'm not throwin' y'all away. I'll be 'round to see 'bout you. If me and James get married, I'll be able bring you back up here."

Her efforts to keep them together had not gone unnoticed. Although he was just as upset as Leotia and Novella, Walter couldn't help but feel sorry for her. *I can't imagine us livin' in the Gulf without her. She's always been there for everybody in our family. When things seemed hopeless, she always found an answer. When everybody else was afraid to speak up or stand up to Poppa, she was more than willin' to do so. During that horrible period when Momma was sick, she took care of her. Even when she moved outta the house, we all knew the minute she was needed, she would come runnin'.*

Going back to the Gulf with her still livin' up here in Pittsburgh is 'bout as foreign to me as me livin' on the moon. Damn Poppa, he's got her backed up against a wall and she can't figure a way out this time.

"C'mon y'all, Maude's done everything in her power to make this work, but she can't keep doin' if Poppa won't help out. Let's go back and don't make her feel guilty. She's feelin' bad enough."

He would go back to the Gulf, but damn it, he wasn't going to stay. The next time he was in a position to leave, it would be for good. Although he had never met him, he felt a certain kinship with Herbert. He was certain about his decision and clearly understood what Herbert realized when he was a young man. In order to be and feel like a real man, you had to distance yourself from Scott. To remain under his roof was an emasculating experience and Walter, just like Herbert, wasn't willing to let him get away with the very thing he held against those who owned him as a slave.

The day the train pulled into the station to take them back to the Gulf was yet another day overcast with sadness and the tremendous sense of loss that constantly dogged them. Maude was more upset with herself than with Scott.

How long does this sadness have to last; how many times do we have to be separated; when will life really begin? Look at 'em – they look like they've lost hope in everybody. I can't blame them. Even I let 'em down this time.

Momma, I'm so sorry. I tried – really I did. I thought I had gotten them away from all that hurt and misery. Lawd, I can't stand to see'em like this, but then again, they're always lookin' hurt, 'cause that man is always hurtin' 'em.

She had to focus on being angry with him. Otherwise, she would have been a mess, sobbing and crying in front of them. She knew they were upset about the separation, but didn't want them to feel as if the world had come to an end. She was determined to get them back to the Gulf in one piece. When Maude was angry, she was fearless. Channeling her anger, she reminded them of a few things.

"Look y'all, we're forever bound by blood and spirit. Ain't nothin' in this world can separate us. All y'all gotta do is call and I'll come runnin'. Y'all know I'll fight the devil and win for y'all. Just remember, as soon as you holler, Maude will come runnin'. I'll visit as much as possible."

"All aboard, All aboard." The train's conductor was instructing them to board the car for coloreds. After giving them each another round of hugs and kisses, Walter, Leotia, and Novella boarded the train. They were on their way back to Scott.

She missed them terribly, but wasn't allowed to wallow in self-pity or sadness for long because James wasn't having it.

"Maude you're one helluva woman. You mean to tell me no man had the smarts to make you his woman before you got outta North Carolina. What's wrong with them boys down there? They blind, cripple, and crazy, is that it?"

"Oh James stop it."

"No, no, I mean it. All this woman and they don't know what to do with you. Girl, you just come on over here and let me hold you real close. Maybe I'll do more than just some holding. You feel like more than holding? Huh?"

He drove her crazy when he spoke to her like this. "James, iffin I come over there, I definitely want more than just some holdin'. What else you got in store for me?"

"Iffin? That Southern drawl just cracks me up. Well iffin you gonna come over here, hurry up. I dare you."

He was in a position to care for and treat her in ways she never even dreamed about. In the past, she never allowed herself to fantasize. Being with him felt like a dream where everything she ever wished for was coming true.

James constantly spoke of his admiration for what she had accomplished despite growing up in the south and in Scott's home.

"Maude, do you know what a special lady you are? Not only are you beautiful, but you are a bold woman. Babe, you've fought and won some battles plenty of men would have been scared to fight. From what you've been telling me, I don't know if I could've survived ol' Scott. Somebody would've died a long time ago. But you survived, and girl you took it upon yourself to raise your sisters and brother. That ain't easy for nobody. I take my hat off to you Babe. If you'll let me, I swear I'll take good care of you for the rest of my life."

She never saw her life as a series of accomplishments, but one with a mountain of responsibility that couldn't be shirked. James was teaching her to appreciate her own beauty and strength. She could totally relax and let down her guard. There wasn't the weight of responsibility of taking care of him. He was only too eager to show her that he was capable of taking care of himself, as well as her.

The long and grueling shift at the mill couldn't even discourage him from stopping by each evening to see about her. "Tell me about your day. I bet the laundry can get mighty hot after being there amongst that equipment for hours."

"Yeah, it's some kinda hot in that place. You know James, as uncomfortable as it is there, it don't even compare with some of the discomfort I've had to deal with during my lifetime. Besides, seein' you after work makes me forget about the heat and everything else. Other than the usual stuff, not much happened."

"Well whatever happened today, just come and rest in my arms. Yeah, just like that. Now tell me, have you heard from your people, and how's everybody doing?"

"Well, I haven't heard anything bad as of today. So let's just hope that means everything is okay. It just breaks my heart that I had to send them back. They were countin' on me and I thought I was gonna change their lives for the better. Sometimes I feel like such a failure 'cause I had to give them back to the very man I was tryin' to protect them from."

"Babe stop beating yourself up. That was a whole lot of responsibility and you are a champion. He's their father and it was his responsibility to at least help you out financially. You had no choice but to send them back. I'll tell you what. If you like, I'll take a trip with you. I know they must be missing you. It'll be good for them to see you. That's so much better than getting letters and telegrams."

Just thinking about him made her feel safe and secure. *My man's a take charge man without bein' overbearin'. He knows how to keep me laughin' without bein' silly. He's debonair without bein' flashy. None of that show-off stuff, just a real fine lookin' gentleman who makes any woman proud to be with him. I didn't even know a man could make a woman feel this way.*

He ain't nothin' like Mr. Harrington or Henry. They were always threatened by somethin' I did or said. Not my James. He's a strong man, and don't have to fight for power with me over every little thing. With him, I can be whatever and whomever I wanna be. Iffin (Oops – he's always teasin' me 'bout how I say "iffin"), but iffin I wanna cry, he lets me cry without takin' advantage of me. If I want some lovin', there he is all ready, willin', and very much able to give me the kind of lovin' I need.

James had more in mind than happy. He wanted a lifetime with her and proposed. Maude had found the man whom she described to Leotia during their conversation about Matthew. There was only one way to respond to the perfect man. They were married in Pittsburgh with only the Best Man and Maid of Honor in attendance.

Immediately after the wedding, they took the train to North Carolina so she could introduce him to the family. This train ride was different because finally it wasn't one of separation.

When the train pulled into Union Station in Washington, D.C., Beolia and Matthew boarded, and they traveled the rest of the way to North Carolina together. Maude could hardly contain herself thinking about the very happy occasion for which they were returning to the Gulf. *I do wish Momma was here to see all of us together for this reunion. She would be so happy.*

When the train pulled into the station, Leotia, Walter, and Novella were anxiously waiting.

"Maude, Beolia, over here, over here. Here we are. Oh my Gawd – I mean God, look at them Otie. Look at them."

They looked elegant. As usual, Maude looked as if she was in charge of everything until her new husband descended the steps of the train car. Walter, Leotia, and Novella rushed to meet them.

James and Matthew collected their luggage and waited patiently. Off in the distance Scott was looking indifferent, and puffing on his pipe. After everybody had calmed down, he started walking towards them. For reasons unknown, a peculiar feeling started to come over Maude.

Oh Gawd, as good as I was feelin' on my way here, the minute he starts comin' my way, I get all anxious and upset, ready for the next fight. I've gotta calm down. My life is too good right now to let him get to me. Maude, just take a deep breath. You've got James with you now and James ain't gonna be scared of him.

When he finally reached them, she started with the introductions. "James, this is... Oh my Gawd." She looked at Scott, then back at James, then back at Scott. The mysterious feeling she sometimes felt could now be explained. Despite everything she loved about him, James' good looks were the same good looks of none other than Scott's.

I must be losin' my mind. How in Gawd's name did I fall in love with someone who looks like the man who caused so much trouble and heartache in my life? What was I thinkin' and why didn't I realize this much sooner? I prob'ly would've run for the door iffin I had realized who James looks like. I wouldn't have let him near me *'cause all I would've been doin' was comparin' him to Mr. Harrington and anybody like him, I don't want nowhere near me.*

She was having an epiphany. *They may have the same good looks, but my man's spirit ain't nothin' like his. If anything, James' spirit is much like Uncle Walt's, and Uncle Walt don't act nothin' like the devil hisself. You know, this only proves a man can be the most handsome creature walkin' Gawd's earth, but iffin his spirit is ugly and twisted, then he be ugly and twisted. Now iffin that same handsome man's spirit be like James or Uncle Walt, then a woman has no other choice but to lose herself in him and love him like there ain't no tomorrow. Yep – that's it. The spirit makes all the difference in the world.*

There was no denying that Scott was indeed a very attractive man. History had proven that for many years. His arrogance, unfriendly nature, and master/slave mentalilty made it difficult to focus on his handsome features unless you were one of the unfortunate women who had fallen under his spell. Beside, Maude knew only too well the devastation that had everything to do with his looks.

I know deep down in my heart I wanna love him. Can't deny that, but he's so damned mean-spirited and unpredictable I can't ever feel one hundred percent secure in the word "love." Now iffin he was just more like Uncle Walt – pleasin' to look at as well as pleasin' to live with then maybe him and me would've gotten along much better. He ain't gonna change though.

"Maude, Baby, are you okay?"

Although Scott tried to act otherwise, she could tell he respected James. *Just like I thought, it's hard to dismiss a man like my James, whose pleasin' to be around and behavin' like a strong man ought to behave. My man is truly amazin'.*

Ya know I'm startin' to really understand this now. Men who are confident and ain't under the influence of Mr. Harrington's reputation can hold their own with him. These are the men he's forced to respect. He wouldn't ever admit it, but he respects a person's strength.

Then there are those times when you least expect it, he comes to your defense and make you believe he actually cares. Like that time he defended my honor with Henry. He did it twice – told Henry that if he put his hands on me again, he would make him pay. He made him pay alright. He made Henry disappear into thin air. Then just when I was gettin' comfortable with my dream of lovin' him comin' true, I find myself drawn into yet another battle. That's when once again I declare I ain't ever gonna let myself get close to him.

Maude was the self-appointed event planner for the reunion. "Walter, Leotia, Novella – y'all come on and join us. We've got plenty of catchin' up to do and I wanna keep y'all close to me while I'm here."

Beolia turned to Matthew. "What did I tell you? She's our momma bear and won't let her cubs out of her sight. Maude, maybe they don't want to stay up under you all the time."

"Beolia you crazy gal. Of course they wanna be up under me all the time. They're my babies. You're my baby too. You just think you too grown 'cause you got Matthew there, but you're still my baby. Y'all ready to go visitin' with us?"

"Yeah Maude." They weren't teasing and feigning agreement to stick close by. They meant it.

The reunion was a week of revelations. Leotia observed Maude's and Beolia's relationships with their husbands and reached certain conclusions about her own life. *Maude and Beolia look real happy. They found husbands who took them away from all this misery, sadness, talk about roots, geechee women, and witchcraft. I'm gonna find me a good man and he's gonna take me away from this miserable life Poppa forcin' us to live.*

Walter, impressed with James and Matthew, was even more determined to carry out his plan. *I can't wait. Soon as I get up north and make my way, I'm comin' back too and they all gonna be excited 'bout the successful man I've become.*

Novella was just happy they were all together again and celebrating. She had no clue about the thoughts Leotia and Walter were entertaining, and how those plans would be life-changing for her as well.

By the time the reunion ended, two of the Harrington children had made up their minds to leave, and soon. Leotia was determined to find a husband to take her away, and Walter was determined to find a good job to take him away.

Scott was losing control over their lives. The time they spent in Pittsburgh had given them insight into life without him. Furthermore, Maude and Beolia had proven that it was possible to find happiness outside of his small world where he was the master and everybody else was relegated to indentured servant, or worse, slave. Leotia and Walter were positioning themselves to move on.

Chapter 23
Beolia – Gone Too Soon

During the ride back to Washington, Beolia kept daydreaming about the family reunion in the Gulf. If she were any happier, she would burst. All of them had been affected by the week together. Their jubilation could not be contained, and new dreams would not be denied.

Unlike so many times before, the tears that constantly flowed throughout the reunion were from joy rather than sorrow. She couldn't wipe the smile off of her face when thinking about how Scott got sucked into the celebration although he tried to act as if he wasn't affected.

She was ready to return to Washington for some much needed rest. It wasn't because she was exhausted from the family reunion. The feelings of nauseousness and malaise had returned.

At first she had been able to control the mysterious cough, and thought the discomfort in her chest was just that – not pain. About a month before they took the trip to the Gulf, the coughing stopped and she was relieved to be feeling better. It returned a couple of days before they left the Gulf.

On the morning they boarded the train to return to Washington it was difficult to control the coughing and she was weak. Her condition was troubling to Maude.

"Beolia, I don't like the sound of that cough. I thought you told me you had gotten rid of it. As soon as you get back to Washington, I want you to see a doctor immediately. A cough from a cold shouldn't be lingerin' 'round like that. Promise me you'll see the doctor as soon as you get back home."

"Maude stop being so overprotective. I'm certain I'll be fine?"

"Well, I'm not gonna stop bein' overprotective, and I got good reason to be concerned. You know we learned early in life what happens when you wait too late to get to the doctor, and I don't want no repeat of what happened years ago. Do you understand me? Matthew, you make sure she sees the doctor, and I want a report."

In between fits of coughing Beolia kept trying to assure Maude she was okay. "Matthew, I keep telling you she's just too bossy, but I love her to death."

"Now Maude, you know for yourself Momma used to cough over everything and nothing was wrong. That was just the way she was made, coughing and sneezing over everything."

She wanted to accept Beolia's explanation for the troublesome coughing, but years after Mary's untimely death, the constant reminder of the tragedy she blamed on Scott's ignorance remained with her.

We've had too good a time to be thinkin' 'bout sicknesses that take people outta here. If Beolia says she's fine, then she's fine. I gotta stop thinkin' bad stuff always 'round the corner.

She decided to change the subject by starting a conversation with James about something totally different.

Within a week after returning to Washington, the cough was much worse and accompanied by blood-tinged sputum. Beolia was running a high fever, while alternating between chills and night sweats. Not only was she left feeling fatigued, the decline in weight started and nothing she ate stayed down. She was terrified at the sight of more blood.

"Matthew, I think we had better go to see the doctor. I found some blood."

"You found blood – where, and how much?"

"It's quite a bit and everytime I cough. What do you think?"

"This doesn't sound good. We had better do what Maude told us to do."

"I'm scared. How soon do you think we can get an appointment? Whatever is going on seems to be serious."

"I'm not taking any chances, and I don't care if we don't have an appointment. We're going to see the doctor right now. Just let me get your coat. I'm not leaving the hospital until they give us some definite answers."

It was serious and they couldn't leave the hospital. The doctors had devastating news. She had contracted an infection called "Consumption." The news got worse when they were told it was lethal and contagious. They questioned Matthew about his health and performed a series of tests. The family tragedy was on a rampage again. He was infected as well, and they both wound up being quarantined.

Maude received a telegram from Matthew's family. She was told not to come to Washington because they couldn't have visitors.

"I'll be damned iffin I ain't gonna go to Washington. I'm not a damned visitor. I'm Beolia's big sister, like her second momma, and ain't nobody gonna apply no rules 'bout visitors to me. They can't keep me from my sister, and iffin I gotta bring her back to Pittsburgh and take care of her myself, then so be it. But ain't nobody gonna tell me I can't come and see 'bout my sister."

When she arrived, she was once again told they couldn't have visitors. Her first encounter was at the nurse's station.

"Excuse me. My name is Maude Wilson, and I'm here to see my sister, Mrs. Beolia Jackson."

"Sorry, she can't have any visitors. She's in quarantine, and nobody but hospital staff can go in."

"I understand she's in quarantine, but I'm family, and need to see her and let her know I'm here to take care of her."

"Look Miss, I said you can't see her. Now leave your name and we'll let her know you stopped by."

"Now look you skinny little heifer, I'm not movin' until you go and get somebody who can give you permission to let me see my sister. Now I know I don't look like no fool, so you had better stop talkin' to me like I'm one. You've got five seconds to get me to my sister or else I'm gonna tear this place up until I get to Beolia. Now move outta my way."

Other hospital personnel came running to the defense of the nurse. They surrounded her and threatened to call the police to remove her from the building.

"Go ahead and call the damn police. I ain't playin' with y'all. I got word my sister is bad off sick, and I'm here to see 'bout her. Ain't nobody, and I mean nobody gonna remove me from this place. Who's in charge anyway? None of y'all look like y'all know what you're doin'."

One of the doctors who were treating Beolia saw beyond Maude's fury. He saw fear, as well as the protective nature usually characteristic of maternal instinct. Although she stood completely surrounded by the staff threatening to take action to remove her from the hospital, she wasn't the least bit intimidated. He saw what everyone else perceived as hostility, but recognized it as the look he had seen on the faces of mothers watching over their children. Moved by her determination, he felt compelled to step in.

"Look Mrs. Wilson, I'm Doctor Foster, and one of the doctors treating your sister. I know you're concerned, and nobody is going to make you leave. Here, come sit with me and I'll discuss what's going on with Beolia. Don't you worry – nobody's going to remove you from this hospital. Let's you and I talk."

They went into a waiting room and she wound up telling him their family's history. He sat there amazed that Maude and Beolia had even survived the story she was sharing. There was no way he was going to separate them at a time like this.

"This is what I'll do. I will get permission for restricted visits. But Mrs. Wilson, you've got to follow my strict orders. I need to treat Beolia and Matthew, and I can't have you getting sick on me too. Promise me you'll do as I ask, and we've got a deal."

Grateful somebody understood, she promised to follow his orders to the letter. He was able to get approval to let her visit Beolia. She was not allowed to go into the room, but watched from an outside room enclosed by glass. The bed was surrounded by a strange looking tent, and the hospital staff that went into the room was dressed in protective clothing from head to toe. She went to the hospital everyday just to stand watch over Beolia and Matthew. She was praying for a miracle.

"My Gawd, I can't believe that's her lyin' there not even knowin' she's in the world. Lawd Jesus, how in the world did this happen? She's been through so much and finally found herself a good man. They've made a good life for themselves and got a lotta livin' left if You'll allow it. Please just do this for us."

After watching over Beolia, she would go over to the waiting room outside of Matthew's quarantined room to support his family. She kept Walter, Leotia, and Novella informed about Beolia's and Matthew's grave conditions. They begged her to let them come to Washington.

"I can't do that. Y'all gotta understand. I had to fight with a whole lotta people. They threatened to call the police on me and everything, but I stood my ground. The Lawd must've been lookin' out for me 'cause he sent an angel in the person of Doctor Foster. He really cares 'bout people whether they colored or white. I told him our story, and he went to great lengths just to let me see Beolia from a distance.

I promised him I wouldn't make him regret his decision to help me. I'm never goin' back on my promise after all that man went through for me. I'll keep y'all informed, and hopefully in a couple of weeks I'll be takin' her and Matthew back to Pittsburgh with me so I can take care of them until they get back on their feet."

James heard the exhaustion in her voice during their conversation over the party-line phone. She didn't sound like his strong wife, but kept trying to put a positive spin on a critical situation.

"Oh James, I'm so glad to hear from you. You don't know how much I miss bein' there with you. I'll be comin' home soon though. Prob'ly will be bringin' Beolia and Matthew with me. They're gonna be needin' somebody to take care of 'em 'til they get back on their feet."

"I'm missing you too Babe, but don't go making all kinds of plans until we hear something definite from the doctors. What're they saying?"

She didn't answer the question because the doctors' reports were in complete opposition with the positive report she was trying to convince him with. The hoarseness and cracking in her voice were blended with a tone of uncertainty. Although she kept trying to deny the inevitable, James could tell Maude had lost all hope, especially when Matthew passed away first.

It was a couple of weeks later when she awakened one morning feeling like she couldn't even get out of the bed. Although no one had said death was imminent within hours when she left the hospital the night before, she sensed the end would come before the day was over. Looking out of the window, she saw an overcast and dreary day. The heaviness in the air was ominous. Breathing was difficult for some reason and she felt light-headed. As she moved around the small rented room, her legs felt weak. She had to keep sitting down to rest just to get from one part of the room to the other.

"My Gawd, I'm feelin' like I'm the one dying. These constant trips to the hospital and a lack of sleep are puttin' somethin' on me. My body's feelin' like I can't take another step, but I gotta get over there to that hospital and watch over my baby – make sure she's bein' taken care of right. I just gotta keep fightin' for her life, 'til the Lawd gives her back her health. If I don't give up, I know she won't give up." She gathered what little strength she had and left the room.

The clicking sound of her heels on the floor tiles in the empty hallway was irritating to her own ears. Each click reminded her that another second had gone by and the end was one step closer. She couldn't tell at what point she stopped hearing the clicking sound of her heels and started feeling the thumping of her heart.

She finally arrived at the window where she had been standing everyday for what seemed like forever. The bed was empty. Her hand flew up to cover her mouth before the scream coming up out of her belly reached her lips. The last ounce of strength was exhausted as she fell back against the glass wall. She tried to pray, but what came out was more like a demand.

"No Gawd. No. You did not take her. They must've moved her, but You did not just take my baby. You didn't take another one so soon. Please, this can't be. I'm beggin' you. You have got to heal my little sister. She's Yo child Gawd. Now take care of this 'cause I can't."

She heard footsteps approaching. When Doctor Foster arrived, she stared at him holding her breath while waiting for the answer. His head moved up and down. Beolia was gone.

Thoughts were coming from every direction and from different periods throughout their lifetime. Her head was spinning as scenes from the past played out as if they were occurring again. After all she had gone through as a child, Beolia made something of herself. Despite her feelings of neglect from Scott, she tried to love and make peace with him. Even when in his ignorance, he made the distinction between the children he fathered and Beolia, she accepted the rejection peacefully and graciously.

Most of all, she was grateful that despite what happened in the Gulf, Beolia dreamed big, pursued her dreams, and became an educated woman who found a man who truly loved her. Although over too soon, she was able to have the life she always dreamed of with the man of her dreams. Unfortunately, 'til death do us part came much too soon because Consumption Disease robbed them of the privilege of growing old together.

She called James. "Oh my Gawd, she's gone. James I just died yet another death. You need to go down to the Western Union office and wire me some money. I made arrangements and the hospital is preparing her body for me to take her home. I'm takin' her back to rest in peace beside Momma. Poor baby, she's been through a lot. She's with Matthew and Momma now, people who truly love her. Nothin' or nobody can ever hurt her again."

He waited to make sure she was finished crying. "Babe, just hold tight. I'll wire the money, but I'm on my way down there. You're not going to do this all by yourself. Just you hold on 'til I get there. I love you Maude."

Chapter 24
Leotia

By 1924, Leotia Harrington had developed into a strikingly beautiful young woman. Her exquisite looks attracted much attention, but she maintained a serene demeanor regardless of what was going on around her. These contrasting qualities made her all the more intriguing. Her personality was like Mary's for the most part. The only character difference was one that surprised everyone given her quiet disposition. She shunned confrontation, argument, and combative interaction, but could hold a grudge. Her grudges weren't fleeting. She could hold on to them forever, or so it seemed to the other person.

She didn't like this about herself because she knew exactly from whom she had inherited it. He refused to let go of the grudges he held against the system that enslaved him to his own father and considered him property rather than a son. His countless grudges caused trouble for anyone who was a part of his life. It wasn't uncharacteristic of him to seek and carry out revenge on those whom he begrudged.

While his overt methods were personally designed to retaliate against the effects of a system of injustice, brutality, and inhumane treatment, her grudges were more effective because she held them in silence, making it impossible for the other person to figure out what was wrong, or how to make amends. Maude spoke often of them.

"Now get Otie wrong and you've got somethin' on yo hands. She's just as sweet as she can be and as quiet as a mouse, but cross her and you pay dearly. I swear that girl can hold a grudge for years."

She knew that until Leotia decided to move beyond the hurt, there was nothing the responsible person could do but wait it out. Walter agreed. "She don't accept no peace offerin's either. You may as well hang yo self out to dry 'til she feels like bringin' you in. All I can say is don't hold your breath."

She abhorred this personality trait and delved into the faith for salvation. *Ain't nothin' but the devil what put that spirit in me like Poppa and I ain't gonna have it. Just gonna do like Momma told me to do. Put my life in the Lawd's good hands, stay in prayer, and live the good Christian life. Don't seem like Poppa took her advice, but that's how I'm gonna live. I wanna see the Lawd. Ain't tryin' to go to hell. If Poppa don't care that be where he's gonna wind up after he dies, then that's on him, but I wanna see the Lawd, Momma, and Beolia again one day.*

She often reflected on past conversations with Beolia when trying to console her for the hurt inflicted by Scott's insensitivity. "Beolia, it ain't you. Poppa just let the devil work a mighty work in him. He keeps bringin' all that trouble in here 'cause he got mixed up with that bad woman name Belle. That's guilt makin' him treat other people wrong. He loves you. He just don't know how to show it."

Just like Beolia, she hated any talk about witchcraft, spells, and the madness that came with dealing with those people who practiced roots. She was adamant in her conviction to never entertain the dark and dangerous practices people said Scott's mistress had brought to their home.

"Beolia, I'm like you. I don't want nothin' to do with anybody mixed up in that world of witchcraft, roots, and all the devil's work. I know that woman is gonna burn in hell fo' what she's done to people who ain't did nothin' to her. Ain't no way 'round it, she's gonna pay for her evil ways."

For years he had been in the dark and was completely clueless about her ability to hold a grudge – especially the one she held against him and Belle. She didn't kid herself into thinking she had the same fight in her that Maude possessed, and said as much to Beolia during one of their conversations out in the barn.

"I may not be a fighter like Maude, but I sure ain't gonna be fallin' all over him 'cause he's grievin' now that his mess with that woman done killed Momma. He's Poppa and all, but from now on, he ain't gonna get my whole heart. No sir. I've learned my lesson. Love him unconditionally and you pay with yo life. Ain't gonna happen to me. I remember that day Doc Moore came over to the house to see 'bout Momma. Even he couldn't believe how bad Poppa let things get. He don't know I saw the look on Doc Moore's face. That sealed it fo' me. Everything I knew in my heart he did to Momma, I saw in Doc Moore's face."

Since Mary had to give her life in exchange for loving him, she swore to love him from a distance. She would never give him all of her when it came to love. Limits were set and she would deny him the unconditional love he denied Mary.

Maude's and Beolia's decisions to leave the Gulf, and good fortune in finding men who loved and married them were the inspiration for the plan to carry out her own exit strategy.

When she was sixteen years old, she met Luther Spruiel, and was on her way to freedom. The road would prove to be long and winding.

When they returned to the Gulf, to their surprise he demanded that they resume Mary's tradition of attending church service on the last night of the year. She was resolute in keeping George Marks' tradition alive.

He held fast to the custom of attending church on the last night of the year. Poppa George used to say, "I swear fo' Gawd, the constant prayers of the righteous slaves moved Gawd Almighty to cause such a stir between them Yankees and these Confederate States of America, President Lincoln knew the only way he could force the Confederate States back into the Union was to sign that document what freed us. Y'all see one of the most impotant days of my life was what we called Freedom's Eve."

"It was December 31, back in 1862. I'll never forget that uplifting service filled with singin' and people jumpin' up all over the place givin' they testimony 'bout survivin' the year with its hardships. Then just before the midnight hour, all of us fell down to our knees and started prayin' in the New Year. All them prayin' voices, they sounded like the rumblin' what come down from the heavens durin' a thunder storm. But if you listened real close, you could hear'em and zackly what they were prayin' 'bout. Some would be thankin' Gawd fo' survivin' another year of hardship, and then a few feet away you would hear somebody else prayin' fo' what they wanted the next year. I reckon all of us was prayin' for freedom."

"A few months down the road, word finally got 'round to these parts tellin' us that back on January 1, 1863, President Lincoln signed the Emancipation Proclamation. I declare, the prayers of them folk on December 31, 1862, was answered. I tol' Gawd that fo' the rest of my days I'd celebrate dat day with my family in His house. Brought my family up, demandin' they be in Gawd's house every year at dat time, praisin' Him for answerin' them prayers of the righteous slaves."

So on December 31, 1925, they rushed into church, out of breath, and anxious to find good seats. Leotia was glad Scott was making them attend Watch Night Service. She had a feeling she enjoyed church services more than Walter or Novella anyway.

In contrast to her quiet demeanor, a different personality came forth whenever she was in church. During the service, she was the one loudly responding to the preacher's sermon. She was moved to jumping up and down, and clapping her hands whenever the lively choruses to the spiritual songs were sung over and over again. She wasn't too shy to do the holy dance. She also took pride in putting on her Sunday best (compliments of Maude).

They had just taken their seats when she felt someone from across the isle staring. When she looked, a young man with eyes that seemed to be laughing was looking her way. Luther Spruiel nodded his head and waved to her. Becoming self-conscious, she slightly nodded in response. She was uncomfortable. *What's he gonna think when the Lawd's spirit get a hold of me? He's gonna think I'm crazy jumpin' up and down, clappin' and doin' the holy dance? Can't worry 'bout that though.*

She had nothing to worry about. Once church service started, he was just as, if not more animated in his worship than she.

"Yes Lawd, he be a man of Gawd and filled with the Holy Ghost."

She startled Walter and Novella with her outburst. They looked at each other knowingly and giggled. Walter leaned over and whispered to Novella, "Whose Otie talkin' 'bout? Who be a man of Gawd, and how she know he's filled with the Holy Ghost?" Novella responded with a jab to his rib cage with her elbow.

Leotia knew they were making fun of her, but didn't care. Turning her attention away from them, she enjoyed the rest of the service worshipping in the spirited way that took her mind off of life outside of the church walls.

Around 11:55 p.m., the Reverend instructed the congregants to go down on their knees and prepare to bring in the New Year praising God.

"Yes Pastor, I'm good and ready to go down on my knees and start prayin' and praisin' Gawd. I have a feelin' the Lawd done answered some of my prayers already." Walter and Novella looked at each other again and giggled.

Once the Watch Night Service was over, she heard a man's voice asking people in the crowd heading towards the door to excuse him. His voice sounded like he was anxious and in a hurry. She could tell he was getting closer, as she heard, "scuse me, scuse me."

She felt the gentle touch of a strong hand as it slowly pulled her around to face the man to whom the hand belonged. It was the young man with whom she had connected earlier in the service. His smile was warm and his eyes lit up with merriment.

"Hello Miss Leotia, I'm Luther Spruiel, but you can call me Luke, like all my friends and family do."

"I'm pleased to make your acquaintance Luke. This is my brother, Walter, and my little sister, Novella.

"And how y'all doin' this evenin'?"

"We doin' just fine." Walter was guarded not knowing who this stranger was and a little irritated that he had pushed everybody out of his way in order to get to Leotia.

Novella was much friendlier. "I'm good Luke and how you doin'?" Before he could answer, she innocently, but bluntly asked him what his intentions were. "Are you interested in courtin' Otie – that's what we call her?"

"Why Miss Novella, I most certainly am interested in courtin' your lovely sister. Who is your poppa and how can I get him to let me visit with Leotia."

"Our poppa is Mr. Scott Harrington and..." Walter shushed her. "Vella be quiet, we don't know him like that."

Leotia then spoke up and provided the information because she definitely wanted to get to know him. "Poppa's name is Mr. Scott Harrington and we live on Jamison. Our house is the yellow one. That be where we live. You can come by 'round 5:30 in the evening and ask him about visitin' me. Just want to let you know that you have to come real respectful or else Poppa won't have no parts of you?"

He wasn't discouraged by her warning. "I will stop by tomorrow evening and ask Mr. Scott Harrington if I can court his beautiful daughter." He was laughing the whole time while talking.

Just then a group of young men who bore a striking resemblance to Luke walked up and were introduced as his brothers. Walter tried to be stubborn, not wanting to give any indication that he approved of Luke's entree into Leotia's life.

By the time they reached home, he found himself laughing along with the happy-go-lucky Spruiel brothers. Luke promised Leotia that he would come around 5:30 the next evening.

Walter and Novella immediately went into the house. Leotia remained at the doorway as she watched the new man in her life walking away. When she finally went into the house, she found Scott standing at the window, apparently having been there all along.

"Hi Poppa, I want to tell you about one of those young men you saw with us. His name is Luther Spruiel, but he likes for people to call him Luke. I met him at the Watch Night Service tonight. He seems real nice, and from what I saw, he loves praisin' the Lawd."

He wasn't impressed. "What's he walkin' y'all home fo', and what do he want?"

She was too excited about the possibility of a courtship with Luke to be discouraged. "He wants your permission to court me and will be comin' by around 5:30 tomorrow evenin' to meet you. I told him it be okay."

"We'll see."

"Yeah, we'll see."

Otie's startin' to sound just like that defiant Maude. He wasn't about to take it from his own flesh and blood. "Gal, what did I just hear you say?"

"Nothin' Poppa."

"I didn't think so." He clearly heard what she said. He just didn't know how to handle it. He had a feeling he was on the verge of losing yet another child, and sensed that this Luke person was the one who would be responsible for his loss. Her defiance placed him in unfamiliar territory.

He was already contemplating tampering with something she wanted badly, but was soon to discover just how stubborn she could be, and how much resentment she had been holding on to with regards to his history with women. His efforts to clip her relationship with Luke would reveal that she was very much her father's daughter and a formidable opponent if driven to the point of warfare.

Sure enough at 5:30 in the evening on New Year's Day there was a loud knock at the front door. He immediately became irritated. *Okay so he's an arrogant nigger that don't know his place, and comin' 'round here knockin' like somebody had better get to the door and get there in a hurry.*

He was trying to get up to answer the door when Leotia came running by, almost knocking him back down into the rocking chair.

"What the hell..." She was too excited to even notice the irritation in his voice or apologize.

He was determined that Luke wasn't going to have a relationship with her. She would receive no prior warning about his plans to undermine the budding relationship. So he resigned himself to tolerate him for a couple of hours, and would concentrate on permanently separating Leotia from her new love later.

She threw open the door to greet Luke, who in turn greeted her with an ear-to-ear smile. The expression in his eyes looked as if something was amusing to him. He immediately took her hand and kissed the back of it.

"Good evening Miss Leotia, it's good to see you again and I'm anxious to meet your poppa. Take me to him."

She took his hand as they walked back into the room where Scott was seated. "Poppa, this here is Luther, I mean Luke Spruiel, and Luke this is Poppa, Mr. Scott Harrington."

Another one of his signature smiles began to spread over his face as he reached out to shake Scott's hand. Leotia was so caught up in the moment she could not see that the smile on his lips never reached his eyes. He kept pumping the hand that was begrudgingly extended towards him, but read and received a much different message than the handshake intended to convey. Leotia didn't have a clue.

This ol' man has no intentions of lettin' me get close to his daughter and he intends to get rid of me somehow. Well I've got news for him. I plan on stickin' around for Ms. Leotia Harrington no matter what he says or think.

Leotia had spent most of the day preparing a delicious supper. She also went to great lengths to make sure her look for the occasion was her prettiest ever.

I just want everything to go right. I feel like I'm on my way to happiness just like Maude and Beolia. They proved we can be happy outside of Poppa's house. All men ain't like Poppa. Uncle Walt ain't even like Poppa.

Lawd knows I tried to be close to him. But lovin' him and bein' close to him is dangerous. Lovin' him is what killed Momma. Must admit though, a part of me wish everything could be different between me and Poppa, but it ain't. Gotta be realistic and stay focused. The best way to love him is to love him from a far off.

"Everybody, supper's ready. Luke do you mind sayin' the grace?"

Scott interrupted. "Since I'm the man of this house, I'll say it." They were all shocked since he had never shown any interest in doing anything spiritual like saying grace before a meal.

Luke recognized the ploy. So he decided to beat him at the game of proving which man was in charge of the evening. "Sir, I think that would be great. Let's bow our heads as Mr. Harrington leads us in prayer."

Scott was caught off guard. His attempt to make Luke look like the weaker man backfired. Luke's acquiescence to the strong-arm tactics made him look respectful and gracious. Scott wanted to steal the stage as the leading man that evening, but his performance was awful as he stumbled over the words. He was uncomfortable and failed miserably since he didn't know what they meant. He muttered portions of the grace with words spoken out of context, and finally ended with an awkward "Amen."

Leotia was embarrassed and glad when he finally finished. When he lifted his head, to his dismay, the look in Luke's eyes was anything but a look of defeat. Not only did he recognize the mischief in them, but saw the slight smile tugging at the corner of Luke's mouth.

Luke was only too happy to let him make a fool of himself, and the expression on his face said "Gotcha." *Look at 'em – he's makin' a complete fool of himself tryin' to make one of me. Who would try to take control over somethin' he knows nothin' 'bout? Only a fool. Oh Gawd, I'm sittin' here lovin' this, and he knows I got him. What a complete fool.*

As much as he wanted to laugh out loud to further humiliate Scott, he was sensitive to Leotia's apparent embarrassment, and wouldn't do anything to make her feel any worse. As they looked across the table at each other, he was more than satisfied knowing Scott received the message. He had lost Round One.

Scott wasn't only embarrassed, but also furious. *You just wait boy, you haven't even begun to see what ol' Scott Harrington is gonna do to you. You wantin' Leotia, but you ain't gonna be gettin' her. I'll see to that.*

Leotia, on the other hand, was just happy to be having her first date. While she was anxious to move ahead with Luke in her life, Scott was anxious to get rid of him.

Throughout supper she chatted about everything she could possibly think of. She asked questions to encourage Scott's acceptance of the relationship. Luke was only too happy to provide the information although he knew nothing he said mattered.

Not wanting to give Scott anything to work with, he announced that the evening was getting late (although it wasn't) and it was time to start walking home.

Hand-in-hand they started walking towards the door to say their goodbyes. Scott was on their heels still trying to intimidate Luke. *He's right up on us thinkin' he can scare me, but it ain't gonna work. When we get to this front door I'm gonna do somethin' else he ain't gonna like. Get ready ol' man, Luke Spruiel is 'bout to win Round Two.*

Luke made his next move to unnerve Scott. He put one hand around Leotia's back and pulled her closer to him. "Leotia, I've really enjoyed havin' supper with you this evenin'. You sho' can cook, and everything tastes so good."

She was thinking *how respectful of him.* Scott was thinking *how pretentious of him.* Luke stunned both of them as he leaned in even closer to do the very thing he knew Scott didn't want him to do.

"I'm ready to go, but before I do, let me just plant a respectful kiss on your lovely cheek. Ummmm – now that was sweet."

This arrogant nigger gonna fix his lips on my gal right here in front of me. I should rip 'em right off of his face and get this over with. He be wantin' me to go off on him and look bad to Otie. I swear fo' Gawd, I'm gonna make him wish he never crossed my threshold.

Luke could see him trembling with rage, but decided to take things even further. He turned to look him directly in the eyes while speaking to Leotia. "Leotia, if it be alright with your poppa, I would be honored if you would have supper with me and my family after church service this comin' Sunday."

Now this hankty young thing be thinkin' he's gonna use the Lawd to get my Otie. I can't stand him, but I can't let her know that 'cause she's gonna fight me on this. I can feel it. So I gotta give in for now and just keep my eye on him and not let him get to her. He won't win – I'll see to it.

Begrudgingly, he agreed, but set a long list of conditions. Neither Luke, nor Leotia cared about the conditions – they had gotten what they wanted.

Supper at the Spruiels was unlike any family mealtime she knew of, and certainly not like supper with her family. It looked like Luke's mother, Cora, cooked enough food to feed the entire Gulf. Looking on in astonishment, she couldn't help but laugh at the huge servings the Spruiel brothers piled onto their plates.

"George, you takin' all the potatoes before anybody else get a chance."

"I'm takin' the potatoes 'cause you took all the greens. A boy's gotta eat to stay strong and if I don't hurry up and get what I want, won't be nothin' left."

Luke's two sisters, Mary and Cora, were the opposite of their raucous brothers. The atmosphere at the supper table was festive, unlike the tension that overshadowed suppertime at her house. Leotia was entertained just watching them enjoying each other. *This is how families ought to have supper together. Why didn't Poppa ever know this was what we needed? Everytime we sat down, we were all waitin' for the dreadful words..."Goin' out – be back in awhile."*

Long before she was ready, Luke took her back home while it was still early evening. He knew Scott was looking for any reason to come between them, and was determined not to give him any ammunition to work with.

The first opportunity to come between them was presented by an unlikely source. Novella came down with a bad cold. She was so weak, all she wanted to do was to stay in bed. After a week had gone by, and she still was spending most of the time in bed he was alarmed. When she stopped eating, he sent for Mama Mame.

"Baby, Poppa ain't gonna let you continue to drag 'round here sick and he don't know what's wrong with you. I'll move heaven and earth to get you well. Walter, hurry up and go over to Mama Mame's and bring her back to take a look at Vella."

Mama Mame rushed over to the Harrington place. The good news was that she couldn't find anything serious. "She's just come down with a nasty cold. Y'all follow my 'structions and she should be up and about soon. Iffin you need me, come quickly and I'll be over here in a minute."

Whenever she wasn't in school, Leotia refused to leave Novella's side. Unbeknownst to Scott, she took it upon herself to send a telegram to Pittsburgh. In the telegram, she assured Maude that she was capable of helping Mama Mame nurse Novella back to health. There was no need for her to come home. Maude sent a response telegram. She was nursing James, who was battling another cold, and was glad Leotia could handle things. She would come, however, if they felt she still was needed.

Leotia's commitment to nursing Novella back to health gave him an idea. By observation he figured out a way to separate her from Luke. Although her temperament was different than Maude's, she reacted to crisis in the same way. He also recalled that his children did everything in their power to keep Mary alive until the end. When he allowed himself to give credit where credit was due, he acknowledged Maude's loyalty and commitment to Mary, and saw these same traits in Leotia, Walter, and Novella. He concluded that during peaceful times, his children became comfortable and started devising ways to move on with their lives – without him. During crises, they rallied around each other and forgot about everything and everybody else.

He was excited just thinking about his strategy. *I finally got the answer. Iffin she see just how much she's needed here at home, she'll do the right thing and won't have time fo' that boy. He'll move on 'cause he only be wantin' one thing, and he ain't gonna get it.*

When Novella started regaining her strength, he discouraged her from rushing things. "Baby, take yo time. You don't wanna fall sick again. If you rush things, you might find yo self back on yo back again. Just take yo time. Otie's takin' good care of you and she wanna make sure you stay well. Ain't that right Otie?"

"Yes sir Poppa, I won't rest until Vella's back up on her feet."

As long as Novella was sick, Leotia wouldn't spend any time with Luke, which was exactly what he wanted. At a distance, Walter watched his manipulative agenda being played out. *That rascal is usin' Vella to keep Otie away from Luke. He's always got somethin' up his sleeve. Damn, don't he ever stop tryin' to rule everybody? Now Otie done finally found somebody that makes her happy and it's a boy in church mind you. Not many of 'em 'round here and still he ain't happy with that. He's gonna destroy this relationship, I just know it.*

At first Luke was patient and encouraged her to concentrate on getting Novella back to a healthy state. The more he learned about the Harrington history, he was determined not to remind Leotia of her father in any way, shape, or form.

It had been two Sundays in a row he hadn't seen her in church. "Walter, how ya doin' man? I haven't seen Otie and Novella in a couple of weeks. Is everything okay?"

"Hey Luke. Vella's tryin' to get over a bad cold. That old bug just won't turn her loose, and Otie won't leave her side. Then on top of everything else, she's got school work and the million and one chores Poppa got for all of us to do."

"Okay, I haven't seen them and just makin' sure everything's alright. Tell Otie I asked about her, and that I miss her."

When he still hadn't seen her for more than a month, he asked Walter if he thought it would be a good idea to stop by, and whether or not Scott would get upset if he showed up. Walter didn't know how to answer the question and didn't have the heart to tell him to stay away.

"Sure Luke, stop by and say hello. Lawd knows she needs a break and to see your smilin' face."

Luke didn't give much thought about whether or not Walter could speak on Scott's behalf. He just wanted someone to say something that would make it okay for him to see her. He missed her, and despite Scott's disapproval, knew she felt the same way about him. He was going to see her.

They were finishing up their weekend chores on the Saturday he showed up. Walter was getting ready to leave to go to his new job, and Leotia had just finished cooking the pot of pinto beans with neck bones, when they heard the loud knock. At first everyone froze in the spot where they were standing. Then Leotia's face lit up with a smile as she started running to open the door.

Walter had made a gross error in not discouraging Luke's impromptu visit. Scott's eyes were ablaze with rage, and he looked as if he were about to explode. His hidden agenda was about to be revealed. *Lawd Jesus, how could I be so stupid tellin' Luke to come on over here? Poppa's 'bout to blow and I don't know how we all gonna come out of this after this fightin' comes to an end.*

His heart was pounding for Leotia. She was getting ready to suffer yet another heart break, and it was going to be devastating. He held his breath as she opened the door. The sight of them locked in each other's arms was all it took for Scott to explode. He rushed over to them and began pulling her away from Luke.

"Boy how dare you show up here without askin' for my permission. You ain't welcomed here, and you be way out of line comin' in here and sloberin' all over my gal. You ain't gonna be treatin' her like some whore."

"Poppa, how could you? He's been nothin' but respectful to me and you. It's just a hug and kiss. 'Sides we're in love and I wanna be with him. I been missin' him terribly…"

"You and him don't know nothin' 'bout no love and I don't wanna hear such talk, you hear me?"

"With all due respect Mr. Harrington, I love your daughter and do have the utmost respect for her sir. Miss Leotia is one of finest young ladies in all the Gulf. I've been lookin' for a lady like her my whole life sir."

His nightmare was on the verge of coming to life. "Looka here boy, I been tryin' to put up with that irritatin' smile on yo face I can't stand. I been tryin' to put up with you gropin' at my Otie here. You think you can come in here and take her away from us, you done lost yo mind. Now I want you outta my house and now."

The depth and breadth of his rage was out in the open. Leotia, who was crying in Walter's arms, pleaded with him. "No Poppa, no. I love him. Please don't do this to us. I love him." Scott was oblivious to her pleas and Luke could no longer dismiss his agenda to separate them. He was an enemy of the relationship and now everyone knew it.

Since Scott had shown himself, he may as well defend his relationship with Leotia. He had nothing to lose, and couldn't walk out without defending the woman he loved. The sight of her shaking and crying in Walter's arms was too much to take. She was his responsibility and he wasn't going to stand there and not attempt to comfort her.

He stepped towards Walter and Leotia.

"Make one more move, and I'll physically pick you up and throw you outta here. I'm tryin' to give you a chance to walk outta that door, but I swear fo' Gawd boy, I will throw you out by the seat of yo pants if you take another step to my gal."

"Then sir, you gonna have to throw me out 'cause I ain't gonna stand here and see my Leotia cryin' and shaken 'cause you offendin' and upsettin' her."

He was expecting the argument to get heated, but quickly discovered the adversary wasn't the type to argrue. Violence was how he handled threats and unresolved issues. The next thing Luke knew, there were hands clamped tightly around his throat. The savagery with which he was being attacked was astounding when his intentions were nothing less than honorable. He couldn't just stand there and allow Scott to kill him.

Then it was Scott's turn to be dumbfounded when a set of large hands came up, and with amazing strength, starting pulling his hands away. Luke's defense further enraged him. He would not be disrespected and allow the enemy to prevail on his turf. This man was the enemy and wanted to take Leotia away.

Walter, Leotia, and Novella watched in horror as the two men fought, knocking over everything in their path.

Walter was the first to break out of the frozen state of horror. "Stop it Poppa, stop it. Oh my Gawd. Stop it Poppa. I said stop, he ain't fightin' you, he's just tryin' to keep you from fightin' him. Stop it. You're upsettin' Leotia and Vella."

He finally exhausted all of his energy struggling with Luke and Walter. Out of breath, he still had a venomous warning to issue.

"Boy iffin you care anything 'bout her happiness, you'll leave her with her family. These chillun been through 'nuff and they need each other. She ain't ready to leave this house, and you tryin' to get her to do something she ain't ready to do. You tryin' to destroy my gal's life, but I swear I'll see you dead fo' I let that happen."

Luke knew the accusation about destroying Leotia's life was a big lie. He sighed with resignation. "Look Leotia, let's just take it easy for awhile. Maybe in time we can figure somethin' out, but right now I don't think it's a good idea for us to see each other."

Her future in jeopardy, she turned on Scott screaming at him. "Poppa, you owe Luke an apology and I'm tellin' you to give it to him right now. Do it."

"Now wait one minute gal, have you forgotten who you talkin' to? You had better be 'pologizin' to me or else I'm fittin' to take this here strap off I'm wearin' and put it to you."

His threat didn't move her. "Poppa, I'm gonna say this again. You had better apologize to Luke right this minute or I'll walk outta here, and you will never see me again. Do it right now, or I start walkin'."

The room was silent. No one knew what to say. Her threat pierced his heart and it took everything in him to mask his humiliation, as well as his hurt feelings over her open display of rejection. She was choosing Luke over him and threatening to walk out of his life in front of everybody.

She had struck a nerve by attacking him with the threat of losing another child. He had never gotten over losing his first son. He still grieved over Herbert walking out of his life, never to be seen or heard from again. He never recovered from the loss of Scott Harrington, Jr. He was suspicious that his relationship with Walter was disintegrating as well.

Without knowing it, she had awakened every fear he held about losing loved ones. He not only carried around the depression of losing his children, but was also carrying around the resentment of having Fondella snatched away from him just because of James Seamore's selfishness and sexual desires.

The grief of losing Fondella never left him. It was compounded by the guilt of losing three wives to early deaths. He could never accept the loss of his children. He created them, and they belonged to him.

Unfortunately, fear was not bigger than his ego and he refused to apologize to Luke. However, he was too afraid to continue the fight with Leotia, and abruptly walked out of the room, mumbling something about ungrateful children.

She wasn't finished and followed him. "Do you hear me? You had better start apologizin' right now or else I promise you I'll walk outta here. I'm not playin' with you. Do it."

Luke couldn't stomach any more. "Stop it Sweetheart. You've gotta stop this fightin' with him Otie. He's never gonna agree with us. Look, let's take a break and settle down some. I'll be talkin' to you soon."

She had the feeling he wanted nothing more than to be done with the Harringtons. Exhausted, she let him go. As soon as the door closed, so did her heart – as far as Scott was concern.

He was tired of waiting for her to come around and time wasn't healing her wounds. He needed Uncle Walt's advice.

"This ain't right. That gal been treatin' me like I'm poison 'cause she don't like what I told that boy Luke. Been a couple of years now, and she's still treatin' me like I'm the stranger in my own house. Walter, I got a good mind to put a strap to her, but knowin' her, she'll turn around and use the damn thing on me."

"Tell me how can I get through to her and make her start treatin' me like I'm her poppa again? She walk 'round the house and I know she's there in body, but her mind and heart somewhere else. Sometimes I don't think she's ever comin' back to me. I reckon her soul walked outta the door with that boy. She ain't been right since."

"You prob'ly right. Her heart and soul was wrapped up in that boy, and when you threw him outta yo house, her spirit left with him. She saw what you did as takin' away her freedom, and you and me both know what that feels like – not havin' no freedom."

"Okay, I understand 'bout freedom and feelin' like a slave and all, but ain't no child 'posed to make her poppa pay for his actions. That be wrong. I'm the poppa – she ain't. She's killin' me with that silence and she knows it. But she's a stubborn gal and you can't break her outta her stubborn ways."

"Whatcha laughin' at Walter?"

"She sound just like her poppa iffin you ask me."

"Yeah – she's a bit of a whip alright. I catch her starin' at me like she got so much contempt fo' me. I even overheard her talkin' to little Vella 'bout how people bein' responsible for destroyin' other folk's happiness and how they gonna burn in hell for it. I knows she talkin' 'bout me and want me to hear it – like darin' me to say somethin'. You ever heard of such a thing? A child darin' her poppa to make a move on her is unheard of. Never thought I'd see the day when my own child condemn me to hell."

Leotia gave him exactly what he had given her and every other woman in his life who tried to love him – crumbs. She showered Walter and Novella with love, making him watch from the sidelines, yearning for her to embrace him again. At times the cunning spirit she tried to keep under control lured him into a false sense of security, believing he was making progress. Everytime he thought he had gained ground, she rejected him again.

The new Leotia was driving him crazy. She was effortlessly behaving towards him in the same manner in which he strategically behaved in order to maintain control over others – cold, aloof, and brutal. He wanted her to love him unconditionally, just like every other woman in his life. This was his child and it was inconceivable that she could be so cruel. Frustrated, he wanted to lash out at her with his belt, thinking he could regain control with corporal punishment, but one encounter specifically warned him of the consequences.

They were coming from opposite ends of the narrow hallway on that night she scared the daylights of him. He saw her coming towards him, but she refused to accommodate him by moving to the side.

"Gal, watch where you goin'. You see me walkin' down this hall? The next time you see me…" He stopped talking when he focused in on her deadly stare. *This gal hates the ground I walk on. She's lookin' at me as if she could kill me dead on the spot.*

He tried to stare her down and scare her back into her place, but the scare tactic didn't work. There was no fear in her eyes. It was, however, all in his heart. He couldn't take the chance of losing her forever, and had no alternative but to retreat.

Not only did he lose ground with her on the night he had the fight with Luke, he lost another child. The night of the big fight was the final straw for Walter as well.

It was during a conversation with Uncle Walt, when he said, "Otie, she ain't never gave nobody no trouble. Her and Beolia always been the peacemakers in the house and refused to get involved when Poppa and Maude was fightin'. Yet Poppa turned on her viciously just 'cause she found love. Uncle Walt, you know that ain't right. She didn't deserve that."

"I know boy. Otie deserves to be happy just like any other young gal. I don't know why yo Poppa's so determined to keep y'all 'way from people outside of this family. I tried talkin' to him, but he is one stubborn mule. He listened, but I could tell he wasn't receivin'."

"Uncle Walt, if he can come after Otie like that, nobody stands a chance with him. I know he thinkin' he could treat Maude and Beolia different 'cause he wasn't their poppa by blood, but sweet Jesus, he's willin' to tear his own flesh and blood apart if they go against his wishes. I can't continue to fool myself. It be impossible to stay outta the line of fire when it comes to Poppa."

Walter suspected that his relationship with Scott was going to suffer the same fate as the fatal relationship between Scott and Herbert. Unlike Herbert, however, he didn't want to permanently sever ties. Although he harbored bitterness and resentment towards Scott, he still couldn't help but wish things had been different. In his heart, he could never give up his yearning for a family life that wasn't lived out in turmoil year after year – all because they were all trying to love and be close to a man whose demons from the past wouldn't let him go.

For years he heard about the short lives of Scott's previous wives, as well as their sad existences trying to stay married to him. He heard about the lengthy and bizarre relationship between his father and Belle involving stories, innuendos, and charges of witchcraft, as well as murder. Even Belle died a horrible death that seemed directly connected to her relationship with Scott.

Walter witnessed Mary's one-sided love affair with him; watched him battle with Maude time and time again as their love/hate relationship played out; watched him all but ignore Beolia; and quietly observed as he strategically destroyed Leotia's relationship with Luke.

"I've had enough. I don't wanna hate him, so I'm gettin' 'way from him 'fore it turns into that. Iffin I'm gonna have any relationship with him at all, it's gotta be from a distance, else I'm gonna follow right in Herbert's footsteps. Uncle Walt, it's time to start puttin' my plan into action."

While Walter was planning his departure, Scott was learning that a fight with Leotia was something a man didn't want to have. Her ability to hold a grudge was unsettling. Always made to feel rejected, he lamented over her unforgiving spirit. *That gal be a stubborn somebody. She's still holdin' on to a fight that happened in the past. That boy wasn't fo' her and she now mad at me 'cause I seen that. Walk 'round here not even speakin' to me half the time. I'm tryin' to make things right again, but she won't give me the chance.*

The mysterious woman who was evolving was confusing to him. He was totally out of his element, and frustrated to discover she was very good at keeping him at a distance. Now that she had his attention, he studied her more closely. Just like Mary, her quiet demeanor belied her strength and resolve when it came to principle. He had robbed her of a chance at happiness, but unlike Mary, she wasn't about to give him that which he robbed her of. He was becoming well-acquainted with her distance and decision to make him pay for breaking her heart. She had gotten underneath his skin.

When he couldn't take it any longer, he offered a concession. "Look Otie, you been a good gal, and I'm thinkin' you prob'ly be ready to start courtin'. You can walk home from church with Luke on Sunday mornin', but that's all. When you walkin' with him, there ain't to be no touchin', kissin', or anything like that. Don't talk to him 'bout anything that go on in this house, and don't ever answer no questions 'bout my bizness."

He thought he was controlling her by adding a long list of conditions, but she knew better and was willing to allow him to think otherwise. She could be patient and when the time was right, he would know who was in control all along. *Yeah, he think that walkin' home with Luke be all I'm gonna do. I've got news fo' him and just at the right time, he's gonna know he lost power over me years ago. I'm just waitin' fo' the right time. Just waitin'.*

While he was consumed with figuring out how to regain power over Leotia's life, Walter was making arrangements to execute his plan. His exit, however, was not the blow that brought Scott to his knees. That blow came from a direction where he never thought to look.

Chapter 25
Walter Seamore Harrington

Walter and Uncle Walt were counting the savings from his part-time job. Although he was excited about his nephew's growing kitty, Uncle Walt was struggling with mixed emotions about Walter's plan to relocate to Maryland. Scott wasn't going to take another son walking away from him lightly, and not taking it lightly was a gross understatement. He only agreed not to breach Walter's confidence because Walter promised that, unlike Herbert, he wasn't going to walk out of Scott's life forever. He just wanted to go to Baltimore and make a better life for himself.

"Uncle Walt, what're you so deep in thought about? First you messed me up with my countin' and I had to start all over. Now you off daydreamin' somewhere? Where are you?"

"Boy, I'm sorry – just thinkin' 'bout things, that's all."

Once they had finished counting, Walter started discussing his dreams for the umpteenth time. "Uncle Walt I'm gonna be successful just like Matthew was fo' he died. Him and Beolia was the main reason why I chose to go to Baltimore. They told me Washington is close by. I'll never forget Matthew as long as I live."

"Now James, he's doin' pretty good for hisself too. He provides good for Maude. Them two men showed me it can be done and I'm determined that be how I'm gonna live my life. Everybody ain't like Poppa. People can live free from tragedy and sadness. I think that's been such a part of Poppa for so long, he think it be okay to live like that. I think he expects to have tragedy and sadness in his life. So when it happens, he just rolls with the punches and expects everybody else to do the same thing. Now me, I can't imagine livin' and thinkin' like that all the time."

"Boy, I understand you wantin' to get away from here and live a better life up north, but you gotta 'member, yo poppa, he done lost every son he ever had and he ain't gonna take kindly to losin' another one. I know you don't think he act like it sometimes, but he care fo' you deeply. Boy, he loves you. He wantin' to be real close to you too. He just don't know how to put that damn pride of his on the shelf where it belongs and reach out to you like he 'posed to. He's gonna take you leavin' as not wantin' him. I know'em."

"I also know times they done changed so much since we was boys. He's gonna have to learn he don't wield the kinda power he used to back in them days. He don't realize his kinda power was always poison and it was gonna kill a whole lotta things 'round him – includin' people. But don't you worry none. You gone on home now and keep gettin' yo self together to make that move. Uncle Walt love you boy."

His train ticket was purchased and the few pieces of clothing he owned had been packed. Earlier in the week, Uncle Walt received a telegram from Maude and the news was good.

"I received a telegram from yo sister. Cora read it to me and it says Matthew's people, they still willin' to honor their agreement to let you room with them. They 'preciate all Maude did for 'em whilst Matthew and Beolia was sick. They feelin' like they're obligated to show their gratitude in some way. So they willin' to let you live in their home. Things lookin' up fo' you son."

With everything now in place, it was time to announce that he was leaving the Gulf.

Scott was sitting in the rocking chair next to the fireplace with his eyes closed. From his peripheral vision, Walter could see Leotia over to the side plaiting Novella's hair. He cleared his throat and at the sound, Scott opened his eyes, looking up at him inquisitively. "What is it Walter? What's wrong?"

"Nothin's wrong Poppa, I just need to have a heart-to-heart talk with you 'bout me and my future."

The scowl of disapproval started forming even before he had a chance to explain. The plans were already in motion and he couldn't back down now. Although he anticipated disapproval, he was more apprehensive about things escalating to the point where the fight became so ugly, he would have no alternative but to make the same decision as Herbert – to permanently sever all ties. A permanent disconnection was not what he wanted. He wanted Scott to understand the move to Baltimore wasn't rejection, and that leaving the Gulf didn't mean he no longer loved him.

"Poppa, I'm leavin'..."

"You leavin' what? I knows you better not be talkin' 'bout what I think you be talkin' 'bout, 'cause the answer is no. Who do you think be anyways comin' in here standin' over me just tellin' me what yo plans are? You ain't asked me one thing and that be why I'm tellin' you no. I don't wanna hear another word. Now get outta my face."

Once again, he was flying off the handle before the other person had a chance to lay out the facts. This was the type of response that reaffirmed to Walter that changing his mind was not an option. It was no longer a matter of wanting to leave, but rather a matter of having to leave. He couldn't take it anymore, and was on the verge of releasing all of the frustration, resentment, and hostility he had been suppressing for years.

I knew it – nobody can talk to this hardheaded bastard. He don't know what my plans are, and that I'm tryin' to stay connected to him in some way. But, no, he's just gonna tell me to get outta his face. He prob'ly said somethin' ignorant like this to Herbert. I don't blame Herbert for walkin' out and never lookin' back. This is the most stubborn son-of-a-bitch I've ever seen in my life

No, no, no – I gotta stay calm. Lawd forgive me. I don't wanna call him a son-of-a-bitch. I love the ol' man. This is my poppa. Lawd Jesus, please give me the right words to say to him. Help me out here Lawd.

Civility prevailed. He wasn't going to allow one of the most important conversations of his life to escalate into a confrontation that could wind up being the last. Nothing and nobody was going to change his mind about leaving. So he stood his ground; not willing to back down, but not willing to be drawn into a vicious fight from whence there was no return.

Scott was terrified by the conversation because he recognized the look in Walter's eyes. He had seen it before. It was same expression in Herbert's eyes the day they had the big fight over Belle. When Herbert told him that he didn't ever have to worry about him speaking to him again, he never imagined the threat was actually a promise. He was now looking at a face with the same expression that had been haunting him for years. He was alarmed but was doing everything within his power to hide it.

"Poppa, I'm goin' to Baltimore, Maryland to live. It's a city close to Washington, D.C., and Matthew's people that live there have offered to let me stay with them. 'Sides, Baltimore isn't so far from the Gulf I can't come back home on a regular basis. You gotta let me go Poppa. I love you, but it be time for me to make my own way in the world. Ain't that what you really want for me Poppa?"

Hell no, that ain't what I want – I want you here with me.

Walter's resolve to maintain peace, as well as his willingness to say what was in his heart without regard to pride finally registered.

This boy is sayin' all the things I wish me and Herbert had been able to say to each other. Maybe that fight wouldn't have been so final. Iffin one of us had been able to back down, maybe we would've been able to come together in a few days. Lawd Jesus, there's just so many maybe's and I'll never have the answers 'cause my boy that I loved with all my heart walked out on me and ain't never looked back this way.

He sensed that he was on the brink of losing another child – possibly for good if he didn't respond differently this time.

Walter gave him room to save face and therefore avoid the dire consequences neither of them really wanted. He wanted Scott to feel like he had some say in the the matter because he knew how important being in control was to him. Extending his hand, he humbled himself and pleaded once more.

"Please Poppa just tell me you're with me on this. I promise, you and me are gonna be alright and I'm not leavin' you for good. I love you Poppa. Nothin's gonna change that – you're Poppa and I'm yo boy. I'm forever bound to you. Livin' in another place ain't gonna change that."

He extended his hand towards Walter, but the handshake never happened because he drew him in and held on to him tightly, rocking back and forth. "Walter Seamore Harrington, yo Poppa loves you and be mighty proud of his boy." He then kissed the top of his head.

Walter pulled back to see Scott's eyes brimming with tears. The show of emotion conveyed much more than he was capable of articulating. He was speechless, but welcomed the ironclad embrace that pulled him close to his father's heart. After all, loving Scott Harrington was all he ever wanted.

The next morning he was surprised to find Uncle Walt sitting at the kitchen table drinking a cup of coffee. Before they went to bed the night before, he told Scott that Uncle Walt would meet them at the train station to say his goodbye's with the family. Seeing Uncle Walt was cause for concern. *Oh Lawd, what happened?*

"Boy he's already gone down to the mill. He couldn't take seein' that train leave with you on it. Give him time, he's gonna come 'round. From what he told me 'bout last night, it seems like he's comin' 'round already. Now get yo things and yo sisters, and let's be headin' off for the train station."

When Walter Seamore Harrington left the Gulf to begin his new life in Baltimore, he was 15 years old. As the train pulled out of the station, his emotions were all over the place. He was feeling a sense of pride because he was following through on a well thought out plan. He was feeling like Maude's and Beolia's husbands must have felt – like he had accomplished something in spite of a world full of odds stacked against him.

He looked out of the window at Leotia and Novella standing with Uncle Walt as the train started to pull away. *Why we always bein' pulled apart just to find some happiness? We should've been able to find it together – all of us in one place. Why Poppa's difficult ways always be the curse of the family? Why, Lawd, did so many women have to die just tryin' to love him? I wanna be happy, but I still feel like I'm walkin' out on Otie and Vella. Why things gotta be like that?*

He took a deep breath and started blowing kisses as the train pulled away.

At the same time the train was pulling out of the station, Scott was taking his lunch break in a small area he had set aside for himself in the back of one of the mill buildings. He wasn't eating lunch, but staring off into space with tears streaming down his chiseled cheekbones. Once again, he was grieving over the loss of yet another son.

Chapter 26
Two Chicks Left in the Nest

He was praying Walter's departure was the final loss of a child he would have to endure. He was losing a lot of battles lately, and quite frankly getting tired of not winning. At present his only comfort was that Leotia and Novella were still living at home. *I know Otie's still mad at me, but she's still here – her and Vella. Oh Gawd, there ain't much else left to go wrong is there? Lawd, ain't it time for you to stop punishin' me?* There had to be a way to keep them happy so they wouldn't start making plans to leave.

As he watched their transformations, he couldn't help but notice their uncanny resemblances to other women in his life. It was if God was teasing and tormenting him with constant reminders of his late wives and the mother he was never allowed to know.

When Novella came running into the house to share her good news, he couldn't help but focus on the distinguishing features she inherited from him, as well as some of the features the old slaves used to describe Fondella.

She dropped to her knees in front of him. "Poppa, you're never gonna guess what happened to me. Try, try and guess what happened. Oh never mind – let me tell you. I won the school relay. I've been winnin' all of'em. Nobody can beat me runnin' down at the school. Poppa, they want me to run against some girls over there in Winston Salem. Can I go? You've gotta let me go."

His finger moved over every part of her face as if to trace and commit each detail to memory. "You're one fine young lady and look like what them ol' slaves say my momma, Fondella, look like. I don't even 'member what she looked like. She ran away 'fo me and Walter got old enough to know what was really goin' on at the Seamore plantation. I reckon it must be the good Lawd wantin' me to see her in the flesh. They say she was somethin' else too. Say slave masters couldn't do a thing with her. Ol' man Seamore was in love with her and never got over her runnin' 'way from him. She had that kinda power Vella. You've got it too. I always say you gonna be a fine lady one day."

She was too naïve to know what he was talking about, and too excited about the track meet over in Winston Salem to really care. "Poppa what're you talkin' 'bout? You keep confusin' me. I thought you said Molly was yo momma. You back and forth with Molly and Fondella. Can't we talk 'bout them some other time, please? I need to know, are you gonna let me go?

He started to issue his standard refusal, but thought about Walter's recent departure. He was also killing himself trying to get back into Leotia's good graces. He had to find a way to keep his two girls happy so they wouldn't leave home.

"Go on over there to Winston Salem and show them gals how fast you be. Show'em nobody's better than Mr. Scott Harrington's baby gal."

He was struggling with, and finding it difficult to adjust to the changes that time was forcing upon him. Although he was trying to keep up with the changes and stay in charge of their lives, his frustration was the realization that it was impossible to keep his children home as his possessions. They were growing up and wanting things grown-ups wanted. They had their own opinions that, for the most part, were antithetical to his. Their evolving personalities didn't neatly fit into the familiar categories that prevailed on the Seamore planation.

He was so focused on trying to figure out Leotia's moods in order to determine whether or not he was in danger of losing her, he was overlooking some gradual and disturbing changes in her physical appearance – at first anyway.

He was shocked at what he saw as she approached the house. When she saw him staring, she was mortified at the expression on his face as she struggled to walk in spite of the terrible pain.

Oh my Gawd, Poppa sees me walkin' like an ol' lady, and he ain't got the patience to deal with anybody lookin' old and crippled. He couldn't stand to look at Momma when she was sick; used to look at her like she had the plague or somethin'. Talked down to her too when she was helpless and messin' all over herself. I gotta straighten up. Oh dear Gawd in heaven, this hurts real bad. What's wrong with my body? Lawd Jesus I hope one day I just wake up and whatever this pain is, it'll be gone.

Everytime she went to church service she made sure that Pastor prayed for her. She was hoping and praying for a miracle from God. She needed the miracle to happen real soon because the pain was getting worse. It got so bad she hated going to sleep at night because the moment she woke up, the pain was there as a reminder of her debilitating condition. Her feet hurt so bad she could barely stand once they touched the floor, and was frightened that one day they wouldn't just hurt, but would no longer be strong enough to hold her up.

She was going to great lengths to hide the pain so he wouldn't view her as weak and vulnerable. He wasn't getting any weaker or more vulnerable despite his age, and was impatient with anybody who was. He was good at making people feeling inferior, but she was determined not to be counted among them.

There was one memory that brought a smile to her face in spite of a body wracked with pain. She still savored the afterglow of standing up to him the night of the fight between him and Luke. Since that night it was he who extended the olive branch trying to restore a father/daughter relationship that had been mortally wounded long before the night of the fight. She still felt a rush whenever she recalled screaming and demanding that he apologize to Luke. She was delayed but not defeated.

But now this mysterious condition was threatening to take away all of her strength. She feared that one day she wouldn't be able to walk at all. Then she would totally be at his mercy and Luke would move on. If that happened, she would always be Scott's prisoner.

She finally reached the porch. "Otie, what be wrong with you gal? You walkin' 'round like you some ol' ol' woman? When did all this start?"

"Oh Poppa, I'm just a little stiff. I think it comes from choppin' that wood up in the back. I'll be alright if I just keep movin' 'round."

"Okay, maybe if you get some liniment from Mama Mame and rub yo self down, it'll get better. We can't have you down and out and not able to help 'round here. There's plenty work to be done."

She knew his advice was good, but was hesitant to let Mama Mame take a look at her. *I just can't bring myself to do it. Be my luck she'll say I got somethin' that's gonna make my arms and legs drop right off of my body. With everything else that's goin' on, I don't think I can bear to hear horrible news like that. If I can just stay up on my feet and keep movin', one day soon I'll be strong enough to carry out my plan. I'm gonna show him he didn't win the battle to rule over my life and keep me away from Luke. I'm gonna marry Luke Spruiel and get the devil outta here.*

Despite her efforts, she was getting worse. The fear of being crippled and unable to walk was just too frightening, and the progression of whatever was wrong made it impossible for her to continue the charade. Whatever condition she was suffering with was much more than stiff muscles.

They were getting ready for bed one night when she let out a moan so laden with agony, Novella had to speak up. She had been noticing the changes in Leotia, but didn't know how to approach her about the troubling transformation. "Otie, what's wrong with you. I've been noticin' you movin' 'round real slow. You've got pain all over your face. What's wrong? Tell me what's wrong."

"Vella, I'm gonna be crippled soon. Somethin's terribly wrong with me. Everytime I get up, change position, or try to walk, some real bad pains go shootin' all through my legs and my back. My feet hurt as soon as they touch the floor in the morning. Sometimes it feels like every part of me is hurtin'. I keep tryin' to walk 'cause it feels a little better when I move 'round. But I can tell its gettin' worse. If Poppa finds out I'm crippled, ain't no tellin' what he'll do. Vella, I don't wanna be stuck here for the rest of my life with him. I'm tryin' to keep the awful truth from him. Please don't tell."

"Don't you worry none. I ain't gonna tell Poppa. You just tell me what to do and how to help you, and it'll be our secret. You can trust me Otie. Now you get some sleep. Good night and sweet dreams. I love you."

Her only regret was that she hadn't confided in Novella much sooner. Novella was quick-witted and sharp when it came to figuring out things. It was like having a younger version of Maude taking care of her. Unlike Maude, she could handle Scott without fighting. He didn't question her motives as he did with everyone else. He usually took whatever she told him at face value.

Whenever he asked about Leotia in passing, she just blew it off. "Oh, she's alright Poppa. She's just a little sore from doin' all her chores. That girl works from sun up to sun down." Her explanation satisfied him. As long as he thought they were working their fingers to the bones, he wasn't interested in the details. So she used her leverage to conceal Leotia's mysterious condition. If she told him Leotia prepared supper, he believed it. She wasn't lying because Leotia did help with preparing supper although she wasn't the one who actually did the cooking.

Whenever Scott assigned the chore of chopping wood to Leotia, Novella would go out to the back of the house with her. Once there, she re-assigned Leotia the task of stacking the wood while she chopped it. "Otie, Poppa don't have to know who chopped the wood and who stacked it. All he wanna know is that it got done. Here put this on. I took some small pieces of fabric and sewed them together. Just slide your arm through the sling. Now, we'll put a few pieces of wood in this part hangin' down like a big ol' pouch. That should make is easier for you to take them back to the fireplace. See, it's workin' and Poppa won't even know the difference."

Unfortunately and despite their efforts, the secret was becoming too serious to remain a secret. "Otie, we're losin' this battle. Your legs and feet are gettin' worse and I don't know what else to do. We've gotta do somethin' before Poppa finds out how bad it is and steps in. Look, I'll sneak into town and send a telegram to Maude. She'll come home. Maude will know how to make you better. I'll tell her to make it look like she just happened to come home for a visit. Poppa ain't gotta know we sent for her. If he finds out beforehand, he may just try and stop her from comin'. So we've got to get to her first before he even suspects anything. Once she knows what's goin' on, can't nothin' stop Maude from comin'.'"

Her plan worked and he thought it was just his misfortune that out of nowhere Maude sent a telegram saying she was on her way back to the Gulf for a visit. "Damn, that's all I need is fo' her to come back here tryin' to boss everybody around. Outta nowhere here she comes. I can't win for losin'.'"

Once he became aware of Leotia's deteriorating condition, he was terrified of the unknown and mystified at the source. How in the world did some mysterious disease come upon her and weaken her to the point where she could barely walk? He was wondering if the rumors about the roots Belle supposedly had put on his wives had somehow included his daughters. He hated to think about such thoughts because he was responsible for bringing Belle into their lives, and further responsible for the devastation his affair with her caused. Although he constantly conjured up lame excuses as to why he did things that resulted in hurting the women in his life, there was no excuse if Belle's dealings in witchcraft had somehow hurt Otie.

Even more frightening than his inability to do something about Leotia's declining state of health was the surprise announcement that Maude was coming for a visit. *I'll bet the minute she gets here, she's gonna blame me for whatever's got Otie down. That gal is gonna make life hell for me. I gotta put up with her this time though 'cause as much as I hate to admit it, if there's a way to bring Otie back to herself, Maude is gonna make it happen or die tryin'. Yeah – I know she's gonna make me answer to some stuff. I can feel it. Gonna have a fit 'cause I didn't call her sooner. I didn't even know how bad things had gotten myself. How she gonna blame me fo' what I didn't even know?*

Chapter 27
The Mighty Maude Returns to the Gulf

When Maude went down to the Western Union office to pick up the telegram, she knew something big, and probably not good, had happened back home. Before she left the apartment, she voiced her concerns to James. "They say I got a telegram from back home. I wonder what's goin' on. Maybe ol' Scott has taken ill. I doubt it though 'cause the last time I saw him, he looked as strong as ever, and was raisin' hell like always. James, I don't think the devil can get sick, do you?"

"Stop that. If he's sick then it's no laughing matter. I know he's a character Maude, but you've gotta understand where that man comes from. He comes directly out of slavery. No buffer there. I don't think he knows how to act outside of that kind of system."

"Oh my Gawd, I sho' hope nothin's wrong with Mama Mame. She's my second momma you know, and I would die if somethin's happened to her. James, do you think...."

"Babe, stop guessing and just go pick up the telegram so we'll know what's really going on. You'll worry yourself sick until you know."

As soon as the thin sheet of blue paper with news from back home was handed to Maude, her hands started to shake. They were shaking so bad James stepped up to steady them.

"What is it Babe – what's wrong?"

"Somethin's wrong with Otie, and she can barely walk. Her condition is gettin' worse everyday and Vella is beggin' me to come home. I gotta go James. I gotta go now." They rushed back to the apartment.

"James, you sure you're gonna be alright while I'm gone? I still don't like that cough you got. I don't want you here by yo self if you ain't well. Oh Lawd, what am I gonna do 'bout my job at the laundry?"

"Babe, will you stop worrying and just go on back home to see what's going on. I keep telling you not to worry about me. I can handle everything here. Even if your job isn't here when you return, I can take care of the both of us."

Just before they left the apartment, a thought occurred to her. "If that damned Mr. Harrington has done anything…"

"Maude, stop it. He wouldn't dare do anything to hurt his daughter."

She was a little ashamed of what she was thinking and saying, but couldn't forget Scott's destructive history and the casualties along the way – including Mary. *James is tryin' to be positive, but he just don't know Mr. Harrington like I do. I'm not gonna argue with him about it. I know how I feel, and right now my blood is startin' to boil 'cause I know that whatever is wrong has somethin' to do with how he handled the situation. He ain't ever gonna do anything right. Wrong seems to be the path he always chooses. If he's got anything to do with what's wrong with Otie, he's gonna hear from me and have to answer for some things. Let's just hope that when I get there, I'll have enough control to avoid another blow-up with that man.*

When the train pulled into the station, there was no one to greet her. She looked around for a familiar face. *At one time there was a pretty big family that would've greeted me. Now that Mr. Harrington has caused so much grief, there ain't nobody left to welcome me back home. They're either dead or as far away from here as they can get.*

She had returned to the Gulf to take care of Leotia and couldn't linger around with self-pitying thoughts. "Maude, get it together. Otie needs you and by Gawd by the time you get finished with her, your little sister is gonna be healthy and back to walkin' anywhere she damn well please." She started walking towards the opposite end of the station to see if she could hitch a ride.

When her ride pulled up to the house, things were quiet. She thanked the driver, gathered up her bags, walked up to the front door, and took a deep breath. "Hmmm. Okay Maude, open the door."

"I'm here. Where y'all at? It's me, Maude. Loud as I'm talkin' I know somebody in here hears me. Where y'all at?"

Novella came running from the back room and rushed into her arms. She was now as tall as Maude. *Gawd she's one beautiful lady. Done shot up like a bean stalk. Momma would be so proud of her. She looks just like... No way, she don't look nothin' like that devil. I guess she does if he was a different kinda person. Anyways she is one pretty skinny gal.*

"Maude, I'm so happy to see you. I know Otie and everybody else is gonna be fine now that you're here, and thanks for not lettin' Poppa know I sent you that telegram. I just didn't know what else to do. Otie's in awful shape. You've gotta do somethin'."

She held Novella's face in her hands. "Don't you worry none, I'm here and we're gonna get to the bottom of this and get Otie back on her feet. You hear me? Maude ain't gonna ever let nothin' destroy her gals. You know that don't you Vella?"

"That's why I called you."

Maude walked back to the bedroom and over to where Leotia was lying asleep. Bending over, she planted a kiss on her cheek. Leotia opened her eyes and smiled up at her. "You're here." She went back to sleep.

When Maude and Novella went back to the kitchen she asked, "Okay baby gal, where's yo Poppa?"

"He's due home from the mill 'bout now. I know he's gonna be glad you're here too. He's just too proud to say it, but I know it's true."

"Guess I'll start supper. I know I'm hungry." She didn't ask where anything was located, but took charge as if it was her kitchen. Supper was on the table when he walked through the front door.

When the aromas of his favorite dishes greeted him, he assumed Novella had done something special to please him. That wasn't the case this time because standing in front of him was the larger-than-life Maude with hands planted firmly on her hips.

"Well hello Mr. Harrington. I can tell by the look on yo face you don't know what to expect. I can certainly tell you to expect that by the time I leave this place, yo daughter and my dear sister will be back up on her feet with legs stronger than those phillies them horse-lovin' white folk like to see race."

He was glad to see her. "Hey Maude, good to see ya."

She could tell that he was sincere, although she was certain his joy was self-serving. However, his selfishness was of no consequence to her.

"Well everybody, get to the table and start eatin'. I'm gonna fix a plate and go feed Otie her supper."

As they were walking over to the table, Novella grabbed his arm and squeezed it reassuringly. "Don't worry Poppa, everything is gonna work out." He responded with a grunt. Novella had a smile on her face, and instead of the anxiousness he felt before Maude's arrival, he was silently thanking God the Calvary had arrived.

The next morning Maude got up when she heard him moving around. For breakfast she served biscuits, grits, and fried fatback.

"Mornin', breakfast is ready." He went over to the table and sat down to eat. She barely heard his "Thank ya."

This man still got a problem with showin' some manners, but I'll keep my thoughts to myself. I ain't here to fight with him.

"Mr. Harrington, I've asked Vella to stay with Otie while I go over to see Mama Mame. I'm gonna bring her back with me so she can look over Otie."

He was now appreciating everything about her that he detested in the past – namely her bossiness. Her take-charge attitude was now more than welcomed.

He noticed that lunch had already been prepared and was sitting on the table, which confirmed what he already suspected. *She still brazen and bullheaded. Ain't gonna do fo' me like the rest and bring my lunch down to the mill at Noon. I know she thinkin' take yo own lunch with you right now 'cause ain't nobody in here gonna bring it to ya later.* He picked up the lunch pail and walked out of the house without mentioning the long-standing requirement that lunch be brought to him.

Maude went into Leotia's room to serve breakfast. "Otie, once you've finished we're gonna get you up from that bed. Then after we get you washed and dressed, Vella and me are gonna take you out for a short walk."

"But Maude, I can't walk at all. This thing what got me down has taken my legs away. I have no strength at all. Maybe if I just rest for a couple more weeks I'll be able to walk some."

"No ma'am. We're gonna do just like I said. You know I'm not gonna do anything to 'cause you more pain. You've gotta trust me. If you want your legs back, then you gotta get up from here and start doin' some walkin'. Don't worry, Vella will be on one side of you and I'll be on the other. Do you think that big strong Maude can't hold you up or somethin'? I've been kicking ass for a many year, so you know I can hold yours up."

They laughed at the crude statement, but Leotia scolded her. "Maude, what did Momma teach us about cussin'? You gotta stop talkin' like that. Gawd's gonna strike you down if you keep usin' cuss words like that. Saved folk don't cuss. You need to get saved."

"Oh gal please. Anyhow, as soon as we come back from that walk, Vella is gonna stay with you, and I'm goin' over to talk to Mama Mame and bring her back. Between Mama Mame, me, and Vella here, we're gonna have you back to walkin' in no time."

For the first time in a very long time Leotia was feeling hopeful. Maude still had the same effect as always. Everything was going to be alright. There was no other option in Maude's book. Leotia was now looking forward to that walk.

Because of the sun's glare, Mama Mame leaned forward squinting her eyes and placing a hand just above her brow trying to make out who the woman was coming up the walkway. She got all excited and started trying to get up from the porch swing when she recognized Maude. "Well bless my soul. Gal how you been, and what you doin' back here in the Gulf? Oh my Gawd, somethin' must be wrong to bring you back here, and have you walkin' up on Mama Mame like you walkin' to a funeral. Oh Lawd, please tell me somebody didn't go and die on us."

"Hi Mama Mame, it's so good to see you too. No, nobody has died, but we've got some very disturbin' stuff going on once again over at the house. Somethin's got Otie down in the bed. She can't walk. She says her legs feel so stiff all the time and whenever she moves 'round the pain is unbearable. Says when it first started, movin' 'round a little bit would ease the pain, but now she can't get up at all without help from somebody."

"Me and Vella took her for a short walk earlier today. We held her up, but I could tell she was in some terrible pain tryin' to walk. I forced her to 'cause I just think she's gotta fight whatever this thing is destroyin' her legs. What could that be? You think them roots that bad woman who was after Mr. Harrington done jumped on my sister, 'cause iffin' they did, I swear fo' Gawd, I'm gonna kill him this time."

"No, no, no Maude, that ain't it. It don't sound like them roots this time. Baby, it sounds like that thing folk 'cause "rithis, arthoritis, arth... somethin' or another." It makes a person ache like the devil and then make the joints in your body lock up on you. I got some liniments we can use on her. If we keep her walkin', keep puttin' them liniments on, and keep prayin', we're gonna get her back. Let me go in the house and get my medicine bag. We'll jump on my wagon and go start workin' on Otie right now. Gal, me and you been doin' this doctorin' thing for a long time, and we ain't gonna lose this battle, ya hear me?" Maude smiled and waited for Mama Mame to get her liniments and other medicines.

Every day Maude and Novella took Leotia for a walk, and every day the distance they traveled got longer. They took turns in applying the liniments made of cod liver oil and kerosene to her legs.

At first Maude's rub downs were painful. "Oh my Gawd Maude, are you tryin' to help me or kill me? Yo big ol' hands feel like they breakin' my bones. Ouch, Maude I'm not playin'. You're hurtin' me. Vella help me. Get her off of me."

"Oh gal shut up. You know good'n' well I ain't breakin yo bones. I'm tryin' to get you better so you can have some strong legs in case Mr. Harrington run you outta here. Now be still and let me rub you down."

"Otie, I know it hurts, but Maude's big ol' hands are what you need right now. Them big ol' hands good for somethin' ain't they?"

Maude shook her finger at Novella, "Okay baby gal, that's enough 'bout my big ol' hands."

The strong massages, application of Mama Mame's liniments, and walks were working. Mama Mame also created a potion including mullein, granulated slippery elm bark, and a teaspoon of cayenne for Maude and Novella to give to Leotia every four hours.

"Yuk – my Gawd. Maude, this stuff is awful. What did she put in it? Are y'all sure she ain't dealin' in some of them roots, 'cause this stuff bad 'nuff to kill a horse."

"Drink it missy and drink it now."

"So y'all gonna stand there and make me take this. Alright – here it goes."

In no time she was back to walking on her own with the aid of a makeshift walker Mama Mame made out of a broken chair. At first she was too ashamed to go outside with the walker. She didn't want anybody to look upon her as crippled.

She dreaded running into Luke on the first Sunday she returned to church. It had been some time since she last saw him. Her conflict was being torn between wanting to be with him, and terrified at the thought that Scott's reprehensible behavior had driven a wedge so deep Luke wouldn't fight to get the relationship back on the right track. She had to find some way to regain the closeness they once shared, but wasn't sure she was ready to face him yet. She didn't want him to see her until she was walking again without help. So she laid out the conditions to Maude and Novella.

"I wanna get to church early enough so we can already be seated when the other people arrive. I don't want Luke to see me hobblin' around lookin' like some crippled ol' lady. Then when service is over, I wanna wait 'til everybody else is gone before we get up from our pew."

"Otie, if that boy really cares 'bout you, he won't mind seein' you use a walker. You've improved a whole lot and any fool can see that in a little while you'll be walkin' again without help from anybody. I know you've got a lotta pride, but trust me, you're still as beautiful as ever."

Novella added, "Yeah Otie, Luke is crazy 'bout you. If he wasn't, he wouldn't have stood up to Poppa like he did."

They arrived at church early, but fate would have it that he was already there. Maude and Novella were standing on each side of Leotia as she attempted to ascend the steps to the church. Before she could lift her leg to step up to the second step, the doors to the church opened and he ran down the steps to meet them.

The smile on his face was in contrast to the shocked look on hers. *Now I've truly lost him. There ain't no way he's gonna want to be saddled with a crippled wife. Lawd just let him walk away. If I've lost him, just let him walk away. I don't wanna see pity in his eyes. Don't let him keep starin' at me.*

He broke the silence. "Hi ya doin' Maude? You take the walker while I pick Miss Leotia up here and take her to where she wants to be seated. I certainly hope that'll be right beside me."

Before Leotia could object, he swept her up in his arms. Maude loved it. "Well I'll be damned..."

She abruptly stopped when she caught Leotia's stern eye. "I'm sorry y'all, I forgot where I was, but it's good to see a real man sweep his woman off of her feet."

She started pushing Luke in the back, urging him to walk down the church isle with Leotia in his arms. "Gone in there boy. Show 'em how it's done."

As they were walking behind Luke holding Leotia in his arms, Maude turned to Novella, "Little Vella, gal, I'll be damned..."

"Maude, be good, or Gawd's gonna strike us all down with you cussin' in His house. We keep tellin' you to get yourself saved fo' the Lawd comes back. Lawd please forgive her – she don't know what she's sayin'."

Maude was having too good a time watching the church members' shocked expressions as Luke marched down the aisle carrying Leotia to think about being struck down by lightening for cursing in church.

As she yanked Novella's arm and was pulling her along the isle, she kept talking. "I'm sorry, I'm sorry. Vella, let's just get in here and praise the Lawd like you and Otie always tellin' me I should be doin'. This here has got to be one of the highlights of this church y'all love so much. I'm tellin' ya, these folks in here 'bout ready to pee in their pants. Always got somethin' to gossip about anyhow. Let's see if they be gossipin' 'bout peeing in their pants. Oh Gawd – this is gonna be good."

The Sunday Morning Service was one of the best and one of the worst for Leotia. It was one of the best because Luke confirmed that his heart still belonged to her, and nothing was going to discourage him from loving her. However, she couldn't concentrate on anything said, sung, prayed, or preached. While she felt guilty about not paying attention in the Lord's House, she was floating on a cloud sitting next to Luke. *Lawd, I'm feelin' like I'm in heaven sittin' here. He still loves and wants me.*

After the benediction was given, he swept her up in his arms again and carried her out of the church. This time, some of the church mothers were grinning ear-to-ear, and the younger women were giggling. Once he was out on the front lawn, he gently put her down so Maude could give the walker to her.

Before they went their separate ways, he kissed her and re-assured her that everything was fine between them. "Don't worry about a thing, ya hear me? Nothin's gonna make ol' Luke walk outta your life. Be patient. In time we'll make this work for us."

The walk home was a breeze. She was riding on the high of being held by him in front of everyone. The conversations with Maude and Novella were about silly things, but true to form, she kept her real thoughts to herself.

I can feel it in these rusty bones – I'm the next one to get outta there. He's gonna see it was him that lost – not me and not Luke I'm more determined now. I'm gettin' outta his house iffin it kills me.

Chapter 28
The Evolution of Novella

While Leotia was recuperating, Novella was still helping Miss Minnie with the laundry she did for the wealthy widow, Mrs. Preston. The pay was next to nothing, but Scott didn't object to the arrangement because of Ms. Minnie's friendship with Mary. "She ain't payin' much, but I guess y'all good company fo' her and all. She missin' y'all's momma, and I reckon seein' y'all does her heart good. I like it when she stop by here on occasion. Prob'ly tryin' to check on me to see what I'm doin'. Ain't none of her bizness, but she's like family so I don't say nothin'."

Doing laundry was such a mundane chore, no one paid close enough attention to question why she was so anxious to go over to Miss Minnie's place and stay for hours. If he had known what she was up to, and the events that were about to take place, Scott would have put an immediate halt to her visits.

She was the family's darling, and they took certain things for granted, like she would never cross or do anything to hurt him. Contrary to their beliefs, she was capable of going after what she wanted regardless of what he wanted for her. She knew how to use her savvy to keep him in the dark.

They were unprepared for the bodacious moves she was capable of and about to make. The new man in her life would capture her heart and be responsible for breaking Scott's. He obsessively invested time and energy into thwarting Leotia's plans when they paled in comparison to Novella's.

It was the year 1927, and Novella would be turning fifteen in September. By July, Leotia was walking without her make-shift walker; Maude had gone back to Pittsburgh; and Scott's world, as he knew it, was on the verge of collapse.

He was finally free from the burden of guilt now that it had been confirmed Leotia's condition had nothing to do with root doctors, spells, or curses. *Things finally gettin' back on the right track. I ain't never believed in them roots like these fools 'round here, but when that thing attacked Otie, I swear fo' Gawd, I was wonderin' iffin them things done jumped on my gal. Wonderin' iffin Belle bein' in the grave didn't matter none. I ain't never even seen that Geechee woman they talk 'bout. Ain't wantin' to see her either. I ain't carin' what folk think 'bout me, but I don't want nothin' like no roots messin' with my chilluns' lives. I love 'em and they're mine.*

So now that Leotia was walking again and Novella seemed happy to be spending a lot of time with Miss Minnie, he was confident all was well on the home front. He knew nothing about Miss Minnie's grandson, Neal Reaves. By the time he found out about him, Novella had discovered a different kind of love – the kind he couldn't compete with. He was so busy manipulating everything and everybody else he underestimated the desires, ambitions, and powers of his beloved.

Chapter 29
Marion and Lizzie Gilmore Reaves

On April 1, 1906, Marion Reaves and Lizzie Gilmore, both from the City of Sanford, County of Lee, State of North Carolina, became man and wife. Marion was crazy about Lizzie although they appeared to be incompatible. Although he was laid back and soft-spoken, her fire was exactly what attracted him to her. He fell hard and asked her to become his wife within the first year of their courtship.

He wasn't from a large family like Lizzie was, but family was first and foremost to him. After they were married, both families occasionally enjoyed eating supper together, or sitting around talking on a Friday or Saturday night telling stories about the old days. His father, Ben Reaves, often visited. Like Scott, Ben wasn't born a free man and whenever they got together, everyone sat attentively listening to his stories about the old slavery days.

In 1908, Marion and Lizzie welcomed the birth of their first son, Johnny. Two years later Lizzie gave birth to Neal in July. The family grew with the births of two more sons, Lonnie and Roscoe. A house full of boys was challenging, but she still wanted to add to the family and often spoke of her desire for a daughter. "We doin' alright with our boys, but I sho' would love to have a little gal."

"It would be nice to have a little gal runnin' 'round here wouldn't it Lizzie?"

Month's later she discovered she was pregnant again, and was anxious about the arrival of her new baby. This pregnancy, however, was different and she was worried.

"I rarely ever feel this baby movin' 'round in there. The others, they kicked and moved all the time. This one, I really gotta be payin' attention to feel anything, and sometimes, I think what I'm feelin' ain't really movin' at all. What do you think 'bout that?"

"Lizzie, this baby prob'ly just gonna be a quiet soul. Everybody don't go 'round raisin' sand all the time. Them boys we got be a handful. It'll be a welcomed change to have a little one who ain't always gettin' into somethin.' Maybe all this mean is that the baby is a sweet little gal. How 'bout that?"

"Yeah – that's prob'ly what's goin' on. She just ain't noisy like her brothas."

On July 19, 1916, she went into labor. When she awakened Marion early that morning complaining about pains, he immediately left the house and rushed over to the Midwife Nanny's house. Miss Nanny's place was much closer than Mama Mame's, and so within fifteen minutes after leaving, he returned home with the midwife.

Lizzie was sitting up in a chair when they arrived looking mad instead of afraid or concerned.

"Lizzie gal, what in the world you doin' sittin' up? Now come on and get in this bed and do everything I tell ya to do. Ya hear me?"

Then Miss Nanny started coaching. "This looks like this gonna be an easy delivery. Thank the Lawd. Uh oh, here we go already. Now push real hard Baby, push, push. Here it comes, here it comes, Lizzie. I've got it, I've got it."

Once the baby was out, the next statement spoke of the worst case scenario.

"Oh My Gawd."

"What do you mean 'Oh your Gawd?' What happened, what's goin' on? What did I have?"

Miss Nanny answered part of the question. "Lizzie, you and Marion had a baby gal."

Lizzie picked up on the operative word immediately. "Why are you saying had a baby gal?"

"Lizzie, she so small, and didn't make it. I'm sorry your little angel is stillborn. She ain't alive." Lizzie was devastated.

Her wish for a daughter became a reality exactly three years later when in July of 1919 she gave birth to a healthy baby girl. She named their daughter after her mother. Marion and Lizzie welcomed Minnie Reaves into their family of boys. After Minnie, she gave birth to three more sons: Walter, Wesley, and Rommie.

Chapter 30
Neal Reaves and Novella Harrington

The day was sunny and scorching hot. Nobody wanted to go outside unless they absolutely had to, and certainly no one wanted to be walking around in the sizzling July heat.

"Neal, go over to Grandma Minnie's house and pick up them fresh vegetables she promised me."

Poppa must be crazy sendin' me out in this heat just to get some vegetables. We got plenty in the house, but he wanna send me out in this heat to get a heat stroke or somethin'. Ain't no vegetables worth havin' a heat stroke over. This is one trip I ain't lookin' forward to takin'.

Shortly after he arrived at Grandma Minnie's house, a tall, slender girl came from around the back of the house and was on her way in. Who was this beauty, and why was she comfortable with going into Grandma Minnie's house as if she lived there? Grandma Minnie never mentioned any young girls coming over to her house so much that it was like a second home.

Okay Lawd, I take back every word I said. This trip was definitely worth a heat stroke. He looked around expecting to see someone else come up beside her. *She's gotta have a boyfriend, or he's some kinda fool lettin' her out by herself. Well – his mistake be my good fortune.* He knew instantly that he wanted her, and he was not about to miss an opportunity to get to know her. No one came up beside her and he breathed a sigh of relief.

Although he was sixteen years old, Neal had already started experimenting with some of the girls around Sanford and the Gulf. Marion was strict but that didn't stop Neal and Johnny from sowing wild oats. They were handsome, playful, and aggressive. They went after whoever and whatever they wanted, and usually got their way.

He had not met anyone who looked like the stunning beauty standing before him and affecting him like she was doing. He could tell that she was different.

I gotta be careful here and not mess this up. She's some kinda pretty, and I can tell she's real ladylike and everything. Nothin' like them girls me and Johnny been runnin' 'round with. Dang, what am I 'posed to say to a girl like her?

He was feeling something he wasn't accustomed to. *My daggone hands are sweatin' and my mouth is feelin' awful dry. What in the devil is goin' on with me? I ain't never felt like this fo' no girl.* He had just stumbled upon the girl whom he dreamed about often, but had not met until now.

"Hey, I'm Neal. What's your name?"

"Hi Neal, my name is Novella Harrington. I'm pleased to meet you."

He was hooked and didn't want to get away. She extended her hand towards him for a handshake, but he was too nervous to take it. He simply stared at it. Still nervous, he asked another blunt question, "Where's my Grandma Minnie?"

"She's still in the backyard. Look, I'm goin' into the house to get another basket for the clothes we're takin' down off of the lines 'round back. Wanna help?"

He was still lost for words, but finally got one out. "Okay."

When she returned to the backyard with Neal, Grandma Minnie smiled at the sight of him holding the basket. Her grandsons usually balked at chores such as doing laundry, believing they were women's work. Now one of them was holding a basket in his hands, grinning from ear-to-ear, and ready to help with the laundry. Novella proceeded to instruct him on how to take the clothes down from the clothes line, fold, and place them neatly into the basket. While Grandma Minnie knew her grandson was attracted to Novella, she was also familiar with his reputation, and felt compelled to put him on notice. This girl was like family and was to be treated like a lady.

When the opportunity presented itself, she stepped up close and whispered a warning in his ear. "If you even thinkin' 'bout doin' anything that could wind up hurtin' this young gal, I swear fo' Gawd, I'm gonna pull yo pants down and whip your hind parts myself. Ya hear me boy?"

Hurting her was not on his mind. As bad as he wanted her, he was intimidated by her.

"Grandma Minnie, calm down will ya. I ain't gonna do nothin' to hurt nobody, especially this beautiful lady right here."

After finishing up with the laundry, he tried without success to convince her to let him walk her home. Fresh on her mind, however, was Scott's determination to break up Leotia's and Luke's relationship. She was learning how to handle such matters from her older sisters' experiences. She wasn't ready for Scott to meet him and devise a way to sabotage the relationship before it had a chance to get started.

Neal watched as she was walking away. *That be the girl for me. I'll have Miss Novella Harrington, and ain't nobody gonna stop me.*

The next time she went over to Miss Minnie's place, Leotia accompanied her. Neal was already there when they arrived.

"Hi Neal, this is my sister Leotia. We call her Otie."

"Hey Otie, how you doin'?"

"Pleased to meet you Neal."

They exchanged pleasantries, but he was anxious to talk to Novella. As they were doing their chores, Leotia observed how close he stuck by Novella, and that he clung to every word she said. She couldn't help but smile seeing how comfortable her genteel sister was with giving this obviously smitten boy orders. He didn't appear to be the kind of boy who took orders from a girl, but she could tell he was willing to do anything just to be close to Novella.

When he left to run an errand for Grandma Minnie, Leotia seized the opportunity to tease Novella. "Why you little sneak, you got that boy Neal runnin' 'round tryin' to please you and all. I think you done found yourself a young man. You look like you pretty sprung yourself."

"Otie, please don't say anything to Poppa. You know how he feels 'bout boys hangin' 'round us."

"Are you kiddin' me, I wouldn't tell Poppa nothin' if he pulled out one of them big black straps he claims come from the old slavery days. Vella, I'm still kinda bitter 'bout how he broke me and Luke up. I'm not 'bout to ruin anything for you. Don't you worry none – I ain't gonna tell ol' Mr. Scott Harrington a thing. Serves him right."

She knew how much he adored Novella and could image his reaction once he found out that his baby girl was interested in a man other than him. *Oh yes. This is gonna be real good. Finally Poppa's gonna get to feel that pain the rest of us have to feel tryin' to love him. He's gonna see this as rejection and won't be able to even stand the thought of Vella lovin' another man 'sides him. Vella's secret is safe with me. I'm gonna make sure Poppa don't get a heads-up. I ain't givin' him no ammunition to tear somebody else's love and life apart.*

Novella was seeing Neal at least twice a week without Scott knowing about the budding relationship. Now that Neal was helping out with the chores, they finished earlier than usual and had plenty of time to devote to each other. Novella and Leotia were careful not to deviate from the time they normally returned home. To do so would have given rise to Scott's suspicions and he would take immediate action.

Miss Minnie was glad to see there was somebody who could bring out a kinder, gentler Neal. Even she didn't know just how serious things had become. Besides, Novella was only fourteen years old and Neal was sixteen. How much trouble could two teenagers get into? The answer was more than anyone ever imagined – especially since the fourteen-year-old girl was Scott Harrington's daughter – the love of his life.

Chapter 31
A Woman Capable of Breaking Him

By January 1928, Neal and Novella had made definite plans and Neal was anxious to execute them. Novella was anxious as well, but scared. Yes, she wanted to be with him on a more permanent basis, but didn't want to hurt Scott.

She was fully aware of the power she held over him. He responded to her in ways he didn't or couldn't with anybody else. He believed she could do no wrong. She showered him with adoration no matter how badly he behaved; didn't battle with him like Maude; had not walked out on him like Herbert and Walter; didn't leave on unfavorable terms like his daughters from his marriage to Iris; and had not engaged in a battle for freedom with him like Leotia did.

Although he was good at alienating himself from those who tried desperately to love him, he was dependent on what he perceived as his perfect relationship with her. *Gawd All Mighty, Poppa's gonna die when he find out I'm in love with Neal, and he's the love of my life. I still get chills just thinkin' 'bout that fight he had with Otie and Luke. Oh well, I just ain't gonna let him find out anything 'til it be too late fo' him to stop me. Otie tried to tell him up front what she wanted to do and look what happened. Not me. I'm not sayin' a thing 'til I'm just about out of the door.*

Back in October, Neal took her over to Sanford to meet Marion, Lizzie, and the rest of the family. They adored and embraced her as their own. She got along so well with them, she started referring to Marion as "Pa Mern", and Lizzie "Momma

Lizzie." As good as she was feeling about her new family, she was dreading the day when she had to tell Scott about them. He would perceive her relationship with the Reaves as abandonment. She knew all too well rejection wasn't something he tolerated, and his response was always brutal.

Although she didn't look forward to hurting him, she was his daughter and possessed some of his characteristics – namely the ability to control a desired outcome. Just like he went after whatever he wanted in life, she was going after what she wanted. In order to have Neal, she would have to devastate him. She was going to walk away from him for another man. He would never understand that her love for him was different than what she was feeling for Neal. Rejection was rejection to him. So she made up her mind not to suffer the same fate as Leotia, but was going to seal her own fate without any interference from him.

When Novella and Leotia got up early on March 9, 1928, they started the day out as usual, careful not to do anything that would cause him to question their schedule. However, this wasn't going to be an ordinary day because before it was over, life would forever be changed for a lot of people – especially Scott. Their chores were completed and they cooked enough food for lunch and supper. Before leaving the house, they stopped by his room to let him know they would be at over at Miss Minnie's place for most of the day.

Leotia was shivering with anticipation. A part of her was nervous just thinking about his reaction, while another part of her was delighted that Novella was getting away with her plan to elope.

Novella was feeling happy about becoming Neal's wife and a part of his large family. They would live with Pa Mern and Momma Lizzie until they could afford their own place.

Space will be tight over there at Pa Mern's and Momma Lizzie's place, but I don't care. As long as I'm Neal's wife, that's all I care about.

Gawd, I'm still achin' for Maude. She's been like a momma to me ever since Momma died. I miss her watchin' over us and tryin' to protect us from everything and everybody. I still miss Beolia. Still can't believe she died like she did so young. Right after we lost her, Walter decided to up and leave the Gulf. I miss all of 'em so much. Poppa, he hurt Otie so bad, she disappeared too. She still be in the house, but her heart ain't there. I just pray to Gawd her heart gets healed one day. But here's my chance at happiness and I ain't givin' it up – not even fo' Poppa.

She kissed him on the way out. He grunted in agreement with the gesture as if it was no more than what he expected.

When they arrived at the spot where Neal instructed them to meet, he was already there waiting with his cousin, George Payne. Unlike Leotia and Novella, Neal and George didn't seem nervous at all. As the sisters approached, Neal abruptly stopped laughing at whatever joke George was telling. She wasn't dressed like she was going to her wedding, but to him she looked downright heavenly.

When she was standing directly in front of him, he reached out and took her hand. "You look real pretty. You ready?"

Although she said "yes," he knew she was struggling with the thought of facing Scott after the wedding. Gently squeezing her hand, he reassured her that everything was going to be fine. "I promise you, it's gonna be alright. You've gotta trust me on this. We're gonna be together forever and nothin's gonna stop us. You just wait and see."

She shook her head up and down, happy to agree with him, but too nervous to say anything. He knew what to say. "Let's go." They proceeded to the Lee County Courthouse.

Things were quiet when they arrived, but that did nothing to calm Novella's nerves. She thought the white people in the main lobby were looking at them suspiciously.

"Neal, maybe we should do this some other time. I don't want any trouble outta these people. They lookin' at us like we're up to no good and I think we better go home."

"No, we're not leavin' but gonna get married today and that's that. Nobody's gonna get into trouble. You just remember to tell them you're eighteen and I'll say I'm twenty-one. Nobody's interested in us colored folk anyhow and won't even bother to go checkin'. So come on now. Don't you want this as much as I do?"

"Oh yes. I'm ready to get married Neal Reaves."

Neal Reaves and Novella Harrington became man and wife, with Leotia Harrington and George Payne standing in as witnesses to the marriage. The Certificate of Marriage stated that Neal was twenty-one years old and Novella was eighteen years old.

After the ceremony, Leotia kept going over the vows in her head. *Those were the most beautiful words I've ever heard. I been hearin' 'bout some colored girls who do get pretty weddins'. They probably got their mommas to help them and all. Plus their poppas ain't nothin' like ours. This wasn't bad at all. As a matter of fact, it was quite beautiful. I can't wait 'til it's my turn to be hearin' those words.*

Plus, them white people Vella thought was gonna make trouble wasn't no trouble at all. The hard part is gonna be explainin' what just happened to Poppa. That war is gonna be just like that Civil War he told us about that freed the slaves. Poppa ain't gonna take Vella's emancipation well at all. Ain't gonna be no President Lincoln signin' no executive order to set Vella free. Poppa wouldn't honor it no how. Vella went ahead and signed her own Emancipation Proclamation in the form of a Certificate of Marriage.

Before she left the courthouse, she pulled Novella to the side.

"Vella, what should I tell Poppa? I hope he don't come lookin' fo you and Neal and kill y'all the minute he finds you. My nerves are all over the place. I'm so happy you pulled this off, but I'm afraid too. Tell me exactly what you want me to say."

Novella, caught up in the excitement about her newly found freedom, waved her hands as if she didn't have a care in the world. "Just tell him the truth Otie. Tell him I'm a married woman. Pa Mern and Momma Lizzie want us to celebrate our wedding day by eatin' cake with everybody. Me and Neal will be over later to pick up my things. Otie I'm so, so happy."

Walking back home, she started bracing herself for the wrath of Scott. *Vella is one courageous gal. I don't know of any woman that's had the courage to defy Poppa. Now the one he seems to love the most has gone and done just that. I hope I'm just as courageous when I break the news to him.*

Her only option was to tell him the truth. Novella wanted it that way. Besides, this was too big to lie about, and by dusk he would be furious that Novella wasn't home. She shivered when she focused on the magnitude of what was getting ready to happen. Announcing Novella's wedding was going to be unlike anything he ever had to deal with. Her initial glee at seeing him squirm over the loss of Novella was turning into dread.

As soon as she walked into the room, he noticed that she was alone. "Where's your sister?"

She had been practicing giving him the news with bravado, but suddenly her voice disappeared and she stared at him with a blank expression on her face. Sensing something wasn't right, he repeated the question. "I said, where's your sister?"

She snapped out of her frozen state and blurted it out. "She got married today."

"Otie, you are not to fool with me gal. Now I'm askin' you a question and I want the right answer."

She saw the familiar dangerous look in his eyes; the look that reduced everyone to nothing; made even white men take a bow; and could burn holes into the soul of the devil.

What on earth am I gonna say?

Then she found the courage that deserted her in the past as images played out in her mind like scenes from a silent movie scrolling on a projector. Suddenly she was standing before him as if it was that day when he blew up, became violent, and threw Luke out of the house. On that awful day he made her feel like less-than-nothing; as if she had no rights whatsoever to have a say in anything about her life. She could do nothing but cry, beg, and plead with him not to drive Luke out of her life. She felt even worse when her crying and begging did nothing to move him to respond favorably to her pleas.

This time, however, she wasn't going to let him destroy another Harrington woman's chance at happiness. She was ready to do battle with him.

"Poppa, I just told you, she got married today. She's now married to Miss Minnie's grandson, Neal Reaves. They told me to tell you they'll be over here later to pick up her things."

He lost it, picked up a chair, and was ready to hurl it through the window when the expression on her face brought him back to the realm of reasonable consideration. *There it is again – the look in her eyes that night I put Luke out and the exact same look she had when we bumped into each other in the hallway. That gal was so mad at me, she refused to move aside. Stared at me with pure loathin' and dared me to do anything 'bout it. My Gawd, she's still holdin' everything she think I did to her against me.*

He felt like such a fool thinking he had gotten comfortably back into her good graces, and that she no longer despised him for what he did to her and Luke. Now here he was getting some of the most devastating news of his life, only to find out that both daughters had been masters at hiding their agendas. Everyone was slipping away.

He was distraught and wanted to tear up everything and everybody. However, if he did, he would lose whatever remnants were left of his relationship with Leotia and possibly Novella. The expression in her eyes also brought back to his remembrance the look in Herbert's eyes before he walked out of his life for good; the look in Walter's eyes before he ran off to Baltimore; the look in Maude's eyes everytime they had one of their big fights; and the resentful looks in the eyes of Irene, Beulah, Fannie, and Naomi when they gave up trying to be close to him, moved out of his house, and ultimately out of his life.

He was now backed into the corner he had been creating for years. Novella dealt him a blow he was certain, until now, no woman was capable of. Then to add salt to his opened wound, he was forced to endure the chastisement of the only child remaining under his roof. She was daring him to make the wrong move. If he proceeded with his ranting or hurled the chair through the window, she would shut him down permanently.

He had taken far too much for granted when it came to Leotia. She was not the innocent girl who, in the past, would do anything to keep the peace. She had discovered one of her greatest weapons and knew how to use it. He was on the verge of losing what little ground he had taken so long to gain.

She, on the other hand, knew he had interpreted what she was feeling in her heart by being the object of her deadly stare. "Poppa, put down that chair. They'll be here in a little while to get her things. Vella wants to be Neal Reaves' wife, and there ain't nothin' you can do 'bout that. It's done. Poppa, do you understand me? It's done. Vella got what she wanted."

Now in a weakened state, he needed to sit down. The rocking chair was only at the opposite corner of the room, but the walk felt like a mile. A lifetime of losses felt like he had a dead man strapped to his back and had been dragging the corpse out of slavery into what was supposed to be his freedom. Would he always be a slave to the loss of loved ones? Was this his cross to bear? Would he ever be free to live and love without the fear of losing those who loved him? He had to do something to end this curse. He couldn't lose Novella, but had to find a way to keep her and Leotia with him. He sat down and waited for them to arrive.

He was asleep when they burst through the front door. As soon as they crossed the threshold, he sprang to his feet, forgetting all about his vulnerable position. He immediately rushed over to Novella and grabbed her by the upper arm.

"Gal what have you up and done? You done lost yo mind runnin' off to get married without askin' me. I don't know nothin' 'bout this slicksta. You had better expla..."

Before he could finish speaking, something with a vice-like grip closed around his wrist. It felt like the steel trap Massa Seamore made the overseer and slave bosses use to catch runaway slaves, but this wasn't his ankle. The excruciating pain was forcing him to loosen his hold on her arm.

He was confused with a flashback. *Was it the overseer's shackles closing around his arm? How and when did James Seamore find out about his plan to run away?*

The grip was a frightening reminder of the overseer's tactics on the Seamore plantation, but he grew angrier when he realized who was now attacking him. Refusing to let go of Novella's arm, he turned to Neal with the intention of scaring him with his signature glare that people swore scared the devil himself. Only this time, his eyes locked with an expression that looked ten times as menacing as any look he was capable of giving his enemy. He was in serious trouble.

"Mr. Scott, if I was you, I would be takin' your hand off my wife 'bout right now. I'm tryin' to respect you sir, but ain't nobody gonna be puttin' his hands on my wife. So before this here gets real ugly, I'm askin' you once again to let her go."

Scott was trapped. It was not his nature to back down from a fight, and instinct warned that he was dealing with a man who was not only physically strong, but was also willing to kill if the fight took him there.

Foolish pride influenced his foolish decision to keep fighting for Novella. "Boy you had better take yo hand off of me. You ain't takin' my baby outta this house. I'll see you dead first. You want me to throw you outta here like I did that pup Luke Spruiel? I got rid of him, and you 'bout to disappear too."

His tirade re-opened an old and ugly wound. Leotia was standing there taking in everything. He only realized his mistake when he heard her say, "Oh my Gawd, you are the devil reincarnated."

The momentary distraction cost him, and he wasn't prepared for Neal's next move. The herculean grip on his wrist tightened as he was about to suffer the ultimate embarrassment in front of Novella and Leotia. Considering his height, it was a long way down to the floor to be brought to his knees. He couldn't live with himself if he had to suffer yet another humiliation. He released Novella.

"Just go. I want you outta here right now."

Under any other set of circumstances, he wouldn't have given a second thought as to how the other person felt when he ordered them out of his house. This wasn't any other person. When he saw the hurt and tears in her eyes, he wanted to wrap his arms around her and beg her not to leave him. He was deflated and asked them to leave again. This time it was a plea rather than a dismissal. "Vella, please leave Poppa alone."

She couldn't ever remember seeing him looking so defeated and wounded. On plenty of occasions she had seen him angry, seldom smiling, dangerously quiet, but never broken.

She reached out and gently placed a hand up to his cheek. "Poppa, I do love you so much. I would never hurt you, and I'm not leavin' you. I love Neal and want a life with him too. The way I love Neal has nothing to do with the way I love you – don't you know that? At some point, a woman needs the kinda love a man who ain't her poppa can give her. That's what comes naturally Poppa."

He removed her hand from his cheek and placed it up to his lips. "Go and get yo stuff Baby. Poppa still love you."

Now that he was in reasonably good shape, she wasn't going to stick around to see things deteriorate again. She rushed off to her room to pack.

When she returned to the kitchen, Neal was standing next to him with a hand on his arm as a gesture of concern.

"Mr. Scott, this ain't bad as you think it is. We won't be goin' too far from here. You ain't losin' her."

Scott shook his head in acknowledgement without saying anything. Novella ran over to Neal and started pulling him towards the door. She was ready to go and start her new life as Novella Harrington Reaves.

After they left, he went over to the rocking chair. There was no fire lit, but he sat there staring into the fireplace. Leotia was silently thanking God Novella made it out in one piece. As she observed him from a distance, she wondered what he was thinking about.

As he sat rocking and staring into the flameless fireplace, he was thinking about his life and all of his losses; How him and Walter were denied a life with Fondella just because James Seamore wanted her all for himself; James Seamore's hypocrisy of fawning over him and Walter, giving them certain privileges intended to ingratiate himself to them, but turning a blind eye when the overseer, slaves bosses, and his nieces abused them;

and how the Seamore nieces only wanted him sexually down in the woods, willing to do anything he demanded of them, including professing their love for him and calling him "master" and "Mr. Harrington", but then treating him like a slave the minute they were within view of any white people. He remembered losing Lillie, Iris, and Mary to early deaths.

Even the stories about Belle and the Geechee woman came to mind. He thought about the havoc people said the root doctor wreaked upon the lives of his family members at the behest of Belle, and how in the end she turned her fury on Belle. Although he ridiculed those people who believed the Geechee had supernatural powers, he had to admit the untimely deaths of three wives, the loss of his sons, and Belle's tormented death seemed more than coincidences. The supernatural had to be responsible for taking every woman he cared about away. What strange forces in the universe had conspired to rob him of every son he fathered?

At one time, he refused to accept the notion that any woman had the powers as it was said the Geechee possessed. Yet history seemed to have proven him wrong. *Maybe the ol' witch do got the powers everybody 'round the Gulf been gossipin' 'bout. If she can tear people away from those that they love, then surely she be capable of bringin' a person back to somebody that love them. I want my baby gal back, and if I gotta go to hell to get her, I'm goin'. Ain't nothin' personal with that boy, but I can't care nothin' 'bout him. He get in my way, then I take him to hell and leave him there whilst I bring my gal back home where she belong.*

I'll make sho' I give that Geechee special instructions. She better not hurt my baby else I'll make her wish she never came up here from South Carolina. Don't nobody like the ol' woman anyhow, and they don't talk to me, so nobody gotta ever know I sold my soul to the devil. His mind made up, he fell into a peaceful sleep.

As Leotia was walking pass him later, she breathed a sigh of relief, thankful he had calmed down and seemed to have accepted the reality that Novella was now married to Neal. Had she known his thoughts before he fell off to sleep, she would have immediately dropped to her knees and started praying again because he was contemplating going to the bowels of hell to bargain with the devil.

Chapter 32
Scott Harrington and the Geechee

When he cleared the woods leading up to the shack, strange and pungent odors filled his nostrils. *What on earth is this ol' woman cookin' up in that shack of hers? Don't smell like nothin' I've ever tasted and bet no one else has.* He wasn't going to let the offensive odors discourage him from doing what he had to do. Novella was too young, in his opinion, to be anybody's wife, and he needed to bring her back home. Besides, he wasn't asking the root doctor to kill anyone – that is unless they prevented him from getting his way.

He shook himself one last time, took a deep breath, proceeded to climb the rickety steps, and knocked.

Before he finished knocking, the door opened. Hazel colored eyes flashing with fire met with light gray eyes as cold as ice. He wasn't intimidated by the piercing gaze of the Geechee.

"Mornin' Ma'am, my name is Mr. Scott Harrington, and I'm here fo' you do somethin' I needs' done. Can I talk to you?"

She cocked her head to the side while staring and sizing him up. *My Gawd, no wonder dat' crazy and 'ceitful fool Belle spent all her money over dem years tryin' to get this man 'way from him lawfully ladies. He be one fine lookin' man. Don't think I've ever seen one like him 'round des' parts.*

What impressed her the most was that she didn't detect an ounce of fear. He was nothing like those who feared her, but were still willing to use her to destroy their enemies. This man knew what he wanted, and since he had come to her, she knew he wouldn't take no for an answer. He was determined to get something done with supernatural powers. He wasn't interested in what was proper or reasonable. He wanted what he wanted at any cost. But what could he want? All of his wives were gone, and she had taken care of that dumb-witted Belle. So what could he need her for?

She finally opened the door wider and step to the side. "Come in suh and tell Ol' Geechee warruh you want."

"I want you to bring my daughter Novella back to me."

Still problems with gals.

"Weh yo gal be at suh?"

"She went off and got married, but she's still so young, and needs to be home with me – her poppa."

"She be in lub?"

"That don't matter none to me. She needs to be home with her poppa, and I want you to make that happen. But whatever you do, don't hurt my baby gal. Do you understand me?"

"Yaas' suh."

She then gave him her price. He, in turn, shoved some bills into her withered old hand.

"Whatever. Just get it done Ma'am."

She didn't take offense to his brusqueness. Her instincts told her that his attitude wasn't personal. This was just how this man handled his business. She took the money and shoved it into her pocket as she watched him walk away.

"Dat man proof that some scars nebbuh heal. Mus'bz some kinda' hard tryin' to lub Mistuh Scott Harrington."

Chapter 33
Promises Kept

Novella wasn't immune to his heartbreak. There just wasn't much time to dwell on his adjustment to life without her. Unlike the house she grew up in, the Reaves household was chaotic because of the number of people living there; not because people were begging, fighting, and dying for love. Still she delivered on the promise not to cut him out of her life. Each Saturday afternoon was reserved just for the two of them.

"See Poppa, I promised you wasn't losin' me. I try to get over here every week, and you see we're still spendin' time together. You got all worked up over nothin'. I'm still here just like I said I would be."

"I know Baby. Poppa just couldn't see his little gal livin' with somebody else as their wife. It tore me up to lose you, but I truly 'preciate you spendin' time with yo ol' man.You kept your promise and I love you for it. Tell me what's goin' on with you and Neal."

Always the chatter box, she talked a little bit about everything, unware that she was sharing too much information. He was storing all of it in his memory bank for dubious reasons. He didn't know when or how, but it was going to be useful some day. It was just a matter of time when the opportunity presented itself.

The sad expression that appeared whenever she announced it was time to leave was back, and it was troubling.

"What is it Poppa? What's on your mind? You do know I love you don't you?"

"I know Baby, I know."

As a matter of fact, the expression on his face went beyond sad. It was haunting, and that was what bothered her the most. What she didn't know was the expression had more to do with guilt than with sorrow. He had collaborated with the Geechee, and she could never find out to what lengths he was willing to go in order to bring her back under his roof and rule.

Gawd, I never thought in a million years I'd even mention my baby's name in the same breath as that evil witch. I just can't have her livin' over there with them Reaves. She belongs here with her poppa. Iffin I gotta bargain with the devil to get her back, then so be it. Money ain't even a problem 'cause whatever it costs to get her back, I'm mo' than willin' to pay the price. Ain't nothin' nobody can do 'bout it now. What's done is done, and I can live with anything but that witch harmin' my baby.

His scheming was precise, but in forethought he was ignorant to the consequences of his actions. He failed to consider that there is usually someone, somewhere who either knows the deepest, darkest secret or stumbles upon it. His one dimensional plot to gain control over Novella's life blinded him to the possibility of losing much more than his hallmark dominance. His secret was not safe.

The kiss to his cheek interrupted his thoughts. "Gotta go Poppa. I'll see you next Saturday. Neal's outside waitin' for me."

As he watched Neal take her hand and walk away, his resolve to win her back was strengthened. He kept staring even after they were so far down the road, they appeared as mere specks. This was war and he had enlisted the help of the most effective weaponry he could find.

It was around October in 1928, when Novella started experiencing symptoms totally foreign to her. "Neal, I'm not feelin' like myself. My stomach always upset no matter what I eat. I stay hungry, but can't keep nothin' down. This queasy feelin' is drivin' me crazy."

"Sorry Novella, I don't know 'bout stomach problems and queasy feelins' in women folk. Maybe you should ask Momma or Grandma Minnie."

Momma Lizzie was also concerned, and went to Grandma Minnie for some answers. "Momma, somethin's goin' on with Novella. She's layin' around a lot not feelin' too good, and that ain't like her."

"Y'all gone over to Mammie's. She'll tell you in a second what's goin' on. She's good at that stuff. I'd say better than Doc Moore."

Everybody in the room darn near jumped out of their skin when Mama Mame took one look at her, and started yelling and running around in circles. "Great day in the monin'. Oh my sweet Jesus, my Mary's baby is havin' a baby. Don't y'all know a pregnant gal when y'all sees one? Lizzie and Minnie, y'all been here befo'. Stop lookin' at me like I'm crazy. Ain't nothin' crazy 'bout me. I knowed it the minute I laid eyes on her. I'm just rejoicin' 'cause Mary's baby is havin' a baby!"

"Baby gal, you have nothin' to worry 'bout. When yo time has come, Mama Mame is gonna bring that beautiful baby of yo's into this world."

The room was now buzzing with conversation and laughter over the breaking news that shouldn't have been news to Lizzie and Grandma Minnie. They were so used to treating her like everyone's little darling, it never occurred to them that she was pregnant. Novella was of mixed emotions.

I'm happy 'bout havin' Neal's baby, but I hope this ain't gonna be a burden on him. He's so worried 'bout findin' a better job to take care of us. Plus we wanna move out and find our own place. He just don't make enough money for us to do what we wanna do right now. Now I've gotta tell him he's got more responsibility with this new baby. I hope he'll be as happy as I am.

While he wasn't the type to get all excited about such things as pregnancies, she could tell he was proud at the thought of becoming a father.

"Novella, don't you go and start worryin' 'cause we're gonna be okay. Soon, I'll get a job that can take care of us. There's a white man I met at the General Store in town who says his brother is a supervisor at a soda plant over in Winston Salem. I can go over there for awhile to make enough money to save up for the baby. Poppa and Momma will look after you real good while I'm gone."

There was a way she could help out as well. Once she started feeling better, she was going to visit the home of that elderly lady Minnie told her about, who needed help with light chores around her place. The job sounded like something even a pregnant woman could handle. This was the perfect way to bring in more money to contribute to their plans for the future.

Chapter 34
The Emancipation of Leotia Harrington

With Novella now married and living with the Reaves, to her disappointment, Leotia was the only one left living at home. She couldn't get over how easily he seemed to have accepted the loss of the apple of his eye to another man. Accepting defeat was not characteristic of him. After the confrontation with Neal, he became quiet about the matter, discussing it with no one. Novella had succeeded in carrying out a covert plan that devastated him – all right under his nose.

Despite his external calm, she noticed the same haunted expression in his eyes that Novella saw. The haunted expression was her least worry though. His disappearing acts had resumed, and there was cause for alarm.

It had been years since he disappeared without warning. Now he had a new secret. She wasn't just concerned, but was suspicious because his secrets usually turned into chaos and tragedy. Any other man his age would have been settling down to a life of peace and tranquility. He wasn't interested in peace or tranquility. The way he saw it, neither one would bring Novella back home. Treachery, immorality, and the willingness to get involved in some very dangerous and destructive schemes were the means to the end he was desperately seeking. The controlling man willing to destroy anyone who got in the way of what he wanted still existed. He was comfortable with doing anything to get his way regardless of who got hurt.

The night Leotia found out what he was up to was the night she gained her independence. She had retired for the night and was sitting on her bed journaling when she heard him moving around and about the house. Until he started disappearing again, there was no reason to be concerned about the noises he made while preparing for bed. She was now suspicious, and out of curiosity, felt compelled to take a peek to see what he was doing.

He was getting ready to leave. *He's up to somethin' and gettin' ready to leave this house in the dark and not say a word to me. I wonder what's goin' on. Whatever it is, it ain't good, I just know it.*

It was time to lay her suspicions to rest. She quickly threw on some clothes. It sounded like he was closing the door cautiously because she could barely hear it squeaking. Looking out of the window, she could see the dim light from the oil lamp moving in the direction of the woods. She then rushed out of the house to follow him. It was frightening sneaking around in the woods after dark, but necessary if she wanted to find out what he was up to.

He emerged from the woods and stood in front of an unfamiliar house looking as if he was undecided about what to do next. Appearing to have finally made up his mind, he climbed the steps to the porch, and knocked on the severely splintered door.

She was crouched down behind the bushes waiting for the unknown to be revealed. What happened next heightened the mystery and ominous air of danger. A frightening looking woman opened the door. Before he went inside, she heard him say, "You gotta hurry up Geechee and do somethin' to bring my

Vella back to me. I'm payin' a lotta money fo' this." The door closed behind him.

"Dear Gawd in heaven. He's plannin' to do something terrible to Vella and plannin' it with that ol' demon that killed Momma. If he's dealin' with her, they're plannin' to kill somebody again, and its prob'ly Neal. He can't get any lower. Maybe Maude was right. Poppa be the devil hisself. I gotta do somethin' but what? Lawd, what am I gonna do? How am I gonna' save Vella and Neal?"

She was frantic trying to come up with a plan of action. Was the right course of action to storm up to the house to let them know she was on to them, or go to Neal and Novella as soon as possible to warn them? But what was the danger? After the door closed, she couldn't hear the details of their evil plan. How could Neal and Novella battle with and win a war against the Geechee, Scott, and the evil world of witchcraft, voodoo, bad spells, and spirits? She thought about bringing Maude in because she would bet her life Maude could handle Scott and the Geechee single-handedly.

"Dear Lawd, you've gotta show me what to do. You're a good and merciful Gawd. It can't be in Your will to let Poppa and that ol' woman do harm to her and Neal."

She was too frightened to travel back through the woods alone, and decided to follow him home. She didn't know how she was going to get back into the house without him finding out he had been followed. The answer came to her as they neared the house.

As soon as he stepped on to the porch, the keen sense of hearing he was forced to develop as a slave alerted him that he wasn't alone. With the sharpness of an owl, he could pick up on sound sources made with the slightest movement, and pinpoint the precise direction of the moving object. Someone or something was coming from among the trees. Spinning around, he faced her standing at the foot of steps.

"Otie, what're you doin' out here in the dark gal? Ain't you 'posed to be in bed?"

"Poppa I followed you to that Geechee woman's house and I know what you're up to. You're evil. You have done or are gonna do somethin' despicable to hurt Vella. All she ever did was to love you, even when the rest of us couldn't stand you."

"Now wait one minute Gal, you had better watch your tongue when you speak to me."

"No – you had better listen to me. If you don't tell her what you've done, and find a way to protect her from that woman, I will. When I tell her you be willin' to use the same woman who killed Momma to hurt her just 'cause she wanna be happy, she'll never forgive you. You will lose her just like you lost Herbert and Walter."

"I declare, I'll walk outta your life along with her, and you will be left with no one. You have stooped lower than I thought you were capable of just to get your way. You're willin' to even hurt Vella – maybe kill her and her husband. I know now for sure you have no soul."

She had him where she and everybody else he ever mistreated wanted him. As soon as Maude, Walter, and Novella found out what he had done, he would be left with no one. He shuttered at the thought of Maude's wrath and violence, and wasn't so sure Walter even wanted to deal with him anymore.

"You're right Otie. I've done this despicable thing you accuse me of. Yo poppa has gone and done it this time. That ol' woman done started castin' her spell and I can't turn it 'round. I made her promise she wouldn't hurt my Vella. She's just gonna bring her back to me – that be all."

"Do you know how outrageous that sounds? That ol' woman ain't gonna be concerned with details. She just gonna do somethin' destructive that's gonna ruin everybody, if not kill somebody. Poppa, I don't know what to tell you, but you had better fix this or else you will lose all of us. I can promise you this, if it don't get fixed, you will never see any of us again."

She then marched on to the porch pushing him aside. "Move outta my way. You make me sick."

She was extremely dangerous now and held the power to destroy the image he held on to so dearly. If anyone found out about his relationship with the Geechee, in no time at all, everyone would know he wasn't the man he portrayed himself to be. They would know how frightened he was to be alone, and that he was so desperate to have his daughter back, he resorted to witchcraft – something he had sworn he was above.

He couldn't win this battle. His only hope was for the Geechee to follow his instructions to the letter. He wasn't concerned about what bringing Novella back would do to Neal. Trapped in his own web of destruction, he went to a woman he absolutely abhorred and paid her to practice evil on the woman he absolutely adored. There was no way out of his conundrum, and Leotia was ready to expose him.

He was beyond humiliated to discover someone, namely one of his children, had been watching as he engaged in witchcraft with the Geechee. He repeatedly dismissed any talk about the root doctor and her dark powers. Yet he reached such a low point after losing Novella to Neal, he was behaving like a pathetic lover who had been rejected rather than the father who swore he loved and would do anything in the world to protect her. He was in a lot of trouble and couldn't figure a way out.

He never imagined the woman least likely to resolve the colossal mess he had gotten himself into would be the woman who wound up saving all of them.

Once again, things were different in the Harrington household and not in a way he was comfortable or pleased with. He had lost any leverage he may have held over Leotia in the past. This became quite evident when he discovered she was seeing Luke again. He had already compromised and given his permission for her to walk home from church with him provided they complied with his list of conditions. Now she had him at her mercy, and was going to outright disobey his orders. She was going far beyond his conditions. He was furious, but more frightened of her retaliation if he tried to interfere again. Not only did she not care that he was aware of her reconciliation with Luke, she even started inviting Luke to supper without his permission.

Luke was surprised when after church she extended an invitation to supper on the following Sunday. Although delighted, he was apprehensive about accepting because he still remembered Scott's violent reaction to any man who tried to have a relationship with one of his daughters. He also recalled how she didn't have any say-so in the matter when her father threw him out of the house. So when the invitation was extended as if the past never happened, he was puzzled

"Luke Spruiel, I miss havin' you over for supper, so I'm invitin' you to join us next Sunday. Be ready for some real good eatin'."

He couldn't imagine what could have changed. "Don't look so worried. Everything's fine now. Poppa's fine with you comin' over. He understands how important this is to me, and he wouldn't want to go disappointin' me."

"Otie are you sure 'bout this? I mean the last time we tried, he had a fit, threw me outta his house and all. Told me that if I cared 'bout you, I wouldn't make trouble and come between you and yo family. He sounded pretty sure 'bout his feelins'."

"Oh Luke, he got over that awhile back. Why do you think he started lettin' you walk me home from church again? He's alright with all of this. Trust me, Poppa ain't gonna make no more trouble for us. He be seein' things my way now. So you just be on time."

He tried to come up with an explanation that made sense. Maybe Scott was mellowing out after all, or maybe he was just tired of fighting with everybody. Luke was wrong on both fronts. Leotia was in a position to destroy Scott with no chance for him to rebound.

While she was confident he had no power over her and Luke, she had no idea how much he feared being alone. He struggled with the constant fear of losing family to tragedies, starting with Fondella. She may not have known the origin or existence of his fears, but she was fully aware of her position of power at present. She was free to invite whomever she felt like inviting to supper. As the woman in charge, she felt like inviting Luke.

The first Sunday was awkward. Immediately he sensed the tension in the air. *I thought she told me everything was okay. The tension in this house so thick, you can cut it with a knife. Ol' Scott still look like he can't stand the sight of me, but he's tryin' to hide it. Since he hates me so much, why on earth would he allow Otie to invite me over here?*

It looks like Otie's in charge now and that ain't how this ol' man operates. Somethin' happened and Otie's got the upper hand. Must be far more strength to my gal than I thought. Whatever it is, I love it.

He didn't want to spend a lot of time on his first Sunday back figuring out how she had gained control. He was just glad to be back in her life. His plan now was to never let her go, and in order to accomplish this he was going to have to get her out of Scott's house.

He was encouraged by the recent events that brought Scott to his knees. Neal was able to court and marry Novella while leaving him clueless until it was too late to interfere. If Novella could escape from his iron grip, then surely Leotia could do the same. Now that she had somehow managed to turn the tables on him, Luke was willing to use whatever leverage they had to free her from the dictatorship she had been living under since birth.

He had to pay very close attention. Throughout the evening she kept dropping threatening, but subtle hints. Something was different, and this time he was sure nothing (or no one) would stop him from having her as his wife.

They were finally moving forward. Luke made her feel special. His sense of humor kept her laughing. Even when he wasn't laughing, his eyes had a mischievous sparkle in them. His lively personality lifted her spirits out of the depths of Scott's cesspool of darkness. They were going to be discussing marriage soon, and she couldn't wait for him to propose. Growing impatient with each passing day, she considered dropping hints to nudge him along. In the end, he spared her the guilt of impropriety by asking him to marry her.

It was after supper and the sun was starting to set. They walked out to the front porch while holding hands. He then wrapped his arms around her. This time when he stared into her eyes, there was no mischief; no silly grins, but rather a serious expression rarely seen on the face of Luke Spruiel. Her heart started racing because she knew what was coming.

"Otie you know how much I love you don't you?"

"Yes Luke. And you know that I feel the same way about you."

"I know you do. I thought I had lost you forever that time your poppa threw me outta this house. I knew you didn't have it in you to fight him, and I couldn't do a thing 'bout that. Now I don't know what it is exactly you got on him, but I do know you got somethin' hangin' over his hard head. Whatever it be, you don't have to keep holdin' on to it 'cause I'm ready to take you 'way from here. Otie, what I wanna, what I mean to ask you is…"

"You're takin' too long Luke to get that question out. So yes, yes, yes, I'll marry you. The sooner you make me your wife, the better." They started laughing.

Back in the house, the rocking chair was moving back and forth as if a mad man was sitting there. He couldn't sit still. The laughter coming from the porch was infuriating. *What's that laughin' hyena so damned happy 'bout? He's laughin' like a fool and got Otie laughin' 'bout as hysterical as him.*

When she floated back into the house to make the official announcement, he found out that, at least for him, it was no laughing matter. His last child was walking out on him. She was going to marry Luke.

He was emotionally exhausted, but asked anyway, "When's all this 'posed to happen?"

His less-than-thrilled tone of voice could not diminish her joy. "Don't know. Me and Luke, we gotta start plannin', but Poppa, it's gonna happen. I'm gonna be Mrs. Luther Spruiel. I'm so happy, and ain't nothin' nobody can do 'bout that."

There she goes again bein' disrespectful. Otie ain't the same no more. She's turned against me too. She's as bad as her brothers. At least I still got my baby Vella. She's gonna come back to me soon, I just know it.

Chapter 35
Novella Meets the Geechee

Well into her first pregnancy, Novella looked anything but pregnant. The only noticeable change was the perfectly round ball that used to be her board flat stomach. Once the initial nausea and feelings of listlessness went away, she rebounded, and was once again ready to start the job helping Miss Flora Belle with light chores. They wanted their own place, and she was set on doing something to make that happen sooner rather than later.

Miss Flora Belle lived in a secluded wooded area where few people in Sanford or the Gulf bothered to visit. No one in the family knew that the Geechee's place was enroute to Miss Flora Belle's. Although Leotia had followed Scott there, it was dark and the surrounding area was unfamiliar.

When she found out about the fire and the proximity of Miss Flora Belle's place to the Geechee's, she thought the curse was already being carried out and in full force. It was after the dreadful fire when she learned that the chance meeting between Novella and the Geechee finally and forever separated them from the evil root doctor and her witchcraft.

You could tell the Saturday morning was going to be beautiful. The temperature was crisp, but the yellow/orange glow from the sunrise gave hint that the weather was going to seasonably comfortable for early spring. Novella was on her way to work when she smelled smoke. *Somebody's got the fireplace goin' already. It's a little bit chilly out here. Glad I threw on this sweater. Momma Lizzie keeps tellin' me to make sure I wrap up. Don't want me comin' down with anything that might hurt my baby. Her and Pa Mern sure are good to me. There's so many of them Reaves in that house, there ain't much time to think 'bout all that stuff that happened in Poppa's house over the years. I'm just glad to have a big lovin' family like them.*

She saw flickering flames through one of the front windows to the shabby-looking house she had noticed on her way to work in the past, but never paid too much attention to. The house was on fire and it looked like a serious blaze. She looked around to see if anyone else was in the immediate area, but there was no one. She called out anyway.

"Oh Gawd – somebody please help. This house is on fire. Please somebody, anybody, please come and put this fire out."

Whoever was inside was coughing, but didn't come out of the house. They must have been trapped. Instinct made her run towards the burning building. The billowing smoke and raging flames were accompanied by foul-smelling and strange odors, but that didn't stop her. Someone was in trouble and needed her help.

She was banging on the door. "If you're in there, please get out. This fire is gonna burn everything up. Please, you've gotta open up the door and get out in a hurry. Can you hear me? You don't have much time, so open this door right now. Help, help – somebody's in this house."

The person trapped inside was still coughing, and she could tell they were either close to, or had reached the door, but couldn't escape. Left with no other alternative, she kicked the door. The fire and smoke plume were moving towards the place where she stood. When she looked down, there lay an old woman still coughing and gasping for breath.

It was the Geechee. She looked like she was well over a hundred years old. Her disheveled gray hair was all over her head. Her skin was weathered and looked like the leather hide of an animal. She was down right boney. Her clothes were raggedy and smelled of kerosene and other unpleasant odors.

Although she was a fright to look at, Novella reached down and started dragging her out of the house. Before they got out flames caught onto the Geechee's tattered skirt. Novella grabbed a moth-eaten blanket and threw it over the burning skirt. As soon as the flames were smothered, she resumed her rescue efforts. Relief was short-lived when she realized they weren't safe yet because more flames were spreading towards them.

This time she couldn't be cautious or gentle. So she grabbed the Geechee, who had passed out, by the shoulders and drug her down the steps. After banging the root doctor's body against everything and anything, Novella finally pulled her away from the burning building.

By then, the horse drawn fire wagon had arrived on the scene with a group of men ready to battle the blaze. They had to move quickly in order to extinguish the fire before it spread to the surrounding trees.

While they were fighting the fire, Novella pulled the Geechee further away from the house. Confident they were at a safe distance, she sat with the old woman's head in her lap. She wasn't put off by the haggard face, unruly hair, and skeletal frame. She gently stroked the withered face and consoled her.

"Ma'am you're safe now. You're gonna be fine. We made it outta that burnin' house over there. Don't worry. I know I've bumped and bruised you up some kind of terrible, but we made it out."

The Geechee's eyelids fluttered as she was regaining consciousness. "O' my Gawd, O' my Gawd, it's you."

Novella thought she was talking out of her head. "Ma'am we got out and you're gonna be okay."

"O' my Gawd, it's you."

When the Geechee first opened her eyes, she thought she was staring into the face of Scott, and was wondering why he was holding her in his arms. She didn't remember him being in the house with her when the fire started. Then she realized it was not a man who pulled her from the burning house, but a woman who risked her life for a complete stranger. Because of the striking resemblance, she recognized the woman holding her as the same woman who Scott had paid her to work roots and destroy her marriage.

She felt a slight bump between their bodies. Looking down, she could see that Novella was pregnant. She then looked back up at her.

Dis' mus'bz one of dem' angels dat' da' Mastuh done sent down from heavin' to save Geechee. Dat' man Scott Harrington mus'bz crazy iffin' he t'inks I gonna mezz wid' Gawd. Even I knows muhself don't nobody go messin' with Gawd. 'Dat man got an angel for a gal and spec me to help him harm her. He mus'bz crazy, but I 'ent. I be daingus, but I 'ent crazy.

Out of nowhere Leotia came running towards them screaming. "Get away from her Vella; get away from her right now. Please get away from her Vella. You don't know who she is."

She tried to pull the Geechee out of Novella's arms, but Novella held on refusing to let go. "Otie, what on earth are you doin'? This lady almost died in that fire back there. Can't you see she's shook up? You know Momma taught us to respect old people.You're way past disrespectin' – you're bein' downright vicious. Girl, I declare. What's wrong with you?"

They struggled in a tug of war using the Geechee's body with both of them refusing to let go. Eventually Novella won. Leotia conceded and stepped back, but spoke with emphasis on each word. "Please Vella. You have got to do what I tell you to do right this minute. Do not question me, but put that old woman down and step away from her. I need to tell you who she is, and when I tell you what she's been up to, you just might wish you had kept walkin' and let her perish in that fire."

Before Novella could respond, the Geechee turned to Leotia and spoke up. "Gal, I knows dat' you know who I be. Dat be why you so tarrified fo' her. But know dis' – Geechee knows the Scriptuh and I taint 'bout to mezz wid' the Mastuh's 'n'int angel who He don sent to pull me from da' dey killer fiyah."

"I know the Mastuh's mussy when I see it. Now you can break her heart or you can leabe here and go back obuh yonder where y'all come from and know that yo life gonna be furh'ebbuh peaceubble. I knows you lub her and you jis' tryin' to putek her. But I tell you now, dis' angel jis' puteked yo fambly from enny tink Geechee was t'ink 'bout doin'. "Dis' gal here be Sabeyuh and I don't mess wid' the Sabeyuh."

"Gal, b'leew me. Ent no reason fo' Geechee to lie. Now take dis' angel an' gone back obuh yonder. 'E don' need to no 'bout t'ings don mattuh. "

The truth would destroy Novella if she found out Scott had schemed, collaborated, and paid to have her marriage destroyed. The Geechee kept staring at Leotia willing her to interpret what she was trying to say. In her own way, she was assuring her that she realized the magnitude of what Novella had done in saving her life, and in turn she would never bother them again. Leotia accepted the goodwill gesture from the agent of evil.

As she led Novella away she offered up a silent prayer. *Lawd, thank You for workin' through Vella to free us from that ol' woman. For generations she's been causin' nothin' but misery and death. Who would've known this is how we would get her outta our lives for good. Belle couldn't do it. Poppa's first two wives couldn't do it. Momma couldn't do it, and even Poppa himself, the mighty Mr. Harrington, couldn't do it.*

Momma always did say this was in Your hands and in due time You would fix it. You used little Vella to break the curse. Poppa used to tell Vella one day she was gonna be a great lady. He never knew how great. I thank You for everything Dear Lawd.

"Otie, what on earth was that all about? You were actin' like that ol' helpless woman was the devil himself. I've never seen you act like that.You said you were gonna tell me. So who is she?"

Leotia's first thought was, *baby girl, that there was the devil himself.* But she just pulled Novella closer to her. "She's nobody Vella. I thought I knew her, but realized I don't. She's nobody. Let's just get you home."

When Leotia arrived home that evening, he could tell something had happened. Her clothes were disheveled, soot was all over her face, and she smelled of smoke. As she approached, he saw the same menacing look when she confronted him about his bargain with Geechee. His legs were shaking so bad, he wasn't confident he could stand up as he attempted to rise from the rocking chair. He never took his eyes off of hers in spite of the menancing look in them.

His heart was thumping and the ringing in his ears was piercing. As terrified as he was to ask, he had to know. The scent of Leotia's smoke-filled clothes was too much to bear.

Oh Gawd, oh Gawd, did that evil bitch go and burn my baby up? Iffin she did, I will skin her alive before I boil her scrawny body in a kettle over a lit fire like the masters used to do to teach rebellious slaves a lesson. I will make sure she has a long and agonizin' death.

She wouldn't allow him ask, but in turn gave him the details. "No she didn't kill Vella, although that could have been the outcome thanks to you. Poppa, that lady name Miss Flora Belle lives just a little ways past the Geechee's place, and whenever Vella was walkin' over there to sit with her, she had to pass by that evil woman's shack. Today she discovered that old woman's place was on fire. The Geechee was trapped inside, but Vella risked her life and went in there. She pulled her to safety."

"The Geechee knew who she was, and thought the Lawd had sent Vella to save her. That bein' the case, she has sworn to never bother any of us again. Do you hear me Poppa? Vella did what none of the people who have been caught up in your evil web were able to do. The Geechee was partly right. It was divine intervention that after all these years has released us from that evil woman. Poppa, you should be ashamed of yourself. Vella could have been killed. Her kind heart led her to help the very person you were payin' to harm her.You were dealin' with the same roots that prob'ly killed Momma and the rest of them wives you had before her. Are you satisfied? The evil you've been dealin' with yo whole life been killin' people yo whole life. How many more people gotta die Poppa? You tryin' to kill all of us."

"Oh Gawd Otie, I never meant…"

"I don't care what you never meant. Any dealins' with that evil witch would have ended up in the ruination of all of us. I have to say the blaze that went through her house scared the daylights outta her and she is forever indebted to Vella. She knows that and has promised never to bother us again. Normally, I would be suspicious, but I know Vella saved us all from the misery that's been followin' us all these years because of you."

His shoulders slumped as he exhaled a sigh of relief and walked away. His daughters may have been safe for now, but he was going to to make sure they never had to deal with the root doctor again. Unlike Leotia, he wasn't convinced their problems with her were over, but was going to settle matters once and for all. He was going to pay her a visit Sunday morning while Leotia was in church. *After I get finished with her, she won't ever wanna come near my family again. I'll make sure of that.*

He hadn't been able to sleep all night, and was up before dawn. Once he was sure Leotia was well on her way to church, he left the house, heading in the opposite direction. *Otie, she's naïve and ready to take that witch's word, but I've been dealin' with devils like her for a many year and ain't gonna leave nothin' to chance. It be time to let the ol' gal know her reign of terror over my family will end today – or else.*

He could smell smoke as he stood taking into view the damage caused by the fire. *My Gawd, how did Vella pull that witch outta a place that burned this bad? Why would she even waste her time on this piece of trash? That's my baby gal, always wantin' to do the right thing. Iffin it was me passin' by, I would've just kept walkin' and heard 'bout it later without any damned regrets. I know it ain't pretty what I'm thinkin', but that be zackly how I feel. She dealt dirty, so she got dirty. This witch has been in my life far too long, and I'm sick and tired of her. Iffin I had my way, she'd be in hell right now dancin' with all them demons she been keepin' company with.*

As he came closer, he could tell that the smell of smoke wasn't totally attributable to leftover embers, but there was actually a burning fire around the back of the gutted out building. There he found a crudely constructed shelter without a door, but old heavy blankets that partially hid the interior. *I'll be damned. This is one devil that just refuses to lie down and die. She be too evil to even leave her hell hole that caught fire yesterday. Here she is stayin' in this thing that look and smell like an outhouse.*

"Geechee, this here is Mr. Scott Harrington wantin' to talk to you 'bout somethin'. Come out here right now."

She was stooping down over a fire mixing liquids that smelled awful with strange objects that looked like the body parts of a small animal. At the sound of his voice she became angry. She could tell he was mad, and was anticipating a fight.

"I 'bout sick of dem Harringtons and dey mess. What he comin' 'round here fo? Got odduh 'tings on my'own mind. 'Ent wantin' no bodduhr'um."

Lifting the smelly old blankets, she looked into eyes that held the same viciousness reflected in her own. "'Smattuh?"

"What's the matter is that you damned near got my baby gal burned up in this here mess with you? I asked you to bring her back to me, and I left you clear 'structions that she was not to get hurt. Now I'm 'bout ready to finish what that fire started yesterday. Tell me just what the hell was you thinkin'?"

"Okay, so you be as crazy as dat yalluh heifer Belle that comes to me all dem yeahs back. I don' know'um nutt'n' 'bout y'all or y'all's mez. I only does what I'm paid to do. So I got rid'of that piece of trash when she t'aw't she could cross ol' Geechee. I be's glad y'all finally outta my life. Then you comes back 'round heah askin' fo' mo' trouble jis 'cause you wantin' to control dat gal of yo's. Well Mistuh Scott Harrington, I was gonna do jis what yo wanted me to do b'fo the fiyah yistiddy."

"I sway 'fo Gawd, I dunno how you wind up makin' babies as pooty and precious as dat gal. Eb'n dat one dat came heah to putek her is a mighty fine lookin' and actin' gal. 'Least when she came heah, she came fo the right cause. Nebbuh t'ink I gret enny tink like git mixed up wid you and dat debble'ub'uh crazy heifer Belle you messin' wid over dem lawfully ladies of hunnuh. Eb'ry tink y'all tuch turn to ashes, 'cludin my place. Yo lawfully ladies 'served bettuh dan dem got, fsutt'n."

He grabbed her by a scrawny arm. "Come here, come here witch. Don't you pull 'way from me. I said to come here. Looka here, you messin' with the wrong man now. You evil devil, who do you think you be talkin' to? I came here to make you back off of my bargain with you."

"Stand still when I'm talkin' to you. Hear me and hear me good. I don't need you doin' nothin' 'bout my gal. I'll take care of that myself. Yeah I made one big mistake comin' to you. As matter of fact, I was willin' to sell my soul to get her back. You make me sick to my stomach, and I'm no mo' sicker of you than I am of myself 'bout now. But I promise you, if one more thing happens to any of my gals, I will have you pleadin' and beggin' me to send you to hell quick and in a hurry. Do you understand me?"

She was filled with as much contempt for him as he had for her. "Looky, I 'ent 'f'aid of hunnuh old slabe. Iffin I hadn't promised Gawd on yistiddy dat I would for ebbuh leave hunnuh fambly 'lone, I'd sho'ly be happy to fight hunnuh to the death. But no madder what hunnuh tink of me, I onnuh my wu'd wid Gawd. He send hunnuh angel to sabe me yisstiddy and I 'ent goin' back on my wu'd wid the Mastuh. Now get out'uh heah and leabe me be. T'engk'Gawd fo' dat angel and consider dis our last meetin'."

She paused, but on second thought had to have the last word, "On dis' side of hell enny how."

He wasn't going to let any woman have the last word in a conversation with him, especially one he hated. "One more thing bitch, iffin I have to come back here, I'll make sure you bust hell wide open. I dare you to try anything – and I mean anything." He then shoved her away from him to the ground.

Once he was gone, she went back to stirring up her latest concoction. Gradually a tingling sensation began to move up her arm. She attempted to shake off the uncomfortable feeling, but it wouldn't go away. Determined to finish her brew, she kept stirring, but then a more intense sensation started to spread throughout her chest. It was becoming difficult to breathe. This was more than discomfort because now her chest felt as if it was on fire and the fire was moving up through her throat.

She tried to get up, but fell back onto the dirt. While thrashing around in agonizing pain, her entire body felt as if it was on fire. She started chanting spells to get rid of the burning sensations, but the heat intensified. Her chanting became erratic as she kept switching spells trying to find one that would save her, but nothing worked.

A thought suddenly occurred to her as she was trying to get up once again. "Oh Gawd, did dat man have some kinda powers? Mabbe he...." Before she could finish what she was about to say, she fell back onto the dirt. For the first time, the look in her eyes was one of terror.

Several days later, a teenager was on his way to Miss Flora Belle's place when he was overwhelmed by a rotten smell more pungent than anything he had ever smelled coming out of the Geechee's place. Curiosity got the best of him and he went around to the back of the burned out shack to investigate.

He found her badly decomposing body with flies swarming and maggots crawling all over her. She was lying on her side with eyes still open. To satisfy his morbid curiosity, he got up close to the rotting corpse and bent down to take a look. In death and in a decomposing state they were the eyes of a terrified woman.

Instead of going to Miss Flora Belle's place as originally planned, he ran into town yelling, "Y'all ain't gonna believe this, but Geechee's dead; the Geechee woman is dead. Found her lyin' in some makeshift tent she built behind her old burned out shack. She half rotten, but her eyes look like Satan himself scared her to death. Somethin' more evil and powerful finally got a hold to her. Guess them powers of hers couldn't keep her 'round forever."

Leotia overheard the news and ran home to share the gruesome details. His response was simple. "Best fo' everybody. She ain't never meant nobody no good no way. She's in hell where she belongs. Prob'ly happy to be there, and I'm happy fo' her."

Chapter 36
Neal Reaves, Jr.

By June 1929, Novella was due to deliver her first baby, and Momma Lizzie was pregnant as well. Mama Mame had her hands full with two pregnancies in the Reaves family and was concerned about Lizzie. "Looka here Lizzie, you take it easy now with this baby. I know it's been 'bout ten years, but I ain't never forgot how you was so upset 'bout losin' that baby gal and them other babies that didn't make it as far as her. You up in the age now, but 'parently you still fertile."

It was on June 29, 1929, about 10:30 in the morning when she heard a knock at the door. She opened it to find Neal looking nervous and impatient. "Mornin' Mamma Mame. Novella's in pain, and we think it's time. Can you please come over now?"

When she arrived at the Reaves place, Novella was already lying in bed struggling with labor pains. Sweat was pouring down her face, and her expression was that of a frightened child attempting to be brave.

"Don't you worry now 'cause Mama Mame ain't gonna let nothin' bad happen to you or that baby. We ready to bring your firstborn here. I just want you to help me. Okay?"

"Yes ma'am." The labor was long and hard, but by 6 o'clock that evening, Neal and Novella were parents. After Mama Mame finished cleaning Novella and the baby up, she introduced Neal to his son. "Neal Reaves, let me introduce you to...."

He finished the announcement for her. "This here is Neal Reaves, Junior. My first son, but I'm gonna father many sons Mama Mame. Just you watch."

The Reaves household was busting at the seams. There was Marion, Lizzie, Johnny, Neal, Novella, Lonnie, Roscoe, Wesley, Minnie, Walter, and a new grandson, Neal Reaves, Jr. As Momma Lizzie's delivery date was quickly approaching, Neal and Novella were anxious. With yet another baby on the way, they had to find a place to live as soon as possible.

"Novella, I just gotta come up with a way to make more money. With not much education, ain't too many folk willin' to hire me, but I'm gonna keep lookin'. We gonna be fine."

They may not have had much money or education, but she had plenty of faith in him. "I keep tellin' you not to worry 'bout things like that. I'm happier than I've ever been. Things will happen in due time."

"That's one of the things I love 'bout you. You're always lookin' at the bright side. But remember this – I promised you a better life and I'm gonna deliver a better life to you."

"Neal, I don't ever want you feelin' like you're not doin' enough for us 'cause you are. I can't go over to Miss Flora Belle's as much, but the little bit she can afford to give me is at least somethin'. We just gotta put our heads together and come up with some other ideas."

Lizzie gave birth to Rommie Reaves on November 16, 1929. It was the Saturday following Rommie's birth and Novella was arriving to have her weekly visit with Scott. He heard the baby's cooing before they reached the house, and was already out on the front porch waiting for them.

They barely had a chance to settle in when he started probing, trying to determine exactly what the state of affairs was over at the Reaves' place. "How y'all doin' over there Vella? I gotta say, this little fella lookin' real fat and happy. Ain't that right Champ? They feedin' you real good over there? Ya almost too heavy for Poppa to hold ya."

She didn't want him to get any ideas about her decision to marry, and wasn't going to let him give her an "I told you so" look, or even worse, actually say it.

"Poppa everything's fine. I'm so happy to be with Neal. He's a good man. He works really hard tryin' to provide for us and everything."

He went along with the small talk. "Vella sometimes its hard fo' me to see you as somebody's momma. I still be seein' you as my baby gal. I know it's crowded over there at the Reaves' place, so are y'all doin' alright – gettin' 'nuff to eat and all?"

His efforts to show interest in her life didn't go unnoticed or unappreciated. She knew how much her decision to get married hurt him. "Poppa, we're doin' okay. But I just need to tell you it feels real good to be sittin' here with you and Junior. Look at you sittin' there all proud and holding your grandson.You're one handsome granddaddy. I'm serious when I tell you that I really cherish this time I get to spend with you. I have to say I'm so proud of how well you've handled all of this."

Ever since the fire at the Geechee's place happened, he was seeing her in a different light. He had always viewed her as his delicate angel. However, since Leotia shared the details, he had a new respect for her. Not only did she save old woman's life, her heroic deed convinced the Geechee to back out of her deal with him.

Sitting in his rocking chair with Junior on his lap, he observed as she moved about tidying up things.

She turned into a real fine lady, just like I said. I do miss her some kinda awful though. Wish she would come back and live with me, but I know talkin' 'bout that to her will only stir up more trouble. Neal, he's too serious, even fo' me and iffin' I bring it up, he's prob'ly gonna go off sayin' I'm tryin' to take away his manhood. I swear, that boy be somethin' else. But he love Vella and will kill anybody he think tryin' to hurt her.

Things right peaceful now so I gotta be happy with that. She sayin' she's proud of the way I handled things. She must never find out how I really tried to handle this. If Otie don't tell her what I did, she'll never find out. Otie's always prayin' 'bout everything else, I hope she prayed 'bout this, and the good Lawd told her to keep her mouth shut.

A miracle was starting to unfold as Novella described, in detail, the crowded situation over at the Reaves' place. His prayers were being answered because Neal's dilemma was his opportunity to have her close to him again.

"Vella, I've got an idea. Ain't nobody here with me now since Otie's gettin' married and movin' out, there's plenty of room 'round here. My grandson here can run 'round as much as he wanna. You and Neal can have some privacy too. Plus, it won't cost you nothin'. Listen, listen, this makes good sense. Y'all come live here and there'll be more room fo' everybody. I can't see why anybody would have a problem with what I'm offerin' y'all."

"Poppa that's a great idea, but I'll have to ask Neal first. If he agrees, we'll be movin' in with you. I love you for lookin' out for us like this."

Once again, things were looking up, and he was about to have a family back in his home.

Chapter 37
A Home Again

"Luke, we're finally gettin' married? I know we're not havin' much of a weddin' ceremony. We ain't even havin' cake like Miss Lizzie and 'em had for Vella, but I'm happier than I can ever remember bein' in my life. Poppa's so glad Vella has agreed to come back home, he ain't had the time to mess 'round in our business or come up with one of his schemes to ruin the day. I think he knows better by now. I wasn't gonna let nothin' on earth keep me away from you again."

"Otie gal, you're somethin' else. You're that same mousy little gal who let yo Poppa throw me outta the house. How could you let that happen, huh?" They laughed at his joke.

"Now that you're gonna be my wife, tell me, what's the big secret? What you got on Poppa Scott?

"Don't have nothin' on him Luke that people don't already know. He's a rascal. I'm just kiddin'. Poppa saw the light, that's all."

"Naw, you've got somethin' on him and he's runnin' scared. It must be good, so tell me. What you got on ol' Poppa Scott?"

As angry as she was with him, she wouldn't give up his secret. It was too ugly, and she couldn't stand the thought of Novella finding out to what lengths he was willing to go in order to destroy her marriage.

"I just told you Luke Spruiel, I ain't got nothin' on Poppa. He just sees things different now."

"Okay, you ain't gonna give your ol' man up, but I know better. You've got somethin' on him, and he ain't 'bout to make you mad enough to tell on him. That much I do know."

In February of 1930, Leotia and Luke were married at the county courthouse. The same reverend who presided over Neal's and Novella's marriage presided over their ceremony. Unlike Novella's wedding day, Leotia's departure was uneventful.

He couldn't and didn't want to stop her from leaving in the end because she had turned the tables on him. His secret was her ammunition, and she would use it if he interfered in her life again.

All was well because back in January, Neal accepted his offer to move in. He was beside himself with joy since Novella was coming home. There was no need to upset anyone by voicing objections to a plan he knew Leotia was going to execute anyway.

Otie's dangerous now, so it's best to let her go in peace. Otherwise, she'll destroy anything I've got left just to make me pay for what I did. Vella's movin' back in and that's good 'nuff fo' me. I love Otie, but it's time to let that gal go.

With Neal, Novella, and Junior living with him, home was once again alive with good chaos. It had been years since the sights, sounds, and aromas of family life resided there because for years people had been walking out on him for one reason or another, and the departures were never on good terms. The light of his life was home again, and that was more than good enough. He wasn't too proud to tell her how happy he was to have her back.

"Vella, you're a great wife. You've made this place come alive again, just like my Mary did when she first came here. You cook, clean, and take care of everybody just like yo momma. You lost her so young, I often wonder how you learned all this stuff."

"Poppa, Maude taught me and Otie lots of stuff. She was always givin' us directions on how to cook just like Momma did. She told us how Momma liked things clean and in order. Maude is somethin' else Poppa. She knows somethin' 'bout everything and made sure me and Otie learned a little bit of everything too. Maude is a real smart woman Poppa, not to mention strong."

He couldn't disagree with her, and was forced to credit Maude with nurturing and mothering his children, especially when he was too lost in grief to give them any attention. They no longer battled as in past years, and during times of reflection, he had to admit she was the strong force that kept them from being destroyed by circumstances that would have destroyed most families.

That gal's a warrior if I ever seen one, but she's got a big heart too. She looked out after my Mary like she was the momma and Mary was her chile. She even had the nerve to stand up to me when she didn't like something.

Truth be told, after Mary died I was a mess and couldn't let anybody know just how tore up I was over losin' another wife. But that gal, she stepped in and took them chillun with her to Pittsburgh and took care of 'em like they were hers. Don't 'preciate how she shipped them back here just 'cause I didn't send her money when she thought I should. I was gonna send it in my own time. She just didn't want me to think I was in charge. She had to go and prove a point. Hope them days behind us. I'm gettin' ol' and tired of fight'n with her.

Things got even better when fate decided to smile down on him again. His position of power was strengthened because Novella was pregnant again.

Another baby's on the way and that be the kinda news that's good to hear. That means they got more responsibility and Neal ain't got the money to handle more of that kinda responsibility. I think they'll be here for awhile. This is where she belongs – home with her poppa. He gladly offered his financial help and home in order to keep what was left of his family close.

Chapter 38
Things Have Changed Back Home

If there was such a thing, Maude and James Wilson's marriage was perfect. The only thing missing was children. But after plenty of trying, and although disappointed, she came to terms with her lot in life.

"James, you know I've made my peace that we won't be havin' babies. Maybe the good Lawd didn't fix me so I could have my own 'cause He knew Momma was gonna leave hers to me. I'm feelin' real good these days 'bout where they're at in life. Walter's now livin' in Baltimore, and doin' pretty good for himself. Every holiday that boy sends me somethin' real special tryin' to show me how much he loves me and I appreciate it. Iffin he didn't send me a thing, I wouldn't love him any less."

"Otie's now married and still livin' in the Gulf. Ya know she was always the spiritual one. I think it got a lot to do with them scars she bore from livin' with Mr. Harrington and all that Belle mess he had goin' on for years. She ain't never forgave him for Momma's death. I guess her consolation was in the church. Just like Beolia, that gal could never stand to hear anybody talk 'bout witchcraft, voodoo, or spells, and she won't have nothin' to do with folk that believe in that stuff."

"Now my little sweetheart, Vella, she married that boy Neal right from under Mr. Harrington's nose. She pulled a big one over on the ol' man when she ran away and got married without askin' fo' his permission, and you know how he is 'bout people gettin' his permission. You would've thought he would be mad as hell and never forgive her for doin' that to him. Somehow, she's been able to keep him wrapped around her little finger.

When he heard about that crowd livin' over at the Reaves' place, he opened his home up to them. I got a feelin' his generosity had a lot to do with his own selfish reasons. Anyhow, his offer was good, Vella's fine with it, and so I'm happy with it."

The letters and stories from back home absolved her of the guilt that occasionally crept up. It was hard to forgive herself for sending them back into the torture chamber when life with James was so good.

The saving grace was that Leotia and Novella evolved into strong women with their own unique brands of independence. They were remarkable, resilient, and possessed an indisputable ability to survive the madness, heartache, and danger Scott had exposed them to for most of their lives.

Leotia's letters were amusing and suspenseful. They spoke of a big mystery that left Maude guessing how she found a way to turn the tables on Scott. Never in a million years would she have ever imagined Leotia controlling him rather than the other way around.

"James, I wonder what Otie's got on him. It just gotta be good 'cause I ain't never seen that man scared of nobody. He's still tryin' to act all big and bad, but she's got 'em walkin' and talkin' real careful 'round her. Have you noticed he won't cross her?"

"Yeah, it looks like she's working the old man instead of the other way around. I mean the way things used to be. I agree – she's got the goods on him. I would just love to know what it is. You know Babe I'm surprised she hasn't told you or Novella about it."

"You've got a point there. They never keep anything from me. That's why I know whatever she's got on 'em, it could do ol' Mr. Harringon in for good. Yeah, she's got him by the you-know-what and he's feelin' the squeeze. But Otie, she's got her own set of principles, and I know she still loves him in spite of whatever it is she's holdin' over his head. I ain't gonna press her though. I just get a kick out of seeing her mess him around."

Other than Scott, no one else knew that Leotia found out about his dealings with the Geechee. When Maude heard her account of Novella's chance encounter that turned into an act of heroism, she was stunned, but in awe.

"Well I'll be damned. Of all the women in the world, it was little Vella who permanently got that demon Geechee outta our lives. Must admit, there were times when I was losin' faith. Vella proved to be more powerful than all that voodoo. Poor Momma – she loved him despite his flaws and I still grieve 'bout that. She loved that man so much, and wanted more than anything to live a long life with him. Me and her thought she was gonna get the chance after Belle passed away. But for some reason, it wasn't Momma's destiny."

"For years I resented Gawd, fate, or whatever it was that took her and spared him when he was the one who deserved to die. A whole lotta people died tryin' to love that man – a whole lotta people. Now, I'm finally feelin' like Momma did win in the end 'cause her seed settled a score neither Momma nor any other woman in Mr. Harrington's life had been able to. Vella did it all by herself. That gal may be skinny, but I tell you, she's packin' a whole lotta power, a whole lotta power."

Maude's life was about to take yet another turn in an undesirable direction. James' condition wasn't improving and something about that was unsettling. At first he kept coming down with what they thought were colds or maybe the flu. He would eventually get over the bout, but in no time, the coughing and congestion came back. The bouts of whatever was going on with him started re-occurring more frequently and with more severity.

She couldn't ever recall hearing anything that sounded as distressful as James' chronic coughing and difficulty with breathing other than when Irene and Beulah, as well as Beolia and Matthew, came down with that dreaded Consumption Disease. *Gawd, I pray that ain't what James got, 'cause none of them folks survived. That can't be, it just can't be true. I heard that disease is highly contagious. But I don't know of anybody in our circle of friends who got it. Plus, when we all went back home together, we were 'round Beolia and Matthew. So why didn't the rest of us get it? Maybe it do got somethin' to do with workin' at that steel mill cause what he been tellin' me sounds like that place be infested with somethin' unhealthy.*

He occasionally mentioned other men down at the mill who suffered with the same espisodes of uncontrollable coughing as he did. "I swear Maude, everytime I turn around, I'm hearing about another guy who keeps coming down with whatever this is. Maybe we just keep passing the cold back and forth among us. I haven't heard anybody mention Consumption Disease or know somebody who has it. That work down there is so dirty, everybody's coughing all the time anyway."

No one could dispute the fact that the environment at the mill would cause anybody who stayed around for a little while to cough and labor with breathing. When James arrived home in the evening, he was filthy, and his clothes were covered with dust and dirt he said came from furnace blasts, as well as clouds of steam and smoke that billowed from the mill's stacks. They dismissed the dust and dirt as harmless.

His persistent coughing and the debilitating congestion turned into something more serious. Maude wanted him to stay home, but the mill wouldn't pay for days off. The once large man she loved to cuddle up to was now as thin as a rail. His breathing was laborious, and his raspy voice occasionally faded away completely.

She was frightened and could no longer hide her fears or appear to be strong. Whatever was going on with him was bigger than the both of them. It was time to be honest, and honestly she was terrified.

"James, we've gotta find a doctor to take a look at you. I know you love me and wanna take care of me, but you're the one who needs to be taken care. Please let me ask 'round at the laundry. Maybe somebody there will know 'bout a doctor who can look at you and get you well again."

She didn't find any answers at the laundry, but one day while at the corner store buying groceries, she started talking to the store's owner about James' condition.

Mr. Dave Rabinovich, who was a Russian Jew, was known to give the coloreds in their neighborhood deep discounts on food items, as well as lines of credit. He would allow them to pay for groceries in installments. Sometimes Mr. Dave, as they called him, would throw in extras, especially when children where in the home. Whenever Maude or James came into the store, they would hang around to chat with him.

Maude appeared to be distracted. "Hi Maude."

"Hi Mr. Dave."

"I haven't seen James in awhile. How's everything?"

"Oh Mr. Dave, I'm so scared for him. Somethin's wrong and he's gettin' sicker and sicker by the day. He don't even look like himself no more. I asked 'round on my job if anybody knew of a doctor who could take a look at him, but nobody could help me. I don't know what to do."

"Look Maude, I'll speak to my friend, Doctor Barr, who works down at the mill. Maybe we can make arrangements for you and James to come upstairs to my apartment. He'll take a look at James. This sounds like something he's mentioned to me before. He'll know what to do. You just go back home and let James know I'm working on this for him."

When Doctor Barr saw James, he had a pretty good idea about what was wrong, but dreaded giving them a diagnosis without first examining him. "Let's get started. Just go into the bedroom and take off your shirt. I'll examine you and see if I can determine exactly what's going on."

Doctor Barr took out his stethoscope and proceeded to apply the instrument to different areas of James' chest and back. "Cough. Okay cough again. Tell me, how long have you had this cough?"

"Doc, it's been so long now I really don't know. At first I didn't pay too much attention to it. I thought it was a cold or something."

"What's your normal body weight?"

"I've got a range. It's usually between 225 and 230 pounds."

He interpreted Dr. Barr's blank expression as shock. "I know I'm a real scarecrow these days Doc. For years I was teased about being a big man, and now I look like a bean pole."

"You can get dressed now. I'll see you and Maude back out in the living room, and tell you what I think your next move should be."

She was looking for a sign but couldn't read anything on his face that was encouraging. *The news ain't good and he's tryin' not to let on, but I can feel it – it ain't good. Dear Gawd in heaven I'm scared for my man.*

"Mr. and Mrs. Wilson, I think we need to get James into a hospital as soon as possible. Things look pretty serious and he needs to be where he can get proper care. There's a hospital I know of that treat coloreds, so it won't be a problem getting you admitted immediately. We have to start working on you as soon as possible."

Doctor Barr had seen a lot of men with the same symptoms as James who worked at the steel mill for long periods of time, and he suspected James was suffering from the same illness.

"Doctor, if James checks into the hospital as soon as possible, how much of a chance does he have of survivin' this?"

"There's always hope and there's always the possibility of a miracle."

Once James was checked in, their worst fears were confirmed. He had contracted a terminal lung disease. After days of crying with Maude, he accepted the diagnosis, but was determined to pull it together for her sake. Knowing what they were facing, he had to be strong for her.

"Look Babe, I'm not gone yet. Now you and me both are strong, so we can't go getting weak on each other now, can we? Come on Maude, I know you can do it. My baby's a strong woman and she's been through too much to go falling apart now. Even if I don't get well, you've got to hold on to what we've had with each other."

"James, don't you dare talk like that. You've gotta get well. I just couldn't see myself goin' on if somethin' bad happens. So you've gotta get well."

"Girl, listen to me. We've loved each other like no body's business, and we've been very, very happy. I didn't know I could be this happy with a woman, but I still can't get enough of you after all these years. I know you can't get enough of me either. See I knew I could still make you laugh. Keep thinking about the way we lit up the jazz clubs. How about them fancy pictures you kept sending back to the Gulf, hmmm? We were having a ball Maude, and that's how I want you to remember us."

In no time his condition deteriorated to the point where he couldn't even speak to her. The sight of him lying in the hospital bed laboring for breath and staring off into space with a body ravaged by the killer lung disease was devastating, as well as heartbreaking.

One evening while visiting, she started talking not necessarily expecting him to answer. During this particular visit, however, he surprised her. "Maude, will you get into this bed with me right now? I want to hold you close."

"James Wilson, shame on you. I can't do that. If my big fat behind get into that skinny bed with you, it'll break down and these folk are gonna put me outta here."

"Girl, do what your man tells you to do and get in this bed right now."

There was something commanding in his voice despite the raspy whisper. So she complied, slipped into bed, and put her ear up close to his lips. A tender kiss brushed her earlobe. When she pulled back to look at him, there were not only tears in his eyes, but a brilliance she couldn't discern.

He couldn't leave her without bringing clarity to the moment. So he fought through the pain and pushed back the hand of time long enough for the two of them to become one in the spirit. As soon as he connected with her for the last time, she recognized the tears and glow in his eyes as the joy when love is complete; when nothing has been held back. They were the tears of a man who truly loved his woman and didn't mind showing her that having her as the joy of his life had moved him to tears. The only sadness was the sweet sorrow of saying goodbye to the love of his life.

"I love you Maude Wilson. Never forget that." Then he closed his eyes, but she whispered back, "I love you James Wilson, and don't you ever forget that."

When the hospital staff came into the room to check on him, he had passed away and was lying in bed with his arms still wrapped around his wife, who was at peace with the years she had spent with the love of her life, James Wilson.

It was time to make some decisions about life going forward and without him. Staying in Pittsburgh was no longer an option. When she first arrived in the Hills, she was surrounded by Leotia, Walter, and Novella. As James' wife, she enjoyed a new level of fulfillment where there was never a dull moment. Now Leotia and Novella were back in the Gulf; Walter was in Baltimore; and James was in heaven.

She needed her family, and it was time to go back to the Gulf. Going back to Scott's place wasn't an option, so she reached out to Mama Mame. She would stay until she was ready to execute her plan. Maude was going to build a home on the lot she purchased.

When Leotia and Novella found out she was coming back, they were beside themselves. "Otie, she's on her way back. I'm so happy I'm about to bust wide open. Maude is comin' back home. I know how much she misses James, but she's got us. Everytime Maude turns around, she's gotta take care of somebody else. Now it's her turn. We're gonna take care of her. We're gonna see to it she's happy."

"I know, I know. Oh my Gawd Vella. Here we are married women jumpin' 'round like children, but I'm so excited. Just when I couldn't imagine myself bein' any happier now that I'm married to Luke, we find out Maude's comin' home. You're absolutely right. We're gonna take care of her now. After all she's done for us, we've gotta be here for Maude."

Although Maude was on her way back to the Gulf, once again, life would not play out as everyone anticipated.

They were having the time of their lives living together. Mama Mame was reflective as she looked at Maude gliding back and forth on the porch swing. *Lawd knows there been plenty of times when I've had to rein this gal in, but I love her spirit. She ain't takin' nothin' off nobody that's full of it – includin' Mister Scott Harrington. I know I've gotta make her respect him 'cause he's her daddy, although she don't like to hear nobody say that. Yet, that gal protected Mary and them chillun from that man a many a day. Naw – ain't no way I wanna see this gal's spirit broken. I'd rather see her fightin' than broken in spirit.*

One of their favorite past times was reminiscing about Mary. "Mama Mame, I sho' do miss Momma's good cookin'. That woman could make a mud pie taste like chocolate cake. I liked everything she put on the table in front of me. Maybe that's why I'm so big."

"Gal, that can't be the only reason why you so big in the saddle. Looka' here, I was eatin' Mary's cookin' for years too, eatin' like a horse and I'm still as small as a sparrow. You was eatin' Mary's cookin' and a whole lotta other folks' cookin' too."

"Now tell me 'bout that house you gonna build again. I don't ever get tired of hearin' 'bout it."

"Oh Mama Mame, it's gonna be a quaint little house. In every room I'm gonna have somethin' that'll remind you of Momma. You'll swear fo' Gawd she's livin' there with me. Of course she'll be there in spirit, but you're gonna think you've stepped back in time and into Momma's house."

"Gal, I love hearin' you describe that house of yours. It be soundin' so beautiful – almost make me cry. After all these years, I still can't believe she's gone. I miss her so much, but I got you gals to remind me of her. Can't go questionin' the good Lawd's decisions after all this time though. He knows best Maude. He knows best."

"I can't wait. Tell me again when you say you gonna start buildin'?

Although Maude was always talking about the house, Mama Mame noticed there wasn't much that was actually being done to build it. This was unlike Maude because whenever she set her mind to doing something, she didn't waste time getting started and seeing the thing through to completion. She seemed distracted. The distraction wasn't negative, but noticeable. She was writing a lot of letters back to her friends in Pittsburgh and Mama Mame thought maybe she missed her life in there, as well as James. She said as much to Maude.

"Oh Mama Mame, I'm happy to be back home with all y'all. Well with most of y'all. I'm gonna start buildin', but I gotta take my time."

When Novella and Leotia came to visit, the family of women talked about everything while patching quilts. Maude would look around the circle reflecting back on their individual and collective journeys. *So much time has gone by, and so much has happened that should've never happened. These gals have been through too much, all because of somebody's attempt to love their poppa. They still love the man though. They're just like Momma on that front. He put 'em through hell and they still love him. No matter what he did, they always found a way to re-connect with him.*

I wonder what's goin' on with Otie though. That gal's got somethin' she's holdin' on to and over his head, but I know she loves him. She just don't wanna. Gotta say though, I admire both of them. They're not like me, but they found the courage to stand up to him when they decided to have a life outside of him. Mama and Mr. Harrington's other wives, as well as that damned mistress, Belle, may have found it impossible to deal with him, but these gals found a way. They learned how to handle him in their own way.

Chapter 39
Mary Della Reaves

In 1930, Novella gave birth to her second child. When the labor pains began around Noon on February 26, she was surprised because based on Mama Mame's calculation it wasn't time.

"Neal, somethin's goin' on. I'm havin' pains and don't know whether or not we should get Mama Mame now."

Scott overheard the conversation. "Boy you gotta get outta here right this minute and get over to that midwife's place. We ain't takin' no chances with my baby gal."

He wanted to add *...and make sure you don't bring back that bossy Maude with y'all 'cause she's gonna be takin' over like she's the midwife, daddy, and everybody else.* Since he didn't want to bring up negative conversation and jinx the delivery, he kept quiet.

Gawd, I hope Neal already know how bossy Maude can be and iffin' he don't keep her in line, she'll run all over him. I just hope he knows who he's dealin' with when it comes to Maude. I'mma ol' man now and tired of fightin' with her. Time fo' somebody else to take up arms against that gal. I ain't sayin' nothin' though 'cause I ain't gonna take no chance with Vella and that baby 'bout to come into this world.

Neal had left the house, and he was pacing the floor back and forth. "Vella baby, don't you worry none. When Mama Mame get here, she's gonna make sure she bring that baby into this world safe from all harm. Poppa ain't gonna let nothin' happen to you, ya hear me?"

"I know Poppa."

He was doing his best to comfort her, but was so jittery he needed somebody to comfort him. *Lawd Jesus, the deaths of wives and babies throughout my lifetime have worn me completely out. Everytime one of 'em was bringin' a baby into this world, there was a whole lotta cryin', pain, and dyin'. You wouldn't think all that misery and death would be goin' on with just tryin' to come into this world.*

Seems like the struggle for colored folk start the minute the youngin' starts tryin' to come into the world. Whole lotta chillun makes it though. Sometimes I think that kinda bad luck was reserved just fo' me. Lawd, I don't know what You got against me. You got me so 'fraid now, I can't even stand to hear a woman announce she's with child.

Just when he thought his nerves couldn't take another moment of waiting, Neal, Mama Mame, and Maude burst through the door. Mama Mame and Maude went directly to Novella.

Oh Great – I should've known better. She's not 'bout to let anything go on in her sisters' lives without bein' there and takin' charge. That gal must've taken after her poppa Daniel and his people 'cause I swear fo' Gawd Mary wasn't bullheaded and difficult like Maude turned out to be. Matter of fact, I take that back. That gal didn't turn out to be bullheaded. She came to this house six years old and bullheaded. Whoever heard of such a thing?

From the kitchen they could hear Mama Mame coaching Novella. "Baby just do like Mama Mame tell you to do and everything's gonna be fine. Push when I tell you to and rest when I tell you to. That's it. That's it. Now push again. Yes, yes – that's it."

Another contraction hit her. "Ooooowww, ooouuuch. Oh my Lawd, that's hurts so much."

They ran over to the door, simultaneously banging and asking what went wrong. Mama Mame was irritated at the distraction. "Ain't nothin' wrong. Will y'all just be patient and let me do my job here? I swear, men folk can sho' nuff get on yo nerves. Never strong when you need 'em to be."

A few minutes later, however, they heard the faint and short cry of a baby. Then everything went silent. Scott was on the verge of panic. *Oh my Gawd not again.*

Then Mama Mame emerged from the bedroom holding a bundle so tiny that at first they thought the blanket was empty. She walked over to Neal with a smile on her face, and was about to hand the blanket to him when Maude jumped in front of him with her arms held out. Mama Mame stared at her with an expression that she clearly understood. "Oh, scuse me Neal, I don't know what I'm thinkin' bout. Let me get outta the way here."

Mama Mame was terse in her response. "Thank ya ma'am."

"Neal Reaves, this here is your first daughter. She be unusually small for even a newborn, but she made it. We gonna have to keep a close watch out on her. She's what they call a premature baby. So it's critical we watch her real close. I can tell this here little gal has the strength to make it. What're you gonna call her?"

He took the baby from her, opened the blanket, and looked down into the tiny face of his daughter. She was stretching her arms and legs in every direction. As tiny as she was, he was surprised at her strength.

He then walked back into the room where Novella was resting and sat at the edge of the bed.

"We have a little girl. What do you wanna call her? She's a tiny little thing, but stretches like she got the strength of a man."

His comment made her think of Mary and how despite her gentle spirit, she was a woman of strength. "I think we'll call her Mary."

"Do you wanna give her a middle name?"

"Let me think about it. No – how about if you give her a middle name."

He blurted out the first name that came to mind. "How about Della? Yes, we'll call her Mary Della."

What on earth is he thinkin' 'bout callin' my baby Della. Ain't Della that rough woman his Uncle Rommie is married to? For Gawd sakes Neal Reaves, that's not what I wanna call my little girl.

Oh Lawd, I've gotta let him have his say in this. Forgive me little Miss Mary, but your momma's 'bout to let your daddy call you Mary Della. I'm so sorry baby.'

"We'll call her Mary Della. Now Neal, give me my baby so I can get to know little Miss Mary Della. My goodness – Mary Della sounds like a mouthful for Junior. How 'bout if we just call her 'Sister'?"

They were nowhere near as happy with their growing family as Scott was. His ecstasy was for different and selfish reasons. While they were anxious and not-too-comfortable with their dependent status, he was beside himself with joy over their status in life, as well as his mounting leverage.

Chapter 40
Fighting For the Right Reasons

In 1931, two major events occurred in the lives of Neal and Novella. The first was Maude's surprise announcement that she was once again leaving the Gulf.

Mama Mame was devastated, and her reaction to the news shocked everyone else. She started getting suspicious when a man by the name of George Lee started coming to town. Maude introduced him as the brother of one of the women she worked with when she lived in Pittsburgh.

"Maude, What's that man's intentions? Everytime I turn 'round, he's back here in the Gulf. What kinda money does he got that he can keep comin' down here from up north? He's nice'nuff, but I know he's got somethin' up his sleeve and that ain't sittin' well with me."

"Yes Mama Mame, George is a very nice man and I want you to treat him as such. Everybody's not like Mr. Harrington. You know how I loved James more than anything. He was everything I ever dreamed of in a man, and I'm so grateful for the years I had with him. I didn't think I could ever love again. Didn't think my heart would ever heal after losin' him, but it has. George isn't James and I don't expect him to be. But he's good to and for me. So you be good to him."

Although she was cordial, Mama Mame kept him at a safe distance. As it turned out, she did have reason to feel threatened. He was in love with Maude. When he proposed, she accepted.

The proposal of marriage wasn't the bad news that devastated Mama Mame. It was the plans after the wedding.

"Mama Mame, George got a new job and the company is located in Passaic, New Jersey. Sweetheart, you know I love you and want you with me forever, but I'm gonna be leavin' the Gulf to live in New Jersey."

"Otie, I'm worried 'bout Mama Mame. She's not talkin' much to anybody and barely eatin' anything. You know as small as she is, she eats like a horse. But since she found out about Maude leavin' again, she's walkin' 'round like she's got no spirit. Maude's not even gone yet and she looks so sad."

"I'm worried too. She's always stuck close to this family, treatin' all of us as if we were her very own. Vella, you've gotta understand she's up in the age now and bein' alone might be gettin' kinda scary for her. I don't care how independent a woman is, at some point in life she's gotta think about a husband and children, and if she didn't have either one, then why. She just covered up so much of what she was feelin' by takin' care of other people and bringin' babies into this world. She ain't doin' much of that stuff anymore, and so she's got time to think about her life now more than ever. We're all movin' on with our lives and she ain't blind. She's human and she's feelin' what human beings feel at one time or another – lonely."

Mama Mame's depression was unfamiliar territory and no one knew what to do in order to bring her out of it. Then Maude unknowingly offered a remedy. "Hey Mama Mame, I've got an idea. Why don't you come to New Jersey and live with me and George?"

The challenge proved to be the cur, and immediately she recovered. Having never been out of the State of North Carolina, Mama Mame wasn't interested in a change in lifestyle or state of residence.

"Listen gal, I really 'preciate yo offer and all, but I've been in these parts all my life and people 'round here highly respect me. They need me. Even Doc Moore hisself always talkin' 'bout how I'm as good a doctor as him. At this age, I ain't tryin' to move nowhere that nobody don't know me. Startin' over is too much for me."

"But Mama Mame, you can do it. If anybody can, it's you."

"Naw Gal. Now hear me out. Look, this is what we'll do. You can come and get me sometimes. Take me back to New Jersey, and I'll stay for a few days. How's that? And as for you, George boy, you better treat my gal right, or else I'll be up there and take a broom to you."

She couldn't fool them. They would have to come to North Carolina for the visit. She wasn't going anywhere.

The second major event occurred on November 12, 1931, when Neal and Novella became parents again with the birth of their third child.

Neal was working at the Coca-Cola bottling plant over in Winston Salem, packaging soda pop. With a growing family, the pressure to make enough money so they could find their own place was getting intense. With limited education, there wasn't much he could do in the way of earning a living. Scott wasn't complaining because as long as Neal couldn't take care of his family on the money he earned, they couldn't leave.

Neal stumbled upon a way to make extra money and it came by doing something he actually liked and didn't require an education. The brawn displayed when he put an iron grip on Scott for trying to prevent Novella from leaving home was an asset for which others were willing to pay him.

His physical strength was well known around Sanford. He feared no one, and this fearless attitude is what concerned Pa Mern and Momma Lizzie the most. They were colored people, living in the south, and if Neal didn't fear crossing certain boundaries, he was likely to get into the kind of trouble that came with major consequences.

Whenever he was drawn into confrontation, there was hell to pay. Minnie often repeated her observation concerning his temperament. "When Neal gets mad, you know it, 'cause you see that steam comin' right off the top of his head."

Johnny explained what a physical collision with his brother felt like. "When a man bumps into that boy, the fella feels like he ran into a brick wall. I've seen 'em bounce right off of him. I swear, I ain't never looked forward to fightin' with him myself. I'd prob'ly have to kill 'em."

Lonnie corrected him. "You mean he'll prob'ly kill you. Everytime some boy is stupid enough to get into a fight with him, the poor sport come away battered and bruised like nothin' you ain't ever seen before."

So when Neal started hearing about this man name Jack Johnson who was a professional boxer, he took notice. He felt a certain kinship with him because Jack was colored, and he too left school very early in life. Jack also came from a large family. Whenever he heard anybody describing Jack Johnson's fights, he listened closely using the accounts of Jack's fights to develop his own fighting style.

Avery Baines had an old barn the owner no longer used. It was a place where colored boys sparred and fought boxing matches on Friday nights. Like Neal, most of them had limited or no education and jobs that paid meager wages. So fighting for money was the perfect way to make some extra money. Avery's Friday night boxing matches even gained the attention of some of the whites in Sanford. On fight nights, the barn would be crowded with spectators cheering or booing the boxers who stepped into the makeshift ring.

Neal was confident in his skills, and so it seemed like an easy way to make some extra money. Not only did the Friday night boxing matches proved to be easy money, they proved easy to win. He was also enjoying the notoriety he was gaining around Sanford.

"Johnny, Lonnie, y'all hear what them white boys was sayin' down at Avery's place? They say I'm Sanford's Jack Johnson. They say I'm a celebrity in these parts."

Once he experienced the thrill of celebrity and the benefits of the money earned from fighting, he wasn't going back to his inconspicuous status. Everytime he stepped into the ring, he saw the opponent as the imaginary wall between him and the life he envisioned. He wasn't going to let any opponent stand between him and the goal of moving his family out of Scott's house.

So now facing his latest opponent, he knew what he had to do. The other guy's nose was already bloody and there was swelling around his left eye. The crowd was cheering. Someone was overheard saying, "His nose may be bloody, but he ain't backin' up. Go and get 'em boy. Go after Jack Johnson and whup his ass."

It was if the opponent heard the challenge and charged in like a raging bull. Neal saw the hunger in his opponent's eyes. He recognized this look because it was the same way he felt. His mind was made up.

It's time to put him down and put him down for good. I can't leave anything in him to come back at me. Right now he's the only thing standin' between me and that money I need. Ain't no way I can leave him standin'.

He started pounding on the opponent's body with relentless blows. Someone else in the crowd yelled out, "Get him. Get him Jack. Show him what it feels like to be in the ring with Sanford's Jack Johnson."

The crowd's taunting was the fuel Neal needed. He kept delivering blows to the torso of his opponent. The guy had very little wind left in his lungs. It was time to take him out, and so Neal delivered his signature upper cut. The crowd knew what to expect and it sounded like everyone in the barn yelled in unison, "Timber." The opponent landed on his face. Neal would be getting paid again.

As menacing as he was in the boxing ring, the minute the match was over, Neal became a different man. Each time he got paid, he was one step closer to leaving Scott's house. Nothing pleased him more than when he returned home late at night after a boxing match to hand the money over to Novella. He could tell she felt the same way. More money meant eventual independence, but more money was becoming harder to come

by because of the declining state of the economy throughout the
country.

Chapter 41
The Great Depression

By 1931, the entire country was feeling as if the life was being sucked out of it. Life had always been hard for the coloreds in Sanford and the Gulf, but now with this thing whites were calling the Great Depression, some coloreds were feeling as if the world was coming to an end. It wasn't unusual to hear conversation about the end times, like the time Luke overheard some older men talking over at the bottling plant in Winston Salem.

"This world is comin' to an end. Ain't no other explanation fo' what's goin' on all over the place. I swear fo' Gawd, everywhere you look, white folks' biznesses are closin'; their factories and mills are closin'. Otis, I even hear that banks, where they keep their money are closin' too."

"Man I heard the same thing. Now I feel like iffin life for white folks is turnin' for the worse and they lookin' as poor as we colored folk, that gotta mean things are comin' to a head. This world's 'bout to come to an end for sure."

Despite the Depression, Scott and Walter Harrington held on to their jobs at the mill. James Seamore's deathbed directive was the insurance they could count on to survive in any situation, including an imploded economy. Had it not been, the devastating consequences of the Depression may have forced James Junior and Clayton to sever all ties with them in order to survive.

They were in a meeting discussing how to keep the mill operating. For most of the meeting certain conversation had been avoided, but Clayton had to finally address the uncomfortable, but necessary subject.

"Junior, things are getting hard and we've gotta make some changes. We're gonna have to let some of these workers go. It's costing us too much damned money trying to keep everybody else employed because we don't want to see them begging and starving. If we're not careful, we'll be in the food lines along with everybody else. There's just no other way. We can't keep everybody on. If we do that, we'll surely go down to nothing like all these other businesses around here seem to be doing."

"I don't disagree with you Clayton, but we've gotta be really careful about how we're going to handle layoffs. I think we can let a lot of the coloreds go. You know these white men won't take too kindly if we let them go, and see us keeping coloreds on at the mill. I don't want to offend them by doing something like that. I say we let the coloreds go first."

"That may be the case, but you know what Daddy told us before he died. Whatever we do, we had better take care of Walter and Scott. You know how our ol'man always felt like he had to make things right with them. I really don't mind keeping Walter. Now Scott is another story altogether. That's one mean rascal. I tell you – I'm scared of him myself. I hate looking into those piercing eyes. He looks at you like he's willing you to drop dead right there in front of him. If we've got to let one of them go, I say let's get rid of that snake."

"No, we can't do that. Daddy specifically said that both of them were to be taken care of real well until the day they die, and that's what we're gonna do. Look, we'll just make them take a temporary pay cut. We had better clearly say the word 'temporary' or that son-of-a-bitch Scott will be waiting for us with a piece of rope, ready to string us up."

"So it's settled, we can keep both of them if we give them a pay cut. Most everybody else has got to go though. Remember, coloreds first and then whites if things don't get any better."

Scott wasn't disturbed by the angst of the Depression because he had guaranteed income for life. Even the pay cut didn't bother him. Despite everything that was going on in the world, and the total upheaval affecting everybody, he was still in a financial position to control the lives of Neal and Novella, thereby keeping Novella close to him.

I ain't depressed 'bout nothin' – got everything I want.

He may have been satisfied with his guaranteed income for life, but Neal was growing increasingly nervous about his ability to provide for his family. The part-time job over at the Coca-Cola bottling plant in Winston Salem and the little bit of money he brought home from his boxing matches was decent, but he was fearful that the job at the Coca-Cola plant was getting ready to go away.

He voiced his fears to his cousin, George. "Have you noticed everyday them supervisors over at the bottlin' plant announcin' they're gettin' rid of more men? They're lettin' them white boys go as fast as they're gettin' rid of the coloreds."

"I know what you mean cuz. Most everybody you talk to outta work – whites and coloreds. This is one dark day. Makes you reconsider callin' some of these folks crazy that swear the world is comin' to an end."

Food was scarce, and hope was even scarcer. People were forming long lines to get food rations at some of the churches. Neighbors and families started sharing meals. Momma Lizzie would fix a pot of pinto beans; Mama Mame would show up with the ham hocks; and Grandma Minnie would throw in a big pot of collard greens or a pan of cornbread.

Neal was worried. He wasn't oblivious to Scott's euphoria over their dependency. If he lost the job at the Coca-Cola plant, there was no way the boxing matches alone could put enough money in his pockets to at least contribute something to household expenses. As long as he was making some contribution, he didn't feel completely beholding to Scott.

Neal and George were on their way over to the bottling plant in Winston Salem when they saw men who looked destitute coming towards them. "Neal, Neal look. Would you look at that? There's some more white men walkin' along the side of the road. The poor bastards lookin' dirty, worn out, and confused. Slow up, one of 'em is comin' into the middle of the road. I wonder what he wants."

"Okay. I'm just gonna roll down the window a little bit. He looks too weak to start anything." As they were pulling up next to the man in the road, George cautiously rolled down the window about halfway.

"How y'all boys doin'?" George immediately took offense to the reference to 'boy', but Neal put a firm grip on his arm, warning him to shut up. He then answered, "We doin' fine, what do you want with us?"

The answer confirmed the rumors about how bad whites were also suffering. "I was hopin' y'all could help me out. If you got some corn bread or leftover food y'all don't want, I'd appreciate it. I haven't worked in days, and haven't eatin' in as long. Can y'all help me?"

"George, look in there and see if there's some extra pieces of cornbread. I think Momma even threw in some extra beans."

George looked through the bag and pulled out a piece of bread. "We don't have no extra beans. Want me to just give him the bread?"

"Yeah, and let's get on over to Winston Salem before we're the ones walkin' in the road beggin' for food."

At times like this, it was hard for him to dismiss the fear of remaining under Scott's roof and control. If things were getting this bad for whites, what was going to become of coloreds? Just how bad was this Depression going to get? Was it possible that they could wind up back in the state Scott and Grandpa Ben described when talking about the old slavery days? *If things be this bad, at this rate, we'll never get out of the ol' man's house. I'll bet he would be just fine with that.*

He came to the conclusion that in order to keep Scott at a respectful distance, he couldn't appear vulnerable or desperate in any way. Scott harbored a slave/master mentality, and if a person fell for his method of control, he assumed the behavior of master and the other person was relegated to the position of slave. Neal made up his mind that person wasn't going to be him. Although Scott liked being in control, he respected those who stood up to him, and respect was good enough for Neal. He figured out a way stay at a safe distance, but couldn't control the antics of his small children, and one incident in particular brought them to blows a second time.

He was sitting alone on the back porch trying to figure out exactly what it would cost to move his family out when he heard Scott yelling. "Who in Gawd's name done went in my pocket and stole my money?" No one answered. *He's just blowin' off steam and talkin' 'bout somebody down at the tobacco mill.* The next comment got his full attention.

"Junior, Sista, y'all better get me my strap and get in here. I knows y'all the ones took my money."

He was already in route to the kitchen when curiousity changed into the clarion call to protect his children.

"No Poppa, no Poppa, Daddy, Mother, help, help, no Poppa, no Poppa." They were yelling for help and crying from what was now obvious; the contact between a leather strap and their flesh. Just as Scott raised his hand and swung the belt out into mid-air on its way down to the behind of either Junior or Sister again, Neal caught it.

In a flash, he wrapped the belt around his wrist several times as he violently reeled Scott's body so close to his that his nose was pressed into Scott's shirt. The difference in height didn't matter to him. Scott, on the other hand, had forgotten about the risk of getting into a fight with Neal.

For the second time, he landed in the vulnerable position of humiliation. He tried to talk his way out by intimidation. "Boy you had better let go of my belt so's I can teach these chillun not to steal."

"I ain't lettin' nothin' go before we get somethin' straight. If they stole from you, I'll take care of them, but you ain't gonna beat my children like they some slaves. I'm tellin you Pop, don't try it again or I promise, you're gonna be sorry."

"Then how you gonna teach them not to steal, huh?"

"Like I said Pop, don't touch my children again or you'll be very sorry."

"How you gonna teach them not to steal Neal. Just tell me that."

Neal was lost for words because he was thinking about how Pa Mern disciplined him, Johnny, Lonnie, Walter, Roscoe, and Weslie. Although he was basically a gentle man, his discipline was brutal. He often repeated his belief, and quoted the biblical scripture about sparing the rod and spoiling the child. Scott wasn't governed by biblical scripture and his methods of punishment were without boundaries.

He didn't have an answer. "Okay Pop, you've spanked them and that be enough – no more. How much is missin' – I'll give it back to you?"

The answer was so ridiculous, he didn't know whether to laugh or cry.

"One of 'em took a penny. I knows I had at least ten pennies in my pocket and now there only be nine."

He dared not risk laughing in his face. That would send him off again and he wouldn't think twice about striking out. Without turning his eyes away from Scott's glare, he gave directions to Junior and Sister. "Y'all gone on outside. Me and Poppa still talkin'. Once they left the room, he dropped the belt, reached into his pocket, and gave him a penny.

Novella was sitting quietly listening to the whole thing. "Do you believe that Novella? We gotta get outta here as soon as possible. I know you're not supposed to spare the rod, but I can't take lookin' at him beatin' my children. Pa Mern do the same thing, but coming from your poppa, it just seems too brutal and too much like a slave bein' whipped by his master. My children ain't nobody's slaves."

"I know Neal, I know. I don't like my babies being hit either, but Poppa's just trying to make them see right from wrong. Somethin's gonna work out for us where we can get our own place."

Chapter 42
The Not-So-Perfect Time to Move On

Luke received news from Baltimore and was anxious to share it with Neal. "Guess what Doc? I just got a letter from Mary. She says Ernest found a decent payin' job at a steel mill located at some place called Sparrows Point."

This was exactly the kind of news that piqued Neal's interest. "Novella, ain't that where Walter moved to?"

"Yes, yes it is. Everytime we hear from him, he seems to be doin' quite well for himself."

"Sound like there's opportunity up in Maryland. So why don't you write a letter to Mary and ask her if Ernest could be on the lookout for me and Deak – maybe get us a good payin' job at the steel mill."

She sent the letter. Although the response wasn't the one they wanted, it was promising. "I got a letter back from Mary today. She says the mill's not hirin' any new men right now, but word's been goin' 'round that in a little while they might be. Mary says Ernest is gonna look out for you and Luke. We just gotta keep the faith and wait patiently."

So in the meantime Neal continued the hour and a half trip to Winston Salem during the week, and fought in boxing matches on   Friday nights. He could only hope by way of a miracle to hold on to both jobs.

Finally the country was starting to feel optimistic. Now that Franklin D. Roosevelt had defeated President Herbert Hoover, everybody was hoping for some sign of recovery or improvement. President Roosevelt was signing executive orders and Congress was passing new laws creating new programs to include those aimed at recovery in employment. Neal was hoping and praying the New Deal would provide the break he needed to land a real job – preferably in Maryland.

He couldn't give up hoping and praying for this much needed break because in 1934, his family was extended yet again. In November Novella gave birth to their fourth child. Neal would have to wait another year and a half before getting the break he had been praying for.

Most of Neal's and Luke's conversations revolved around their plans to leave the Gulf. "Ya know Doc, I can't see for the life of me a light at the end of this very long and dark tunnel. It must be somewhere further up north."

"I know what you mean. I've tried everything and although everybody's sayin' things are gettin' better, I'm barely keepin' my head above water. I'm grateful for that, but the little bit of money I'm makin' ain't enough to get outta Poppa Scott's house. If we can just get to Baltimore things will start to turn around for us. Look at Mary and Earnest. Even Walter's doin' pretty good for himself, considerin' the Depression and all."

"Look Deak, ain't no use in holdin' out and waitin' for a better day before we make that move to leave here. We might as well do it now. We've gotta step out on faith. It's time to do something drastic if we wanna see drastic results."

Their minds were made up. It was time to tell Scott that his daughters were leaving the State of North Carolina.

They were having supper when Neal started the conversation for the umpteenth time about the hard economic times through which they were living. Scott wasn't complaining because many of the circumstances that were presenting problems for everybody else were the same ones providing him with leverage over the lives of Novella and Leotia.

The fear of not being able to provide for their young family kept Neal and Novella living in his home. Even when Leotia and Luke came up short, unbeknownst to Luke, he occasionally slipped money to her. She had to keep his contributions at a minimum because Luke hated taking anything from him. He often expressed his sentiments about accepting help from him in any form.

"I'd rather suffer than to ask that ol' man for anything. That's exactly what he wants – people beggin' and pleadin' with him. He made my life miserable years ago, and if I have anything to say about it, he won't get the chance to ever humiliate and control me like he did back then."

Leotia wasn't about to suffer, and was still holding on to the secret about Scott's bargain with the Geechee. She had no concerns that they would be beholding to him now that she was calling the shots.

 Looking around the table, she could see that Scott wasn't bothered by the conversation. The arrogant look on his face was evidence of his confidence that he was in control of the situation. There was no question – they needed his financial assistance, and as far as he was concerned, there was no way out.

Neal was describing the indigent white people he saw whenever he rode over to Winston Salem. Luke also gave accounts of the despair he was witnessing. "I know exactly what Doc means."

Scott was once again irritated at the nicknames they had given to each other and interrupted Luke to express his annoyance. "Why y'all boys callin' each other them silly names? Ya'll's poppas didn't name ya Doc and Deak, so why keep callin' each other them strange names?"

Luke got pleasure out of seeing him irritated over something that wasn't even his business. "We ain't got no problems with what we call each other. Anyway, like I was gettin' ready to say, I know what Doc mean cause I've seen plenty of white folk beggin' and hungry just like some of us. I know folk sayin' things are gettin' better with President Roosevelt now in office and all, but this Depression has been so bad, everybody's feelin' it. It's gonna take us colored folk a whole lot longer than whites to improve the way we live."

Scott wasn't interested in what they had to say, and was intentionally acting clueless. Neal became impatient, and finally dropped the bomb.

"Poppa Scott, me and Luke got jobs up north in Maryland at a steel mill and we're all leavin' in about a month or so to go and live in Baltimore. The fork full of food hung in mid-air as he looked around the table.

"Stop talkin' stupid boy. Whose gonna hire y'all colored boys with no schoolin'? Where you gonna live with dem chilluns? How you even gonna get up north?"

His scare tactics weren't working, and he was upset when the line of questioning didn't produce the discouraging effect he was looking for. *Now these boys think they so smart and determined to go through with these stupid plans of theirs. They ain't leavin' the State of North Carolina with my gals 'cause they can't make it without my help, and I ain't helpin'.*

The determination to execute their plan was much stronger than their fear of any downside to relocating to Baltimore. Luke had more details to add to the conversation. "My sister, Mary, and her husband are gonna let Otie and me stay with them. Doc, Novella, and the children are gonna stay with Walter and his wife. Sides, Ernest say the steel mill pays good money to colored men. Plus, Doc and me been savin' our money fo' train tickets. We worked it all out Mr. Harrington."

He still refused to address him by any other name but, 'Mr. Harrington', which was good enough for him. *He get so much of a kick outta folk callin' him Mr. Harrington, that's exactly what I'm gonna call him. I just can't bring myself to say, Poppa or none of them endearin' terms. Endearin' this ol' man ain't.*

I can't wait to get away from him and his controlling ways. Here we are in the 1930's and he still actin' like this some slave/master relationship, with him bein' the master and everybody else bein' his slaves. All I can say is good riddance once we get outta North Carolina. I ain't never gonna 'cept another penny from him if I can get me and Otie outta here.

He then sat back in his chair with a sly grin fixed on his face knowing they had gotten the best of Scott. He loved seeing him squirm. Scott hated seeing the grin on the face he wanted to slap. He lost his composure and threw down his fork. Food splattered all over the table.

"I'm saying no. There's this Depression and Vella got little chillun to look out fo. Y'all don't know iffin them white folk up in Maryland gonna give y'all jobs that can pay fo' takin care of yo families. I say it ain't a good time, and I don't want my gals sufferin' in this Depression."

Neal almost laughed out loud. *Now Pop been struttin' 'round here like the Depression don't touch him none. He knows he's got us while we stay here in North Carolina, and he's been usin' his money to keep us bound to him. Actin' like there's no Depression at all. Now all of a sudden he's concerned 'bout the Depression. This ol' man is somethin' else. These girls been tryin' to love this stubborn man for a many year and he ain't been nothin' but a handful – a handful of trouble and heartache. Can't stand the thought of me and Deak leavin' here, and havin' control over our own lives. Well, we're goin' and ain't nothin he can do about it.*

Rather than voice his thoughts out loud, which he knew would add fuel to the fire, he responded with a conciliatory promise. "Poppa Scott, we'll be okay. If we need you, we know how to come back."

He couldn't win this battle and to save face, his only alternative was to accept Neal's acknowledgement that they may still need him and if so, they would come back to North Carolina. Neal was only making concessions to appease him for Novella's sake. He, just like Luke, had no intentions of ever coming back.

Chapter 43
1936

In January 1936, Neal Reaves' young family, along with Luke and Leotia, arrived at Penn Station in Baltimore. They were exhausted from the long and uncomfortable ride in the car designated for "Coloreds Only." The children were cranky and hungry. Thank God Walter and Bernice, along with Mary and Ernest, were already at the train station waiting for them.

Neal and Luke reported to the steel mill for work on the following Monday. There was no anxiety about starting new jobs because they were too happy celebrating freedom from the sufficating oversight of Scott. They were confident his power and influence didn't extend beyond the Gulf.

Walter's house was crowded, and Novella, self-conscious about the imposition, kept apologizing about the cramped space. "Vella, will you stop worryin'. I'm just happy to be helpin' y'all out. I'm so glad you and Otie finally got outta the Gulf, and are here close to me. So stop worryin'. I know you appreciate everything."

"Look, since I been here in Baltimore, I joined a group for colored men called the Sugar Hill Club, and one of the members told me that he knows of an apartment available over on the eastside. I told him I would talk to Neal 'bout it and if Neal is interested, I'll take y'all over there to look at the apartment next weekend."

Things went well and the landlord offered to rent the apartment to them when he found out that Neal had just been hired at the steel mill. The apartment was small, but to them it was perfect. For the first time since getting married, they were living on their own.

After settling in, the first thing Leotia did was to inquire about a church. "Mary, where can I find a church for me and Luke to join? I learned a long time ago, when I was a little girl, how much I needed the Lawd in my life. I'm sure Luke has told you 'bout some of the things we went through growin' up, and what a handful my poppa is. I try to believe he loves us with all he's got in him. But he's also got plenty of devil in him and Satan has made him do some bad things to a lotta people. I know the only thing that's kept us was the Lawd. So now that He's answered my prayers, I've gotta find us a place to worship to give Him somethin' back. Only Gawd Himself could make a way for us outta Poppa's legacy of slavery, mistresses, roots, geechie women, and all the other darkness that was a part of him.

"I know the perfect place Otie. Me and Ernest belong to this church located at the corners of Eden and Monuments Streets. I'm tellin' you, the services there are spirit-filled just like you and Luke like e'm. I want y'all to come and go with us. Let me know what you think after service."

Leotia was sold and couldn't wait to join. Mary was right. The storefront church was everything she had been looking for in her place of worship. The next Sunday, Leotia and Luke joined the church. She was so excited about their new membership, she invited Neal and Novella to attend a service with them.

On the following Sunday, she was surprised that it was Neal who seemed to be affected by the service, and not Novella. She sat quietly, and didn't appear to be moved by anything other than what was going on with the restless children. Leotia was baffled.

Oh my goodness, I would've thought Vella would be overjoyed 'bout escapin' Poppa's System of Slavery. I can't contain myself. Look at Neal – he's even rejoicin' like he understands what it means to be gettin' his freedom. If she only knew what Poppa tried to do to her, she would be runnin' 'round this church like a crazy woman thankin' Gawd she got away from him. That Geechee woman was right 'bout one thing. Its best she don't know. So I'll do all the rejoicin' for the both of us.

Novella was struggling with conflicting feelings. Although she was glad to be out from under Scott's dictatorship, their relationship was different than his relationships with the others. She was acquainted with his tyrannical style, but knew she had always been his favorite. The only incident of conflict was on her wedding day. Since she was still in the dark about his dealings with the Geechee, as far as she knew, he had come to terms with her new life. So although she was happy to be living in Baltimore, nothing could change the truth. She missed him

Their good fortune kept getting better when Neal and Luke accomplished something else that went against conventional wisdom and under most circumstances would have been considered unattainable. They became land owners in a place called Sun Valley. The sun was shining down on them, and their good fortune must have been a miracle from God. What other explanation could there be? They would have never imaged that in 1936, during the Great Depression, they could become land owners in Anne Arundel County.

On the day the good news was announced, he burst through the apartment door talking about something Novella couldn't quite grasp. "Neal Reaves, would you please calm down for a minute? I can't understand a word you're sayin'. I know nothin' 'bout pieces of land for sale, and what all that has to do with us just arrivin' here in Baltimore."

"Novella, Baby, you'll never guess what happened to me and Deak today down at the Point. There's this fella down there who told us about some undeveloped property in a place called Sun Valley. Says the land has been in his family for years, but they're all goin' back to South Carolina and wanna sell. Get this. He told us the land is big enough to build houses on. His family is tryin' to leave town in a hurry, so he's willin' to let us have it for next to nothin.'"

"Neal how we colored folk gonna buy some land and we hardly got any money? You know there ain't no banks that gonna help us. Tell me how we're supposed to do that? Do you want me to ask Poppa for..."

"Ain't no way I'm askin' him for another dime. This man said he would work somethin' out for me and Deak, and I'm just gonna trust Gawd like that pastor told to us to do last Sunday."

Although she had reservations, she wanted to believe what he was telling her about the real estate deal, as well as God working something out.

The deal came through, and Neal and Luke purchased the land in Sun Valley for $300 each.

"Novella, when a man owns land, he owns power. People who know 'bout these things been tellin' me for years that since the beginnin' of time, men have been fightin' wars over land."

She had to admit to hearing about the power of owning land from Scott.

Once the grandeur of their most recent accomplishment sunk in, she rushed to the telegram office to send a wire back to the Gulf. He would be shocked, but proud of them. She remembered how he bragged about the land the Seamore's owned, and what kind of power came with owning land. She was confident he would be impressed by what Neal and Luke had accomplished. Her husband, a young colored man, who had just come to Maryland, with very little money, was now a proud land owner. He would see that she was in the very capable hands of a man who loved her. She never received a response.

Luke was the first to execute his plans. He enlisted the help of his brothers and they built from the ground up, the dream home Leotia had described to him. It was a modest home with two-bedrooms. They added a front porch inspired by the homes in North Carolina she was always talking about. Immediately out in the front yard close to the house, a well was dug for access to water, and further away they constructed an outhouse.

He continued to work at the mill, but also decided to act upon one of his other dreams. He and Neal purchased a used plough and borrowed the horse of the neighbor down the road to break and turn over the soil for planting fruits and vegetables. He also built a chicken coop, and near the end of his property line, a pig pen.

He had defied the odds that Scott repeatedly told him were stacked against him. The country boy had trumped his father-in-law, who for some reason, despised him and wouldn't accept that he was capable of succeeding at anything.

"Doc, I know that ol' man got Novella's telegram, and he's itchin' in the seat of his pants with jealousy. He was sure we were gonna get here and have to come crawlin' back to him for help. He can't stand the fact that we did somethin' big like buying land. You know how he's always braggin' 'bout the land them Seamores own. I know he be tryin' to hint that it's his daddy that owns the land, even though that daddy ain't never acknowledged him 'til he was on his deathbed. Now, the two of us really own some land and not through our daddies. He can't stand that. So of course he does the hurtful thing and ignores Novella's telegram. She was all excited when she ran down there to that telegram office. Otie says everyday she could tell Novella was lookin' for a response. I know his silence was disappointin' for her."

"Ain't no questionin' we made the right decision. I'm determined Novella will never have to go through what she went through growin' up. I'm not kiddin' myself. It's gonna be hard, but hard is way better than bein' at the mercy of Mr. Scott Harrington. He's so ornery, he couldn't figure out any other way to hurt her but with his silence."

"Man I'm tellin' you, that's exactly why I'm so glad we moved outta North Carolina. I know at first we was tryin' to wait for the perfect time to make the move, but it became clear that wasn't gonna happen. I know ol' Scott was prayin' it wasn't gonna happen."

"That ol' man ain't the kind to humble himself enough to go before Gawd 'bout anything but controllin' the lives of his children. I thought he was gonna kill all of us rather than let us out of the Gulf. Look at us now. We got our own place to live, own land, and farm. Plus people are willin' to pay us for a little bit of those fruits and vegetables we growin' on our land. Who would've thought – all this good stuff happenin' durin' these hard times."

Speaking of the odds being stacked against them, Neal and Luke had accomplished what Scott had sworn they never would. They had taken the last two people under his roof and rule away and out of the State of North Carolina. Everybody who had been enslaved to loving him had finally been set free from the dictatorship of Mr. Scott Harrington. It had taken from 1863 to 1936 to accomplish this.

Chapter 44
Scott's Latter Days

Neal's and Luke's promise never to return to Scott's territory as wards had one major flaw. They couldn't negate the fact that Novella and Leotia still loved him. Novella even wanted to go back to visit, but things were different on that front as well. Despite their feelings, the reality was that Novella and Leotia were not willing to go back to the way things were. They had tasted freedom and were not willing to relinquish their liberation no matter how much they loved him.

Although he was still in great shape physically, Novella worried that he was lonely without her to fill the void no one else was willing to. She returned to the Gulf to spend the entire summer with him. Within a week he was demanding, overbearing, and obstinate. He constantly struggled, trying to avoid defaulting back to his controlling ways, but was losing the internal battle. He went so as far as to try to convince her that it was in her best interest to come back to the Gulf.

The strain of maintaining peace, feeling sorry for him, and longing to return to Neal was getting the best of her. Regardless of her conflicting emotions, she couldn't risk giving into his unreasonable demands. She was well-acquainted with his persistence and what happened when he didn't get his way. Sensing the direction things were headed, she sent a telegram to Neal, telling him she was ready to come back to Baltimore.

For the first time in his life he found himself alone. While growing up, there were plenty of people living on the Seamore plantation. As a free man, he had a wife and a mistress. When Lillie and Iris passed away, he still had Belle to physically comfort him. While married to Mary, he still clung to Belle, that is until she became so physically and mentally sick he couldn't stomach being around her.

For most of his life, there were one or more women trying to love or make love to him. If it wasn't his master's nieces seducing him as a teenager, it was his mistress; if not his mistress, a wife who was willing to do almost anything to please and hold on to him; if not his wife he had adoring daughters from both marriages vying for his love and affection.

Although losing Herbert was devastating, he hid behind a false sense of security with adoring daughters and young Walter living at home. He became accustomed to having someone around at all times trying to please, get close to, love or be loved by him. He had become a master at giving orders and controlling the lives of others, but had never learned how to be independent. He went from being the property of James Seamore to being a man always surrounded by people who were willing to do everything for him in exchange for his love. He was now placed in unfamiliar territory.

His critics were finally gloating and harboring thoughts such as, *the ol' man's 'bout 90 now, and all of his children have finally got 'way from him. Bet he don't know what to do now that he can't force his master/slave thinkin' onto people whose only crime is tryin' to love him. Ain't none of his kinfolk left here in the Gulf.*

Those people who hated, envied, or pitied him were mistaken if they thought he was finally down and out for the count. They were premature in gloating and dismissing the slave who ruled the Gulf in strange ways for nearly three-quarters of a century, and were in for yet another surprise. His next move had all of them wondering if he possessed the super powers to which the root doctors laid claim.

He found another woman who was willing to take a chance on loving him, and her name was Sonya Morgan. She wasn't a replica of Lillie, Iris, Mary, or Belle. She was a combination of all four women. He had finally found a woman who possessed all of the characteristics that were attractive to him.

It was a Saturday morning when he asked a neighbor's son for a ride down to the General Store. When they arrived, the area was busy with people grocery shopping, visiting the hardware store, and running other errands. Some of the store owners had placed crates on the outside of their small businesses. Inside of the wooden cages were live chickens clucking and flying around in the restricted space with feathers flying all over the place.

He took his time getting out of the parked truck. Once completely emerged from the vehicle, he stood just as tall and erect as a much younger man. Just like in previous years, he still commanded attention, was still very attractive, and women of all ages were still drawn to his strange charisma. He remained the popular topic of many conversations, and the story of his life just kept getting new and intriguing chapters added to the Gulf's grapevine version of history.

Just as he turned around to close the door to the truck, he saw her. Sonya was picking up a small package, and as she straightened up to her full height, dark course hair generously mixed with silver gray strands fell away from her face. He was mesmerized by her beauty. Although she was a beautiful chocolate brown woman, at first she reminded him of Belle. He immediately dismissed the thought because there was something different about her.

While she possessed a sensuous air, the expression on her face reminded him of the peaceful expressions of his three wives. Unlike Belle, she wasn't flaunting her good looks, and moved gracefully without attempting to draw attention to herself. Still she had captured his attention and he wanted her. He reacted in the manner that was classic Scott, and wasted no time in going after what he wanted.

"Good mornin'. My name is Mr. Scott Harrington and you are...?" She greeted him with a pleasant smile. She had noticed him too, and was looking forward to the introduction the moment he started walking towards her. So when he finally reached her, she was ready for him.

His looks and strange charisma had been the topics of conversation throughout the Gulf and Sanford for years. She remembered hearing her mother and her friends gossiping about him and the women in his life. The stories went from one extreme to the other, extolling his exotic allure or bad-mouthing his behavior and history. She was intrigued.

There were many dimensions to her, and included in them was a spirited woman who wasn't afraid of a challenge – even if that challenge came in the person of Scott. Now here he was, at least forty years her senior, coming on to her. _My Gawd this be some kinda handsome man standin' before me. He's old enough to_ *be my daddy, but I know he ain't interested in bein' my daddy, thank Gawd.*

She then extended a hand out to him. "Hello Mr. Harrington. I'm Sonya Morgan, and pleased to meet you. Do you mind if I call you Scott?"

He was caught off guard. While she respectfully acknowledged him as "Mister", the request to call him by his first name was her way of putting him on notice that she considered herself his equal. The bottom line was that her request was actually a condition that had to be satisfied if he wanted her. He wasn't comfortable with any woman calling him by his first name. Yet something about the way she responded only made him more determined to get to know her.

"Yeah – sure. You can call me Scott for now."

She smiled at his stubbornness, refusing to give up the "Mister." *How endearin' and funny. He's so stubborn he just had to put in that "for now" condition, but we'll see. Yes sir – we will see.* She kept smiling.

"For now."

She was a widow with no children. Since the coast was clear, he asked if they could have supper together. They made arrangements for the following Sunday.

She was unlike any woman he had known prior to and after becoming a free man. She was pleasant, soft-spoken, and easy to be with. Unlike his wives, she wasn't willing to submit to a subservient role in his life. Watching and getting to know her was the lesson wherein he was learning that assertiveness wasn't offensive. Belle was rebellious and flippant. Sonya was confident with the right blend of humor and no-nonsense. The assertive nature was just who she was, and he was definitely attracted to her just the way she was.

He was impressed with her job at the hotel located in town up on Horner Boulevard. Belle worked too, but he didn't consider working at the juke joint respectable. Sonya was the head maid, and the hotel owners entrusted her with a lot of responsibility on the job.

She may have wanted him, but since she didn't need him, he had to work harder to draw her into his charm. He had to work harder at showing affection. She was a passionate woman and demanded to be treated accordingly. Although he had to work harder at making her fall in love with him, he accomplished just that. Sonya was well aware of his agenda, and was willing to comply because she wanted him to be just as much in love with her as she was with him. She accepted the challenge, and he fell hard.

Iris had discovered his secret attraction to the lady who had just the right amount of fire in her. An untimely death prevented her from enjoying his secret passion for the almagamation of good girl/bad girl that was his true desire in a woman. Fate would have it that Sonya was the woman who captured the heart of the lover whom his wives and mistress desired and longed for.

He wanted a permanent commitment and decided the best way to seal the deal was to have her move in. The opportunity to lay out his proposal presented itself one night as they were sitting on an upholstered settee and making small talk. She moved over closer and was lying back in his arms.

Nothing about him was characteristic of a man his age. When she was with him, age was the furthest thing from her mind. There was no question that the man whose eyes she was now staring into loved her as much as she loved him. He wanted her. This is what she loved about their relationship – the passion was mutual.

"Mr. Scott Harrington, you be lookin' mighty fine to me this evenin' sir. I must say, you've just gotta have the most beautiful eyes the good Lawd ever put in a man's head."

She was the only woman he knew of who could speak both provocatively and respectfully at the same time. Although she had aroused him, he wanted something from her as well. Rather than submit to his desires and her seduction, he held back. He wanted what she was offering, but now wanted it with conditions. In order to get what he wanted, he needed to use something that would make her seriously consider his offer.

Instead of proceeding with the seduction, he kept the conversation going, but in another direction. "Miss Sonya Morgan, you be a mighty fine lookin' woman, and frankly I can't believe you're interested in a ol' man like me. I know I don't got long to be here. The Lawd ain't gonna leave ol' Mr. Scott Harrington on this here earth forever."

"I done seen so much in my lifetime. Been a slave; then a free man; lost three wives and mo' babies than I can remember; watched my boys walk 'way from me; and my gals all gone from my house. I've done plenty I ain't proud of, but I can't undo those things at this stage of my life. Just when I think nothin' good's left for me, you come along. You young 'nuff for me to be yo poppa, so I understand you wantin' to keep a certain distance.

But fo' I leave this world, which ain't fo' long, I want you to come stay with me."

She wanted to leap at his invitation, but also had reservations. Although willing to take the chance on loving him, she was also cautious to maintain her independence. She was determined not to suffer the same heartaches of the women in his life who preceded her. If not careful, she could become just as lost in him as her predecessors, and would be willing to do the same things they did to have and keep his love. While willing and eager to be close to him, she wasn't willing to totally surrender her life to him. His offer required serious consideration, and she wasn't ready to give him an answer.

"Scott, I think you know how much I love you, but I've been by myself for a long time. I worked my butt off to get that promotion to head maid up at the hotel, and I live quite comfortable for a colored woman in this day and time if I do say so myself. While my heart is tellin' me to close up this here house and move all my stuff over to your place immediately, I gotta think 'bout this before I give you a firm answer. You understand don't you Mr. Harrington?"

He was disappointed, but couldn't afford to show it and take a chance on running her away for good. He had every intention of waiting with patience, but an unforeseeable event changed his good intentions, causing him to default back to his old ways.

He was feeling under the weather – something he wasn't accustomed to. The cold was zapping him of all his energy, so much so that he couldn't go to the mill. Missing time from work was not characteristic of the Harrington brothers.

Another generation of Seamores was now running the tobacco mill. They were amazed that Mr. Scott, as everyone (including coloreds and whites) down at the mill called him, was still working at 90 years old, but were comfortable with him around. He was family, and from the time they were children, were told to look out for Mr. Walter and Mr. Scott.

There was the time when they thought he was going to finally retire. He and Walter were in their eighties and still working. One day Walter didn't return from lunch. The supervisors were concerned because the Harrington brothers were known for their punctuality, and their work ethics were beyond reproach. So they sent mill workers out to search for him.

He was found in a small area set up to privately take lunch similar to the one Scott set up for himself. He was sitting on a small stool hunched over with a partially eaten sandwich still in his hand. As the workers approached and called out to him, there was no response. He was dead.

When Scott was given the news, he ran down to the spot where Walter was found and grabbed the lifeless body up in his arms, holding on for dear life. They tried to comfort him and take Walter away, but he wouldn't let go. His cries hauntingly echoed throughout the mill buildings and the surrounding area. The loss of Fondella; the bitter and twisted relationship with the Seamores; the loss of three wives, stillborn babies, and Herbert; the agonizing and tantalizing relationship with Belle; and every other heartbreak from slavery through the present came crashing down on him.

Now the one person he could totally rely on, who never disappointed him, had gone through and understood everything – especially the System of Slavery, promised never to leave him, was gone. He couldn't hide behind pride, arrogance, or indifference. He didn't care what anybody thought as he wept over the loss of Walter.

The Seamores were just as upset. Their employees watched as they wept over the sight of one Harrington brother holding the corpse of the other. Clayton was so distraught, he couldn't even stand up. His children tried to pull him away from the scene, but he fought to stay. His agonizing cries were just as haunting as Scott's. The long, sad, and complicated family history of the Seamores and Harringtons was on open display.

The younger Seamores couldn't remember a time when Walter and Scott wasn't a part of their lives. Each new generation was indoctrinated into the love/hate relationship that originated with James Seamore, Sr.'s obsession with Fondella. There was a terrible sense of loss that permeated throughout the mill on the day they found Walter dead. If not for the truth, no one would have guessed the family's history began as a slave/master relationship sanctioned by law. Mr. Walter was now gone, and Mr. Scott was inconsolable. After a month of mourning, they offered him the option to retire with full benefits. He declined.

After belonging to the Seamores as a slave and working for them as free man, not only did he miss his first day of work, he couldn't even visit with Sonya. When he didn't show up for supper on Sunday, she went over to check on him.

In the old days he would have been enraged if anybody had taken the liberty to come to his home without prior approval. He would have strangled Belle if she even thought about coming up to his front door and knocking. This was not the case with Sonya. As a matter of fact, he was happy to see her.

"Why Scott Harrington, whatever on earth is wrong with you? You lookin' like death warmed over and never sent somebody to come and get me. Oh Sweetheart, you don't have to suffer like this. Move aside, and let me in. We'll get you back up and raisin' cane in no time."

She was true to her word, and in no time had him back up on his feet. Although it took nearly two weeks, they were two of the best weeks of his life. He had the woman he loved staying with and taking care of him. Sensing when he needed it the most, she held him in her arms saying absolutely nothing, and not expecting him to say anything. Her only expectation was that he rest in the comfort she was giving. In Sonya, and at 90 years old, he had found a haven of rest he never knew existed.

When she announced that it was time to go home, he was disappointed. He tried once more to convince her to move in, but she still wasn't ready. She promised not to abandon him, and would still be there to clean house, prepare his meals, and take care of him in any way he needed. Her counter-offer wasn't what he wanted to hear, but was willing to accept rather than lose her.

The bout with the cold affected him more than physically. Because he had been rendered weak and helpless, he was forced to think about things such as his mortality. He was 90 years old and while he had been in pretty good shape healthwise, he was not oblivious to the conditions in which he saw other people who were not as old as him. He couldn't imagine himself sick to the point of needing someone to feed or clean him, nor could he imagine someone having access to his most private parts in his most vulnerable state.

Adding to his insecurities was Sonya's refusal to move in. He couldn't help but wonder if her reservations had something to do with taking care of a sick old man.

Up until the incident with the cold, he had been enjoying an excitement in life he believed was long behind him. He was proud to still have the desires of a much younger man, and the ability to satisfy a much younger woman. He was convinced this was one of the reasons why she was willing to have a relationship with him. He wanted to offer her the man she was attracted to – not an invalid or obligation.

"Scott, I think you're in pretty good shape now. It's time for me to go back home."

"I thought you were feelin' comfortable after bein' here with me these past two weeks and ready to move in. Don't see the need fo' you to keep runnin' back and forth."

"I don't wanna be runnin' back and forth, but I've gotta be honest with you Honey. I'm just not ready yet. Don't worry though, I'm not gonna forsake you. I'll be here to take care of you and this place too."

The old Scott surfaced and panicked. He sent a telegram to Novella, Leotia, and Walter asking them to return to the Gulf immediately. He didn't bother to tell them that his sickness wound up being only a cold from which he had recovered. He framed the telegram with the intentions of pulling one or all of them back under his control. Novella took the bait and wouldn't rest until Walter and Leotia agreed to accompany her back to the Gulf.

As the train pulled into the station, Leotia was reminiscing about her young life. Back in 1936, she was glad to finally be getting away from him, and it was her intention never to return. Living with and loving Scott was too taxing and distressing. Once she and Luke arrived in Baltimore, she felt as though the weight of the world had been lifted off of her shoulders. While she loved him, she couldn't see any other way to deal with him but from a distance. If a person let him too close, he or she would suffer in some way. He wouldn't allow anyone to love him freely. There was always a price to pay. When you counted up the cost, it was never worth it.

She hadn't forgiven him for his attempts to drive Luke out of her life. She almost lost the man she loved and married because of his selfish agenda. He tried to come up with every scheme he could think of to manipulate her into waiving any possibility of finding happiness.

His secret relationship with the Geechee and plots to use witchcraft to destroy Novella's marriage solidified the charges of many that he was a dangerous man. This was yet another unforgivable sin. If he was willing to bargain with the devil and involve his own daughter – the apple of his eye, he was capable of anything.

Walter returned to the Gulf more out of a sense of obligation than panic over Scott's health. He was in a financial position to visit occasionally, and everytime he came home Scott looked reasonably healthy to him.

He met Sonya during one of his visits and really liked her. He just couldn't understand how Scott was able to catch a woman like her at his age. It was understandable why he was attracted to her. He was even more baffled when he learned she had been living in the Gulf her entire life, heard the stories about his father, and still wanted to come anywhere near him. After he got to know her, he decided she could handle herself, as well as Scott. So he wasn't really falling for the old, sick, and helpless storyline.

Once they got off of the train, Novella was happy to see that he looked much better than the telegram described. When he started walking towards them, she took off running. She flew into his arms and immediately planted kisses all over his face. He was pleased. At least she was still the same.

She would like Sonya. He had to be careful though, and couldn't appear too happy with his new love because he was trying to convince one of them to come back to the Gulf. He had to be careful with Sonya as well because he didn't want to offend her in any way that would convince her to give him a firm "no" to his request just in case his plan didn't work.

After a week, Walter returned to Baltimore, leaving Leotia and Novella in North Carolina. They bonded well with Sonya. When Scott introduced her as his housekeeper, she wasn't offended because she was still trying to keep him happy with the arrangement they had agreed to and not badger her about moving in. So his official introduction gave her the excuse she needed to avoid making a decision she wasn't ready to make.

Walter's departure back to Baltimore answered any questions about his willingness to return to the Gulf as caregiver. He would come to visit, but wasn't going to move back. So Scott had to move quickly and convince Leotia or Novella to commit to returning to the Gulf. He was about to meet with a harsh reality. Relocating back to the Gulf was not an option available to Walter, Leotia, or Novella.

His self-absorption would not allow him to think beyond his personal desires. The only thing that mattered was he was in his 90's, starting to feel vulnerable, and faced with his mortality. Besides, it was taking too long to convince Sonya to give up her place. If she waited too long, he could become a sickly old man and she would never agree to move in.

To cover all bases he had to lay his cards out on the table in order to convince one of them (preferably Novella) to come back to the Gulf. The answer was "no" – from both of them. While hurt and disappointed, he wasn't shocked by Leotia's refusal. He was well-acquainted with the contempt she held for his relationship with Belle. She held him responsible for the misery she endured when he threw Luke out of the house and attempted to drive him out of her life. Lastly, and more importantly, she had the real goods on him when she caught him in the act of bargaining with the Geechee. She was in a position to destroy any and everything he wanted to preserve. She knew too much and wasn't willing to give up her freedom to come back to him or the Gulf.

Her response was straight to the point. "Poppa, I'm not comin' back. I'm married to Luke, and we just built a new home. He's got a good job at the steel mill. Plus, we have a small farm. Maryland is my home now."

He then turned to his savior, but she shot him down as well. "Poppa, you know how much I love you, but Baltimore is my home now. Me and Neal are doin' okay, and we can't keep movin' our children back and forth. We've done that enough already and want to give them a foundation. I want to give my children everything I didn't have."

The last statement felt like a stake had been driven through his heart. She wasn't as starry-eyed when it came to loving him as he thought. She had not turned a blind eye to his sins over the years. The ultimate blow was that although she adored him, Novella knew that he was flawed.

A new era had definitely been ushered in. He would never be able to manipulate and control them again. They had paid too great a price trying to love him. After miraculously escaping from his personal System of Slavery (something three wives, several children, and a mistress had not been able to do), the survivors were not willing to take a chance on returning to the scene of the crime – Gulf, North Carolina. At the end of the second week, Leotia and Novella took the train back to Maryland.

Chapter 45
A Wish Come True

Although he tried to hide his devastation over Walter's, Leotia's, and Novella's refusals to return to the Gulf, it was apparent he was a different man. He was distant, condescending, and impossible to be around.

Sonya tried to be patient, but the dual personalities of the loving man she adored, and the slavedriver who treated her as if she was a total stranger were making life a living hell. She kept her end of the bargain and did everything she had done while he was sick, with the exception of moving in. He was unappreciative, and barked out orders as if she was the hired help, or to be more accurate, his personal slave. If she stayed away in an attempt to defuse the mounting tension, he hurled false accusations about other men. Things deteriorated to the point where nothing pleased him.

The final straw came on the night when he demanded that she address him as Mr. Harrington.

"I helped everybody out during this Depression and they wind up some ungrateful chilluns. Them gals of mine run off to Baltimore and think they don't need me no more. Them boys actin' all high and mighty cause they bought some land. I ain't ever asked for much from nobody. Yet all I got was cryin', whinin', and accusations 'bout everything. I tried to take care of my chilluns and wasn't gonna let nobody hurt 'em. Them gals of mine don't understand. All I ever wanted to do was to protect them. Ain't that what a poppa 'posed to do?"

"Oh Scott, they love you. They're now young women with families and have to look out for their husbands and children. Those are their priorities as they should be."

Already feeling rejected, he couldn't take the perceived criticism and pounced. "Don't you dare tell me about where my gals' priorities ought to be. I'm gettin' tired of you direspectin' me too. Don't think you're gonna sweet talk me by callin' me Scott. I told you some time ago, my name is Mr. Harrington and you're to call me that. I'm the man of this house and iffin you wanna be comin' 'round here, you had better start talkin' to me proper."

He was now screaming at the top of his lungs. "Gal, my name be Mr. Harrington and that be what you call me from here on out. Do you understand me?"

"I understand I'm gettin' outta here right now. I love you, but I'll be damned if I'm gonna stand here and let you talk down to me. I know who I am and what I'm worth Scott. That's right, I didn't say Mister. As of right now, consider yo self my past 'cause I ain't about to have no kinda future with a disrespectin' ol' fool like you. The way you behavin' now, I can't say I blame your children for not wantin' to come back here and live with a tyrant like you. Goodbye and good riddance."

With that she snatched up her purse and shawl to leave. Before she even reached the door, he was filled with regret. She was too furious for him to speak another word, and would have slapped him had he attempted to touch her. He had no choice but to let her leave.

He had to get her back. She had brought something special to his life at a time when he didn't believe it was possible. She made everything that happened in the past a distant memory. She was everything in a woman he had tried to get out of several women. She was his last hope, and he wasn't going to give up on his last hope.

He showed up at the hotel and pleaded with her to let him walk her home. The first two weeks she turned him down, refusing to take one step with him. He was determined to win her back, and refused to let her rejection turn him away.

On the third week, he was waiting when she left work that Monday evening. As soon as she came out of the hotel, he jumped in front of her and blocked her path. She attempted to move around him. "Look Scott, I've told you I'm movin' on. I don't wanna be bothered. Please just leave me alone and go away."

"Sonya, you were right. I'm an ol' fool. I shouldn't have talked to you like that. I knows you deserve much better and I was just boilin' mad 'cause my gals don't want me no more. Plus, I was gettin' scared 'cause you don't wanna live with me. Can't say I blame you, 'cause you deserve a young man like yo self. I got carried away when you started lovin' me and guess I thought that meant you would wanna stay with me all the time. I should've just 'cepted what you offered. Havin' you come 'round like you offered was better than anything I ever had."

His apology was raggedy at best, but it was heartfelt, and he was putting himself at her mercy by admitting his true feelings. She still didn't give in immediately.

Starting on the second month after he began pursuing her, she let him walk her home every evening. They resumed having supper together on Sundays, and he was forced to court her for the next six months. She finally agreed to move in with him.

By October 1939, they had been living together quietly, peacefully, and in love. He was 93 years old and she was 53 years old. There were times when they disagreed, but he never let the arguments escalate to the point where she walked out on him. He could still be manipulative, but while irritating, she considered him harmless.

Although he was still working down at the mill, he was slowing down and spending a lot more time sitting in front of the fireplace in his rocking chair. There were times when his gaze into the fire seemed to take him far away to some other place in some other time. If she asked about his thoughts, the response was usually, "Not much. Just thinkin." He was stubborn, and it was pointless to press him for more conversation than he was willing to share. His short responses were enough. This time of reflection was obviously needed, some things needed to be worked out, and it was time to make peace with unresolved issues.

It was the last week of October when he asked her to run an errand. "Sonya Honey – can you pick me some stamps up at the post office? I wanna write to Otie and Vella."

He was proud of his most recent accomplishment. He had never given much thought to the necessity or importance of communicating through writing. That all changed once everybody had moved out of the house and left the Gulf. At Novella's insistence, he learned how to read and write a few words. She told him not to worry about misspelling because misspelled words weren't important to her.

That's just like my baby gal to come up with a way to talk to her poppa even when she can't come back to the Gulf. Even Otie seem to be willin' to talk to me through writin'. Still can't believe that gal ain't opened her mouth and tol' Vella 'bout me and that Geechee woman. Gotta say she'll stand on one of them principles she's got like she's standin' on the Rock of Gilbraltar.

Sonya was delighted to hear that he was in touch and communicating with Leotia, Walter, and Novella again. She was happy to run the errand.

He lit a fire to knock off the October chill that could be felt throughout the house. He then sat in his rocking chair and began to stare into the flames. Eventually his eyes closed and he drifted off to sleep.

He and Walter were young boys. They were standing outside of the Seamore's huge kitchen peering through the big window at the tall and beautiful woman kneading dough. She looked familiar. They waited anxiously hoping she was going to invite them in. At first her stare was piercing, but gradually the expression turned into a warm smile. Then she said something, and with the wave of her hand, beckoned for them to come in.

"Momma loves both of you so much." She then blew a kiss in their direction.

"Did you see that? Oh my Gawd, Walter do you know who that is? She said, 'Momma loves both of you so much.' Walter, ain't that how you understand what she said?"

Walter's head bobbed up and down, indicating that he too understood her message of love. When they turned back to the window, she was gone. He became anxious. Where did she go?

How could she have disappeared so fast? No – it couldn't be. She had to come back. They started banging on the window trying to get her to come back. That was…

When he woke up, he found himself poised at the end of the seat as if he was about to get up. He had been dreaming. They were not boys. He was 93 years old and Walter was dead. Disappointed he sat back in the chair and drifted off to sleep again.

This time they were teenagers and running through the woods as fast as their legs could carry them. He wanted to stop because his chest was hurting, but they couldn't. If caught, they would be dealt with brutally. They had to keep running. Off in the distance the barking dogs could be heard. It was the overseer, slave driver, and some other white men who were sent out to hunt them down. They were told never to try to run away again or else, but decided to take their chance on "or else." They kept running putting more distance between them and the sound of the barking dogs.

Confident they had reached a safe place Walter decided that it was best to settle down for the night. "We've gotta save our strength for the days ahead iffin we gonna get up to Boston. Once we make it, we'll be free men and free to look for Fondella."

"Yeah Walter, Massa's gonna see we ain't acceptin' them crumbs he always tryin' to throw our way. Ain't nothin' takin' the place of the momma he first took from us and then drove her away. He's gonna see that we won't settle for less. We're willin' to risk everything for freedom – just like Fondella. When we all meet up, we can live as free people up there in Boston." They fell asleep thinking about the long awaited reunion with Fondella.

Just as the sun was coming up, they opened their eyes to look into the ends of very long rifles. Vicious and snarling dogs strained at the leashes holding them back. The overseer and his men had found them. They would be taken back to the Seamore property to learn what "or else" meant.

They started fighting for their lives, determined not to go back even if it meant not going back alive. The dogs were released, but Walter pulled out the machete he kept buried beneath the floor in their quarters and slit their throats. He rejoined Scott in the fight. The overseer and his men were no match for them. Scott managed to wrestle a rifle away from one of the men and killed him with his own weapon. Bodies were flying all over the place from the shots Scott fired and the blows Walter was delivering. The slave driver then snuck up behind Scott and started striking the bull whip across his back. The searing pain from their torn flesh made them fall to the ground. While they were being shackled, they still refused to give up and kept fighting.

It was another bad dream. He then got up and made himself a cup of black coffee. The coffee was strong, but soothing as it went down. He sat back down to finish his drink and resumed staring into the flames. Once again he fell asleep.

This time there was music and singing voices. A group of people appeared. At first the figures were mere silhouettes, but as they started to take on definition, he saw Lillie, Iris, Mary, Herbert, and several young children who looked familiar, but their facial features remained distorted.

They were singing a beautiful song that brought tears to his eyes. He had never heard music so beautiful with voices sounding so angelic.They floated closer and formed a circle around him. The volume of the music and singing voices started to get louder. Why was this unfamiliar song affecting him so much that it brought tears to his eyes?

As the singing continued, Lillie broke away from the circle and floated up to him. She had a peaceful smile on her face, but her smile only made him want to cry. She reached out and touched his cheek. He tried to apologize. "Lillie, sweet Lillie, I'm so sorry. You had just gained your freedom when your life was taken away for no reason. No – that's not true. You lost your life because of me. Can you ever forgive me?" She smiled and then reached up again to touch his cheek. She nodded her head – yes she forgave him. She then floated back to the circle.

Iris then broke away from the circle and floated up to him. She reached over and slightly touched her lips to his. As their lips touched, their eyes locked, and they stared into each other's eyes. His heart was pounding because he didn't know what to say to her, and for some reason, was afraid of what she might say to him. He recalled not wanting to look at her when she was terminally ill with a grossly emaciated body.

"Oh Iris, you were such a strong gal.You tried to fight fo' our marriage. I didn't marry her – I did keep that promise. Iris, I need you to forgive me." She answered, "I do forgive you" and then floated back to the circle to join the others in their song.

Mary was next. He was prepared to apologize and ask for her forgiveness as well, but she wouldn't break away from the circle. The time had come to make peace with everyone who loved him, and he was almost there. As soon as she granted him clemency, all of his affairs would be in order. She still refused to break the circle. He was confused because her favorable response was deadline sensitive and time was running out. He beckoned for her to come to him with haste, but she wouldn't.

What was happening to him and where he was? The music and the voices started getting soft again. However, he could clearly hear the lyrics as they were repeated over and over. "Loving Scott Harrington, Loving Scott Harrington, all I ever wanted to do was to love Scott Harrington; Loving Scott Harrington, Loving Scott Harrington, all I ever wanted to do was to love Scott Harrington."

Sonya was praying he wasn't too hungry and angry with her for taking so much time away from home when all he asked her to do was to pick up some stamps. After leaving the post office, she ran into old friends, got caught up in gossip, and the time just got away from her. Now she was anxious to get home. She would make it up to him.

"Scott Harrington, I'm home." There was no answer. *Oh no – he's got an attitude, but I'll love him back to happy.* "Oh Mr. Harrington, Honey, I'm home. I know you're mad 'cause I took a long time, but I'm make it all up to you. The time just got away. I apologize." Still there was no answer.

"Please forgive me." *Oh no. He must really be mad at me.*

She was now in the room where he was sitting in front of fireplace. He was asleep. She walked over to run her hand through his beautiful white hair. *I ain't never known a man who got a woman in love with him at 93 years old like I love this man. He's a rascal, but I love him. He's a long way from perfect, but I love...*

As she was running her fingers through his hair, he started to fall over. She scrambled to get a good grip on him before he fell to the floor. He was not asleep. While sitting in front of the fireplace watching the fire and dreaming, Scott Harrington passed away at the age of 93.

Chapter 46
All I Ever Wanted

crowd gathered at the gravesite as the reverend committed the body of Scott Harrington back to the dust. Leotia thought it interesting how even in death he commanded a crowd, although it was mixed with people who loved, disliked, adored, hated, feared, or envied him. Also in the crowd were those people who were curious about the 93 year old man whose life as a slave and free man had been the topic of Gulf gossip for generations, being laid to rest. She was trying to focus on the individual faces in the crowd in order to avoid the tears that kept welling up in her eyes. Her heart was so heavy, she couldn't stand up much longer. She was actually looking forward to a mental or physical collapse just to ease the weight of her grief.

Poppa was larger than life, so how could he be dead? No matter how old he got, Poppa seemed to be as strong and alive as he was when we were children. I stayed mad at him for most of my life, but I can't imagine him dead. If anybody was gonna live forever, it was gonna be Mr. Scott Harrington.

She had to admit that all along she had been yearning for reconciliation, and never imagined they would never get the chance.

Walter stood at the gravesite with both hands shoved deep into his pant pockets because they were shaking so bad. The only time he took one out was to catch the tears streaming down his cheeks or snot running from his nose.

Why couldn't I ever get close to Poppa the way I wanted to? Gawd I loved that man. He could get me madder than anybody on earth, but I was always wantin' things to be different. All I ever wanted to do was to love Scott Harrington.

Novella was standing with Neal on one side of her and Maude on the other. They were each holding an arm, trying to keep her standing upright.

A month earlier, she had delivered another baby boy whom they named Johnnie Ed. She claimed he looked like a real doll baby and went to great lengths to dress him up and plait his long locks. She was comfortable with life in Baltimore, enjoying her marriage, first apartment, being a mother, and the new baby. Finally everything seemed to be going their way. She was unprepared to receive word that Scott was dead.

Now here she was unable to stand up without the help of Neal and Maude. She was crying so hard, she could barely catch her breath. The pain of losing Mary was different than this loss. This felt raw; like an open wound; like something was left unresolved – unanswered.

They shared something special. As difficult as he could be with everyone else, she knew that he was crazy about her. Guilt was eating away at her. *Dear Gawd, did I miss something? Was he sick back then and we overlooked it? He seemed happy and content with Miss Sonya. Oh Poppa, did I desert you in your time of need?*

Maude saw him first. She happened to look over near some trees at the back of the cemetery when she saw a face among the crowd. It was the face of a man who looked exactly like Scott. He was tall, thin, and had a head full of glistening white hair. Even from a distance, she could see the piercing gray eyes.

I know I ain't seein' things. Mr. Harrington is right there in that coffin, so I know I ain't seein' what I think I'm seein'. Maybe I'm grievin' more than I wanna admit. This is one tough man I thought would never die. Thought he was too mean and stubborn to give up the ghost. She shook her head as if to clear any cobwebs and went back to giving Novella her full attention.

Then it was Leotia's turn. She was still trying to look at anything or anybody rather than the coffin about to be lowered into the grave. Her eyes fell upon the stranger who looked exactly like Scott. *Who in the world is that? It can't be Uncle Walt 'cause he died a few years back.*

"Luke, who is that man standin' over there? Don't he look just like Poppa?" Luke looked in the direction where she was pointing, but there was no familiar-looking man.

"Where Otie, who are you talkin' 'bout?"

Finally, the stranger moved closer to the crowd. This time it was Walter who noticed him. He had taken a hand out of his pocket again to wipe away the tears when he saw him. "Oh my Gawd, oh my Gawd. It's you. After all these years here you are. Oh my Gawd, it's you. Jesus Christ. You look just like him."

The stranger stared back at Walter with tears running down his face.

Before she took a good look at whomever it was that had interrupted their goodbyes, Novella asked, "Walter, what on earth are you talkin' about? You actin' as if you've seen a ghost or somethin'."

"Look at him y'all, look at him. He's the spittin' image of Poppa, but must be 'bout twenty years younger. Oh my Gawd, don't y'all know who this is?"

Maude, Leotia, and Novella started to understand, but were still trying to get over the shock. Walter then stated what everyone else was afraid to say out loud for fear this was all some cruel joke. "This is Herbert Harrington, Poppa's oldest son who left all those years ago."

Leotia and Novella just kept staring. He did look exactly like Scott – more than Walter or either one of them.

Maude said, "I'll be damned."

"Yeah. I'm Herbert, and Scott Harrington was my father.

Maude then asked, "Well Herbert, how did you know he passed away?"

"The Seamores told me. They been keepin' me up-to-date about Poppa's life ever since the day I left the Gulf."

"Why on earth would you wanna stay in contact with the Seamores and not just get back in contact with Poppa?"

"Let me explain Walter. No – everybody listen to me. I know y'all will prob'ly understand what I'm about to say. All I ever wanted to do was to love Scott Harrington, but the ol' man made it next to impossible to do that. So I did what I thought was the next best thing."

"I had to leave if I wanted to feel and be free. I couldn't bring myself to make contact with y'all. I was figurin' he most likely was puttin' y'all through all kinds of hell too, and to come back into that picture was just gonna make things much worse."

They did understand. Dealing in Scott's circle of madness could be draining and hazardous to the health of the people who tried to love him. They could attest to the casualties along the way in the war between freedom and slavery; love and hate that was his life.

The people in the Gulf thought a very long, sad, haunting, and painful chapter had finally come to a close, but Scott wasn't finished. Even from the grave, he was still capable of delivering devastating blows to those who were guilty of loving him.

The Seamore family requested a family meeting to include Herbert, Maude, Walter, Leotia, and Novella. Leotia and Novella brought Luke and Neal along to the meeting. Once they arrived at the big house that had been familiar to Scott since he was a young slave, they were taken to and seated in the library along with several Seamore relatives and a man who was introduced as the Seamore's attorney.

The attorney started the meeting by announcing that Scott had a Last Will and Testament, and the purpose of the meeting was to read the Will. They were confused as to why the Seamore relatives had to be present.

Herbert thoughts were that Scott was trying to make amends after all the trouble, pain, and suffering he had caused. Walter was excited to find out there was even enough money to warrant reading a Will. Novella and Leotia were curious. Although neither one of them had ever given previous thought about his death or any money that would be dispersed per the directives of his Will, they were now anticipating some extra money. With Johnnie's birth, Neal and Novella now had five children, and any extra money would definitely be welcomed.

Even before the attorney began reading the Will, Maude started feeling as if something wasn't right. *Now he done called in all these white folk 'cause he don't think his children smart enough to know how to handle whatever he left behind. That's just like him, still tryin' to control everybody from the damn grave mind you. Somethin's not right and now they 'bout to find out what.*

The attorney started by explaining the laws of the State of North Carolina. The law required the testator of the Will to leave at least one dollar to his or her heirs before bequeathing his or her personal assets to anyone else.

He then proceeded to read the Last Will and Testament of Scott Harrington. Scott did exactly what the law required him to do – nothing more. They sat frozen as the attorney read the stipulations that left each one of them a single dollar – that is with the exception of Walter. For reasons unknown, Scott excluded him from the Will. The Seamore family; the family of the man who fathered and owned him as a slave; and owned the tobacco mill where he worked up until the time of his death, inherited everything.

Clearly shakened hurt, and confused, Leotia and Novella grabbed each other's hand in instinctive support. Neither one of them wanted any trouble. They just wanted to get out of the room and the State of North Carolina as soon as possible.

Leotia leaned over to Novella. "Vella, we've got far more than he could ever leave us. We have Gawd, our husbands, you have your children, and we have each other.You've got everything that matters. You loved him like nobody else. Trust me – much more than he deserved, but you did the right thing."

Tears were forming in Novella's eyes, but she was determined to walk out of the room with her head held high. "I know you're right. I don't understand why he did this, but I'm okay with his decision. I still love him."

As if on cue, they stood up together looking like twin towers of strength. They were getting ready to walk out of the room when Novella had an idea. "Otie, let's walk – no, let's trot 'round this entire room before we leave. When I was a girl runnin' in those relay races, the winner always took a victory lap at the end of the race. Let's take our victory lap. This particular race has been run, and I do believe we've won. What do you think?"

She took Novella's hand again and raised it in victory. "Yeah Vella, let's do just that."

It was time to move on. There was nothing left in the Gulf for them to turn back to.

The Seamores looked on as the two sisters began their victory lap. Maude stood to the side with tears in her eyes, a smile on her lips, and pride in her chest as she watched. *Oh Momma, I know you're lookin' down on them right now. You've gotta be real proud of them, cause I know I am.*

As he watched them trot the victory lap, Walter spoke to Mary. "Now Momma, them gals right there be your seeds. They won Momma, they won. They fought hard and won. Yo' gals overcame." This time he didn't try to stop the flow of tears or snot.

Herbert looked on imagining Lillie, Iris, and Mary taking the victory lap with Leotia and Novella. He honored them with an ovation as he clapped and recited Iris' favorite passage of scripture.

"When thou passest through the waters, I will be with thee; and through the rivers, they shall not overflow thee: when thou walkest through the fire, thou shalt not be burned; neither shall the flame kindle upon thee."

"Momma, you said sometimes the scriptures was all we would have."

After Leotia and Novella finished their victory lap, they walked out of the Seamore's Library without looking back.

Maude stayed behind because she had something to say before leaving. She was not leaving quietly and didn't care who heard it, or whose feelings were hurt. The Seamores were startled once again when she spoke.

"That mean son-of-a-bitch has hurt my sisters for the last time. He died the same ignorant slave he was born. He ain't never been set free and all he ever did was loved a bunch of folk that owned his sorry ass. Y'all just saw my sisters walk outta here in victory. Remember that. He can take his money, y'all Seamores, and rot in hell for all I care." The Seamores looked embarrassed and uncomfortable. *Good cause they need to be embarrassed. They probl'y had somethin' to do with all this foolishness.* Satisfied with having said her peace, she walked out.

Herbert ran out of the room to have a word with them. "I know it hurts to hear somethin' like that, but don't take it too personal. I hate to admit it, but Maude is right to a certain degree. Poppa was ignorant to many things in this world and the power he had, he used it in all the wrong ways. So in the end, he had no power at all. Y'all seem to have pretty decent lives, so go ahead and live in peace. Y'all ought to be proud of yourselves."

"I swear fo' Gawd I saw my momma, Iris, Miss Lillie, and Miss Mary takin' that victory lap with Leotia and Novella. Thank y'all for provin' good triumphs over evil when it's all said and done. Each one of y'all standin' here survived the ol' man. There are plenty of people who didn't live to survive him and the madness of slavery that wrapped itself around his heart and life. Some people were able to move on and leave that stuff behind, like dear Uncle Walt, may his soul rest in peace, while others, like Poppa, couldn't get rid of the gruesome stain. But y'all made it despite the demons that followed him into what was supposed to be his freedom, and attached to him as dark and dangerous affections. Y'all survived. That's worth more than any amount of money."

His words of comfort and wisdom seemed to have calmed everyone down, including Maude. But Walter was still back in the library with the Seamores and their attorney. There was nothing no one could do or say to comfort him. He was furious. He didn't walk away as Herbert had done. Even after moving to Baltimore, he kept his promise to come back to the Gulf. Although there were plenty of times, while growing up, he was bitter over the calamity Scott brought into their lives, as well as the carnage left behind, he fought to continue loving him because all he ever wanted to do was to love Scott Harrington. Mary died trying to love him. If the rumors were true, she died because his mistress consorted with the Geechee to destroy her. Even after Mary's death, Leotia and Novella tried to love the old man although he constantly stuck his nose into their business, attempting to destroy their relationships and maintain control over their lives.

After all this, the bastard leaves everything to that white family what owned him as a slave. His parting shot filled the room with question.

"Y'all listen up real good. Walter Harrington's got somethin' he wanna say, and I ain't leavin' until I've had my say. If that ol' man thinks he's won the last round, he's got another thought comin'. Yes sir – Mr. Scott Harrington, Walter Harrington's got somethin' in store for you. This time you won't be able to do a damned thing about it either."

The Seamores and their attorney started leaving the library quietly, but were confused by the angry statements made by Scott's boy as he stormed out of the room. What on earth could he be talking about? Everything had been settled. They were entitled to everything Scott bequeath to them. The Last Will and Testament was clear and there were no more battles to be fought. Why would he argue with a legal and binding document?

The answer was disclosed 62 years later when everyone who attended the reading of the Will had passed away, with the exception of one person – Scott's beloved Novella.

The End

What Really Happened

62 years after Scott Harrington's death, and 42 years after Walter Harrington's death, a family member broke his silence when he unveiled Walter's secret. Walter contested the Will and won because Scott failed to include him. The Will was not binding because it was in violation of the laws of the State of North Carolina at the time of Scott's death.

According to Novella Harrington Reaves, Scott was 17 years old when he became a free man.

Scott demanded that all of his wives call him Mr. Harrington.

He kept the same mistress throughout all of his marriages. It was rumored that his mistress was responsible for the death of his first wife and their unborn child.

Mary Marks Harrington died when Novella was 9 years old. According to Maude, she was 10 years old when she ran a distance of 10 miles in order to get the midwife who delivered Leotia Harrington in 1908.

Mama Mame was a midwife and life-long family friend.

According to Novella, at the sound of the recess bell, every day at 12 Noon, she ran home from school to get Scott's lunch pail, and then took it to his job at the mill.

According to Novella, Herbert, who was a son from Mary's previous marriage, left the State of North Carolina, and was never seen or heard from again by family members. Someone claimed to have seen him in New York City in the early 1930's.

According to Mary Reaves Jackson, Scott spanked her and Neal, Jr. for stealing one penny. Scott counted his money by carving symbols such as ||||| into a wall.

Neal Reaves' mother, Lizzie Gilmore Reaves, lived to be 100 years old. She passed away in March, 1980.

Marion Reaves, Neal's father, died on December 25, 1941.

Marion Reaves, Lizzie Gilmore Reaves, and Mary Marks Harrington were all born within 20 years after the abolishment of the System of Slavery.

Minnie Gilmore (Lizzie's mother) and Ben Reaves (Neal Reaves' grandfather) were not born free people. According to the family bible, Minnie Gilmore and Ben Reaves both passed away in 1938.

With the help of Scott's brother, Walter was able to save enough money to relocate to Baltimore, Maryland.

Scott passed away at the age of 93 in 1939. He sent the woman who lived with him at the time to the post office for stamps. Upon her return, she found him dead, sitting in his rocking chair. Stamps were already in the house.

Walter Harrington died in 1959 from an asthma attack while sitting in a hospital Emergency Room.

Maude was born on February 29, 1898, and passed away at the age of 84 in 1982.

Luke and Leotia Spruiel were married for 55 years.

Luke Spruiel became an ordained minister and a pastor.

Leotia passed away at the age of 78 in 1985.

Neal and Novella were married for 60 years and 8 months. They renewed their wedding vows with a wedding ceremony on their 50th anniversary, and another ceremony to celebrate their 60th anniversary in March of 1988, eight months prior to his death.

Neal became an ordained minister.

Neal and Novella had ten sons and five daughters together. Two sons were stillborn. Neal had one son from another relationship. In total, he fathered 11 sons.

Neal Reaves, Sr. passed away on November 7, 1988, at the age of 78. Left to cherish his life, legacy, and memory were four generation of descendents: nine sons, five daughters, three sons in law, seven daughters in law, twenty nine grandchildren, seventeen great grandchildren, four great great grandchildren, two brothers, two sisters in law, one aunt, and a host of other nieces, nephews, and cousins.

Novella Reaves Harrington enjoyed a long life as a mother, homemaker, seamstress (self-taught), pianist (self-taught), missionary; and creative artist. She passed away on March 3,

2002, at the age of 89. She would have turned 90 years old on September 14, 2002. When Novella transitioned, she was survived by five generations of descendents to include: seven sons, four daughters, four daughters in law, four sons in law, twenty-six grandchildren, thirty great grandchildren, six great great grandchildren, and one great great great grandchild.

Gulf, North Carolina is an unincorporated community located in southwestern Chatham County, in North Carolina, south of the town of Goldston. Gulf is home to a general store and several historical homes. It received its name from its location, at a wide bend in the Deep River. It is the geographical center of North Carolina.

The Practice of Roots. There is no practice that elicits such deep-seeded beliefs, turbulent emotions, and heated debate as "root work." For generations, there are those people who have engaged, or are engaged in the same practices as the Geechee. These practices are prevalent in southern states such as Georgia, Louisiana, South Carolina, Mississippi, and North Carolina. Some call it "Working Roots." Others refer to it as "Voo Doo", "Hoodoo Roots", and there are those who say it is just another form of witchcraft.

Root work is controversial to say the least. Believers say that it has been used to hurt and harm, enslave and set free, protect and destroy. People who acquaint themselves with and embrace such practices hold the practitioners in high regard. Believing in the super powers of the root worker, they are willing to resort to untraditional methods of getting whatever it is they desire out of life.

A traditional scientist stated his position that although he doesn't believe, if someone were to tell him that roots had been worked on him, he would pause with concern.

Roots, voodoo, hoodoo, and witch craft are feared by many. These people view such practices as dark and dangerous. The practitioners are considered con artists, sorcerers, or demonic.

Then there are those who totally dismiss the world of roots. Even if they don't believe, non-believers want nothing to do with these practices, and won't go anywhere near anyone who does believe and practice.

Thank God for the Harrington women who believed in, served, and prevailed because of His Power. Because of them...